Critical Praise for Matthew

High Life

"Stokoe's in-your-face prose and raw, unnerving scenes give way go a skillfully plotted tale that will keep readers glued to the page."
Publishers Weekly

"One of the most unstinting, imaginative, brutal and original contemporary novels ever written about the punishments that come with the prioritization of fame..."
Dennis Cooper

"All of the classic ingredients of Californian noir are here, but Stokoe takes things further than most... This is a compelling and gripping novel."
Black Star Reviews

"...an unholy hybrid of Raymond Chandler's best work and Bret Easton Ellis's American Psycho."
Henry Flesh, Lambda Literary Award-winning author of *Massage*

Empty Mile

"Beautifully written and deeply gripping, Empty Mile is a great read. I'm already looking forward to the next one from Matthew Stokoe."
Michael Connelly, author of *The Gods of Guilt*

"… heartbreakingly powerful contemporary noir…" "Stokoe stays true to a bleak vision of the world as he enmeshes his characters in the kinds of tragic setups reminiscent of a Thomas Hardy novel."
Publishers Weekly (starred review)

"The tension builds unbearably in this magnificent 'Sierras Noir' novel. Stokoe writes damaged people worthy of James M. Cain and Jim Thompson. His star-crossed lovers and broken families will steal your heart, even as Stokoe drives the knife home."
Denise Hamilton, author of the Eve Diamond Series

"This book has everything a good crime novel should: a suspenseful story with violence at its core, characters driven by lust, love and guilt, propelled with prose that's poetic and profound."
Carole E. Barrowman, Milwaukee Wisconsin Journal Sentinel

COLONY OF WHORES

MATTHEW STOKOE

For my wife, Elizabeth, who has been waiting far too long.

Chapter 1

The sky above the city looked like someone had tipped kerosene over it and set it on fire. In the Santa Monica Mountains, up around the Encino Reservoir, the forest had been burning for three days straight and the northern end of the Los Angeles basin now lay under a light gauze of smoke. During the day the light had a flat, metallic quality, but at night, as the sun lowered, the sky above the Pacific was mauve and gold and burnt-rose and charcoal, and crowds gathered on the pier and along the beaches to marvel at it.

Fifty m.p.h. Olympic Boulevard. Tim twisted the Vespa into third gear and crossed into Santa Monica. Inside his helmet, a radio news broadcast: more American casualties in Afghanistan, a fatal gas explosion in Culver City, the Californian deficit, predictions of economic ruin....

Tatters of a daily hangover.

Four years ago, after his last screenplay had gone nowhere, he'd thrown in his writing towel and started drinking a bottle of wine a night.

The shops and the lights and the cars slid past.

Everywhere about him people were lit in the fireside glow of sunset.

But as he breathed in smoke and wove through traffic, the only thing he saw was Jocelyn. Surrounded by a group of men.

A nine-level car park on the corner of Wilshire Boulevard and South Barrington Avenue. Decommissioned in 2008, but still standing because budget cuts by Santa

Monica City Council had delayed its demolition indefinitely. Gray concrete, talentless graffiti, entrance barriers torn from housings.... Nothing Special. Nothing more than another helping of L.A. decay.

Tim had been there once before. A week ago.

When he'd pulled up outside the coffee shop where Jocelyn worked.

When she was already disappearing down the street in the passenger seat of a blue Toyota Prius.

Jocelyn.

Year-and-a-half girlfriend.

Kind of.

They'd met at a weekend screenwriting seminar Tim had signed up for in a half-assed attempt to slap his writing career back into consciousness. By lunch the first day they'd abandoned the course and, rather than continuing to debate the positioning of second-act turning points, were sweating into her mattress instead.

You didn't have to be Einstein to surmise she wasn't quite right in the head. But Tim was still staggering under the weight of Rebecca's death, and moving in with Jocelyn offered at least the illusion that there were other things in life besides grief.

The first six months hadn't been too bad, considering their differences – she, an ex-meth addict, running on Diet Coke and a coruscating mix of rage and self-delusion; he, withdrawn, sedated with wine, a recluse in the making.

The next six, though, had been an ever-accelerating careen down the far slope of their relationship after it became impossible for Tim to ignore the fact that his partner was as gripped by sexual compulsion as she was by her need for over-caffeinated cola.

The casual comments about trying group sex that had started early in their cohabitation became repetitive. There were absences, regular and prolonged, that she did not bother to explain. There were phone calls she took in another room.

He'd moved out, into the flat Rebecca had left him. But he'd continued seeing Jocelyn part-time; the tincture of ennui that then clouded his blood simply made it easier to suffer her infidelities than to end things properly. And, too, she was one of his very few social contacts, a fact which, despite her flaws, made her a valuable commodity in his circumscribed life.

But she was losing value now.

Rapidly.

Absent from the cafe again. Same day of the week. Same time. Hadn't been too hard to figure where she might be.

Tim bounced over the fractured concrete of the car park's entrance ramp and began the spiral climb upwards. There was no lighting on any of the floors, but the faint evening glow lingering outside and the beam of his headlamp were enough to reveal the desolation which had settled on the building during four years of abandonment.

On the lower levels: mounds of trash and landfill, illegally dumped by private sanitation companies. Higher up, above the smell of rotting garbage: small clusters of mattresses and cardboard cartons, shopping carts drawn into loose crescents to form illusory, wagon-train protection. Homeless people, some in families, looked up briefly from the weak light of lanterns and cooking stoves as Tim passed.

On the eighth floor, empty of both garbage and people, he parked the Vespa and took off his helmet. A hollow silence. Breath in his ears. Steeling himself. Knowing what he'd find on the level above.

He walked quietly up the final ramp, hid behind a pillar, watching.

At the center of the floor: six cars grouped haphazardly, two with their headlights on, most with their doors open. People inside the cars and around them, moving against the light, caught briefly as they drifted from one place to another, one partner to another. The British had given it a name. *Dogging.* Fucking strangers in secluded public places.

In the back of a Camry the torsos of two men were visible in silhouette, pumping at something between them. Three other men stood grouped around the front of an old Taurus, shirts open, pants rucked at their ankles. Splayed diagonally across a corner of the hood, head hanging backwards over a fender, Jocelyn lurched as they went at her.

She was naked, her skinny body made skinnier still by her arching back. Her face was hidden but her forehead and short red hair were visible between the legs of one of the men.

Beyond the cars, where the light thinned to a mesh of shadow, a blond woman stood behind the open door of a blue Prius, hand between her legs, watching Jocelyn. Same as she had when Tim had followed them there the week before.

When the men were finished with her, Jocelyn picked up her clothes and walked naked to the Prius. Headlights caught a liquid sheen on her face and breasts, down the insides of her pale thighs.

The blond woman stepped forward into the light and met her with an expression of frightened wonder on her face, as though Jocelyn had returned from some dangerous journey which the woman herself longed to undertake but did not have the courage for. She ran her hands over Jocelyn's body, then reached into the car for a towel.

When Jocelyn was dried and dressed she vamped a little and held her hand out. The blond woman took some sheets of paper from the glove compartment and gave them to her. There was just enough light for Tim to see that they were yellow.

Tim on a bench in a small park. The day gone and dark. Thin traffic on Wilshire. A string of movie billboards in front of a construction site, bouncing hard, mercury light across the boulevard. The smell of grease from a fast-food joint and the hot dustiness of day-long baked concrete masking any scent of grass or leaf that might have survived in this sad simulacrum of nature.

Tim had hoped for birdsong, a small reminder that some slender thread still connected the city to a wider world where human passions were not so thoroughly twisted.

But there was none of that either.

He stared numbly out at the road.

Across Wilshire, a girl on a red-and-white Triumph Thruxton swerved to the curb and dismounted. Tim watched her. She wore a one-piece black leather catsuit and SWAT boots, and when she pulled her full-face helmet off he saw that her hair was a short chop of dull blond.

She stood for a moment, looking up at one of the movie billboards – a lurid advertisement for a big-budget action flick with a lot of explosions. She checked the street both ways, then took something from a pannier at the back of her bike.

She held it out, away from her – a bottle with a rag stuffed into its neck. And then the rag was alight, a bright flare fringed with oily smoke, and there was a grin on the girl's face, stretched and crazy as she turned and swung her arm up and over and launched the bottle at the billboard.

The first thought through Tim's head was a tiredly eye-rolling "Jesus, this fucking town...." But then the bottle broke and the billboard was a sheet of flame and Tim, who thought he cared about nothing anymore, muttered in wonder, "That chick just set a billboard on fire...."

The Thruxton roared and Tim looked back at the road and saw the girl tearing toward the first cross street inland. Her taillight flashed as she approached the corner then went dull as she made a low, fast, sweeping turn. And then all that was left of her was the dwindling note of her machine.

Tim watched the billboard burn, watched as the backing board disintegrated to reveal its supporting framework of girders, and thought that in the beauty of its destruction, in the insane outrageousness of the act, there was an echo of what he had hoped to find in the park's missing birdsong.

Chapter 2

Jocelyn's flat was stark. In an attempt to unclutter the inside of her head she had denuded the place of anything that did not fulfill a necessary purpose. No knick-knacks, no flowers, no picture frames.

Lying on her bed, Tim listened to the shower run in the bathroom.

He'd given her enough time to get back to her apartment, then dropped by and casually asked where she'd been. She'd shrugged, said, "Nowhere," and avoided any further conversation by closing the bathroom door.

She came back into the bedroom now, pulled on a T-shirt, drank half a can of Diet Coke and paced the room, smoking, rarely looking at him.

She said: "You should do *The Artist's Way.*"

"I'm not blocked."

"You haven't written anything since before we met".

"Still had two scripts made."

"Digital video. Both of them sub one-mil."

"Better than nothing at all."

"You should see what I'm writing now."

Tim snorted. Jocelyn churned out screenplays in a cigarette- and caffeine-fueled fury, four or five a year, but they were all uniformly shit. Like him, she had shelves of how-to books, had been to workshops with Robert McKee, studied Syd Field on YouTube, but her story ideas were pedestrian and her understanding of structure was nonexistent. She had, so far, failed to attract interest from even the lowest of the lower-rung agents.

When she'd finished her cigarette she took a sheaf of typed pages from a desk in the corner of the room and held them out to him.

"I thought maybe you could polish the dialogue. Don't change anything else. It'd be cool if I could get it back by next week."

Jocelyn left the room. Tim stared at the ceiling, then out of a window that showed black sky and the tops of palms under-lit by streetlight.

There were twenty-five pages. He sat with his back against the wall and read them, more to delay returning to the loneliness of his dead sister's flat than out of any real interest. He knew what he'd find – characters that were undeveloped, a nonsensical through-line, a plot full of holes.... And shitty dialogue.

Only he didn't. What he found was slightly more than the first act of a finely observed and elegantly structured drama. It was marred by Jocelyn's trademark junior-school prose and the dialogue was on the nose more often than not, but the skeleton of the script – the progression and balance of scenes, the turning points punching their way through the narrative, the manipulation of sympathy – was masterfully accomplished.

The story, or at least what he had of it, was a portrait of three aspiring film-makers struggling to establish themselves in the business. Starting out with lofty ideals, artistic integrity and an arthouse sensibility, they are quickly seduced by Hollywood, eventually abandoning character-driven indie moviemaking to focus instead on a break-through mainstream action film.

Once the film has been made, though, they face career disaster when one of the heads of a film distribution company that purchases the rights to their action film wants to shelve it indefinitely. They respond by murdering him, knowing that his business partner will release the film.

Out in the living room, Jocelyn was vacuuming and reciting a personal affirmation mantra. Tim knew it was some bullshit about freeing creativity and achieving success; he'd heard it a thousand times. It occurred to him now, though, that if she finished this screenplay and the rest of it was as good as this sample, there was a better than even chance she'd get her wish.

He put down the last page, wondering how Jocelyn, until now such an abject failure at the craft of writing for film, could suddenly produce work of such quality.

He got off the bed and went into the living room. He waved the pages at her.

"This is good."

"It's going to make me a rock star."

"You got a treatment of the rest?"

She tapped her head.

"In here."

"Really? You started this and you don't have a treatment or a step-outline?"

"Trying a different process."

"What happens in the second act?"

"Haven't decided."

"This guy, Tad Beaumont, the head of the production company—"

"Jesus, what about him?"

"He's going to have some sort of personal crisis, right? Because he's given up his ideals, not to mention become a murderer?"

"Maybe."

"Maybe? Don't you think it's kind of imperative to his arc?"

Jocelyn looked levelly at him.

"You know, Tim, showing me how clever you are isn't the same thing as actually writing something."

She went into the bedroom and closed the door behind her.

Tim suppressed an urge to call her a cunt, to scream that he knew all about her cheating. He looked pointlessly about the room and felt its emptiness creep into him like damp, figured his time there was pretty much at an end. He folded the script pages into his jacket pocket and started to leave.

In the small entrance alcove the leather document case Jocelyn pretentiously used as a handbag hung from a peg by the front door. Sticking from it: the upper edges of five folded sheets of yellow note paper.

Tim checked over his shoulder, the bedroom door was still closed. He pulled the pages out, saw that they were a step-outline for part of a screenplay.

Screenwriters used step-outlines as maps to guide themselves through the construction of first-draft screenplays. Step-outlines did not lay out the internal structure of each shot or contain dialogue as such, and any two screenwriters, working from the same step-outline would produce screenplays which differed in tone and approach. But the story, the characters, the progression of the plot and the final outcome of each screenplay would be essentially the same.

The pages Tim held outlined the rise of a group of filmmakers through the Hollywood ranks after the release of a violent action movie they had produced – obviously the next section of the story for the screenplay he'd read in the bedroom. They were written in ballpoint in handwriting that wasn't Jocelyn's.

Tim replaced the papers and left the apartment.

CHAPTER 3

Gone ten p.m. Traffic on Wilshire Boulevard less than light. The yellow 1967 Camaro easy to tail. Denning hung back a few car-lengths, but he wasn't really worried about being spotted. The driver of the Camaro had no reason to suspect he was being followed and his passenger, Denning's twenty-eight-year-old daughter, Peta, would keep her mouth shut even if she saw Daddy's fifteen-year-old white Crown Victoria in her boss's rear-view mirror.

Denning's windows were closed. Air conditioner off. He was only vaguely conscious of the sweat that ran from his receding hairline and down his cheeks. Peta had been working for Kid Haldane for four months and it was plain to Denning that she was falling for him – the first rent in the web of dark interdependence she and Denning had woven in the ten years since Clara disappeared.

Peta was an attractive woman and the affair was long overdue. But the thought of her climbing into this man's bed, and the changes it would bring to his own life, made Denning want to cry out.

Santa Monica. Westwood Village. Denning had paid little attention to where he was on this route through the western end of Los Angeles. He'd given even less thought to what Haldane's destination might be. So, now, when the Camaro turned into an open parking lot about a quarter-mile past Beverly Hills, it took an effort of will to understand what he was seeing.

He drove on for another hundred yards, his stomach icing with disbelief, then U-turned and drove back, parked on the street a few yards shy of the entrance to the lot, killed his engine and lights.

A long, gray, two-story building bordered the lot at its far end. There was no lighting and the lot was only dimly illuminated by the spill from the boulevard. Two cars – the Camaro and a Maserati. All the other slots empty.

Peta and Kid stood at a service entrance set into the side of the building. Kid pressed a button and put his hand on the door. A moment later it opened and the two of them went through it.

Denning sat rigid in his seat and stared at the building. One part of the wall was covered with a billboard advertising an action movie, the rest of it displayed a giant, illuminated logo – three initials: GHQ.

G...H...Q....

Three letters that had been branded into Denning's brain eight years ago. Now filling him like a toxic wave, sending him tumbling back through the years, back to when the cold winds of disgrace snuffed out what was left of his life.

By 2004 GHQ had capitalized on the runaway success, just twenty-four months earlier, of *Maximum Kill*, its first major release, and had bagged two of that summer's top weekend openings. Any mutterings that *Maximum Kill* had been a fluke for a production company previously known only for a single arthouse flick were forever quieted, and Michael Starck and his two co-owners, the twins Jeffery and Ally Bannister, stepped firmly into the ranks of A-list independent producers.

Denning was working as a features writer for the Hollywood Reporter at the time and caught the assignment to write five thousand words on the company and its spectacular rise. Portrait pieces like this were ten-a-penny in the Hollywood press, and he figured he'd do his career a lot more good if he dumped the usual formula of potted bios and cinema-centric chronologies in favor of something a little more sensationalist.

So, Denning went looking around the edges of the company, searching for connections, relationships, involvements.... Searching for anything, however tenuously related, that might titillate his readers.

He found two things: Big Glass and Delores Fuentes.

In early 2002, the worldwide distribution rights to *Maximum Kill*, essentially a violent, eighteen-million-dollar car chase which Michael Starck had himself directed, were bought at the Toronto Film Festival by a new but pushy distribution company called Big Glass. Big Glass was owned and run by two partners: Theo Portman and Scott Bartlemann. Three months before the scheduled North American theatrical release of *Maximum Kill*, Scott Bartlemann was murdered.

The kill was an easy close for the Los Angeles County Sheriff's Department, because along with Scott Bartlemann's body they found that of his maid, her head blown off by an apparently self-inflicted shotgun blast. In the absence of any information to the contrary, the case was labeled murder/suicide and quickly disappeared from the front page.

That was it. That was the extent of the connection between GHQ and the Bartlemann murder – Scott Bartlemann had been one of the principals of the company distributing their film. Nothing more. But Denning saw that the murder could be used, however spuriously, to draw extra eyes to his planned story.

Hoping for some background color, he'd interviewed a few low-level Big Glass employees. There wasn't much they could tell him, given that they were on the outside looking in, so to speak, and not privy to any of the more juicy details the police might have stumbled across during their investigation. Denning did, however, learn three things: that *Maximum Kill* had been written by Danny Bartlemann, Scott Bartlemann's son and only child; that Danny and Scott had been estranged since Scott walked out on the family when Danny was eleven; and that, at the time of his death, Scott Bartlemann had been planning to delay the release of *Maximum Kill* for up to two years for commercial reasons.

On hearing this last snippet, Denning caught the scent of a Pulitzer nom; a chance to break a case the cops couldn't properly solve: *Son Kills Father Over Delayed Movie Release!* Sadly for Denning, the fragrance of journalistic fame faded into the balmy L.A. air when police case files revealed that Danny had an iron-clad alibi. At the time of Scott's death, he'd been in a Santa Barbara hospital undergoing a minor operation on one of his kidneys – a procedure necessitated by urinary tract complications resulting from a skiing injury he'd sustained in his youth.

Robbed of his chance to count Woodward and Bernstein among his peers, Denning moved on to take a closer look at GHQ itself.

Requests for interviews with its principals, who had been made aware of his earlier visits to the Big Glass office, were turned down – Michael Starck, and Jeffery and Ally Bannister all citing work commitments. This lack of personal contact put a serious hole in Denning's research, but by that time he had other things on his mind. He'd become obsessed with Delores Fuentes.

No examination of GHQ at that point in their development would have been complete without some mention of their most glittering star. She was, if the PR pieces were to be believed, a true Mexican spitfire. Sensual, beautiful, volatile and talented.

So talented, in fact, that she'd taken female lead in both films produced by GHQ after *Maximum Kill*. A feat all the more astounding to Denning because he could find no previous acting history for her – no drama school attendance, no bit parts or commercials, no previous roles. It was as though she had fallen to earth in Hollywood a fully formed star.

In addition to the acres of column inches devoted to Delores' merits as a female version of Bruce Willis in his *Die Hard* period, she'd also hit film industry headlines when it was learned she was signed to a ten-year exclusive contract with GHQ. Long-term exclusive contracts had gone out in the 1950s, but in interviews at the time Delores was quoted as saying that GHQ had made her a star and she saw no reason to ever work for anyone else.

All of this was interesting stuff, but not worth more than a paragraph or two in an article, the primary focus of which was a film production company. Thing was, Denning was still grieving the loss of Clara. And Delores had a body remarkably similar to that of Denning's disappeared wife.

The rational part of his brain knew that this similarity meant nothing, that it did not bestow one iota of who Clara had been upon the posturing female movie star. But there was another part of him, unfortunately, that didn't think quite as clearly.

From stalking her at various hip eateries to going through her garbage, Denning ran the gamut of cracked investigative practice, battering his head against the walls of privacy which either she or GHQ had thrown up around those portions of her life that did not immediately pertain to her current incarnation as movie star.

That wasn't to say there was nothing to be learned about her. There were press releases, of course – shallow descriptions of her previous life in Mexico, her attendance at a GHQ casting call because she had been dared by her girlfriends, the flash-grenade detonation of her success....

But none of these satisfied Denning's desire to *know* Delores, none of these carried the fleshy taste of who she really was.

Finally, after weeks of pestering everyone from the press girl at GHQ, to Delores' personal manager, to Delores herself when he was able to accost her in public, Denning secured an interview with her. Far from serving to establish a special rapport between Denning and his subject, though, this interview went bad from the start.

When he realized that Delores – sitting across a coffee table from him in her Bel Air mansion, displaying curves, skin texture and cadences of flesh that had once, in another woman, been so familiar to him – not only felt no physical attraction for him, but was obviously engaged in a game of subterfuge when it came to her past, Denning reacted badly.

He bored at her relentlessly with questions about her upbringing, her training as an actress, the obstacles she must surely have encountered on the road to success....

But Delores, made of sterner stuff than the average Tinsel Town floozy, blocked him at every turn. And Denning came away with nothing more than he'd already learned from her press releases.

Whether it was something to do with his intrusive probing of her background, or whether it was linked to his concurrent research of the Bartlemann murder, Denning never found out. But a week after the interview, GHQ destroyed his career, disgraced him in front of his peers, and sentenced him to a marginal existence of odd jobs and occasional prescription painkiller abuse.

Now, sitting in his car, sweltering in the GHQ parking lot, Denning could still smell the cool air of the Hollywood Reporter offices, could still see the dim room, its venetian blinds torqued against a carefree sun, where his editor and the security manager had sat him down and played him some footage on one of the early plasma screens. And he could still see the tinted glass of the limo's window sliding up as the two detectives arrested him on the sidewalk and walked him to their car, could still see the face of Michael Starck watching him as it disappeared behind a sheet of dark reflections.

Chapter 4

An unsubtle military palette – olive carpets, khaki walls, sections painted in Desert Storm camouflage. Posters for action movies that had smashed the box office. Displays of military hardware from various productions. GHQ. General Head Quarters. Michael Starck's mission statement: Conquer Hollywood.

This late at night, the place was empty. Peta followed Kid upstairs and along corridors. She was only there to carry his bag, to play her assistant's role, but it was hard not to be excited at being inside a real, bona fide Hollywood dream mill. Even more so when your boss was falling in love with you and the future looked set to hold a whole lot more Hollywood magic.

At the back of the building there was a private reception area for those lucky enough to get face time with Michael Starck. Beyond this, a short corridor lined with assault rifle replicas, and then a set of double doors that gave onto Starck's office.

Kid Haldane asked for his bag, a leather shoulder sack, and she held it open while he took out a small container of film – circular, yellow plastic, like home movies years ago. He put it in his hip pocket, winked at her, told her to wait in the reception area, then went down the corridor and pushed open the doors.

Michael Starck sat behind a desk that looked like a small fortress. More weaponry on the wall behind him. Down one side of the room, a collection of vintage projectors on wheeled stands.

Michael lifted a screenplay from his desk, looked levelly over it at Kid, then dropped it.

"*Antepenultimate.*"

The twang of his Australian accent was noticeable, even though he'd lived in the States for thirty years.

Kid nodded.

"The one before the one before last."

"Yeah. Sesquipedalian.... You know what that means?"

"Uh—"

"You're familiar with our catalogue."

"I've seen everything GHQ's done. I love that stuff, but—"

"The longest word in any of our titles has four syllables. *Antepenultimate* has six. Sesquipedalian is a word meaning a long word, or a word with many syllables. But its root is Latin – *sesquipedalis*, meaning a foot and a half in length. Not to put too fine a point on it, Kid, but that's about the size of the financial dick this film would shove up my arse."

"It's a title, who gives a shit? We'll change it."

"It's two hours of introverted drivel about a guy whose daddy didn't love him."

"It's a Danny Bartlemann script. The first thing he's written in ten years. Yeah, it needs some tightening, but don't you feel it? Doesn't it lift you?"

"Oh, please.... Look, this kind of thing is fine for Sundance. And that girl of yours wants to use it as a calling card? It's fine for that too – a closely observed, intensely wrought excursion into the lives of real people. Yeah, yeah, yeah. But you want three million dollars."

"*Only* three million dollars."

"It's not a lot of money for a film, nobody's disputing that. But it's a fuck-load of money to lose, even for a company like GHQ."

"You won't bankroll it yourself, you'll use private equity funding. And the risk to GHQ will be minimal after foreign sales. Even domestically you'll recoup, what? A million when you sell it to Big Glass?"

"Big Glass won't touch it."

"Are you kidding? Big Glass? The company Danny's father used to own?"

"*Part* own."

"Okay. But you're telling me they won't distribute it? What about old times' sake?"

Michael laughed and shook his head.

"Do you have the slightest fucking grasp on reality? *Antepenultimate* is too small. Big Glass is run by Theo Portman, has been since Scott Bartlemann's death. Theo lives to make money. *I* live to make money. The return on domestic distribution for a three-mil film isn't going to top three-fifty. It's just not worth doing. But that's not all. Someone, somewhere is going to lose money if the film tanks. And that's someone, somewhere we can't go to again to finance the films we *want* to make."

"But it won't tank. You saw what Chick did with *Loggers*. We broke even, for Christ's sake. Everyone got their money back. She won Best First Feature with it."

"At Atlanta."

"It's still an award. How long have we known each other? Twenty years? We were on our knees together in that fucking desert, man."

Michael shook his head in disgust. "*Loggers* had a budget of four-hundred K, and more than half of that came from the MPAA's New Director Fund. I'm one of the producers contracted to disburse those funds. I pushed them your way and made up the difference by selling a couple of the cars we used in *Turner's Highway*. GHQ didn't even carry *Loggers* on its books. And that, Kid, is as much as old times' sake gets you."

"Michael, come on. Filmmaker to filmmaker—"

"You've done one film. 'Filmmaker's' a bit of a stretch. And your director, ditto. She's done her student films and *Loggers*. Period."

Kid took a breath and thought about the film in his back pocket. He took another shot.

"Doesn't the quality of the movie mean anything?"

"It's not a movie, it's a script."

"Okay, script. Danny Bartlemann – he wrote *Maximum Kill*, for Christ's sake. That film put you and GHQ on the map. Don't you think there's a possibility a script by the same writer might turn a few bucks?"

"*Maximum Kill* was a flat-out, road-burning action movie with an outstanding body count and a shit-load of sex. It was an anomaly. Danny wrote it as a joke. Before that, he wrote another flick about Daddy: *The Seminal Day*. Lionsgate took a bath on it. *Antepenultimate* is just *The Seminal Day – Part Two*."

"What about *Chrysanthemum?*"

Michael's face turned stony.

"What about it?"

"The first feature GHQ made, before *Maximum Kill*. Your directorial debut. I'd venture to say it was somewhat sesquipedalian. And it was arthouse to its roots. I know, I've seen it."

"You've answered your own question, then."

Michael was a large man. He had a thick head of dark hair, a red face, and a prominent belly. He didn't give a shit about current Hollywood body-aesthetics, he was too successful. The only exercise he took was riding his horse. He kept a private stash of weapons at his house and there were rumors he'd once blown up a cow with a bazooka while filming in Thailand.

His mouth was set tight now and Kid figured the meeting was about to get called to a close. Kid stood up, took the yellow film case from his pocket and walked over to the row of projectors. He selected one and wheeled it out in front of an empty stretch of wall. Michael watched him darkly.

"This is *my* office, Kid."

Kid opened the case, took out a spool of film about four inches across.

"I saw you had one of these when I dropped off the script. Super 8. Retro cool...."

He located a wall socket, plugged the projector in, then laced the film through the gate and onto the take-up spool. He flicked a switch and the bulb came to life, throwing a blurred square of light against the wall. Kid twisted the lens until the edges of the square were sharp. He turned to Michael.

"I've had this film two years. I could have used it anytime I wanted and just asked for a handout. But I didn't. I want you to remember that, Michael. I'm not trying to fuck you. And I'm not going to do this more than once. But you're going to finance my film."

He set the film running.

Michael watched the image flicker on the wall of his office and felt a loose stirring in his bowels. And for the thousandth time cursed Delores and her cunt screenwriter.

When the film was done, as the take-up spool spun and the tail of the film ticked against the projector's tension arm, they came to terms.

Michael said: "A budget of three million, it'll have to go through the company."

"Fine by me."

"Anything over a million needs sign-off by Jeffery and Ally too. Company bylaws. And I can tell you, they won't want to make this."

"I'll take care of Jeffery and Ally. You just make sure you tell them you're signing off."

"You have something on them, as well?"

"I've known them a long time. Jeffery's a freak. I was a porn star. Draw your own conclusions. Ally will do whatever Jeffery wants."

"I want the film."

"I could have copied it."

"I'm sure you have. But Super 8 is reversal stock, it captures a positive image, so there's no negative. To make a good quality copy you'd have to use a transfer facility. Not something you'd risk, I think. Some tech recognizes me, takes a copy for himself, it'd be on YouTube before I could wipe my arse. Then it's worthless to you. That leaves some homemade video cam thing – shitty quality, less authenticity, easier to challenge. In any case, you can't expect me not to ask for a show of good faith if, as you say, you don't intend to use it again."

This wasn't anything Kid hadn't expected.

"How long will the money take?"

"Not long. A week or two. I'll send Business Affairs a memo when I hear from Jeffery and Ally. After that, you sign the papers and give me the film, Business Affairs transfers the funds into a production account."

"Or you transfer the funds and *then* I give you the film."

Michael looked at him without speaking for several seconds and then said: "No. If you can't do this for me, Kid, we need to have a different conversation."

Kid hesitated for a moment, then nodded.

"Okay."

He rewound the film and put it back in its case. At the door he stopped and turned to Michael.

"You renege on the deal, a shitty video copy could still cause you a lot of grief. And if I should wind up in a dumpster and my lawyer sends that shitty video copy to the police along with an outline of the deal we've just made, I think it'd go a long way to shoving a foot and a half of *legal* dick up your ass."

In the reception area, Peta dropped the film back into Kid's bag and slung it over her shoulder. Kid was in a good mood and wanted to have drinks in a bar across the street. On the ground floor, as they headed out of the GHQ building, they passed the door to a restroom. Peta told Kid to go on ahead, asked him for the key to his car so she could pick up her jacket on the way.

When she was finished in the toilet, Peta walked out into the parking lot, unlocked the Camaro and got her jacket. She looked inside the bag, saw only the film, a pad, some pens, a couple of blisters of OxyContin and a protein bar. Figuring Kid wouldn't need any of that stuff in the bar, and knowing nothing of the film's contents or importance, she dropped the bag into the driver's-side footwell.

CHAPTER 5

Denning had his window down. The heat and the anxiety of wondering what his daughter was doing in the GHQ building, of trying to divine what horror this insane intersection would give birth to, had tightened about his chest until he figured he'd better have some air.

But air hadn't made any difference at all.

Peta was now in a bar with her boss and the evening's conclusion was obvious. Denning's head lurched with images of tangled sheets, his daughter's spread legs.... He wanted to scream at the sky. He wanted his chest to blow apart and end his misery. But his ribs stayed knitted together and his heart kept pumping and his fucking brain, this brain that was so battered and worn, disobeyed him and kept on making sense of everything he saw.

Breath in...heart thudding, blood a surf in his ears, the Crown Vic's door open behind him. Breath out...his damp, dark suit clinging to him, pulling at his legs, Denning not feeling it, hearing sounds that weren't there, sounds he'd made two seconds before, only now catching up with him, so that he felt propelled by some motive wave, blown forward by something he'd decided long before.

Breath in...at the Camaro, the world slamming into place, long lines of light becoming objects again. Breath out...nausea, sweat, heat, a headache pushing at his forehead, sensation returning to fingers and hands and feet.

And the feel of the cylindrical rubberized grip in his palm, thumbing the bright steel stud, the pleasing jolt as the extendable baton shot to full-length, four segments of black steel. The weight, the heft, the sudden empowerment. The lozenge-shaped head arcing through the parking lot air. Denning a monster to himself – lips drawn, teeth at full clench, eyes stretched and watering. Around him, a boiling concoction of lights and objects, a spinning wall that set him beyond this pared fragment of Los Angeles. The sound of Wilshire a distant crepitation, as though somewhere there was a beach and somewhere beyond its dunes sea-grass rustled under an uneven wind.

A shatter of fragments, glassy; for a moment, for a heartbeat, for a breath, pausing in their trajectory to snatch light and hold it, bitter and hard, then collapsing in a dimming shower across the Camaro's seats and the tarmac of the lot.

And Denning, circling, smashing window after window, and then, with no more windows left to break, unzipping and pissing past the jagged glass of the driver's-side window. Shaking off, seeing Kid's bag and lifting it out, figuring whatever was in it Kid would miss.

Heading coastward. Denning spent now, his rage replaced by an overwhelming sense of his own impotence. He glanced at himself in the rear-view mirror. Dark, receding hair cut close, heavy moustache. He'd been told he looked like Burt Reynolds, before Burt started wearing a rug. But tonight there was nothing of that good ole boy handsomeness, nothing of that rugged capability. Tonight he looked drained. Tonight he looked like a man who could not understand even the smallest part of what went on in the world.

He pulled into a small court of stores and bought a bottle of Wild Turkey. Back in the car his eyes fell on Kid's leather bag. He opened it, saw the usual detritus – snacks, pens, a notepad full of scribbled reminders. And a couple of things a little more interesting – a circular yellow container that held a roll of narrow film with sprocket holes down one side, and two blisters of 40mg OxyContin.

Denning recognized the type of film. Snatches of his own childhood had been recorded on similar stock. He figured this spool was probably something mundane to do with Kid's movie business, that he'd check a few frames when he got somewhere where the light was better.

The OxyContin was a major bonus. In his early twenties Denning had been prescribed the painkiller for an injured shoulder – the result of repetitive impacts received during college football – and his body had never forgotten the delicious insulation the small pills provided. Denning would never have shot smack or burned meth, but ten years ago, after Clara disappeared, he'd scored his first illicit dispensation of OxyContin on a street corner in Watts. Since then, he'd indulged in week-long binges several times a year.

Denning swallowed one of the pills, chased it with a mouthful of bourbon, aware it wasn't a good mix, then pulled out onto Santa Monica Boulevard and rolled toward the ocean.

In the bar, Kid and Peta sipped jalapeño margaritas and snacked on blow-torched Tasmanian scallops.

Kid was in his mid-forties. He was the Marlborough man with a ten-inch cock; a gauntly lined, suntanned and sun-blonded porn star fuck-up playing the L.A. game – bury the past, incinerate an old life in the transformative fires of movieland, turn himself into something new.

At least he was trying.

And Peta was a necessary ingredient. Someone to love at last. Someone he *could* love.

They kissed over their drinks and he begged her to come home with him, but she said she wasn't ready yet. Strange, in Kid's experience, for a twenty-eight-year-old woman in the film industry.

They had known each other for four months, had been flirting for two of those. And now there were embraces behind closed doors at the office. The groundwork was done, for both of them. And yet she had not made that final move, had not set a match to the touchpaper of their relationship.

He had suspected an existing lover, but she had sworn that she had none. He had asked to visit her at home, but she had refused with some excuse about privacy and personal space and that her father wouldn't like it. He had asked about her life, her history, had gotten next to nothing.

New ground for Kid, the celluloid cocksman.

They talked about *Antepenultimate*, about the excitement of making a movie. Kid said his meeting with Michael Starck had gone well, that things were on track. He avoided specifics, steered her away from the topic of finance.

Walking back to the parking lot they held hands, the carbon dusted air of Wilshire falling about them, warm and pleasantly acrid, Kid letting himself believe that he really could become someone different.

It was only when he saw the Camaro, with its windows smashed and piss on the seats, that he realized Peta was not carrying his bag. When he asked, Peta, feeling like she wanted to throw up, told him she'd left it in the car.

Kid was quiet for a while, looking at the wreck of his classic automobile. Then he took his jacket off, bundled it up and used it to sweep out glass and soak up the puddles in the seams of the seats.

He climbed behind the wheel. Peta slid in beside him.

Kid stared through the space where the windshield had been, his fists balled on the rim of the steering wheel, the muscles at the corners of his jaw bunching. Peta put her hand on his arm and said: "There wasn't really anything in it except that film."

Kid looked at her for a long moment, and then he smiled and rubbed her thigh and started the Camaro. They drove down to Santa Monica, the wind in their faces, so Peta could get her car from out front of the office.

CHAPTER 6

Denning trudged drunkenly through the sand. He'd taken a second Oxy on the way to the beach and his bourbon bottle was half empty. He held it by the neck, swinging it as though it were a scythe, cutting his stumbling way through the night. His head was too heavy to lift, so he watched the sand lurching beneath his feet like a sparkling treadmill, seeing nothing else, finding comfort in its consistency, every step the same.

The drug and the alcohol and the rolling sand. Brain blank. Wanting nothing more than nothingness. Wanting to float away, to feel his feet leave the ground, to drop the bottle, to unsling Kid's bag from his shoulder, to feel his clothes slip away, to rise up into the orange-dusted night sky above the Santa Monica coast, to be blown out to sea, to dissolve....

But Denning's heart was too heavy. It chained him to his own desolation, and all the booze and all the drugs in the world could not cut those iron links. So, when his feet stopped moving, he followed its pull and fell heavily to the sand, ass-first like some giant toddler, legs splayed in front of him, arms cradling Kid's bag, chin on his chest, eyes watching his hands as though they might do something interesting if he stared at them long enough. But when one of them moved it was only to raise the bottle to his mouth.

Tim and Sean in Sean's '78 Trans Am. It had been gold when he bought it, with a firebird logo on the hood, but Sean had had it sprayed matte black to minimize its visual signature on his infrequent journeys across the dark tarmac of the city.

A hideout car for a hideout guy. Recluse didn't begin to describe it. He lived in a converted electricity sub-station off an unused trail in the Hollywood Hills. He called it his bunker. He'd been off the grid for two years. Since before Tim had met him for the first time at Westwood Memorial Park, the day Rebecca had been buried.

Back then, Sean still looked like he was clean, still looked like the up and coming James Dean surrogate he'd been making himself into for the previous ten years. Blond hair, blue eyes, toned, tanned, ripped.

He'd stood at the back of the small chapel where the service was held. Quiet, not knowing anyone there, watching from the shadows. After the service, he'd offered his condolences to Tim, said he'd met Rebecca at a few industry parties. He hadn't known her that well, but always thought she looked like a really nice girl. Tim liked him immediately, grasped at the emotional straw held out by a man who was so obviously sympathetic, so obviously open to friendship.

But Sean had already started shooting smack by then and it didn't take long for those James Dean looks to change. Now, his hair was down to his shoulders and his body was thin and pale. Bar one small role in an indie, he hadn't worked since that day in the cemetery. Hadn't wanted to. What sparked this degeneration Tim never knew and Sean never said. They stayed friends all the same.

At the beach. They were parked in the large parking lot that fronted the sand. Behind them, a few hundred yards, the pedestrian walkway of Ocean Front was empty except for an occasional late-night cyclist and a few ambling loners on the lookout for sexual opportunity.

To the left, across the mostly deserted asphalt, Santa Monica Pier rose against the dark sky, jamming a long, neon finger into the Pacific. The Ferris wheel made patterns of colored light, but it was almost twelve now and its carriages were empty.

There were floodlights at points around the lot, but many of them had burned out and the bulbs had not been replaced. For fifty yards the sand was dimly illuminated, after that the beach was dark, and then there was the faint shine of the ocean.

Sean tied off and shot up, threw the empty syringe out the window. For a few moments he rode the small rush his top-up hit had given him, eyes closed, breath heavy through his nose, then he shifted in his seat and looked at Tim with pinned eyes.

"You gotta wake up, dude. That bitch is fucked in the head."

"I know."

"'*I know*'? She just got fucked by three dudes. You should have walked in there, slapped the shit out of her, and terminated it. Instead you don't say shit? What does it take, man? I know you're still grieving for Rebecca. I get that. But you're getting close to the edge, bro. You don't write anymore, you drink every night, you don't know anyone.... And that gut of yours is getting unsightly, you don't mind me saying."

Sean wore a sleeveless T-shirt and Tim looked pointedly at the small trickle of blood in the crook of his arm. Sean caught it.

"Okay, I'm no role model. But someone's gotta say it, man."

Tim stared through the windshield, stung because he knew what Sean said was true.

Out across the beach, where the shadows started, a drunk man in a suit walked through the sand and collapsed.

Tim and Sean sat in silence.

A couple of minutes later the man in the suit still hadn't moved. From somewhere in the parking lot there came the thud of car doors closing. Tim looked to his left and saw a rusted Pontiac. Two men, one with stringy blond hair, the other gray and balding, walked away from it, heading out across the sand.

Sean nodded toward the drunk.

"Dude's gonna get rolled."

And in that moment, in the matte black car, with Sean's smack-nasal voice throwing away that comment like a guy getting robbed was just one more blip in the L.A. night, Tim felt something break inside him and rage flowed down from his head, through his chest and his arms and his legs and he looked around the car and saw a shifting wrench on the small backseat. And when it was in his hand it felt heavy and right and he got out of the car and started across the lot with Sean calling after him: "Hey, what the fuck, man?"

Out on the sand, the two men like something from a zombie flick – meth addicts for sure – capering toward the drunk, all disjointed limbs and flapping clothes.

And then crouching over him, down on their haunches, starting to pick through his pockets. And Tim coming up on them, dimly hearing Sean's door opening and closing way back behind, not thinking that this was a crazy thing to do, not weighing the consequences, the possible outcome. Just feeling...anger.

The guy on the ground lay on his back, conscious but out of it, trying drunkenly to push away his assailants. He had the strap of a leather bag looped across his chest, the bag itself was underneath him. The blond meth-head was in the process of trying to work it free while the other one held the drunk's arms.

When Tim got there they froze for a moment, looking up. Then the gray-haired one said: "Fuck off, man. We found him. Go do one of the fags on the boardwalk."

And then he saw the wrench Tim was holding and said, "Oh, yeah?" and pulled out a switchblade and snicked it open, smiling like he knew Tim would just go away. But Tim swung the wrench and hit him flat with it on the side of the head and an arc of blood from a small cut vein leapt into the air, pattering against the sand, and the man fell sideways, stunned.

The blond was halfway to his feet when Tim heard the sound of running footsteps behind him and Sean launched himself into the air and kicked the guy square in the face and then barreled on over him and tumbled into the sand, rolled and stood up.

Two fucked muggers. Blood in their hair. Blood on their faces. Both only half conscious. Lying in the sand waiting for the pain to stop. The guy Tim had hit with the wrench starting to puke.

Tim helped the drunk to his feet, noticed he looked a bit like a young Burt Reynolds. The drunk looked around, steadying himself on his feet. When his eyes focused on the gray-haired mugger he took a couple of shaky steps and kicked him in the stomach. Then let Tim lead him back to the parking lot with Sean walking quickly ahead of them, leaving the scene of the crime asap.

Walking sobered the drunk a little, and when they got to the car Tim asked for his address and called him a cab. Sean got into the Trans Am and closed the door. Tim and the drunk leaned against the trunk. The drunk stuck his hand out, slurred: "Alan Denning."

"Tim."

They shook. Denning reached into the shoulder bag and brought out a blister of pills.

"You want some OxyContin?"

"Really?"

"Sure."

Denning passed the blister over then sank back into a stupor. A little while later the cab arrived and took him away. When he'd gone, Sean rolled down his window and said: "You know, Tim, that wasn't exactly what I meant."

The heat of the day hadn't lifted with the night, but now there were clouds in the sky out over the ocean and the smell of smoke from the Encino Reservoir fires seemed lighter, though maybe it was just because of the sea.

Tim gave Sean half the remaining Oxy. Looked at his friend sitting in the black car, noticed how drawn and tired he looked. Tim knew he'd been to rehab three times, knew he'd tried to quit a whole lot more on his own. But it had never taken.

There had always been an unspoken agreement between them that Sean's history was not to be talked about. But tonight, after the violence they'd just shared, after the shit he was going through with Jocelyn, Tim couldn't help asking.

"What happened, man? To the film career...to everything?"

Sean smiled sadly and started the Trans Am, and while the engine rumbled he looked at Tim, still smiling, and then said: "So long, tough guy."

Tim watched him pull out of the parking lot and turn onto Appian Way, thinking that if this once-golden boy could fall so far and so hard, then no one was safe.

On the ride home, Tim caught another newscast – half a street of houses was burning on the border of Topanga State Park after one of the fires had jumped firebreaks and made its first foray into the suburban fringe. Two fire fighters had been badly burned and a family of six was dead after refusing to evacuate their home. On the upside, it was possible there would be rain soon.

CHAPTER 7

Rebecca's flat. His now. All her stuff crammed into the second bedroom at the end of the hall so he wouldn't have to see it every day.

Back from the beach. Late, late night. Stripped raw by Jocelyn's dogging, by what he'd done to the meth addict out on the sand. Standing in the middle of the living room, light from the ceiling too bright, eyes closed; letting in, a little at a time, what the place meant, the pain and the loss.

Rebecca was the success story. A degree in English Lit when she was twenty-two, post-grad diplomas in film production and screenwriting from UCLA, an internship with Fox Searchlight, then the move into full-time screenwriting. She sold the second script she wrote, and pretty much every one after that. By the time she was in her mid-thirties she'd had her name on five features and her reputation in Hollywood was solid.

Tim, on the other hand, two years younger, went straight from high school into a twenty-year string of dead-end jobs and did his writing at night. By *his* mid-thirties the only entries on his screenwriting resume were two straight-to-video cheapies.

Luck of the draw. He didn't begrudge Rebecca her success. She was his sister. He'd grown up idolizing her. He'd grown up a little bit in love with her.

Rebecca had had a wild side. In Hollywood, she decompressed from the pressures of writing with casual sex, mining internet dating sites for men and women.

Tim and Rebecca both lived in L.A. They saw each other every few weeks. A brother in love with his sister, the sister a little loose. Both of them old enough. Both of them not the sort to care what other people thought. It had to happen.

And it did.

One night, after dinner at Rebecca's flat and too many bottles of New Zealand Sauvignon Blanc, with the second bedroom in the process of being repainted, they'd decided it'd be better if Tim didn't drive, if he stayed over. Rebecca had a king, they'd stay on their own sides. Same as when they were kids on vacation.

He'd fallen asleep without incident. A couple of hours later, though, he'd woken up inside her.

They lasted three months. Three months of sex a couple of nights a week, Rebecca digging the freakishness of it. It might have gone on longer, but Tim was in love, thought he'd found his life partner. When Rebecca realized this, saw the heartache that lay ahead, she killed it fast. Drove the point home by playing him a DVD she'd made of herself in bed with various internet-sourced partners. Figured it would save him greater hurt.

But Tim was already hurt so badly that he stopped writing and began a high-speed retreat from life.

They stayed in touch, but their meetings grew less and less frequent until, at the end, Tim knew very little of what was going on in his sister's life.

His last contact with her had been two years ago, when she'd phoned to tell him she was going up to the San Gabriel Mountains to finish rewrites on a screenplay. Said if he wanted to visit he was welcome. Tim had asked what the script was about – he'd read all her others. Rebecca made excuses, said it wasn't the right time to talk about it. Tim had never gone up to visit her.

A cold morning. Sixty-one degrees and rain. The narrow view he had of the sea down an alley from the second-story studio he was renting in Venice at the time showed gray sky and gray water scored with dirty lines of chop.

The two cops were detectives from the Sheriff's Department. They'd driven down from the San Gabriel Mountains. They stood at the top of the external stairs, wearing raincoats that didn't look like they were doing much good.

Tim was off work with a hangover. He'd drunk a bottle of ginger beer and swallowed 120mg of codeine, but his head still throbbed and his liver felt like it had been fried in a pan. When he opened the door, the cops told him his sister had been murdered.

Inside the flat. One of the cops, Jessup, spoke. The other didn't.

"She was renting a vacation property outside a village called Mule Ridge. You know what she was doing there?"

"Working on a screenplay. She was a screenwriter. What happened?"

"Someone shot her. Four times, close range. Looks like a handgun."

"When?"

"Close as we can tell, around mid-afternoon yesterday. August twenty-third. We're going on the assumption it was a robbery gone bad. No cash, no credit cards in her purse. You say she was a screenwriter – she'd have a laptop with her, right?"

"Yeah, she never went anywhere without it."

"We didn't find one. Maybe someone heard about a Hollywood screenwriter on vacation and figured she'd be worth taking down."

Tim nodded numbly. Jessup continued.

"We've started canvassing, maybe we'll turn up someone who saw or heard something. But the place is pretty isolated, about two miles outside of town...." Jessup shrugged. "You know what she was working on, specifically?"

"Just another script. She was successful, she was always working on something. Maybe her agent would know. Was she raped?"

"No sign of it. Looks like whoever it was just walked in, shot her, took some stuff and left. Why?"

Tim told them about his sister's promiscuity, her use of internet sites. Jessup said they'd pull her ISP records.

Jessup talked to Tim awhile longer, getting details about Rebecca, her agent's name, the people she knew, checked that the address on her driver's license was still current, asked if he had a key to her apartment because they hadn't found any keys with Rebecca and they'd need to check the place and secure it.

Two days later Jessup came back and drove him to the Lincoln Heights building of the Los Angeles County Department of Coroner for a formal ID.

A cold alcove. A body on a gurney. Green fabric screens. On the other side of them, the sounds of trolley wheels, drawers opening and closing, men working quietly. Tim had known there was no chance of a mistake, that the cops would have identified her from the fingerprint on her driver's license. But he'd hoped all the same.

No mistake.

His sister.

When he pulled back the sheet, three holes between her breasts, black around the edges. A patch of gauze below her eye.

The last minutes with the physical body of a loved one. The last time you will ever see that form, that face, those hands, the lips that spoke a thousand things to you, trivial and profound.... How to leave that last connection? How to say that final, irrevocable, obscene goodbye? How to hold the pieces of your heart together, to walk away with your own blood running between your fingers?

Outside. Sunshine and a sky washed clean by last night's rain. Sitting in Jessup's car, driving to Rebecca's flat in Santa Monica. Jessup wanted Tim to take a look at the place – the absence of house keys at the scene bugged him a little.

Inside Rebecca's home, another sledgehammer of grief – a thousand small evidences of her, of her likes and dislikes, of her work and her life, of who she had been.

In the living room, Jessup said: "We had the locks changed because of the missing keys. There's no computer here, so our assumption that it was stolen at Mule Ridge looks to be correct. We also spoke to Rebecca's agent. He said she was working on something, but he didn't really know what. Said all she told him was that it was a personal project and that she didn't need him to rep it. A spec script?"

"It's where you write a screenplay and hope someone will buy it, rather than getting commissioned to write it."

Jessup looked uneasily around the room.

"Did she have more than one computer?"

"No, just the laptop."

"As a screenwriter, particularly a successful one, she'd have copies of what she wrote? On paper, I mean."

"Of course."

"Yeah, that's what I thought. We couldn't find any here."

"They're in her study, first door off the hall. She kept them in a cabinet."

Jessup shook his head.

"Not there."

They went into the study. A bare room, walls painted white. A desk, a chair, a set of glass-fronted bookshelves. Every other time Tim had been in the room the top shelf of the bookcase had held a collection of screenplays, titles written in black marker on their spines. The shelf was empty now.

Tim opened the draws in the desk – pens, toner cartridges, a couple of reams of blank paper. Nothing screenplay-related. No notes, no outlines, no treatments. There was a gray filing cabinet in the corner of the room. He opened this too – bills, receipts, tax papers, contracts. But no screenplays. Tim turned to Jessup and shrugged.

"Well, they used to be here."

"Would she have thrown them away?"

"Unlikely. When you write a screenplay it's like it's your baby. Do you think someone took her keys and came here and stole her screenplays? What for? They aren't worth anything. It'd be like stealing a bunch of books."

"I don't know. There's no sign of a break in, but then there wouldn't be if keys were used. On the other hand, there's quite a bit of expensive stuff in the place – TV, ornaments etc. So if someone *did* come here, why didn't they take any of that? We dusted the place and we've been able to eliminate all the prints we found – all friends or business acquaintances, people with legitimate reasons for having been here. So.... I don't know. Maybe she just moved the screenplays to a storage facility that we'll turn up later. We'll factor it into our investigation."

"Do you have any leads at all?"

"To be honest, no. Unfortunately our canvass was unsuccessful. No one in the village or the surrounding area heard or saw anything. We found hoof prints about a hundred yards away from where she was staying, but there are riding trails all around there and the property is a right-of-way for riders, so that hasn't led anywhere. We got viable slugs from the scene, but ballistics couldn't match them to anything in the database. We're still looking into the hook-up site she used."

Jessup had a slim manila folder with him. He tapped it against his fingers and looked at Tim for a moment before speaking again.

"Look, I don't know if it's something that would be useful to you, but I have photographs here of the scene. I have to warn you, they're distressing, but sometimes relatives feel they need to get a visual grasp on what happened. To be clear, some of them do show your sister's body."

Tim took the folder. It held several large color photographs of the interior of a small rental property. Shots of various rooms. Different angles. In two of the pictures – a body on the floor, covered with a sheet. Tim closed the folder quickly and handed it back.

"I don't want this."

Jessup nodded.

"The scene has been cleared now. If you want to visit it, I can arrange access for you. Sometimes it helps with closure."

Tim looked at him like he was insane.

Jessup nodded again and apologized. He looked at his watch, then said: "I know I haven't been able to give you anything concrete, but it's early days yet. We're working the case as hard as we can and there's a good chance we'll find something that leads us to whoever did this. Sometimes just one little thing is all you need. You know, maybe somebody from around there just went on vacation and when they get back they'll give us a license plate, a description, something...."

But the case had never been solved. The police didn't locate the missing screenplays or the laptop, and the hook-up site didn't give them anything more than a bunch of people possessed both of over-active libidos and alibis. And they didn't turn up a suspect. When he'd been told of his sister's death, Tim had had fantasies of revenge, of tracking down and murdering her killer. But these eventually dissolved under a river of white wine, impotence and time.

Now, two years after Rebecca had had the life blown out of her, Tim stepped into the second bedroom of the flat she had left him.

Boxes of clothes stacked against the walls, piles of books, ornaments, pictures, jewelry.... What he wanted sat where he'd put it when he'd moved in six months earlier, a burned DVD in a plastic case, propped in the corner of a windowsill.

He'd swallowed 40mg of OxyContin before he left the beach and the drug was warm inside him. But not so much so that he couldn't feel the charge of excitement building in his stomach and groin. He'd thought about this DVD ever since he'd found it among Rebecca's things, but he hadn't played it yet, frightened of the price he knew it would exact. The last time he'd watched it was when Rebecca had broken his heart. Now he didn't care. Now his need for contact with her was too strong for wine or painkillers or common sense.

In the lounge. Windows closed, the apartment overheated and stuffy. He stripped off his pants, pushed the disc into the slot. Sat on the couch in his briefs, one hand holding the remote, the other on his crotch.

A parade of lovers. An encyclopedia of fucking. A guy with a heavy tan and slicked-back hair, a surfer, a slender man with an expensive watch, a tattooed woman with dyed-black hair, a girl with freckles and pink nipples…. Grasping arms, locked legs, the slapping sound of flesh against flesh.

Tim hard, squeezing himself, sobbing at the infinite distance that separated him from his sister.

And needing more. Needing more than an image of her. Needing to taste her, to smell her again, her sweat, her scent….

And then an answer to this need. A scene with Rebecca and another woman, shot in the second bedroom which, at that time, had been empty of furniture save a futon on the floor and a large mirror on the wall. Rebecca getting up from the bed, laughing, saying: "You want dirty? I can do dirty."

And moving to the foot of the futon, and out of shot. Passing beyond the camera's field of vision but her reflection appearing in the mirror. Tim watching as she opened a small closet, then crouched and peeled away a square of carpet and lifted a small trapdoor. She looked over her shoulder at the woman on the bed and Tim heard her say: "My goodies."

When she walked back into shot she carried a large pink vibrator and wore a pair of tight black leather briefs with a zip between the legs.

Tim froze the video and ran from the lounge. It took him a couple of minutes to clear the closet of the boxes he'd crammed into it. He lifted the carpet, saw a trapdoor with an inset brass ring.

A small compartment, about the size of two shoeboxes. Goodies indeed – a selection of vibrators and dildos, a strap-on, a small bottle of amyl nitrate, two pairs of split-crotch panties in a frilly material, and the leather briefs from the video. Tim pulled them out one by one, his sister's intimate stash.

There was a trace of scent on one of the dildos, but it was faint after two years and no use to Tim. The panties were clean and smelled only of the material they were made from. But the leather briefs had never been washed and even now smelled strongly of her.

In a corner of the compartment Tim found one more thing, a USB stick. It seemed incongruous, this little piece of technology amongst a collection of sexual paraphernalia. Tim figured it probably held more vids of his sister and put it in his shirt pocket to check out later.

Back in the lounge. The DVD playing again. Kneeling in front of the TV, leather briefs pressed against his nose, into his mouth, her smell around him like a fog, closing out the world, taking him back to the nights when she lay beneath him.

And afterwards, the sadness came as he knew it would, and the DVD played out and the screen went dark and Tim lay curled on the floor, naked except for his shirt.

Chapter 8

Denning woke face-first on the couch. The sun came in at the window in an angular fan that lanced his eyes and scoured the inside of his head. Last night's passage across the worn carpet was marked by a discarded jacket, a shoe, an overturned side table and a leather bag. He tried to remember entering the bungalow. His bedroom was only a few yards further inside the house – obviously too trashed to make it.

He rolled onto his back and forced his eyes to stay open. The paint on the ceiling above him was peeling. There was a ceiling fan, but it didn't work. He traced the jagged curls of paint as he pieced together the events of the night before.

A fight on the beach, rescued by a couple of Good Samaritan types – he groaned as he realized he'd have to take a cab down there later to get his car – smashing the windows of a yellow Camaro, Peta with her boss, the heart-stopping memory of the GHQ parking lot. Even now the shock was enough to set a wave of nausea roiling through his bourbon scorched stomach.

He hadn't checked on Peta when he got in last night – he was certain she would not have come home. The thought made him feel hollow. He sat up and felt the two halves of his brain part, the sensation so distinct that he actually pressed his hands to the sides of his head. Denning did not drink as a rule, hangovers were something which terrified him.

He had been staring at the leather bag for a full minute before a sunburst of hope broke within him. OxyContin! Savior of the tired, the sore, the wounded, the lost, and those sad assholes who on occasion dove too far into the bottle.

He crawled across the floor and opened the bag, saw with grateful disbelief that one of the blister packs had survived the night. He swallowed a pill, bit half from another and swallowed that too. The action made him feel how thirsty he was.

In the kitchen, Denning stripped off his clothes and threw them through the door to the laundry room. The air against his hairy, naked body revived him a little. He watched the news on a small TV while he drank a pint of cherry juice, then went back through the lounge and started down the hall to his bedroom.

Two rooms gave off the right side of the hall, first Peta's, then his. As he passed hers, the sound of her voice calling to him made him catch his breath. He tamped a quick flare of happiness before it could turn into hope, and opened her door.

The curtains were drawn, but behind them a window was open and a breeze coming through it made the fabric billow, periodically splashing the floor and part of the double bed with clean hard light.

Peta lay alone, propped against a pile of pillows, covered by a sheet. She nodded at his nakedness and sighed.

"I thought we agreed...."

"I was just about to take a shower. I got home kinda late."

"Yeah."

"Yeah...."

Peta looked at him angrily. "What the fuck were you doing?"

"Drinking?"

"I saw you following us. You pissed in his fucking car! You smashed his windows. It's, like, a classic or something. What the fuck were you thinking?"

Denning felt his own anger rise.

"Did you fuck him?"

"If I'd fucked him I wouldn't have bothered coming home, would I? We've talked about this." Peta took a breath. "Look, I know this isn't easy for you. It's not easy for me either."

"That place you went to last night? You know what it was, right?"

Peta sighed.

"Yes, I know. GHQ. Michael Starck."

"They destroyed me."

"I know they destroyed you, Daddy. I was part of the fallout, remember? What do you want me to do? I'm Kid's assistant. He had a meeting there. It's my job."

"A meeting about what?"

"Kid's looking for finance for a film he wants to make. He knows Michael Starck somehow, so he's leveraging that connection. I stayed in Reception. I didn't even meet him."

"Kid's talking finance with GHQ?"

"So?"

"They're A-list. Big budget, big stars, opening weekend grosses. Your asshole boss—"

"Daddy...."

"This guy, this...ex-porn star, what's he done? An art film no one's seen."

"Everyone has to start somewhere."

"Yeah, but you don't get money from a company like GHQ when you've done next to nothing. They exist to succeed, not to gamble."

Denning sat on the edge of the bed beside her. He could smell traces of her perfume, the nighttime scent of her. He crossed his legs.

Peta's voice softened.

"You should give his bag back."

"He's a drug addict."

"He's not a drug addict. He had some Oxy, like everyone else. Big deal. There was a reel of film. He acted like it was important to him. Will you give it back? Or let me take it?"

"Fuck him."

Peta sighed and shook her head. Denning, now floating on the dreamy edges of an Oxy high, rolled onto the bed beside her and stretched out.

Peta said: "We're not doing that any more, remember?"

"I know, I know. Just let me lie here a minute."

Clara had been missing for three months when it started. Denning had come home with Peta, then eighteen, from a late dinner and they'd sat in the kitchen drinking decaf together, talking about nothing in particular. After the coffee was finished, Denning washed the mugs. When he turned from the sink, Peta was standing behind him. Thinking she was about to go to bed, he bent to kiss her cheek, but she turned her head, their mouths met, and she opened her lips.

It was something they could have stepped back from, a slip, a faux pas. But this kiss, this simple thing, had no chance of remaining an innocent moment of play, not when their grief for Clara was such a potent excuse. Not when Peta had had a crush on her father since she'd been old enough to think about boys. Not when Denning saw in her so much of his missing wife.

So, that night after coffee, Denning and Peta slept together and began a new relationship that was neither father and daughter, nor man and wife, but some strange hybrid, at once more profoundly intimate than a normal love affair, and more prosaic than any romance between strangers.

For nine years it worked. They were partners in bed and companions in grief, finding in each other the illusion of a balm for their loss. But by the time Peta turned twenty-seven her youthful idolization of her father had burned itself out and the grief for her mother had at last faded. She assessed her situation, saw a smart, attractive young woman with a bitter, grief-damaged man twenty years her senior. It was not a recipe for a fulfilling life. There were opportunities out there, there were relationships that didn't need to be kept hidden, men who weren't ruined by their pasts, lives to be lived that were open and free and full of possibility. She wanted more.

Denning, too, knew that things could not remain as they were. His relationship with his daughter was illegal and abhorred by society, fraught with the tensions demanded by secrecy. That it had survived as long as it had was a source of happy amazement to him. But in its latter years he had come to see that this longevity carried a price.

Peta was the closest thing he had to a copy of Clara, and to lose such intimate access to her would be to lose the last thread of physical connection to a woman who had been everything to him. The flipside, of course, was that Peta anchored him to his grief, that he would never move beyond his loss while he was lying in his daughter's bed.

So, a year ago when Peta told him the sex was over, although his initial reaction had been one of horror, he'd known that she was making the right choice, that there was really no alternative if either of them was ever to have any chance at genuine happiness again. The problem was, when Peta found one of those opportunities she had been longing for in the shape of Kid Haldane, it had not been quite as easy for Denning to see the bright side as he'd hoped.

When Denning woke it was late afternoon. Peta had gone to work and he was alone. He looked at her side of the bed, at the impression she had left in the rumpled sheets. It seemed a metaphor for what they had now – a messy imprint of something that used to be real.

He got up. The bag was where he'd left it in the lounge. The film was housed in a round, yellow plastic container. There was a Kodak logo on the lid, but nothing else, no label indicating what the film's subject might be.

Denning took the spool out and unrolled a few feet – a narrow strip of celluloid with an 8mm frame, sprocket holes down one side only. Super 8 – what amateur cinematographers had made movies on before video cameras were available to the public.

He wondered why a so-called filmmaker would be carrying around a type of film that was rarely used today. He wondered why, according to Peta, he would be particularly upset when that film was stolen.

Denning held the film up to the light. The frame was so small it was difficult to see clearly, but it looked like the image was of a wall of trees, a forest, perhaps; the air a little hazy as though there had been fog on the day it was shot. He unwound a few more feet – same scene, trees, a little more haze.

Denning had an 8mm projector at the back of a closet somewhere. It had been in the family since he was a kid, and if he wanted to see with any clarity what was on the film he'd have to dig it out. But right then he was too exhausted to be bothered.

He went into the kitchen and sat in the breakfast nook, elbows on the Formica table, staring at a window covered by a net curtain that the angled sun had turned luminous.

GHQ.

Kid Haldane.

What connection could there be between a company that had taken away his career, and his daughter's new employer?

He put his head on his arms and closed his eyes and drifted, thinking about Clara, remembering how she used to smell in the mornings.

CHAPTER 9

Morning. Tim walked heavy-footed and bleary into his kitchen and made coffee. On the radio, an announcer read his way through the news: a windstorm had caused a power outage in the San Fernando Valley, leaving 200,000 residents without electricity; fourteen Californian cities had filed for bankruptcy protection over their inability to pay pensions to retired city employees; forty percent of Los Angeles sidewalks needed repairs they were never going to get.

At the rear of the kitchen a door opened onto a set of external stairs. Tim drank his coffee on the small landing at the top. The flat was in Santa Monica, and somewhere off to his left there was the sea. But he couldn't see it. His view was of other buildings, walls, small gardens and an alley.

Los Angeles. Twenty years ago he'd loved the place. It had been exactly what everyone around the world believed it to be – a place of palms, long scallops of beaches, movies, glamour; a wide-open free-breathing nexus of energy and talent, a place where anything could happen to anyone who had the guts to try. When had it changed? When had the city's skies become gray more often than blue, when had moving through its streets become less an adventure played out in balmy summer breezes and more like taking a shower in dirty water? When had it become a place of constant threat?

In the alley behind his building a girl in her twenties walked in the direction of the beach, speaking on her phone. She wore a brightly colored dress. She laughed, and every now and then skipped for a few yards and pirouetted.

Tim watched her, wondering if maybe the old Los Angeles was still there after all. Wondering if it was he who had changed and not the city.

He went back inside the flat and plugged the USB stick he'd found in Rebecca's sex toy stash into his laptop. When it loaded, he was surprised to find not a collection of pornography, but a single Final Draft file. Final Draft was a screenwriting software package widely used in Hollywood. Tim owned his own copy and was able to open the file.

A one-hundred-and-ten-page screenplay. A title page with the heading: *Wilderness*. Under the heading, Rebecca's name, a note that the file was a second draft, and a date in August two years previous.

He knew Rebecca's working pattern – a second draft would be the story complete in all its major aspects. She'd do another one or two drafts before she was finished, fixing inconsistencies, refining turning-points, polishing dialogue.

It took Tim an hour and a half to read the whole thing.

Story outline: three filmmakers form a company called Pillbox Productions. They make a character-driven indie film, holding true to an initial vision of artistic integrity. But it doesn't make them famous, doesn't get them to the top of the Hollywood pile, which, it turns out, is what they want a whole lot more than artistic integrity. So, Pillbox acquires a script for a balls-out action movie. Brandon Kane, the leader of the three, directs it and it turns out so well the filmmakers know they have a breakout movie on their hands, one which will catapult them into the A-list.

Only trouble is, Beau Montgomery, one of the two heads of a distribution company that acquires the North American rights to the film, changes his mind and wants to shelve it for at least two years because it isn't flattering to returned Afghanistan War veterans.

The filmmakers, knowing the other principal of the distribution company loves their film and will certainly release it without the veto of his partner, murder Beau Montgomery.

They get away with the crime, the film is released to huge success and they go on to become one of the most successful production houses in Hollywood.

The latter part of the screenplay went on to chart the course of their moral decline as their abandonment of all artistic honor took its toll on their personalities.

Before he was five pages into the script, Tim recognized what he was reading. He went to the bedroom and took the folded sheets of screenplay that Jocelyn had given him the day before from his jacket pocket. Back in the lounge, he compared them to the screenplay on the computer. Jocelyn's pages matched, in all important points, the first act of Rebecca's *Wilderness* screenplay.

The two versions, of course, were not word for word copies. Scene description was different, dialogue was different, character names had been changed – for instance Rebecca's Beau Montgomery, the film distributor, had become Tad Beaumont in Jocelyn's script – but the personalities were the same, the characters had the same goals and they moved through the same sequence of knowledge and events. Though Rebecca's was more efficiently put together, more beautifully written, someone watching a movie of either screenplay would experience essentially the same story.

The date on the title page made *Wilderness* the screenplay Rebecca had been working on at the time of her death – the screenplay she'd refused to tell her agent anything about. A screenplay which Tim, who had read everything Rebecca ever wrote, had never seen before.

So how had Jocelyn gotten hold of it?

Tim hadn't met Jocelyn until six months after Rebecca's death, and it was unlikely that Jocelyn would ever have met Rebecca by herself before then. Rebecca was successful, Jocelyn was most definitely not. And even if they had met, there was no way Rebecca would have shown a head-case like Jocelyn a screenplay which, seemingly, she'd been keeping off the Hollywood radar.

That Jocelyn was plagiarizing *Wilderness* was obvious. But Tim didn't think she had access to the whole thing, not yet. If she did, she would have waited until she had copied out the entire screenplay before crowing about it to him. And there was her seeming ignorance of the progression of the screenplay's story, her inability to answer questions as basic as the direction of the second act or the arc of an important character.

Tim wondered about the handwritten notes on yellow paper that he'd found in Jocelyn's document case – a continuation of the pages she'd already typed up. Same color paper the blond woman had handed Jocelyn in the parking lot on Wilshire and South Barrington.

Not a huge leap to figure the blond woman was the source of Jocelyn's new-found cinematic skill. But how had *she* gotten access to the screenplay?

CHAPTER 10

K id Haldane and Christo Ramirez had known each other since the nineties when they starred in porn flicks together. Their on-screen collaborations hadn't lasted much more than a year, though. Christo was already spending more time working as muscle for the owner of one of the largest of the San Fernando Valley porn mills. And Kid, by that time, had started to believe that the acts he performed on camera were beginning to erode his soul.

By the start of the new millennium, Christo had relocated back to Mexico and established himself as a coyote, specializing in transporting young women from rural villages across the border into the States. Kid, porn-vid career dead in the wake of a smorgasbord of chemical dependencies, was making ends meet by giving occasional private porn performances for some of Hollywood's dissolute elite.

Unlikely that they would ever have seen each other again. Except that during those dark days when Kid was living from one hit to the next, he'd scored a gig slapping Jeffery Bannister across the face with his flaccid cock – some kind of humiliation thing Jeffery needed, made all the more bizarre by the fact that Jeffery wasn't gay.

Kid's soul was in deep hibernation by this point, and when Jeffery and his sister, Ally, had asked him to find them girls to rape, had offered him the kind of money a junkie couldn't turn down, Kid figured he had nothing left to lose by saying yes.

The first time, he'd done it himself, in Los Angeles. But bundling a girl into a van, having to render her unconscious, to feel her and hear her, was too much for him, made him feel too *responsible*. But he needed the money, needed the hydro-codone and crack cocaine it would buy. So he'd gotten in touch with Christo and suggested a variation on the Mexican's coyote routine, offered him an additional revenue stream.

The arrangement had lasted more than ten years. Four girls a year. Christo making money at both ends — when the girl paid to be smuggled across, then a whole lot more when she took an unscheduled Hollywood detour.

For a long time the drugs insulated Kid from his part in this horror. But then he met Chick again and his soul woke up, and he saw that what he was doing with the girls was an abomination. It took six months, but he stopped the drugs — his motivation: a small chance at redemption.

He could have stopped the girls too, terminated his arrangement with Christo, told Jeffery and Ally to fuck off. But he needed the money. Not for drugs now, but to buy his way into a new life. He gave himself a time limit — one year, two max. Closed his eyes and procured the girls, put the money into Kid Haldane Productions.

And so today. An abandoned refrigeration works off the 101, a few miles north of Solana Beach. Two hours south of Los Angeles, forty minutes north of the Mexican border. A perfect spot for this kind of exchange.

They drove identical, States-registered, white vans, the cargo bays of which were windowless and separated from the cockpit by a solid partition.

Get out, hand over the money, swap vans and drive away — Christo back to Mexico, Kid north to Los Angeles. They talked for a couple of minutes. Christo was a light-skinned Mexican with a heavy build and a face badly scarred by child-hood chicken pox. They'd been friends a long time ago, but there wasn't a lot to say now. Apart from the girls, about the only thing they had left in common was that they both had ten-inch dicks.

Chapter 11

Malibu Hills. The end of a dusty trail leading through an acre of chaparral that formed the grounds of the property. A mansion called Raintree. Owned at various times by a silent movie star, a newspaper magnate and, until it burned down in the mid-eighties, a Hollywood producer. Secluded. High in the hills. Surrounded by empty land.

At each end the structure still rose to its full three stories, but in the middle it was charred and gutted, as though something had taken an enormous flaming bite out of it. Jeffery and Ally Bannister had more than enough money to clear the site and rebuild. But, apart from reconstructing the garage and a staircase down to the undamaged basement, they'd never bothered. They only ever used the place when there was a girl, the rest of the time they lived in Bel Air.

Kid drove around back, pulled into the garage. A black Escalade was already parked there and the steel door that gave onto the basement stairs was ajar.

The girl in the van was handcuffed, her eyes and mouth sealed with duct tape that had been wound around her head like a mask. She was only half conscious, a result of the intravenous Valium Christo had shot her up with on the other side of the border. As Kid guided her down the stairs to the basement she stumbled and banged against the wall and made small noises behind her gag.

A long corridor, a couple of rooms. At the end, a screening room, its décor largely unaltered since it had been installed by the property's first owner. Walls paneled in dark wood, a sixteen-foot screen recessed above a shallow stage, the floor rising gently toward the rear of the room. The original seating layout had been four double rows of twin-seat leather couches, but Jeffery and Ally had had the first two rows removed.

Kid uncuffed one of the girl's hands and closed the free cuff through a ring that had been set into one of the walls. He crossed the room to a utility closet, dragged out an object like a large saw-horse, used bolts to fix it to lugs in the floor – four splayed legs to which leather wrist and ankle cuffs had been fixed, a padded horizontal bench at hip-height, long enough to support the torso of a woman.

The woman twisted and flailed about with her free arm. Kid took a contact Taser from the pocket of his jacket. He waited until her movements turned her away from him then pressed the jaws of the Taser against the back of her neck and thumbed the button. She convulsed, then collapsed, landing heavily on her knees. She turned so that her chest and face lay hard against the wall. The handcuff cut into her wrist as it took her weight.

Kid worked quickly, uncuffed the woman, stripped her naked, lay her face-down on the saw-horse, cinched the leather restraints tight about her wrists and ankles, made sure that her legs and arms were stretched to full extension and could not move.

He stepped back and checked his work. She was secure. The tape around her eyes and mouth in place.

Kid left the room, headed back along the corridor to one of the other rooms as the woman regained consciousness and started to make gagged pleas for release.

Jeffery and Ally were twins, scions of old-school Hollywood. Their grandfather had been an independent producer with a first-look deal and a permanent suite of offices on the Warner Bros. lot. He'd made a fortune from lowbrow movies with lots of explosions. When the twins were twelve he'd become their guardian after their parents had been killed in a light-plane crash.

Brother and sister, both in white robes, sat now, holding hands on a green velvet couch in a windowless room off the basement corridor, waiting.

In their early forties, they were both pale, slightly built and coppery blond. They were equal partners with Michael Starck in GHQ, but for the last few years they'd played an increasingly backseat role in its day-to-day operations – a result of Jeffery's declining mental health.

Kid entered and said: "She's ready."

Ally took an envelope from the arm of the couch and held it out to him – forty-five grand. Minus Christo's fee, twenty-five thousand for a day's work.

Ally disengaged herself from Jeffery, folded her hands in her lap and looked directly at Kid.

"*Antepenultimate* is a good script. But it won't make a cent, you know that."

"These films can find their audience if they're handled right. Look at *Crouching Tiger, Hidden Dragon*."

Jeffery snorted. He had a high-pitched voice that tended to run away with him.

"That was a fucking kung fu movie. Of course it made money. Only an idiot would have been surprised."

Kid said: "I got Michael's sign-off."

Ally nodded. "Yes, he called. Surprising. How did you persuade him?"

"We go back a long way."

"You go back a long way with us, too. But we have a reason to be persuaded to help you. You supply something very important to us. Not so with Michael."

"I have my thing with you. I have something else with him. You promised me you'd agree to GHQ financing the film if I got Michael to sign off. I got him to sign off. Who gives a shit how I did it?"

Jeffery blurted: "I should have worn a hat."

Ally ignored him, said: "Very well, but Michael must have asked you the same thing. What did you tell him about us?"

"Nothing he doesn't already know. I told him that Jeffery pays me to humiliate him. I told him I could embarrass you."

Ally looked at him measuringly.

"You know, Kid, being in the middle of two camps, I'm sure you think it's terribly advantageous. But it can also be very dangerous."

Jeffery stood up and started pacing the small room. He said: "All this talking is making my head hurt."

Ally continued speaking to Kid.

"You plan to use the girl who directed *Loggers*?"

"Chick? Yes."

"What's her background?"

"Before *Loggers*? A year at UCLA, then she shot a couple of shorts. She's a genius."

"She's competent, but she's a long way from genius. You don't want to look for someone with more of a track record?"

"I'm using her."

"Why?"

"She's right for the material."

"It's a story about a young man's relationship with his father. She's missing a necessary body part don't you think?"

"She's part of the package, end of story."

Jeffery shouted: "Ally, come the fuck on!"

Ally stood. "Michael didn't involve us in *Loggers*, so we never met Chick. You bring her to meet us and if she's halfway competent we'll sign off. Didn't Michael want that too?"

"He trusts my judgment."

Ally snorted, then took Jeffery's hand and together they walked out of the room and down the corridor.

Raintree was a wonderland. Jeffery and Ally had been allowed the run of the place – the arched basements, perfect as dungeons for mad scientist games; the attic for dreaming away soft autumn afternoons; the vast rooms full of movie memorabilia and curios from around the world; servants to bring any food they wished. If there was ever a retreat where two recently bereaved children could heal from their loss, this should have been it.

But a few months after their arrival, Trevor Bannister, their paternal grandfather, sixty-three years old and semi-retired after a glorious movie-producing career, made certain additions to life at Raintree that punctured any sense of fantasy the twelve-year-olds might have managed to weave about themselves.

Tuesdays and Thursdays were 'bed nights', nights when Trevor, virile still in his sixties, fucked first one of them and then the other in his king-size bed. The twins were never made to touch each other, but they were made to watch.

The bed nights continued until the twins were sixteen years old. By then they were big enough physically to put up a fight. A point Jeffery underlined by smashing a vase across the back of Trevor's head one night when he was in the process of mounting Ally.

Jeffery and Ally waited two years after that to exact their revenge. They needed time to process what had happened to them, to understand how badly broken they were. And they were not stupid. They were Trevor's only living relatives and he had mentioned their primacy in his will as sexual leverage on more than one occasion.

So they waited until a month after their eighteenth birthdays, and then they set fire to Raintree.

Their grandfather was in the habit of using sleeping pills. He also smoked cigars. How easy, then, to wait until he passed out from his nightly dose, light one of his half-smoked Cubans and drop it on the bed cover.

The blaze spread from the bedroom and burnt out the entire center section of the mansion. The isolated location of the property ensured that both the house and Trevor were beyond salvaging by the time the fire trucks arrived.

The fire was ruled an accident, the twins inherited the bulk of Trevor's estate and their abuser was dead. The future should have been rosy.

But the images stayed stuck in their heads, the feelings of worthlessness grew stronger and their lives, rather than turning out toward the world, became inward focused, governed by the damage that Trevor Bannister had done to them.

When they turned thirty and it became apparent that the various therapists they had employed were incapable of helping them, they took matters into their own hands. They began to practice the Ritual of Freeing.

The woman Kid had delivered was fully conscious now. Like all of them, except the very first, she was Mexican. Her skin, normally a smooth amber, was a play of moving color. Jeffery had set the projector running and the two-hour selection of clips he and his sister had pieced together from the most moronic car chase, shoot-out, fist fight, exploding building segments of their grandfather's films played on the screen and spewed lurid light out into the dim screening room. The girl couldn't see anything, of course, her eyes were still taped, but the volume was high and each time something exploded she flinched.

Jeffery and Ally sat on a couch in the front row and watched the girl, remembering back, back to all the nights when they had been the ones at someone else's mercy. Week after week, year after year, each of them filled to the brim with pain. And that pain now at such a level that the only way to live with it, the only way to find even temporary relief, was to transfer it, to drain some of it into the girl twitching in fear in front of them.

In the beginning the ritual had been planned as a simple episode of rape set to the background of their grandfather's movies. Jeffery and Ally had figured the movie clips would add the necessary resonance, the necessary *connection*, to an otherwise mundane invasion of orifices. That had all changed, though, when they saw the hardon Oscar, when Kid brought it to them along with the First.

The hardon Oscar was an exact replica of the thirteen-and-a-half-inch award handed out by AMPAS, except that in place of a sword it had an erect phallus jutting from its crotch. Sex and movies. Combined into an insertable object. How much purer than Jeffery just banging away, or Ally using a strap-on? How much more sacred? The instrument had changed everything, had become the cornerstone of their ritual.

Ally rose from the couch now, walked across the room to a wall, opened a concealed cabinet by pressing a section of wood paneling, and brought the hardon Oscar back. She and Jeffery stood behind the girl, holding the golden statuette before them with one hand each. And as the noise of the movie clips howled around them, recited a litany they had refined through various iterations over the last twelve years:

> *"No pain*
> *No history*
> *No guilt*
> *All that was him leaves us."*

They lowered the Oscar and the girl whimpered as the head of it touched her. And then screamed as they drove it in, shrieked through her nose and strained and hunched her back and prayed to whatever village saint she had placed her faith in when she handed over her money to the coyote for a new life in California.

The twins held the statuette on its side. As they rammed it in and out the jutting phallus split the girl's right labia and a narrow stream of blood ran down the inside of her thigh.

By the time Kid got to Griffith Park it was early evening. He found an unpaved trail, drove along it for half a mile then stopped and guided the girl out of the van. He left her with a thousand dollars, a map of Los Angeles, a bottle of water, a disposable cell phone and a small pair of nail scissors so she could cut the tape away from her head. He told her to count to fifty before she used them. Then he got back in the van and drove away.

The things he'd given the girl were from him, not Jeffery and Ally. Their only stipulation, made in unequivocal terms, was that the girls be released alive and no more harmed than when they'd finished with them. This condition was not the result of any particular kindness of spirit on their part. It was just good sense – dead, raped Mexican girls turning up at regular intervals in Los Angeles would eventually draw heat, even if they were illegals.

On the other hand, the girls had paid to be smuggled over the border, to get into the US, so by giving them what they wanted, albeit with an unpleasant stopover, there was a good chance they'd simply disappear into whatever barrio they'd been headed for in the first place.

Kid left the van in a Westwood Village storage unit on the outskirts of the UCLA campus. From there he drove the Mustang he was renting until the Camaro was fixed back to his apartment on Wilshire Boulevard.

On the way he thought about the stolen Super 8 film, no doubt lying in some Los Angeles gutter or wherever else it had been tossed by the junkies who had trashed his car. It was his leverage with Michael, the keystone in his plan to launch *Antepenultimate*. Jeffery and Ally sign off, Michael signs off, the money flows. If he couldn't figure some way to bullshit Michael about the film's loss, to come up with a believable reason for not handing it over, *Ante* was going to be a very short-lived project indeed.

And the missing film was not the only threat. Jeffery and Ally wanted to meet Chick. He'd figured he could keep them away from her, that they wouldn't bother themselves with the details of such a small film. But they were more interested than he'd expected. Maybe because they didn't understand how he'd been able to force Michael to agree to the film. Maybe because their rape-girl boy had the temerity to want to carve a better life for himself.

Now, he didn't have much choice. Putting Chick in front of them was a necessary gamble – they'd made it plain they wouldn't sign off on the finance without meeting her. All Kid could hope was that enough time had passed. That they wouldn't recognize her.

Chapter 12

Jocelyn's flat. Sepulveda Boulevard near Mar Vista. A shitty stretch of apartment complexes and small office buildings. Not far from the drone of the 405.

Tim had the section of screenplay she'd given him. He hadn't bothered to re-type it, had just polished the dialogue and made corrections and suggestions for improvements in blue pencil directly onto the manuscript pages. He'd figured he'd swing by unannounced, hand it over, then grill her about the whole Rebecca plagiarism thing. He had a full copy of Rebecca's screenplay with him. But Jocelyn wasn't home. She hadn't been at the café either, his first port of call.

Early evening. He could guess.

He'd stapled her pages together. He scrawled a short note on the cover and wrote his name, pushed them into her mailbox. Then rode his Vespa to the abandoned parking building at Wilshire and South Barrington.

She was there. This time on a dirty mattress someone had dragged up from one of the levels below. Five guys running a train. The blue Prius there again. The blond woman watching from beside it.

Tim stayed hidden and watched the show, made the decision he was finished with Jocelyn, that he'd never see her again. There was no point in talking to her about the screenplay. She'd lie to any question he asked. She'd ignite and explode. And it was more than likely she didn't know the truth about it anyhow, that the blonde kept secrets.

Tim filmed a few minutes of the action and then, when it was finished, filmed the blond woman handing Jocelyn another sheaf of yellow pages. When the Prius exited the building he was sitting on his scooter, waiting fifty yards up the street.

Wilshire. Sepulveda. Easy to follow. He'd guessed where they were going. Jocelyn's ride home. The blonde parked the Prius and the two women walked upstairs, their hands moving impatiently over each other.

An hour later, the blonde climbed back into the Prius and Tim fired up the Vespa again.

Bel Air smelled of orange blossom. It was evening, but the sky was still light and evenly spaced pepper trees threw soft shadows across the grassed edge of the street. Denning could hear crickets and birds.

He hadn't seen the house for eight years, but nothing had changed. The white mansion, a little further down the road from where he was parked, was still hidden from sight by a twelve-foot wall, still protected by wrought iron gates and security cameras. He'd been inside it once, sat with Delores Fuentes on a white brocade couch and asked too many questions.

He'd been watching the place since mid-afternoon, chilled by a minimal 20mg dose of OxyContin, pissing in a Tupperware container when he could force anything past the dick-tightening effects of the drug. The Bel Air Patrol had cruised past him twice so far, but Delores Fuentes' home was no stranger to fans and the private cops had let him alone.

Around five o'clock he saw her. Driving herself in a convertible Mercedes 500 SL, silver, top down. She was still beautiful, but more muscular now. She hadn't made a movie in four years; no one was really sure why. Gossip rag stories had her working out obsessively – gymnastics, Krav Maga, Pilates, a Hollywood nutjob over-identifying with the action heroes she used to play.

What he was doing here on this perfumed evening, what he hoped to achieve, he didn't know. But two nights ago, in the GHQ parking lot, his past had exploded into his present – and Delores was every bit as much a part of that past as Michael Starck.

Blue Prius. Driver driving dreamily. Wilshire. Beverly Glen Boulevard. Through Westwood Village to Bel Air and one of the small, billion dollar streets around

Brown Canyon. Tim hung back, pulled to the side of the road and stopped as the car slowed to enter a driveway. A pair of ornate iron gates slid apart and the Prius entered the grounds of a large white mansion.

Further up the road, beyond the gates, a white Crown Victoria faced him, the shadow of a man behind its wheel. Maybe a courier waiting for a pick-up, maybe a ride for a maid or a cook.

Tim took his helmet off and did his best to look innocent. Across the road, opposite the mansion, the canyon fell away and there was a view across the lights of western Los Angeles to a slice of red-lit ocean and an incendiary sky.

Tim figured two things: one, that the woman driving the Prius did not own this house, she just didn't have the poise; two, that buzzing the intercom by the gate and asking to talk to someone about sex and screenplays probably wasn't going to be too productive.

The streetlights were on and the sky was beginning to fade. Tim felt exposed and out of place. The Crown Victoria hadn't moved. Tim was worried that sooner or later someone in one of the houses along the street would make a call about a guy sitting on a scooter in the dark. But he figured if he'd come this far he might as well hang around until he got moved on or the woman showed again.

Denning watched a blue Prius turn into Delores' mansion, saw a guy on a scooter putter up the street behind it. Denning had followed enough celebrities to enough hillside retreats to recognize a tail when he saw one. Someone else was interested in Delores. Denning figured, probably just some hack looking for something to fill a few column inches. But then the guy took his helmet off and Denning recognized him as one of the men who had rescued him at the beach, the guy he'd given some OxyContin to...Tim?

A level of coincidence strong enough that when the Prius re-emerged from the mansion fifteen minutes later and the scooter rider took off after it, Denning joined the caravan.

An old court of stores at the junction of Beverly Glen and Sunset Boulevard. Palms along both streets, dusty, their fronds lit from beneath by streetlights and passing cars, picked out like the skeletons of fish. A parking lot out back, through an arch. Unchanged since the 1940s, poorly lit, a handful of cars. The blond woman returning to the Prius, an unwisely chosen spot in a far corner, carrying a paper sack from an organic grocer. Tim sitting on a low wall there, watching her come, holding Rebecca's screenplay.

When the woman got to her car, Tim pushed himself off the wall and stepped in front of her, holding up the screenplay.

"You dropped this."

The woman, about forty, worn around the eyes but slim and well dressed, jumped and clutched the grocery bag tight against her chest.

"I didn't drop anything."

"Take a look at it."

Tim shoved the screenplay at her. The woman fumbled behind her for the door of the Prius and got it a little way open.

Tim stepped closer and kicked it shut.

"You're going to talk to me. If you don't, I burn a DVD of a video I shot earlier tonight in a parking lot on South Barrington and drop it off at the place in Bel Air you just came from."

The woman blanched. She didn't say anything, but she stopped trying to get into her car. Tim figured she needed a little more persuading and took his phone out. He played the footage of Jocelyn being fucked, the woman clearly visible in the background, masturbating. Then he played the second video, the woman handing Jocelyn the pages of yellow note paper. He put his phone away, forced the grocery bag out of her arms and pushed the screenplay at her again. This time she took it.

"Read it."

The woman flipped the title page, scanned pages one and two. Tim watched her face sag. When she looked back at him, though, she did her best to look blank.

"Recognize it?"

"No."

"Yeah, you do. Don't lie to me again. What's your name?"

"Skye. Where did you get it?"

"Isn't that my question?"

"Look, I'm not selling it or anything. I'm not trying to make any money out of it. Who are you?"

"Someone who knows who wrote this. Where did you get it?"

The woman didn't say anything. Tim continued:

"The person who wrote this was killed while they were working on it. Now *you've* got it."

Skye's lips started to tremble and she looked quickly about her.

"I didn't know that. I don't know anything about it. I promise. I just found it."

"Where?"

Skye hesitated a long time, then, in a rush, let go: "My boss. I had to get a computer fixed. The guy at the store backed the files up on an external drive while he was working on it. He assumed the computer was mine and gave me the drive. He hadn't put a password on it."

"And the screenplay was just sitting there."

"No, it was hidden at the bottom of a folder tree, labeled like it was a system file."

"You must have been looking pretty hard."

"I just used a Windows Explorer search, keyword: *screenplay*. It found all the scripts on the drive. Everyone puts *'a screenplay by'* on their title page."

"Who was this one by?"

"The name had been deleted, or never entered in the first place. That's why I chose it. I met Jocelyn in a club. I liked her. She said she wanted to be a screenwriter, I told her I had a brilliant story I'd been thinking about for years. We made a deal. I'd write an outline for her if she'd let me watch her having sex."

"Pretty weird definition of 'liked'."

"This is L.A., you asshole."

"You didn't think someone would recognize it?"

"I didn't think anyone would ever see it. I've read Jocelyn's stuff, she can't write for shit. Look, I won't give her anymore. I promise. I made a mistake. Can you please just let me go? Please...?"

The woman was on the verge of tears. She knew what was coming.

"Who's your boss?"

"I can't."

Two men had entered the lot through the archway. Skye looked like she was about to run. Tim grabbed her arm.

"Who is your boss?"

"If they find out I'll lose my job. I'm a personal assistant. I'll never work again."
She tried to twist her arm free. Tim held her tighter.

"You won't be working very long if your boss gets to see what you like to watch in parking lots."

"If it comes down to that, I'll take my chances."

Skye tugged her arm sharply and shouted, "Let me go! Let me go!" And then, when she saw that she'd attracted the attention of the two men, yelled, "HELP!"

The men paused for a moment then moved quickly across the parking lot.

Tim let her go and walked away, head down, the screenplay gripped tightly in his hand. Skye wrenched open the door of the Prius, hit the go button and fishtailed out of the lot.

Denning, parked on the same side of the lot, but nearer the entrance arch, had watched the scene through his open passenger-side window. He'd seen Tim hold his phone in front of the woman's face, he'd seen a chunk of paper shoved into her hands. And he'd caught the note of threat in Tim's voice, the cadence of fear in hers.

And now it was obvious what was going to happen. Tim would be intercepted by the two well-meaning men, a couple of soft office-types in khakis and polo shirts. He'd try to shake them off, things would get physical, the cops would be called....

When the two men put themselves in front of Tim, then held him when he tried to step around them, Denning got out of his car and jogged across the lot.

Tim was tall, a little heavy around the waist, brown hair with a scatter of gray at the temples. The men spoke to him in firm but reasonable tones, convinced of their own righteousness, demanding an explanation for the unacceptable behavior they'd just witnessed. Tim, on the verge of panicking, told them to fuck off.

Denning stepped up and said loudly: "It's okay, I'll take it from here."

He flashed a fake cop I.D. he'd had since his journalist days, put it quickly back in his pocket. A look of recognition crossed Tim's face. Denning used a cop voice: "I saw what happened. The woman in the Prius. It's downtown for this fucker."

He took hold of Tim's arm and pulled him firmly away from the men. Before he'd taken two steps, though, one of them said:

"Shouldn't you put cuffs on him? Can I see that I.D. again?"

Denning shook his head.

"I want to get this perp to the station, question him before he clams up."

The two men looked at each other. *Perp? Clams up?*

Denning pulled Tim another step away. The men were ready to escalate, flabby chests puffing up, indignation flushing their cheeks.

"Hey, wait a minute, Mister."

Denning stopped and faced them square-on. He took his extendable baton from his coat pocket and pressed the stud. Eighteen inches of segmented black steel. The men looked at it like it was a deadly snake, took in for the first time Denning's solid body, his close-cut hair, his thick moustache....

And figured they'd done enough superhero work for the night. They lifted their hands, backed off a couple of steps, then turned and walked away, looking over their shoulders, one of them muttering: "This town's going down the toilet. I knew I should have taken Mimi and the kids to Colorado when I had the chance...."

Denning closed his baton and nodded at the script in Tim's hand.

"Working on a screenplay?"

Tim retrieved his scooter and followed Denning down Sunset until they found a cheap diner just north of the 405. Denning had black coffee, Tim had coffee regular and a slice of lemon pie.

Denning thanked Tim for the beach rescue. Tim bounced it back for the parking lot. After that, they sat silent for a while, the hard fluorescent light of the diner cutting lines into their faces. Each of them turning over questions, trying to figure out what game had just been kicked off here.

Tim started: "You followed me to the market."

"I followed you following that woman."

"Why?"

"Do you know whose house that was?"

Tim shook his head.

"Then why were you there?"

"Like you said, following the woman. She has something that doesn't belong to her."

Tim's canvas satchel was beside him in the booth, the top of the screenplay poking from it. Denning pointed to it.

"Anything to do with that?"

"Yeah. My sister wrote it. I wanted to find out how that woman got hold of it."

"Why didn't you ask your sister?"

"She was killed two years ago."

"Killed, like murdered?"

"Yeah."

"Jesus, I'm sorry.... What did the woman say?"

"That she copied it off her boss's computer. Stole it, basically."

"But she wouldn't tell you who her boss is."

"No. Why did you jump in back there?"

"You did the same thing at the beach. Quid pro quo."

"Not the same thing. You were getting rolled. As far as you knew, I was threatening an innocent woman."

"You look like a good person."

Tim snorted. He ate a mouthful of pie. He took a swallow of coffee and watched Denning carefully.

"Who are you?"

Denning looked around the diner, said the first thing that came into his head: "A writer. I'm researching a book."

He leaned forward, put his forearms on the table. "That woman is Skye Peterson."

Tim looked at him blankly. "Okay."

"Skye is Delores Fuentes' personal assistant."

Tim blinked. "Movie star Delores Fuentes?"

"Movie star Delores Fuentes. I used to be a reporter. I met Skye when I interviewed Delores once, a long time ago."

Tim absorbed the information. It made a certain sense. More sense than Rebecca's screenplay being in the possession of some random sex freak, at least. Delores Fuentes was a big star. It was perfectly feasible that Rebecca might have sent her a copy of the *Wilderness* screenplay in an attempt to pave the way to a sale – attach a star and studios start paying attention.

Denning said: "So, Skye's stealing your sister's screenplay from Delores Fuentes. Your sister must have been pretty good, working at that level."

"She was very good, very successful."

"You didn't know she was working with Delores?"

"No."

"And Skye's trying to pass the screenplay off as her own now?"

"She's feeding it to my girlfriend."

Denning looked confused.

"For sexual favors."

Denning laughed. "Seriously?"

"I know...."

"This town, huh?"

When Denning had intervened in the shopping court parking lot he'd been after one thing – info, anything at all that he could use against GHQ. But this stuff about Tim's sister's screenplay was simple Hollywood venality. The only person at fault, some sexually skewed personal assistant.

The two men sat in the diner with nothing left to say to each other. Tim pulled the screenplay from his satchel and flipped through it despondently.

"Maybe I'll see if I can speak to Delores Fuentes, see how far they got with it."

"Good luck."

"What do you mean?"

"Okay, picture this – you're you, and you want to go sit down with Bruce Willis and have a sandwich. Sound even remotely possible?"

"Well, no, but—"

"That's exactly what you're talking about here. Eight years ago it took me two months before they even responded to my request for an interview, another six weeks after that before I got in. And I worked for the Hollywood Reporter."

Tim dropped the screenplay on the table. He finished his coffee, it was cold now and tasted greasy. He wanted to go over to Sean's place and drink a bottle of wine, get bombed enough to kill the aching memory of Rebecca, to sandblast away the remains of Jocelyn's sexual insanity.

Denning thought about the screenplay. It was probably just that – a screenplay, nothing more, not something that could be used to attack GHQ or Delores. But it was there in front of him. And Delores had had it on her computer.

"Hey, I always wanted to try writing a screenplay, but I've never read one. That's a copy, right, you've got more?" Denning pointed to the screenplay, "You think I could...?"

Tim slid the script across the table to him.

"Knock yourself out."

After that the two men stood, shook hands and exchanged contact details, even though neither of them expected to see the other ever again.

On the way to Sean's, Tim swung by his flat. He wanted to check something.

Delores Fuentes. Rebecca. A screenplay.

A number of ways to connect the dots: Rebecca writes the screenplay, circulates it around town and Delores winds up with a copy for no special reason. Or Rebecca writes the screenplay with Delores in mind and sends her a copy to see if she's interested. Or Rebecca pitches the story to Delores and they develop the screenplay together – Rebecca writing, Delores giving notes.

A memory of something he'd seen over a year ago.

In the second bedroom he rummaged through boxes.

After probate was granted, Rebecca's bank records had been forwarded to Tim. At the time, he'd skimmed them without interest and stored them away. But he remembered seeing something which he wondered about now.

He found the pages, ran his finger down lines of figures. Rebecca's income came in chunks – long periods of nothing, then a payment when she sold a screenplay; or an advance and, later, a completion payment if she was writing for hire. Made it easy to find.

Two months before she'd been killed, seventy-five thousand dollars had been credited to her account. The description beside the figure showed that the payment had been made by a firm called Hastings & Kottle, the accompanying description simply: *Screenplay*. It was the last payment Rebecca had ever received, before that there hadn't been one for more than six months when Sony Pictures Entertainment had paid her two hundred thousand for an adaptation of *Jane Eyre*.

Hastings & Kottle. Tim had no idea who they were, had never heard Rebecca mention them.

Google time.

He found their site. Hastings & Kottle was a business management firm. They worked with high earners, taking care of income and outgoings, managing investments. On one page they had photos and short bios of some of their more illustrious clients. Delores Fuentes was near the top.

Tim figured there was only one thing the seventy-five grand could have been for. Whatever way Rebecca had approached the writing of *Wilderness*, she'd been paid for it by Delores Fuentes via her business managers. On Rebecca's scale that amount of money would just have been an advance payment. Made Tim think Rebecca must have pitched the idea, maybe worked on it with Delores. She would have collected the balance of her fee when she turned in the final draft. Only she didn't live that long.

Tim printed out another copy of the *Wilderness* screenplay and stuck it in his satchel.

Chapter 13

Evening. Sean's bunker, near the south-east corner of Laurel Canyon Park. Down a narrow private track that led off the end of Elrita Drive. A deco-embellished stone box the size of a small bungalow, surrounded by scrubland. No windows. Across the canyon the slopes below the park were punched out here and there with squares of golden light from the handful of homes that had been hammered into the hillside.

Inside, a single open space, drywall across the far end where a bathroom and kitchen had been built. A flat-screen on one of the long walls, a couple of couches, a stone floor with holes where large machinery had once been bolted.

Tim and Sean sat opposite each other, the flat-screen played muted news footage of massive waves pounding the San Diego coastline earlier that day.

Tim had brought wine. He drank it alone. Sean, veins warmed by brown Afghani heroin, never touched alcohol. They chewed the fat, they shot the breeze, Tim debriefed on the Jocelyn situation.

"...and now the bitch is ripping off one of Rebecca's screenplays."

"Seriously? What's the point? They've already been sold and made. She'll just end up in court."

"This is a new script, no one's seen it."

"How'd Jocelyn get it, then?"

"The woman who watches her fucking. That's the deal – sex for installments of the screenplay."

"And *she* got it, where?"

"She got it, get this...from Delores Fuentes."

"Delores Fuentes?"

Despite the smack, Sean's face tightened. Tim figured it for celebrity name-drop shock.

"Yeah. This woman's her personal assistant. She stole it off her computer."

"But Delores Fuentes hasn't been in anything Rebecca wrote. Why would she have one of her screenplays?"

"I think they were developing it together. Rebecca was working on it when she was killed. Two months before, she got a payment from Delores' business manager. Obviously, the project never went ahead."

Sean stood up and got a Coke from the kitchen. When he came back Tim thought he looked a little pale.

"You okay?"

"Just the junk. And you've got a copy?"

"Yeah. Here, take a look. Rebecca hid it, I only found it by accident."

Tim pulled a copy of *Wilderness* out of his satchel and handed it to Sean. Sean flipped through it, spent some time closely reading two or three scenes, then dropped it on the couch next to Tim and went and stood in front of the TV. Started flipping channels. News, movies, ads, cartoons scrolling across the curved surface of his corneas.

After a while he turned back to Tim.

"Jocelyn's got all of this?"

"Just the first act and a bit more. So far."

"You should talk to her, man, tell her it's ripped off. If Delores Fuentes paid Rebecca, she's got rights to the screenplay. Same as I said before, Jocelyn will get fucked on plagiarism."

Tim shook his head. "A, she wouldn't listen to me. B, I'm done with her, I'm never going to see her again – like you said, terminate the fucking thing. And, C, I couldn't care less if someone sues her."

Sean looked pensive.

"You're not going to try to sell it yourself are you, dude? Put it out under your name or anything?"

"Fuck, no."

Sean nodded to himself. Tim thought he was going to say something else, but right then someone started hammering on the front door.

Sean glanced across the room uneasily. He went to the door and looked through the peephole.

Tim had seen the girl before. Once. On Wilshire, at night, hurling a petrol bomb at a movie billboard, riding away on a Triumph Thruxton.

Leather catsuit, SWAT boots, gloves stuffed into the helmet hanging from her hand.

Late-twenties. Lean body. Not immediately pretty. But the whole fuck-you package making Tim's heart race.

Tim wondered at his reaction. She was not Rebecca. She was not his age. What was there here for him – a failed screenwriter in his forties, a man with a paunch, an alcohol problem and too many memories of a dead sister? He watched muscles slide against each other under the tight black leather, saw her labia separate against a seam, noticed a faint salt ring around her crotch. Realized the answer, of course, was LIFE and YOUTH and ANOTHER CHANCE.

Sean had had a small part in a film she'd directed, something called *Loggers*, the only bit of film work he'd left his bunker for in the last two years. He introduced her simply as Chick.

Chick paced, shifted weight from foot to foot, stood, feet apart, firing her arms into the air, speaking, mouth on full-auto, dropping small hard stones of laughter into the spaces between sentences.

"Yeah, Sean-o, I know I should have called first. But I'm making another film, man. *Antepenultimate*. A fucking Danny Bartlemann screenplay! Three-mil budget. Kid's producing. There's a part for you. Not a big part, I know you don't want anything high-profile. Come on, man, you were soooo good in *Loggers*."

Chick was speaking to Sean, but she'd been watching Tim, had turned her body toward him. Now, as she paused to breathe, their eyes locked, and in that instant Tim felt the giant wall of impossibility that for so long had surrounded his goals and desires crumble to dust. And he knew, just *knew*, that he had a chance with her.

Sean made noncommittal noises to Chick's offer. She spun on one foot and shouted: "It's going to be great!"

Then slapped in another clip and turned her machinegun mouth on Tim.

"What do you do, Timbo? Actor, author, director, DoP, model for the more mature demographic – you got a handsome face, you get told that a lot? Is that your Vespa outside? Or is there another girl here somewhere? Only joking, man. I applaud the sentiment, reduce your footprint and all that. But it doesn't exactly scream 'cock', you know what I mean? You should see what I'm riding."

She stopped speaking abruptly.

Tim took a breath and risked: "I'm a screenwriter."

"Cool, Daddio. Had anything made?"

"Couple of straight-to-video things."

"Don't you think it's so cool starting off? I mean, at the beginning, man, there's a million ways to go, all that possibility like, what's going to happen to me? What mark am I going to make? When we all go Scorsese and it's like, oh yeah, we're all rich and super-duper important, these are the days we're gonna look back on. I guarantee it. What directors you like? I like seventies movies. Y'know? *Easy Riders, Raging Bulls*, that kinda thing. You like John Cassavetes?"

And Chick carried on for another few minutes, switching targets halfway through, back to Sean, badgering him for a commitment when she got *Antepenultimate* off the ground. Sean told her to come back when it was firm, that he'd think about it then. Tim spent that part of the conversation stealing glances at her camel-toe.

The Thruxton's red and white paintwork gleamed in the light from the spot above Sean's door. Chick sat on it, revving the engine. She'd removed the shell that covered the rear portion of the seat and stowed it in the bike's pannier.

"860cc, DOHC parallel-twin engine, sixty-eight brake horsepower."

She looked at Tim steadily for a moment.

"You like action movies?"

"Not really."

"Good, 'cause I fucking hate them. You want to take a ride? See what a bike's supposed to feel like?"

"Sure."

Tim put his helmet on, kicked the pillion pegs down and sat behind her, pressed himself against the black leather skin, felt the firmness of her body, her ass nestled between his thighs. When she lifted her hands to pull on her gloves he saw that the tip of the little finger on her right hand was missing.

The way Chick rode was no surprise – as fast as the roads would stand, hard downshifts into the corners, ramming up through the gears on the other side. Tim held her around the waist, leaned into her, sensing weight-shift as she set up another corner, moving his body with hers.

Streetlights, house lights, store signs, oncoming cars, red taillight streaks. Hot air and exhaust fumes slipstreaming around them. Chick whooping at every near-miss, the big British engine howling beneath them. And the sense that if he just let go he would be taken by the air, lifted up and up and up, to float above Los Angeles, above the lights and the sea and the mountains and all the cars and all the people. A sense that something in him was starting to wake.

They pulled to the curb outside a large house on the slopes of Beverly Hills. The place was severely geometric, hip minimalism played out in a series of stacked concrete and glass boxes behind a polished concrete wall and a flat steel gate. Chick pulled off her helmet and climbed off the Thruxton.

"You ever seen *The Killing of a Chinese Bookie*?"

"No."

"Fucking brilliant. If I could go back to the seventies, I would, man. You know, before fucking Spielberg did *Jaws* and started the whole blockbuster mentality. Can you imagine, movies used to play in theatres for months back then? You could go and watch something that some guy had poured his soul into, see it over and over again, really absorb what he was trying to say. Where did all those guys go? All the Coppolas, the Schraders, the Scorseses?"

"Well, Scorsese—"

"I know, I know. But *Gangs of New York? Hugo*? What do they say? They're not *Mean Streets*, they're not *Taxi Driver*. Who's out there now? With real film? Shooting *life*? When did you last see a real fuck scene? Where the girl wasn't interested and the guy spent the whole time worrying about the size of his knob? I mean, *Bob and*

Ted and Carol and Alice had more reality than J. J. Abrams' entire fucking catalogue. There's more conflict, more emotional complexity, more human statement in *Dog Day Afternoon* than all three puke-inducing installments of *Lord of the Rings* put together."

Chick punched the air and made a high-pitched growling noise.

"I mean, Jesus fuck, when did you see a comedy like *Harold and Maude*? Where the sadness, the reality, the *truth* is so close to the surface it rips your fucking guts out?"

She shook her head, then opened the pannier on the back of the bike and took out a manila envelope.

"All these special effects movies, all these action movies, they're wrong, man, they're wrong. You can't learn anything from them because they're empty. And they're empty because they're made by empty people. Empty writers who've never lived, who don't give a shit about anything except hitting their turning points and selling a screenplay. Empty directors who are so fucking lost they think a fifty-mil opening weekend is a failure. There's no art, man, not any more. Not in cinema."

Chick walked toward the gate, waving for Tim to follow.

"And it won't change by itself, you know why?"

"Money."

"Exactly, Timbo, exactly. The financial structure of the studios is completely dependent on having these monster hits – go for the lowest common denominator, capture the biggest audience. If they don't have at least one or two a year they become insolvent."

Chick buzzed the intercom on the gate pillar. When someone answered she said: "Courier. After-hours delivery for Mrs. Sandy Fagel."

A moment later the gate slid open and Tim and Chick started up a short driveway.

Tim asked: "What are we doing here?"

Chick tapped the envelope.

"Community service. The guy who owns this place, Ron Fagel, works exclusively in the mega-budget-CGI-action-bullshit arena. He's shooting tonight, but his wife's home."

A maid met them at the front door and held her hand out for the envelope. Chick refused to give it to her, saying that the sender had insisted it be handed directly to Mrs. Fagel.

The maid went away, then came back and showed them down a long, softly-lit corridor of molded concrete and variegated wood to a large room that had a spectacular view of the city through floor-to-ceiling glass.

A woman, about forty and wearing silk lounging pajamas, sat on a white leather couch. She had dark hair that curled below her shoulders. She was beautiful but there was a heaviness to her hips and middle that aged her.

Sandy Fagel looked a little alarmed to see two people delivering the package, but she couldn't help herself running her eyes jealously over Chick's catsuited body. She took the envelope and looked questioningly at Chick when she didn't move to leave.

"You should open it now."

Sandy frowned and said dismissively: "I'll open it when I want. You can go."

"It concerns your husband."

"So, when you go, I'll look at it."

"And me."

The woman stared at Chick for a long moment, then tore open the envelope and tipped out a burned DVD. She sighed. As she crossed the room to a large flat-panel, tears were already dissolving the makeup at the corners of her eyes.

Tim looked around nervously. Whatever they were about to watch, it was a safe bet it wasn't going to be accompanied by a laugh track. He tried to catch Chick's eye, but she was locked on the woman, mouth clenched in a hard smile, eyes glittering. He noticed a tang in the air, a slight, acrid scent of ammonia and fish. It took him a moment before he realized it was coming from the crotch of Chick's catsuit.

The screen came to life, the DVD played. Full HD. Chick in an expensive hotel room, on her hands and knees at the edge of the bed. A man behind, scrawny with a flabby gut, fucking her in the ass. Ron Fagel, of course, grinding deep, shuddering and moaning when he finished.

Sandy watched it six feet from the screen, her hands over her mouth. When it was over she vomited on the floor. By the time she had straightened and wiped her mouth, Tim and Chick were already back on the Thruxton, shattering the quiet of residential Beverly Hills with British-made thunder.

Hollywood. Chick stopped the bike. Tim bought a couple of bottles of cold New Zealand Sauvignon Blanc and a pack of plastic cups.

They rode to Griffith Park and sat on the downhill slope of a hairpin bend on a trail below the observatory. It was late. The observatory was closed, the park all but deserted. Below them the floor of the L.A. basin was an immense tapestry of light, threaded with the glowing lines of freeways and highways and boulevards. A front of heavy cloud had moved in from the sea and its belly was silver in places and black in others and in the air there was the first cold-metal scent of coming rain.

They lay on the still-warm dusty earth, drinking the crisp wine, staring at the view, their bodies close to each other, sounds of the monstrous city distant, separate, as though coming from somewhere Tim and Chick had escaped.

The alcohol soothed Chick a little. She was silent for a while before she spoke.

"In case you get the wrong idea, him fucking me in the ass wasn't his choice, I didn't give him an option. You probably won't understand it, cause I know what all you guys like, like it's the holy grail of fucking and all that, but for me it was another way to attack him. A man like that deserves to be smeared with shit. I used to take codeine the day before so I'd be constipated."

"Did you know him long?"

Chick laughed. "Are you kidding? I did it just long enough so he couldn't brush it off as a drunken one-night stand when his wife found out."

"Because of his movies."

"What else, dude? Jesus, you think I want to fuck something like that? Of course because of his movies. That's what it's all about, man. Fucking his marriage won't stop him making them, I know that. But they don't have a pre-nup so he's going to lose a shitload of money. Score one for art."

"Hard on the wife, though."

"Really? Timbo...really?" Chick turned on her side and lent on her elbow facing him. "If this pig is out picking up girls half his age, taking them to hotel rooms and fucking them in the ass, do you think it's better she knows, or not?"

"Point taken."

Chick drank a cup of wine straight down, filled it up and drank some more. When she spoke again her voice was small, almost frightened.

"I got hurt pretty bad when I was fifteen. I don't fuck very often. Like, I mean, I don't fuck many people. What you saw on that DVD wasn't me, it was just a means to an end."

Chick put her cup down and moved so that the front of her body was against his. She put her hand on the side of his face and ran it up into his hair.

"I like the gray. I like the lines around your eyes. How old are you?"

"Forty-one."

"I like that, too."

And Tim thought, fuck it, what did he have to lose? If he did the wrong thing, if he wasn't any good, if she was only some crazy girl who wanted to get banged on the side of a hill, he'd at least have the memory of being with someone who wanted to be with him.

He pushed her back against the dust of the hill and kissed her. He smelled again that ammoniac tang, put his hand on the soft, split bulge of her crotch, slick already with glit that had leaked through the stitching in the seam there.

Then the rain began to fall, heavy drops that made small craters in the dust, that soaked him in seconds, so that he stood, intending to run for cover. And Chick stood with him, but didn't run, stood in the rain and kicked off her boots and unzipped her catsuit and peeled it off with nothing on underneath, and then lay down on the ground that was now mud and opened her legs to him.

Rain falling, backwash light from the observatory caught in the heart of each drop, pattering her body, making it shine. Pale skin, blond pubic hair. Chick's legs high around him, mouth open, lips twisting and stretching, trying to work, trying to release the noise inside her, hands balled, punching his ribs, over and over until he had to pin her wrists above her head and she was at last able to scream:

"Fuck me, Daddio. Fuck me, fuck me, fuck me!"

The wild world above them, the city below. How could either of them not see this as ordained by the Californian fates?

Chapter 14

Magnolia Boulevard. North Hollywood. Chick's place was a two-story ex-commercial building made of cinder blocks painted a sickly green. At street level there were large glass windows that had been painted over. Above them there were marks where some sort of sign had been ripped down. Inside, a warehouse area on the ground floor and a one-bedroom flat upstairs.

Morning. In bed together. Tim went down on her, the smell of her used pussy cutting him off from the world. When they were done, he pulled his face away and noticed for the first time that her right labia was raggedly split in the middle, as though it had been torn and had healed without being stitched. She saw his glance.

"War wound. I told you I got hurt when I was fifteen? Bit of a euphemism. This place used to be my mother's store. She sold movie memorabilia. I'd mind it for her a couple of nights a week. One time, someone starts banging on the Roll-A-Door at the back of the shop. When I go to see who it is, a guy in a ski mask jumps out and Tasers me. I came to blindfolded, gagged, taped up in a van going somewhere. When we got wherever it was, they tied me over a bench and two people went at it and tore up my cunt."

"Jesus."

Chick got out of bed, went into the adjoining bathroom and wiped herself with a wet cloth. She came back and pulled on her catsuit.

"All the time they were doing it I could hear clips of movies. They were so fucking loud. And all of them the lowest kind of shit – explosions, gunfights, car chases, stupid macho dialogue...."

Chick blew air out sadly, crossed her arms over her breasts and rocked a little where she stood.

"When I was eighteen my mother died of breast cancer and I got this building. I was growing up, I had my own place to live. I thought maybe I'd forget about it. Guess what? There are some wounds time doesn't heal."

Then she laughed and let go of the memory.

"Full disclosure, Timbo: I'm fucked in the head. Hey, what's that?"

Chick pointed to Tim's satchel lying beside the bed. It had fallen open and the *Wilderness* script had slipped halfway out of it. The rain in Griffith Park the night before had found its way into the bag and the script's cover page was wrecked.

Tim, feeling so close to Chick at that moment and wanting to keep her for ever and ever, wanting to impress her and have her think him better than other men, said: "Oh, just something I wrote a while ago. Kind of a Hollywood murder thing." Then tore off the cover page, on which his sister's name was still partially legible, and passed the screenplay over.

"You can read it if you like."

"Totally, dude. But not now. We got things to do."

Downstairs. The Roll-A-Door at the rear of the warehouse. Chick beside her Thruxton.

She said: "Long ride on the back of a bike."

"We could swing by Sean's and pick up my Vespa."

"Or you could ride that."

Chick pointed to something standing against the wall. It was covered with a tarp. Tim went to it and pulled the rough canvas away: Triumph Bonneville, 790cc, chrome, two-tone fuel tank, for years the flagship of British bikes.

"What I used to ride before I got the Thrux. Okay?"

"I think so."

Tim had ridden bikes for years before his declining self-image had convinced him that the Vespa was a better fit for his personality. Nothing classic or expensive, but he was an experienced rider and he knew he'd be able to handle the Triumph.

Chick crossed to a stack of boxes piled in a corner, pulled out a black leather jacket and tossed it to him. It was nicely weathered and smelled of cologne.

"Bought it at an auction for Kid. But he doesn't ride. Used to belong to Ron Jeremy. Maybe another reason he didn't want it – cock rivalry. Try it on, get rid of that fucking sport coat."

Tim wasn't sure what she meant about cock rivalry, but the jacket fit well. He pulled on his gloves and helmet.

Chick pressed a remote on her keychain and the Roll-A-Door rolled up. Tim swung his leg over the Bonneville. The key was in the ignition. He twisted the accelerator a couple of times, checked the bike was in neutral, then thumbed the start button. Chick hit hers and they peeled out of the warehouse, into the alley that ran behind it, the noise of their engines bouncing off walls in one long explosion.

101. 405. 10. There were shorter routes. But on bikes, on a day where the temperature was seventy-two degrees and the sky was clear and clean after last night's rain, taking Pacific Coast Highway as far as they could was kind of mandatory.

From North Hollywood to the coast the ride was nothing special. The 405 was clogged with morning traffic because of lane closures due to work on a damaged bridge. Chick rode between the lines of crawling cars and Tim followed, looking for cops, ignoring drivers who got pissed off and yelled when the bikes passed too close. Freeway ridin', it wasn't.

But at Santa Monica they curved off the 10 onto PCH, and the traffic was suddenly gone. Ocean on one side, the whole country on the other. Water, gulls, whitecaps. Sunshine a powdered yellow pigment in the air.

Throttle back, clutch in, down a gear, clutch out, fuel on again hard, engine howling. Accelerating out and around a station wagon full of kids. And the road opening up, then gas-clutch-gear again, up one cog, and another, and the engine breathing deeper, steel frame flexing, the whole machine reaching out, lengthening its stride. Vision feathering at the edges. Chrome and polished paintwork. The wind a solid hand on Tim's chest.

And Chick beside him, whooping, keeping pace, and then blasting the lighter Thruxton out ahead, just to show that she could, but the speed too much for her and falling back to match him again, and Tim slowly testing the big engine on the long straight by Point Mugu State Park, taking her with him, m.p.h. by m.p.h., to teach her a lesson, and Chick staying with him, refusing to back down, and both of them laugh-screaming in their helmets, and the world electric around them, and their cells changing, and their hearts changing....

Pulling over, breathless, laughing and clutching each other, outside a roadside diner, somewhere maybe ten miles from Oxnard, too full of adrenaline to speak, too full of the connection they had just made, all wide eyes and mouths, their skins too small to hold them. And doing the only thing they could do right then, fucking in the toilet of the diner. Chick on a sink, Tim hammering it in, both of them collapsing when they came.

Afterwards, they sat in a booth and had one cold beer each, smiling, touching hands, speaking softly, making idle talk.

Chick said: "This guy I'm going to see, Danny Bartlemann, he looks kind of... worn out, but he's fucking brilliant. Have you seen *The Seminal Day*?"

Tim shook his head.

"Amazing film. If you need proof that Hollywood is designed to eradicate anything meaningful, *The Seminal Day* is it."

"I'll put it on my list."

"Not surprising it's so good, though. The guy's suffered."

"Hey, us artists...."

"No, I mean for real. I don't know the details, but apparently his father was murdered. Never solved."

Tim thinking he could match that, but not wanting to get into something so dark with this girl, on a day this beautiful.

Outside, Chick still happily chattering.

"There's a rumor he doesn't have a cock."

"Huh?"

"That's what I've heard."

Chick grabbed for Tim's crotch then laughed and ran the rest of the way to her bike.

Back on the road they took it easy, following the 33 inland, past Mira Monte and Meiners Oaks, up to Los Padres National Forest – a hilly, two-million acre swath of forest that stretched from Ventura to Monterey.

Danny Bartlemann owned a half acre inholding off Matilija Canyon Road, about seven miles inside the park's southern boundary.

Danny Bartlemann had written and directed *The Seminal Day* – a thinly disguised account of his troubled relationship with his father, the film distributor, Scott Bartlemann – when he was twenty-eight. Praised by critics and the filmmaking community at large, hailed as a work of filmmaking genius, it was nevertheless an unmitigated commercial failure.

Two years later, the result of blogosphere goading after he'd posted a particularly virulent exegesis on *Lethal Weapon*, he'd written *Maximum Kill*. It had been a joke, a throwaway piece intended only to give him the credentials to continue savaging Hollywood dross. He'd sold it for a song and, when it was released, had publicly ridiculed the story.

When *Maximum Kill* became one of that summer's top earners, Danny left L.A. and disappeared into the forest. He continued to blog movie reviews and post rants against mainstream Hollywood, but he hadn't written a screenplay in over ten years. Until now. Until *Antepenultimate*.

The bikes bounced over the rutted red-earth trail that led from a five-bar gate to a large log cabin flanked by stands of Jeffrey pine. The property stood on the slope of a canyon and the house had a view across a mile of valley. Tim killed the Bonnie and looked back the way they'd come – trees, outcrops of rock, more trees. A sense of peace, of isolation. He could understand how a writer might come here to repair himself, to outrun the expectations the world had of him. Or those he once had of himself, perhaps.

Chick had brought the final version of the option agreement for *Antepenultimate* with her. Danny didn't believe in agents and they'd thrashed it out in emails and meetings over the last month. Danny was something of an indie film idol to her and she wanted to do the signing in person.

The three of them sat in a large room at the center of the cabin drinking tea. Danny Bartlemann was a thin man with wire-rimmed glasses, a thin moustache like matinee idols had in old movies, and receding hair tied back in a ponytail. Chick handed him the option agreement and read through it aloud.

Tim had signed two of these agreements himself and the points Chick listed were pretty standard, except that where most option agreements ran for six to eighteen months, the option period for *Antepenultimate* was only thirty days.

Additionally, unlike many screenplay agreements which stipulated that only ten percent of the purchase price would be paid at the time the option was exercised, with the remaining ninety percent due on the first day of principal photography, the deal Chick was offering Danny allowed full payment at time of purchase.

This was a particularly advantageous clause for Danny as only about ten percent of purchased screenplays ever went into production, meaning a whole lot of screenwriters never got more than ten percent of their potential pay check. And even screenplays that did get made could often spend a year or more in development and pre-production before the cameras rolled for the first time.

What Chick got back for these concessions was a much smaller up-front option payment than the writer of *Maximum Kill* might otherwise have commanded. A useful trade given that her producing partner hadn't quite locked down the film's finance yet.

When they were finished with the read-through, Chick handed over a check drawn against Kid Haldane Productions for $8,000. Danny folded it and put it in his shirt pocket. Chick left the room to use the toilet and Tim, casting about for some topic of conversation, asked:

"What was your inspiration for *Antepenultimate*?"

"My father's murder."

Tim figured: bad start.

"Oh, shit, I'm sorry."

"Don't worry about it, it was ten years ago. We weren't close."

"What happened? Do you mind talking about it?"

Danny shook his head.

"He had a weekend place in Isla Vista, north of Santa Barbara. Maid went crazy one night and shot him with a pistol, then took one of his shotguns and blew her own head off with it."

"Jesus!"

Danny made a face and shrugged.

"He left us when I was eleven. After that, there really wasn't much meaningful interaction. So, you know...spilled milk, and all that."

Danny looked at his hands for a moment, then roused himself and smiled weakly.

"*Ante's* not an account of the murder, though. It's about loss, about having something taken from you that you can never get back. It's about how fathers destroy their sons. I set the story in a 1970s hippie commune. You know, like they had in Northern California? And the leader, right, the meta-father figure? He goes off hunting in the mountains with his son. So we're able to look at the one-on-one dynamic as it affects this poor kid, right? And we also see the effect of his absence on other members of the commune – the pseudo-children. And of course, on an even more meta-level, it resonates with the whole Watergate thing that was going on then. Abandonment on a national scale. Nixon as failed father figure."

At any other time Tim's eyes would have glazed over. But he wasn't listening to Danny's pseudo-psychological exposition. He was listening to a series of switches clicking shut in his head – a Hollywood executive shot dead in his weekend house, the maid with her head blown off by a shotgun....

Chick came back in sniffing her fingers, said it was time they hit the road for L.A.

Danny paced the floor of the cabin. *The Seminal Day*, *Maximum Kill*, *Antepenultimate*. Three screenplays in twelve years. Where had the time gone? What had filled the holes between those three bursts of activity?

As writer/director on *The Seminal Day* he'd been certain he was the harbinger of a new wave in cinema, an Orson Wells for a generation who had been so emotionally defoliated by MTV and franchised action movies that they were crying out for some sort of psychic sustenance. But then there was Afghanistan and 9/11 and all anyone wanted was more explosions and more buddy movies.

And so, a period of confusion that had eventually turned to resentment, *Maximum Kill* hurled as an insult at the film world, and then retreat. Retreat to this cabin, and the long years rolling by, thinking of stories to write, plotting outlines, developing characters, but somehow never sitting down to page one. The money from the sale of the share of Big Glass that his father had left him an insidious financial cocoon.

And in this cocoon – turning over the anchor points of his life, reliving the lightning-bolt memories that had shattered a life he knew could have been different, could have been better.

His father.... His father.... Did it all come down to that? To the withdrawal of this man who had been such a presence during the early years of his childhood, such a thing to look up to, to love. But withdrawal wasn't enough, wasn't a term that adequately covered it.

Three days after Danny's eleventh birthday, Scott Bartlemann had left – left Danny, left his wife, walked out of the family home and never returned. Danny and his father had not been close for a long time by then, but still, so dramatic and final a severing of ties was a wound from which Danny knew he'd never truly recovered.

He referred to it as *The Abandonment* – the point after which all life had changed.

He'd lived on with his mother in the house, had seen his father on birthdays and at Christmas – strained occasions, during which his father was eternally preoccupied, that made Danny feel more abandoned than ever. He'd logged the bulletins that made it across this no-man's land of disinterest: his father's sale of the dry-cleaning business he'd spent ten years building, the move into film distribution, the famous people his father was sometimes photographed with....

Even after Danny's accident in the snow there had been little change. Flowers sent to his hospital room, a card prepared by a secretary that Danny imagined his father had signed as perfunctorily as he signed his checks.

But Danny hadn't hated his father for any of this. There was a part of him that was too desperate for what his father could have supplied, a part of him, he understood, that kept hoping his father would change.

Had Danny become a filmmaker because of his father? Was his decision born of a desire to impress, to attract attention? Probably. Was *The Seminal Day* an attempt to understand what his father had done to him? Without question. Danny was fucked up, but he wasn't so fucked up that he didn't know how fucked up he was.

In the end, though, that chance to impress, to change things, had never materialized. There had been some contact after *Maximum Kill*, but by then the dynamic between them had turned to stone, and even a potentially successful Hollywood movie could not make Scott Bartlemann love his son. And then Scott Bartlemann was killed.

Danny had been in hospital at the time, was discharged early so that he could identify the bodies. In the morgue his predominant emotion had been that of relief, relief that he could now stop hoping for something he'd never had any chance of getting in the first place.

But Scott didn't let Danny off quite that easily. When the dust settled and Scott's will was read, Danny found himself Scott's sole heir and, therefore, owner of Scott's share of Big Glass.

Would any man leave his stake in a company he'd helped build from the ground up to anyone but someone he loved? Danny wanted to believe it, but he couldn't shake the feeling that the bequest was a huge joke. He was not a man who could run a film distribution company, even with a partner. His father had known this. Being left a controlling interest in Big Glass, then, was a challenge Scott knew his son was certain to fail.

Danny figured, if you didn't play the game you couldn't lose, and when Theo Portman, already somehow aware of the contents of the will, came to Danny a week after Scott's death and made an offer for Scott's share, Danny was only too happy to agree to sell once probate was granted. So happy in fact he signed a letter of intent, didn't bargain about the price and never paid any attention to the company again.

Danny's suspicion that his father's will was not the product of love was somewhat confirmed several years later when, on a rare trip to Los Angeles, he bumped into Michael Starck and was told, not entirely without malice, that Scott Bartlemann had been planning to delay the release of *Maximum Kill*, a film written by his only son, for up to two years.

So, Los Padres, and the long years rolling by. And then, one day, waking up, blinking, seeing that wasteland of time behind him, realizing that to end things, to escape the cycle of failure and introspection his father had set him upon, he would have to write his way out. And wanting to do it for his talent as well. Wanting to not let the sum of his creative life be two films he'd done ten years ago. Wanting his loneliness, if it had to continue, not to be something he hadn't tried to change.

Antepenultimate had taken him three months to write, start to finish, rewrites included. And Chick had come to him before he'd even tried to shop it around. She'd seen a post on his blog about a new screenplay. She thought he was a genius. For his part, she fit the material perfectly, fit his image of who he thought should direct a film like *Antepenultimate*. And he loved *Loggers*.

But none of this was why he'd signed her option agreement. He'd signed because the project was being financed through GHQ. And finance through GHQ meant a pathway back to Ally Bannister.

Danny and Ally had met during the production of *Maximum Kill*. They'd fallen for each other immediately.

But women, for Danny, were an exercise in masochism. When he was nineteen, he'd lost control while skiing at Tuolumne Meadows and run body-first into a deeply snowed pine. Forty m.p.h. Knocked unconscious. Most of his penis torn off by the broken end of a crotch-high branch.

He'd almost bled out. Two hours lying hidden in the trees before Mountain Rescue found him. By that time the shredded blob of flesh they'd found halfway down the leg of his North Face ski pants was no longer viable for reattachment.

In the years after the accident he'd allowed himself to get close to a handful of women. But he'd always cut the relationships short, unable to face that hideous moment when clothes had to come off.

Ally had been different.

Ally was damaged. He didn't know the details, but there was about her a palpable sense that she'd been deeply hurt.

So he'd hung in there, seeing her for far longer than his previous temporary attractions, surprised when the issue of sex didn't surface to torpedo their attraction for each other.

Until one night when she'd told him she wanted to sleep with him, but confessed that she could not stand to be penetrated. She gave no explanation and Danny, overjoyed to have found a woman who didn't need a penis inside her, didn't ask questions. She was the first woman he'd had sex with since high school.

A fairytale scenario, but it didn't last.

Because of her brother.

As Hollywood nutjobs went, Jeffery Bannister was in a league of his own –
emotionally dependent on his twin sister, grandiose in self-image and only tenuously connected to the real world. He lived in constant fear that Ally would be
taken away from him.

Over the six months it took to get *Maximum Kill* shot, edited, and sold to Big
Glass for distribution, Jeffery's antagonism toward their relationship, and toward
Danny personally, grew to a point where it was impossible for Ally to fit both men
into her life.

Danny lost out.

Two days after his father was murdered, she told him it was over. Told him she
loved him, that she was heartbroken, but that Jeffery was ill and needed her more.
Some might have said her timing was lousy. The truth was, Danny felt next to
nothing about losing his absentee father. But he felt a hell of a lot about losing her.

CHAPTER 15

Delores' Bel Air mansion. A room overlooking the pool and the garden. Delores in her action hero gear – black combat pants, black sleeveless top, tactical boots. Standing in front of a wall mirror, flexing the muscles of her arms. Mexican skin tight and glowing, a cascade of dark curls past her shoulders. Trademark unshaven armpits.

It had taken Sean two days of phone calls to get there, to get past secretaries, security guys, assistants....

Delores spoke to her own reflection:

"It's been a long time, Sean."

"Two years."

"We were together almost that long."

Delores' accent had been elocuted to non-existence by a succession of vocal coaches and her voice now was a husky generic American.

She glanced over her shoulder at him, then started pacing about the room, stopping here and there to pick up and hold some object or other, as though it was a prop in a film, something she should interpret as significant, meaningful.

Delores said: "I was in love with you."

"We were both in love. Trouble was, we were in love with ourselves, too. And because of that, a woman died."

Delores looked at him directly for the first time.

"Did you pull the trigger? Did I?"

Sean didn't answer. He knew blame was not something she was prepared to accept, her narcissism made everything someone else's fault.

Delores moved closer to him.

"I tried to find you, Sean. But you'd disappeared."

Sean wasn't sure she was telling the truth, but her words skewered him nonetheless. How many nights had he longed to be with her? How many times had he told himself that he could be made whole again if he could just be with her?

"You said it was final. You said it was over forever."

"You went to Michael. You betrayed me."

"Jesus, Delores, do you think things would have turned out differently? You were going to show it to him eventually, anyhow."

"*Wilderness* was mine. It should have been my decision when and how Michael got to see it."

Sean saw anger flare in Delores' eyes. But it was gone the next second and she smiled seductively and said: "Let's not talk about the past. It can't do us any good. Let's talk about us. I missed you. You're looking very thin, you know. Have you been pining for me?"

"*Wilderness* is out in the world again."

When Delores had terminated their relationship Sean had been all but destroyed. He took some pleasure now in the look of horror that replaced Delores' sultry pout.

Delores sat down abruptly.

"Impossible. It can't be. I have the only copy."

"On your computer?"

Delores tossed her head. "What does it matter where I keep it?"

"Because it can be copied."

"By who? I have a password."

"Does Skye still work for you?"

"Skye?"

"She has a copy. She's passing it to her girlfriend page by page. The girlfriend's rewriting it, calling it her own."

Delores' lips trembled. She bit down and made them stop.

"Are you sure?"

Sean had known this moment was coming since Tim had told him about the screenplay. Jocelyn and Skye were involved already. But he could save Tim. He wove a story out of bullshit, hoping it would count for something when it came time to weigh his soul.

"I go to a writers' group. We read out what we're working on. Last week a girl called Jocelyn read the first act of *Wilderness*. She'd changed it a bit, but it was still *Wilderness* – a group of filmmakers, a movie, the exec doesn't want to release their picture, the filmmakers, *three of them*, go to the exec's house and kill him. Even the maid.... The same fucking story. I followed her after the meeting. She met up with Skye. Skye gave her some pages. Skye works for you. You're the only person who could possibly have a copy of Rebecca's screenplay. Skye's the source of the story."

Delores threw herself on the floor, did a rapid series of push-ups, then stood up, panting.

"I'll fire her."

"It'll take more than that. Jocelyn already has the part that matters. She wants to be a big screenwriter. She's going to circulate the script when it's finished, for sure. Michael will find out. And when he does, he'll think you're behind it. He told you last time he'd kill you if you crossed him again. And he'll kill me too. I've only ever been a loose end to him. Why do you think I disappeared?"

Delores started to crouch, getting ready for another set. Sean reached out and stopped her, held her arms.

"The only way to stop Michael coming after us is to tell him about Skye and Jocelyn before he finds out himself."

"I don't suppose you want to play any part in that conversation?"

"I'm not the idiot who kept a copy."

"There'll be more blood."

"But it won't be ours."

For a moment, Delores stayed rigid under his hands. Then she melted against him, turned her head up and kissed him. They held each other for a long time, then Delores pulled away and went and stood by the window, looking out at the garden.

Sean wrote down Jocelyn's address. As he was leaving, Delores asked him where he lived. But Sean shook his head and gave her the number of a disposable cell phone instead.

Chapter 16

Santa Monica. Eighty-two degrees. The living room with rain falling outside. Air sticky and humid. Wet tarmac, wet buildings. Steam from the roads in the brief pauses between rain. No happy, laughing girl in the alley today.

Tim with the *Wilderness* screenplay in front of him, putting pieces together.

Danny Bartlemann had said his father was killed in Isla Vista, shot to death with a pistol, that his Mexican maid blew her own head off with a shotgun.

Google time again.

The murder there loud and clear, mirroring Danny's description.

At the time of his death, Scott Bartlemann was co-owner along with his business partner, Theo Portman, of Big Glass – a company specializing in the domestic distribution of non-studio-produced movies.

The cops suggested murder/suicide but they never closed the case, primarily because no one was able to figure a motive. Best guess around Hollywood was that Scott had been fucking the maid and the shooting had stemmed from something to do with that. The maid, never identified, was presumed to be an undocumented illegal immigrant.

In the *Wilderness* screenplay, Rebecca had a group of filmmakers murdering a distribution company executive at his weekend house, also in Isla Vista. A maid, also Mexican, interrupts the scene and has her head blown off by the filmmakers with one of the executive's own shotguns.

Two different scenarios. But an executive shot to death in an Isla Vista weekender and a Mexican maid with her head blown off – what were the odds?

Of course Rebecca could just have used the Bartlemann murder as a starting point and built her own story around it. That would have been the obvious explanation.

Except for one thing. Except for the fact that Rebecca had been murdered while she was working on the final draft of the screenplay. Except for the fact that it looked like she'd done her best to keep the screenplay away from Hollywood eyes.

Tim added up: Rebecca writing a screenplay that exposed the truth of a murder. Plus Rebecca dead. Equals Rebecca killed because of the screenplay.

It wasn't conclusive, and Tim had no idea how Rebecca could have discovered the truth, if truth it was, about the Bartlemann murder, but it had one great advantage over the random kill scenario that the cops had pasted on his sister's death.

It gave him a target.

He thought about Chick. About her wild, burning energy. Setting billboards on fire. Destroying the marriage of a man she despised. Vicious, maybe. Insane, at least to some degree. But pure. And honorable. True to what she felt and the changes she wanted to bring about.

Tim went into the kitchen. He opened the fridge. He bought his wine by the case and there were eight bottles left from his last purchase, laid out on the shelves. He opened all of them and tipped them down the sink. Then stood and looked out the kitchen window.

Rebecca had been killed because of the *Wilderness* screenplay, he was certain of it. Her killers had to be those who had the most to lose if the screenplay entered the world, i.e. the murderers of the distribution company co-owner – Beau Montgomery in the screenplay, Scott Bartlemann in reality.

His drinking, Jocelyn, the failure of his screenwriting ambitions, his sister's rejection of him, and then her death...all of this had taken something from him. Finding the killers would be his version of Chick's vendetta, would be his truth, his purity of action. His way of rebuilding himself.

Back in the living room. Looking for clues. The screenplay killers: three filmmakers – a brother and sister, Chad and Chloe Standish; and Brandon Kane, the leader. Googling those names got Tim nothing useful. Not surprising. He already knew Rebecca had changed Scott Bartlemann's name to Beau Montgomery.

Tim made notes, short character sketches. Chad and Chloe Standish were portrayed as the unhinged adult children of a wealthy investment banker – rich kids hungry for Hollywood glamour. Brandon Kane was a British ex-pat whose impoverished childhood had made him desperate to succeed at any cost.

Without real names to hang these descriptions on, though, they were next to useless. Tim's earlier determination took a hit. He began to wish he hadn't thrown the wine away.

CHAPTER 17

E vening. The rain had thinned to a depressing drizzle. The air was still warm, but all
Denning felt was cold.

He'd known it was coming. They both had.

"I fucked Kid."

Said by Peta when she got home from work.

It had happened in Kid's office, her on the edge of his desk, him plowing her
with his monster cock. Of course, she hadn't put it quite that brutally to Denning.

They sat in the kitchen. There were banana palms along the fence that separated them from their neighbor. The palms were close to the house and the thin
rain dripping from their fronds made an insistent, papery tapping.

Denning said very little. He wanted to scream, he wanted to beg.

But he kept his mouth shut.

So she could go.

And Peta, across the table from him, understood his silence and took it as the
gift it was. And felt all the worse for it. Because she knew that if she had not stood
close behind him that night in the kitchen ten years ago, if she had not put her arms
around him and opened her mouth, he would not be in such pain now.

Later. Peta in bed asleep, dreaming troubled dreams of change. Denning, still in
the kitchen, counting backwards.

Twelve years ago they'd moved to L.A. from Las Vegas where Denning had
been working as an entertainment reporter for the Las Vegas Sun News. It had

looked like a fabulous new start. Denning had landed a job with the Hollywood Reporter. Clara and the then sixteen-year-old Peta were overjoyed to swap the neon and the gambling and the artificiality of casino-town for the beaches and glamour of California.

Clara had started a mobile dog-grooming business as soon as they were settled. A small truck with a dog Jacuzzi on the back. Flea treatments, canine shampoos, nail clipping, dog massage.

Denning had always felt the dog thing didn't quite fit her. She had the body of a swimsuit model and it seemed incongruous that she should be scrubbing down British Bulldogs or blow-drying Great Danes.

But the business was her baby. She scraped the cash together for the truck, she built a client base from the ground up. She was first generation and the poverty of her Mexican parents had left a mark she was determined to scrub off. Plus it brought in a steady income, a bonus with the mortgage they had on the two bedroom in Westwood.

Two years into their brand new life, Clara had noticed a white van following her dog truck on Mulholland Drive. She told Denning about it that evening. Denning asked for the license plate, but Clara hadn't been able to get it.

Next morning, though, Denning got to see the van first-hand. It was parked across the street from their house. Clara thought it looked like the one from the day before so Denning walked over to speak to the guy behind the wheel. But the van took off before he could get there. Even so, Denning got a look at the driver – Mexican, late thirties, wraparound shades, a shattered question mark of chicken pox scars on the side of his face. He got the license plate, too.

He told Clara to stay home, but she brushed the whole thing off. She had important clients that day, a rich set in Pacific Palisades. They argued about it a little, but ended up laughing at their paranoia. And she went off to work.

Her truck was found a day later, abandoned on Latimer Road, a quiet street in Pacific Palisades that served the back entrances of expensive houses.

Denning gave the cops a description of the man driving the white van and he looked at mug shots, but there was no record of the guy. He gave them the license number, but it turned out the plates were stolen. A member of a Japanese gardening crew was located who had seen a man in a white van drive past him on

Latimer. But he could give no useful description because the driver's face had been obscured by a ski mask – an oddity the gardener hadn't bothered to report at the time due to his fragile immigration status.

The cops traced her movements that day. Clara had kept her first three bookings, all in the Palisades area. Her fourth scheduled stop was the house of the ex-wife of the owner of a chain of discount shoe stores. It was outside the service entrance of this residence that her truck had been found. Clara hadn't made it inside to wash the ex-wife's Labradoodle.

The woman was checked and cleared. Every customer on Clara's books was interviewed. But these were people who ranged from rich to super-rich and none of them turned out to be a sociopath with a deadly taste for Mexican-American women.

Most of them weren't even home at the time Clara made her calls. And the maids, who generally handed over the dogs, could add little to the investigation beyond confirming Clara's arrival and departure times.

Similarly, an examination of Clara's truck yielded nothing forensic-wise that helped.

No one was ever arrested, no one was ever even identified as a plausible person of interest. And neither Clara alive, nor her body, ever turned up.

Now. Late night, present day. Denning felt himself to be thoroughly fucked. GHQ had destroyed his career, his wife was gone, and his daughter had found another man. A man who was somehow connected to Michael Starck. A fucking ex-porn star.

Denning went to his bedroom and got the reel of Super 8 film. In a closet at the end of the hall he found a Bolex projector and a collapsible screen that had belonged to his father, took them into the living room and set them up.

He threaded the film and flipped the switch.

The film was in color, silent, somewhere out in the country. Shot from maybe two hundred yards away. The camera panning across trees, the trees shrouded in smoke, and then more of them, on fire, flames jetting from trunks. And a small cabin in a clearing, the trees behind it not yet on fire, but the fire moving steadily closer.

The door of the cabin opening and a man stepping out onto the porch, a back-pack over his shoulder, looking quickly about, looking off to his left at the burning trees. And the camera zooming in, framing the front of the cabin, close enough for Denning to recognize the man.

The man walking quickly to his right, to the end of the porch, jumping down, jogging along a faint trail, away from the burning trees. Reaching a nervous horse tethered to a pine. Mounting and riding away.

Listening to the projector whirr as the film ran out, Denning wondered what he'd just seen. Some candid footage of a Californian forest fire? Some campers, perhaps, in the right place at the right time, camera at the ready? The cabin and man just an added bonus, a dramatic counterpoint to a seasonal forest fire?

Maybe.

Maybe if it hadn't been shot on Super 8.

Maybe if the man coming out of the cabin hadn't been Michael Starck.

There was nothing in the film that could help Denning identify where the cabin was located. There was nothing to tell him when it was shot. And, most importantly, there was nothing that gave any sort of significance to the film as a blackmail tool. Guy walks out of a cabin in a forest – so what?

Denning rewound the film, took his phone, set it to video and pointed it at the screen. Not the most professional way to make a copy, but his phone shot in HD and the film was sharply focused against the screen. He figured the quality would be okay.

Later. Denning in bed. Alone in his room. He tried to sleep but thoughts of Peta made it impossible.

He got up and turned on the light, took the Super 8 film out to the kitchen and left it on the counter where he knew she'd see it in the morning.

Back in his bedroom, he looked about for something to read. And saw the screenplay that the guy from the market parking lot had given him.

By the time he finished reading it he knew what he was going to do with the next part of his life. He'd said it as a quip, a throw-away lie to explain his presence outside Delores Fuentes' house to Tim. But now it was the truth – he was going to write a book.

CHAPTER 18

For Jeffery and Ally she was always The First – the beginning of the Ritual of Freeing, the start of their self-prescribed healing process. For Kid, though, she was a line in the sand separating good and evil. A line he hadn't stepped across, so much as pole-vaulted over.

He'd known, when Jeffery and Ally had come to him with the offer of all that money, what he was doing; known that he would not be the same person afterwards. But he'd done it anyway and all the regrets in the world couldn't change what had happened that night twelve years ago in a North Hollywood alley behind Magnolia Boulevard.

After Jeffery and Ally had placed their order, he'd trawled Los Angeles looking for a girl who'd pose the least difficulty for an inexperienced abductor. He'd found her in a movie memorabilia shop, had seen her as soon as he walked through the door, dealing with a customer. He'd taken a quick photo with his phone and stepped back outside before she noticed him.

Kid's photo wasn't good. The girl had moved as he'd taken it – her head was bowed and her face was not visible. But her body was, and when he showed it to Jeffery and Ally they said she was good enough. There was something else in the photo, though, that they went bat shit over.

A gold statuette on a shelf behind the girl. An Oscar. The pinnacle of movie achievement. Only, instead of a sword, this one had an erect phallus. A hardon Oscar. Kid's shopping list grew by one item – they wanted the girl *and* the statuette.

After that, it was just a matter of watching and waiting. Of checking out the shitty industrial two-story that housed the store, of finding the Roll-A-Door service entrance in the alley out back, of plotting the safest route from there to an unused property Jeffery and Ally owned in the hills above Malibu.

He spent ten days at it, and once he'd learned that the girl minded the store alone a couple of nights a week he crossed that line in the sand.

A quiet Tuesday around 9.00 p.m. The store empty. The girl bored, sitting at the counter flipping through magazines. Kid parked a stolen van up close to the Roll-A-Door, the van's sliding side door open. Banged away with the heel of his fist like he was making a delivery.

Ski mask on as the door rolled up, standing off to one side, out of sight. Contact Taser to the neck when she stepped out. Drag her into the van, slide the door shut. Tape her wrists and ankles. Tape her mouth and eyes. But not before taking a long look at her face, imprinting it on memory as an icon of regret.

She was younger than he'd thought, maybe around fifteen. Not particularly pretty. Dyed-black hair, bad skin, slim body, the tip of her right little finger missing.

He remembered the hardon Oscar as he was about to drive away, ran back into the still-empty store and snatched it from the shelf.

When it was over, when Jeffery and Ally had finished with the girl, Kid took her to Griffith Park, still blindfolded and gagged, put some paper towels in her pants to soak up the blood, then slit the tape on her wrists and got away from there as fast as he could.

He'd abducted a girl so she could be raped by a pair of psychos. It kept him awake at night. It flashed in his psyche like a huge neon sign – *Bad Man, Bad Man, Bad Man....* Kid was traumatized. But not traumatized enough to throw away this new income stream – he just needed to find a way to distance himself from the actual doing of it. So he called Christo, down Mexico way.

Crazy thing – two years ago, ten after he'd dragged her into the van, he walked into a coffee shop in Hollywood and saw her behind an espresso machine. Her hair was blond and her skin was clear, but he recognized the face, still. And the tip of her little finger was missing.

He knew it was a sign, that he was being offered a chance to make restitution. A chance at a new life.

Casual conversation. An engineered friendship. She'd done a course at UCLA. She wanted to direct films. Bingo, he had his mission. He couldn't un-rape her, but he could make her dream come true. He used his money from Jeffery and Ally to rent office space in Santa Monica, started to call himself a producer. She found a screenplay she wanted to make. He leveraged his connection with Michael Starck to finance it.

Loggers had a three week shoot and a shoestring budget. It won an award at a small film festival and played the arthouse circuit. It was a start, but it was more calling-card than breakthrough. He couldn't pretend that his task was done. And so, *Antepenultimate*.

Kid had spent the last few days shitting himself over the stolen Super 8 film. No Super 8 meant no finance, meant no *Antepenultimate*, meant no dream-come-true for Chick, meant no alleviation of the guilt he carried.

He'd told Chick everything was fine, that the finance was still on track. But he'd begun to think of contingency plans, of buying a gun and holding it to Michael's head.

And then this morning he'd sent Peta to pick up the Camaro from the auto-glass shop. And she'd come back smiling, pleased with herself. Handed him the yellow container of film. She'd found it under the seat. It must have fallen out when the bag was stolen. It had been there all the time.

He wanted to laugh his head off. He wanted to tell someone, to shout it to the world. But contented himself with feeling relieved, took it as a sign that he was destined for change.

But another problem now – Chick's introduction to Jeffery and Ally. He'd tried to get out of it, phoned Ally and told her his director was a very private person, that she didn't want to taint the creative process by getting involved with the business side of things. Blah, blah, blah. But Ally had insisted.

On the drive up there, Chick sat next to him in the car as pleased as punch. For her, this was tangible evidence that her project was moving forward. These guys were bona fide, big-time movie producers. These guys were Hollywood.

She babbled away about how unreal *Antepenultimate* was going to be, how she was single-handedly going to reverse the dumbing down of contemporary cinema. Kid tuned it out and drove, ticking off the things he had to be thankful for: she was twelve years older, her hair was blond now, her skin was clear, her body had lengthened a little. And back then, most of her face had been covered with tape. He wished he could have thought of a convincing reason to ask her to wear gloves.

Bel Air. A mansion on a one-acre promontory. Unobstructed sea and city views. Clean and white. A wholesome flipside to the horrors of the place in the Malibu hills. They sat by the pool, a maid served pastries and fruit, organic coffee and imported water.

Chick in leather. Ally in white linen. Jeffery in some insane version of a 1940s private eye outfit, his gaze wandering as though he was following things the rest of them couldn't see.

Ally played host, relaxed and cool. She and her brother had both seen *Loggers* – they liked it very much, she said. They'd read *Antepenultimate* too. It annoyed Kid that psychos like these could be so professional.

Jeffery let his sister speak.

"Name a director, a point of reference."

Chick said: "Hal Ashby."

Ally shook her head.

"*Antepenultimate* is not Hal Ashby."

"Well, from the point of view of really nailing relationships, you know?"

"You think 'relationship' pictures grab people these days?"

"You mean people who've been de-educated by all these bullshit action movies? People who don't understand how to watch anything that doesn't have an explosion or a fuck scene every ten minutes?"

Kid killed a smile. Chick knew these were exactly the type of movies GHQ specialized in. Despite this artistic friction, though, things seemed to be going well. Neither Ally nor Jeffery had given any indication that they recognized Chick.

Ally smiled a little at Chick's righteousness.

"Narrative engagement depends on structure and on the conflicts inherent within and between characters. Importantly, people want to follow a hero, whether he's dodging explosions and having sex, or whether he's some weed trying to unravel the relationship he had with his father. *Antepenultimate* has a number of problems in this area. Primarily, you don't have an active protagonist. The Terrence character doesn't make things happen, things happen to him."

"But that's why it's so real."

Chick raised both her hands and spread her fingers to emphasize her point. Kid saw Ally take in her missing finger joint. It was nothing dramatic, just a subtle tightening around the eyes. But it was there, and Kid felt the first small fissure of uncertainty work its way into the morning.

"It might be real, but you run the risk of a disengaged audience."

"Not if it's done well. If it's done well you get a remarkable film." Chick leaned forward, got earnest. "Look, as a director, you make someone interesting, worth following, when you find the emotional heart of that character. When you unlock this, when you get to the very core of what drives him, what informs his decisions, what makes him act the way he does, then there's a truth to the story that audiences instinctively recognize. And once you get there, even the mundane becomes interesting, even passive characters hold our attention."

"And you can get to that place?"

"Terrence is a man who has been so shattered by the shitty relationship he had with his father that it's like he's been emotionally raped."

Kid saw where this was going and inside his head screamed: *"Nooooooo!"*

But Chick kept talking.

"And I *know* I can get to that place because I've been there. I've been raped. I've experienced how it infects everything that comes after."

Ally looked shocked.

"Oh, you poor thing. What happened?"

"I was abducted from my mother's store when I was fifteen. Taken somewhere and...." Chick shrugged.

"Oh, my God. Did they catch him?"

"Them. Man and a woman, I think, from their voices. No. I was blindfolded the whole time. Crazy thing was, they played clips from old action movies while they were doing it. I could hear the soundtrack. Afterwards, they dumped me in Griffith Park."

Ally reached across the table and took Chick's hand, said to Kid: "You've got someone very special here, you know that?"

"From the first time I met her."

"And when was that, exactly?"

"Two years ago."

Chick said: "In a cafe. I was working as a barista. We hit it off immediately."

When Ally spoke again she was still looking at Kid.

"I bet you did. I bet it felt like you already knew each other somehow."

Chick smiled gleefully, figuring she and Kid were acing this meeting.

"Yes! How did you know?"

Ally turned to Chick.

"That emotional heart thing? I'm pretty good at it, too."

Jeffery stood up, said: "I have to go inside. I've got the wrong hat on."

He left without saying anything else.

Ally smiled brightly. "Well, I think we've got ourselves a film. I'll call Business Affairs today and give them our okay. Hey, you know who would be perfect as the mother Terrence lusts after? Delores Fuentes. I think the cougar thing she has going on now could really work in that part. I'll set up a meeting for you."

And all Chick could say was: "Wow...."

And all Kid could wonder was what Jeffery and Ally were going to do, now that they'd recognized Chick as one of their rape girls.

Ally found Jeffery in the dressing room of his suite. He'd taken off his jacket and hat and stood now in front of a full-length mirror wearing pegged trousers and a close-fitting waistcoat. He wore an old leather shoulder holster which held a .38 snub-nose revolver. Around him the floor was covered with hats, all of them bought from auction houses specializing in costume department sell-offs.

In his hand he held the one he prized most – a trilby worn by Fred McMurray in Double Indemnity. He ran his fingers around its brim, put it on his head and took it off, put it on and took it off again.

"I wish everything was in black-and-white."

When Ally didn't say anything, he dropped the hat on the floor with the others.

"They don't work anymore."

"What do you mean?"

"I used to be able to be anything I wanted – a private eye, a cop, a newspaper hack...."

Ally put her hand on his neck and started to knead the muscles there. Jeffery looked at the floor like he was standing on the edge of a cliff.

Ally had known for a long time that her brother was drifting away from her. Like some child's balloon lost at a carnival. And as high as she jumped and as fast as she ran, she knew her days of bringing him back to earth were almost over.

What had started in his twenties as a simple interest in film noir had morphed over the years into a delusional landscape where two realities overlapped – the day-to-day mundane, and some other twilight invention where tough guys and femmes fatales waged their wars against each other in a black-and-white world where the calendars always read 1940.

And in this mythical Los Angeles a murder lived forever. It was always there, in newspapers, in the collective consciousness, in the lore of the place. For a man who struggled to define the outlines of his own existence, the possibility of instant inclusion in the annals of the city held a powerful attraction, held out the tantalizing possibility that, with just the pull of a trigger, he could rank alongside such timeless sensations as the William Desmond Taylor and Black Dahlia cases.

Jeffery walked away from the mirror and sat on the edge of his bed and said: "The girl."

"The First."

"I think it's a sign, don't you? If we use her the right way we'll be free, the ritual will be complete."

Jeffery lay down on the bed. Ally stood at the floor-to-ceiling window and stared out over the city to the ocean. Jeffery rolled onto his side to look at her.

"I've been good, haven't I?"

"Not mentioning Danny."

"Yes."

"We're not producing *Antepenultimate*. We're just the money. There's no reason he and I should meet."

"He wanted to take you away."

"But I didn't go. I stayed with you. Go to sleep now."

Jeffery took the .38 out of its holster and put it on a nightstand beside the bed. It was eleven-thirty in the morning. He swallowed two Zopiclone, lay on his back and crossed his arms over his chest.

Ally looked out the window. She listened to Jeffery's breathing change.

Danny.... She hadn't seen him since *Maximum Kill*, had never expected to see him again.

But she had thought about him.

And since Kid had sent them the screenplay for *Antepenultimate*, she had thought about him even more.

•

CHAPTER 19

Late morning. The day after rain. Sunshine and a warm breeze through the windows, moving the curtains. Denning had phoned, said he wanted to talk about the *Wilderness* screenplay, wouldn't take no for an answer. Tim figuring the guy wanted writing tips. No skin off his nose, happy to talk about what he knew best, even if he didn't do it anymore. Said come on over.

Denning arrived. Handshakes and a little awkwardness between the two of them. Tim immediately sensing that screenplay structure was not a topic uppermost in Denning's mind. He offered coffee. Denning said yeah. But when Tim opened the fridge he found that he was out of milk. He left Denning in the flat while he walked to a convenience store, figured a guy who'd saved him from a couple of assholes in a parking lot wasn't going to rip the place off.

Denning killing time, wandered into the living room. There were shelves of books, mostly how-to texts on screenwriting and histories of the film industry. There was a flat-screen TV and a DVD player. One wall was hung with photographs, the same woman in all of them, sometimes alone, mostly with Tim.

Denning looked at the photos wondering: girlfriend? But he didn't think so, the family resemblance was too strong. Weird, though, if she was family, if she was the sister Tim had mentioned. Something too close, too intimate between them. At the back of Denning's mind the synaptic catgut of recognition began to thrum.

Denning sat on the sofa, unsettled and fidgety, anxious to begin his conversation with Tim. He picked up a remote, absently pressing buttons. The TV/DVD combo came to life. Denning expecting Hollywood gossip, expecting news or a wildlife show. Finding instead the woman in the photographs – a DVD that had been left in the tray, now playing. The woman masturbating. With another woman in bed. With a man hammering her from behind.... A whole selection of clips.

And then, unheard, Tim back in the room, carrying a carton of milk in a plastic bag. Holding his hand out for the remote, killing the screen, heading back to the kitchen, calling over his shoulder that Denning should follow.

When the coffee was made they sat at the kitchen table. Denning eyeing Tim, thinking there was more common ground under them than he'd thought.

He put the copy of the *Wilderness* screenplay that Tim had given him on the table between them and said: "You and I can help each other."

He tapped the screenplay.

"You said your sister was murdered while she was writing this. Skye's feeding it to your girlfriend—"

"Ex-girlfriend."

"Understandable. Skye got it from Delores Fuentes, which implies a possible connection between Delores and your sister. Which explains why you're so invested, why you'd hang around outside Delores' place and threaten a woman in a parking lot."

"Because she stole the screenplay."

Denning shook his head. "No. Because murder. Your sister's. You think this screenplay had something to do with it."

"You must have been a hell of a journalist."

"If you didn't, you wouldn't have threatened that woman. And if you think the murder in the screenplay might have led to your sister's, then you've probably figured out who the guy is who gets killed. In real life."

"Why do you care about my sister or some guy in a screenplay?"

Denning ignored him.

"Scott Bartlemann."

Denning's words made Tim catch his breath. In that one name there was instant support for his own interpretation of Rebecca's screenplay. Someone else had drawn the same conclusion. He nodded slowly.

"Yes.... I think the Beau Montgomery character is Scott Bartlemann."

"How did you figure it out?"

"You didn't answer my question. Why do you care?"

"Tim, listen, I think we want the same things. I'll explain why I'm so interested, I promise. But can you tell me why you think it's Scott Bartlemann?"

Tim hesitated for a moment, then figured what the fuck and told Denning about visiting Danny Bartlemann with Chick, about how Danny's description of his father's murder matched that of the murder in *Wilderness* too closely to be a coincidence.

Denning asked: "And do you know who the killers are supposed to be?"

"No."

Denning nodded and took a sip of his coffee, put his cup down and said: "There's a film company called GHQ—"

"I've heard of them."

"Okay. So let me tell you a story. Eight years ago I was a features writer for the Hollywood Reporter. They asked me to do a portrait piece on GHQ. I wanted to make it more than just a run-of-the-mill bio, so I looked around for something to spice it up. What I found was that GHQ had had their first hit film, *Maximum Kill*, distributed by a company called Big Glass. And Big Glass was the company Scott Bartlemann co-owned at the time he was killed. *Scott Bartlemann*, right?"

Denning raised his eyebrows to make his point.

"Now, this wasn't a secret or anything, and there was never any suggestion that GHQ was involved in the murder, but I was a journalist. I got paid to sensationalize shit. So I revisit the Bartlemann investigation, get to read some of the case notes the cops have. Murder/suicide, the maid did it. There were a couple of oddities, like the maid had traces of duct tape adhesive around her wrists and ankles. Like the lab tests showed gunshot residue on the maid consistent with shotgun ammo, but nothing that could be matched to the ammo from the pistol Bartlemann was killed with. They also couldn't find the shotgun shell that blew her head off.

"None of this was new or anything huge. It's the kind of thing that gets explained away if there's nothing to contradict it. Maybe Bartlemann was playing fucky-fucky with the maid and liked to tape her up while he was doing it. And the pistol GSR? Maybe the lab just couldn't pick it up underneath the stuff from the shotgun.

"So I try something else. I go visit the Big Glass offices hoping maybe I'll find something about GHQ there. Best people to talk to are the secretaries. In an office, they know everything that's going on. Only problem was, there weren't any still working there from the time of the murder, two years before. So I get a few addresses from the HR department and go track down some previous employees. And one of them has something to tell me.

"This girl, Tyler, she's a complete nutjob speed freak – shit all over the place like she's a hoarder, do anything for a pipe, scabs on her face.... Anyhow, a couple of hundred bucks is big money for her and she's happy to talk. What she tells me is this: back when she's working for Big Glass her habit was just starting to take hold, but she was still a good worker. A little too good, because she used to take work home to type up in the evenings and on weekends – it was strictly forbidden, but she didn't give a shit, she needed something to fill all those extra speed hours.

"Anyhow, her work comes in the form of mini-cassettes. She's an audio typist – listen to the tape, type it up, sneak the docs and the tapes back the next day, make herself look like Super Secretary. Only, on one particular day, couple of days before Bartlemann is killed, she gets workplace drug tested and fired. She's already dropped the documents off, but the tapes are still in her handbag when she's escorted out of the building. Amazingly, she still has them buried somewhere in the piles of junk she's got around her apartment. I listen to them. One's just internal staffing bullshit, but the other was dictated by Scott Bartlemann."

Denning took a Dictaphone out of his jacket pocket and put it on top of the screenplay, clicked Play. Tim heard background hiss, the sound of a man clearing his throat, and then a male voice:

"July twenty-sixth, 2002. Strictly confidential; in-house only. Attention: Theo Portman, Joint CEO; Steve Holdsworthy, Marketing; Lionel Weerasinga, Domestic Booking; Pete Meers, International Booking; Trisha Chin, Publicity and Exhibitor Relations....

Re: Maximum Kill....

Test scores for Maximum Kill in demographically indicative theatres in Santa Monica, Des Moines and White Plains all fail to exceed seventy-five. Evaluation of score card comments indicates audiences perceive the film as inappropriate during this time of war with Afghanistan. Further, the fact that the lead character is both a returned serviceman and a sociopath is perceived as insulting to our armed forces.

It was initially felt that the action elements of the film and its ultimately redemptive ending would neutralize any such patriotically based opposition. This, unfortunately, has proved not to be the case.

It is my feeling as Joint CEO and head of Domestic and International Booking that the shallowness of the film's characterizations, the lack of any theme beyond that of revenge, its overt misogyny and excessive use of explicit violence in place of a satisfying and enriching story arc, make Maximum Kill at best an extremely risky proposition for the summer vacation and/or Christmas markets. The film is therefore to be shelved until the war in Afghanistan does not loom so large in the public consciousness, or until such editing as may be required to tone down the unnecessary brutalism of the picture can be performed. In either case the picture should not be released for at least two years.

All abovementioned departments, please liaise to terminate whatever promotional efforts are in train.

Scott Bartlemann, Joint CEO, Head of Domestic and International Booking etcetera, etcetera...."

Denning turned the Dictaphone off and looked heavily at Tim.

"Scott Bartlemann shelving *Maximum Kill*. It matches what your sister wrote about – the Tad Beaumont character refusing to release the screenplay film. Back then, I thought maybe Danny Bartlemann might have been involved in the murder. You know he wrote the *Maximum Kill* screenplay?"

Tim nodded.

"Well, his relationship with his father was poor to say the least – maybe he found out about the delay and went crazy and killed him. You know, some fucked up Hollywood family thing? But Danny had an alibi, he was in hospital at the time, so that never went anywhere. And GHQ? Like everyone else, they'd been eliminated as suspects by the cops. And a production company murdering their own distributor? It seemed just too counterproductive to take seriously."

"But now it doesn't."

"Now there's this screenplay. And that tape, or the letter from it, works as a possible motive."

"Only if GHQ knew about it. And you've got to figure Big Glass would get their ducks in a row internally way before they gave that sort of news to the filmmakers. And even if GHQ did somehow get hold of a copy of that letter, Scott Bartlemann was killed July twenty-ninth. The date on the tape is the twenty-sixth. Add maybe another day for it to get typed up.... Makes things pretty tight."

"But not impossible. And look at all the other parallels." Denning ticked off points on his fingers. "In your sister's screenplay there are three filmmakers, two of whom are brother and sister. The filmmakers have their own production company and they make a film they're sure is going to make them all famous. But one of the heads of the distribution company – there are two – wants to shelve it, directly citing Afghanistan. The filmmakers kill him, the film is released by the other distribution head and everyone goes on to be super successful.

"Now, GHQ. Three filmmakers own that company: Michael Starck, the driving force behind it, and Jeffery and Ally Bannister. And Jeffery and Ally Bannister are twins. Ten years ago GHQ made *Maximum Kill*. They sold it for distribution at the Toronto Film Festival to Big Glass. Big Glass was owned by two guys: Theo Portman and Scott Bartlemann. Scott Bartlemann was killed and, even though Tyler's audio tape shows clearly that he was planning to shelve the film, *Maximum Kill* was released and went on to be hugely successful."

"Knowing they'd get the film un-shelved would have to have been a done deal *before* Bartlemann was killed. No one's going to commit murder on an off chance."

Denning shrugged. "After Bartlemann was killed Theo Portman took over the company, bought Bartlemann's share off Danny, and started running Big Glass as a one man show."

"You think there was some sort of collusion between Theo Portman and GHQ?"

"Who knows? But as joint CEO he would have known Bartlemann was planning to can *Maximum Kill* well before that letter was ever dictated. And in the not so long run, both GHQ and Portman benefited from Bartlemann's death."

"There's no collusion between the Portman character and the filmmakers in Rebecca's script. He just lets them know he likes the film and they take a chance that he'll release it. It works in a screenplay, just, but it's too weak for reality."

"Maybe she didn't know about that side of things. Maybe she was just working with what she had."

The two men were silent for a while. Tim got up and took the coffee mugs to the sink, ran himself a glass of water. When he sat down again he looked squarely at Denning until Denning started to speak.

"You want to know why I give a shit about a screenplay and a ten-year-old murder. The reason is, before I ever got to write that article, GHQ destroyed my career and what was left of my life. I mean, completely. I was never able to work as a journalist again. And, they humiliated my daughter."

"How? They're a film company, not the CIA."

"Ten years ago, my wife was abducted. She was never found, but I know she was murdered. In my heart, I know. A few months after it happened, my daughter and I began an affair. Out of grief, loneliness...I'm not even going to try to explain it. But it happened. And before you freak out, she was eighteen at the time and it was completely consensual. In fact she initiated it. It's finished now."

"I wasn't going to freak out."

Denning smiled gratefully for a second.

"I didn't know it, but sometime during my research for the piece on GHQ they put a camera in my house. In the bedroom. They sent the footage to my boss at the Hollywood Reporter. And to the police. Anonymously, of course."

"How can you be sure it was GHQ?"

"Because the only thing I was working on at the time was the GHQ piece. And because when the cops marched me out of the THR office, Michael Starck, GHQ's main man, was sitting in his limo outside the entrance. He had his window down, he wanted me to see him. He wanted me to know it was a warning. The irony was, at the time, that I had absolutely no idea what for."

"You were arrested?"

"Yeah, and my daughter. They dropped the charges eventually. Consensual adult incest isn't often prosecuted in California. But it was six months of living hell, and the damage was more than done."

"And now you figure you've found a way to take revenge."

"If what I was doing eight years ago made them nervous enough to attack me, then maybe there's something they want kept secret. And maybe that something is what your sister's screenplay is about. Tell me about her murder."

"It happened two years ago. She was shot while she was staying in the San Gabriel Mountains. She was up there finishing rewrites on a screenplay – *this* screenplay as far as I can tell. When I spoke to her a couple of days before it happened, I asked her what the script was about. The weird thing was, she wouldn't tell me. And she used to discuss *everything* she wrote with me.

"When they found her, her computer was missing. No notes, no copies of the screenplay. Nothing. It also looked like perhaps someone had gone through her apartment as well, taken anything screenplay-related. The cops said she could have just put the stuff in storage, but it didn't turn up. In the end they logged the whole thing as a robbery gone wrong. They never got anyone for it."

"What was your sister's connection with Delores Fuentes? How did she get a copy of the screenplay?"

"I don't know for sure, but when Rebecca died, her bank records showed a payment from a financial management company called Hastings & Kottle. Their website lists Delores as a client. And the payment was about what Rebecca would get as an advance for writing a screenplay. So it's a reasonable guess that they had some sort of arrangement. But whatever it was, it was something out of the ordinary, because it didn't go through Rebecca's agent."

Denning frowned. "I interviewed Delores Fuentes for the piece on GHQ. She's one of the weird things about them. Came out of nowhere, big star from the get-go, works only in their films, has this 1950s-style exclusive contract with them. I couldn't get anything out of her. The shit she gave me about her background, how she got into the business, her life back in Mexico, it was all just empty PR bullshit. It's not unusual for a movie star to massage their past, but this was like a brick wall."

Denning was silent for a moment, then said: "Do you know where Rebecca got her version of the story?"

"The murder's a matter of public record. She could have just worked up a film around it."

"But that's not what you think."

"I think writing a screenplay about a real-life murder and then getting murdered yourself before the screenplay can make it out into the world is way too much cause and effect."

Denning glanced through the open doorway into the living room, at the large black TV.

"You were...close?"

Tim thought of all the possible responses he could make, then just said: "For a time, yes."

Denning stood, put the Dictaphone in his pocket, picked up the screenplay.

"This is what *I'm* going to do. I'm going to find out if the screenplay is true, and then I'm going to write a book about GHQ and the Bartlemann kill – a novel, true crime, I don't care how it turns out. But I'm going to expose them, fuck them, and make a million dollars at the same time. I don't know what you want for your sister. But you want *something*, I know. You wouldn't have confronted Skye if you didn't. And whatever it is, Tim, it's cool with me. *Whatever* it is."

Denning stepped onto the steps outside the kitchen door, looked back at Tim.

"The first thing to lock down is if there was any way GHQ could have known about that letter Bartlemann dictated. We find that, then we really do have a solid motive. I've got Tyler's address somewhere. I'll call you."

Chapter 20

Michael's mansion was A-list. He'd made sure of it. From the thirty-yard pool, to the half-acre of tended gardens on the slopes of Beverly Hills, to the three-story marble foyer. A declaration of his status in the filmmaking community. An expunging of his past as a poor boy who'd grown up selling newspapers on the dry, heat-baked streets of Adelaide.

Delores there on a sunny day. Delivering Sean's bombshell. Figuring this kind of thing was better done in person.

Michael had bought the place four years ago, a month after she'd left him. Before that, they'd lived together in an over-sized Malibu beach house. It was there that he was placed most firmly in her memory. There in glass-walled rooms that faced a blue Pacific, with the sun hot and white – a light both of them saw as a badge of success. California. Film. Money. Their childhoods long distant. The people they had been, dried up and blown away by the Santa Ana winds.

And there had been another place before that. Ten years ago. Before the money, before the success. An apartment in Venice. More a base for Michael's work than a place to live. But it had been there that he had fallen in love with her, had promised her a Hollywood life. There, while his wife was out, that they'd made love.

She'd thought they would last forever. Michael had believed it even more. With a relationship forged in blood and murder, they pretty much had to. Michael held true to his belief. He divorced his wife for her. He made Delores a star and they'd lived together as Hollywood gods. Wealthy, famous, adored. Free of the fetters that bound the rest of the world to lives of repetition and despair.

And yet not free at all. Shackled to each other, to Jeffery and Ally, to the horrors of their past. To things done so that they might rise to this illusory Mount Olympus. At least that was how Delores came to view their life together.

When had it begun, this necrosis of the soul? When she made the decision to pay a coyote to smuggle her across the border? When he drugged her and blindfolded her and passed her to some unseen Americans to be raped and torn within a day of leaving her village? When she picked up the phone and said that Scott Bartlemann was alone? When another woman died so that she could see her name in lights?

The things she had done for her career she had done willingly. But they were not things she could let herself examine too closely. Not if she wanted to maintain the fiction that she deserved the best the world had to offer.

And it was this aversion to self-examination, to accepting what she had done, that had eventually killed her relationship with Michael. Because Michael was a mirror in which she saw herself too clearly.

In the early days she thought his ruthlessness, his overwhelming desire to succeed – to be better and richer and more powerful than his peers – was a transitional phase, something that would be jettisoned later in favor of a more accountable and humane personality.

But after six years together, Delores realized that Michael's avarice was central to his identity, that the ruthlessness and the greed were not parts of a phase. And because she had this same selfishness at her core, but could not admit it, she left him.

She had been a big star by then, big enough, she thought, despite her exclusive contract with GHQ, to survive Michael's anger. An assumption, it turned out, that couldn't have been more wrong – Michael reacted by refusing to allow her any further work in movies at all.

After two years in this career desert, Delores had had enough and decided to get herself a little screenplay leverage. When that plan, too, turned bad, it was only Michael's love that had saved her from Jeffery and his gun.

Now, as they sat together in the formal garden behind his house, she hoped there was still enough of that love left to save her again.

Evergreens. The sound of water falling from fountains. Birds in the trees, brightly feathered, a contrail high up, breaking apart as an air current took it.

Michael in striped shirt and white slacks. His thick middle, rather than making him look overweight, seemed only to make him more formidable. He started to make industry small-talk, but Delores cut him short, told him that the *Wilderness* screenplay had resurfaced, that her personal assistant had stolen it from her computer.

"You kept a copy? Are you fucking brain dead?"

"I had to. You I trust. Those two Bannister freaks, I don't. What other insurance did I have?"

"I would never have let Jeffery near you."

"He might not have given you the choice."

Michael ran his hand through his hair.

"Skye has it? Jesus Christ!"

Delores gripped the arms of her chair and engaged her core.

"I've fired her. But that's not all of it. She's been giving pages of it to her girlfriend. The girlfriend is a screenwriter."

Delores knew Michael would be angry, would be apoplectic, and she was prepared to be frightened. But not as frightened as she was when he spoke quietly and clenched his fist so hard it shook.

"How many pages?"

"Everything that matters." Delores felt a small trickle of urine dampen the gusset of her briefs. "Michael, this is nothing to do with me, I promise. I mean, really, do you think I'm that stupid? As soon as Sean told me about it—"

"Sean?" Michael's ruddy face went gray. "That pretty-boy piece of shit?"

Delores figured uh-oh, but it was probably a non-starter trying to keep Sean out of it anyhow. Plus it would split Michael's anger.

"He wanted to do the right thing, like me."

"You're still seeing him?"

"Not for two years. We split up after last time. He came to see me. He goes to a screenwriters' group. A girl there, Jocelyn – I don't know her last name – read out the first act of a screenplay with exactly the same storyline as *Wilderness*. Sean followed the girl and saw Skye handing her some pages."

Michael scoffed: "A screenwriter's group, Skye as Deep Throat. Don't you think it sounds a little too pat?"

"Skye's doing it because she's fucking this girl. Why would Sean lie? He came to me because he was scared you'd hear about the screenplay and think it was me, again. Or him."

Michael stood up. He was angry with Delores, of course, but he was even more angry with himself for still loving her too much to simply get rid of her. For a truly ruthless man, love like this was a dangerous weakness.

He knew it wouldn't make anything any better, he knew it would push her even further away from him. But he also knew it wouldn't make a shit of difference, because she had no intention of ever coming back to him. He hauled her to her feet and turned her toward the table. When she started to struggle against him he slapped her hard across the side of her head.

He swept the food and the coffee onto the ground and bent her over, lifted the short dress she wore and jammed himself into her – pounding, hammering, doing his best to kill what he felt for her. If he had been a weaker man he would have sobbed.

When he was finished Delores cleaned herself with a napkin and cursed him. But she knew this brutality, this degradation, was just the cost of doing business with a man like Michael.

Before she left, she gave him Jocelyn's address.

"Skye was renting my guest house. She moved out when I fired her. Her forwarding address is the same as Jocelyn's, so I assume they're living together."

"I want to talk to Sean, too."

"No."

"His address."

"I don't know it. He wouldn't give it to me."

"A phone number, then."

"No. He tried to help by warning you, that's enough. You don't need to go anywhere near him."

Michael followed her through the house. He watched her drive to the gate, the top on her Mercedes down, her dark hair lifting in the car's slipstream. And knew there was only one way he'd ever really be free of her.

Chapter 21

Sean took a long time to answer the door of his bunker. When he did, it was obvious to Tim that he wasn't too long out of a borderline fix. His pupils were nonexistent and he moved like an old man with a back problem.

Denning had said GHQ. Sean was the only actor Tim knew. Wouldn't hurt to ask.

The day was beautiful. Tim wanted to sit outside under the trees that overhung a patch of wild grass running along one side of the bunker. Sean wouldn't hear of it, opened the door halfway and pulled him inside.

Tim said: "What's wrong, dude?"

Sean looked blank for a moment.

"I don't know, man. The sky's just too fucking bright."

"You ever think it might be time for rehab again?"

"Have you seen Jocelyn? Did you talk to her about the screenplay?"

"Nup. I'm done with her, I told you."

"At least tell her it's Rebecca's. Give her a chance to do the right thing."

"She's fucking guys in parking lots. There's nothing left. If she gets sued, she gets sued. What the fuck do you care? You met her, like, three times and you couldn't stand her."

Sean shrugged and didn't answer.

Tim continued: "Anyhow, listen, there's something a lot more important than Jocelyn. I think that screenplay had something to do with Rebecca getting killed."

Sean had been sitting on one of the couches in the bunker's living area. He got up now and walked quickly to the bathroom. Tim heard him throwing up through the open door. A couple of minutes later he came back, wiping his mouth.

Tim asked: "You okay?"

"Too much smack. So you were saying...Rebecca?"

"You don't look good, man."

Sean waved his hand.

"I'm fine, I'm fine. What about Rebecca?"

"There's a murder in the screenplay. A group of filmmakers kills the executive of a distribution company. I've done a bit of research and I think it's kind of a *roman à clef* thing of a real murder."

"Of who?"

"Scott Bartlemann. You heard of the guy? Happened about ten years ago."

"Wasn't he killed by his maid?"

"That's what the cops thought, but the case was never closed. The screenplay puts it as a double murder – the maid and Bartlemann killed by the filmmakers. And if that's the way it really happened, then maybe the filmmakers killed Rebecca as well so no one would ever get to read the screenplay."

"Wow."

"Yeah, I know."

"No, I mean, really? There's a whole conspiracy thing about Rebecca being killed? I don't want to sound like a cunt, but do you think this might just be your grief talking?"

Tim felt like he'd been slapped across the face. He'd expected at least a little excited interest from Sean, even if Sean didn't fully believe him.

"You do actually sound like a bit of a cunt."

"I'm just saying. Some Hollywood filmmakers kill a suit, Rebecca writes a screenplay about it and then the filmmakers kill her? Don't you think it's a bit farfetched? How would Rebecca have ever found out about the murder in the first place?"

"I don't know. What I do know – and thanks for your support, by the way – is that there actually is a group of filmmakers who could be the ones Rebecca wrote about. GHQ."

"GHQ? Are you serious? They're one of the biggest independents in Hollywood. Tim, dude...."

"Okay, fuck it. You don't think I'm right, just humor me. What do you know about them?"

"What do you mean, what do I know about them? Why the fuck would I know anything about them?"

"Because you're an actor. You've been in the business. I'm just looking for some background, anything...."

"I haven't worked in two years. I don't know what I can tell you."

"I'm not asking for a fucking stock market valuation. Just anything. I don't know...did you ever work on any of their productions?"

"Actually, yes. I had a small part on *Turner's Highway*. Five or six lines. A fucking blip."

"When was that?"

"About three years ago."

"You know anyone connected to them? Like anyone at all?"

"I was a featured extra, man. Who am I going to know?"

"Anyone who might know something about them, or how the company works. Anything."

"Sorry, man. I went to set, did my stuff and left. I had, like, two days. That was the extent of me and GHQ."

"You know anyone else I could go ask?"

Sean shook his head.

Any other time, Tim might have hung around for a while, but there was an edge to Sean today that made him uncomfortable. The reluctance to accept his theory about the screenplay, to talk about GHQ.... Tim didn't understand it. They drank a soda together, barely speaking, then Tim said he had to go.

At the door Sean put a hand on his shoulder.

"Dude. Rebecca's gone. It's a terrible thing. But don't cause yourself anymore pain than you have to."

When the door closed behind Tim, Sean stood for a long time, looking at it. Then he went slowly back to the sofa and sat with his elbows on his knees, staring at the floor.

His friend, Tim. A relationship that started as a way to make himself feel less guilty, but one which he had genuinely come to value. He had no others.

Two years of hanging out, of Tim drinking wine and Sean shooting smack, of talking about life's ups and downs. But really, Sean figured, two years of lying, whichever way you cut it.

Just like the lies he'd told Tim five minutes before.

He'd done what he could about Jocelyn and the screenplay. Done his best to nip it in the bud. But Tim was determined. Tim was driven by Rebecca's death. And that was as it should be. But it meant, now, that it wasn't just Michael Sean had to fear.

He made a decision. There would be more horror, it couldn't help but come. And he'd already played a part in it – he'd thrown Jocelyn and Skye to the Hollywood wolves. But he wouldn't do the same to Tim.

He lay down on the sofa and closed his eyes, drifting, remembering the taste of Delores' kiss, the first in two years. Smack-dreaming that maybe...maybe they could get back together.

Chapter 22

Kid's office suite in Santa Monica had a cheap, temporary feel. Set in the upstairs part of a small strip mall off Santa Monica Boulevard – three rooms, a shared washroom down the hall. They came as a package – phone lines, internet access, generic office furniture, coffee machine and a cleaner once a week. The kind of place a real estate scam artist or a terrorist cell might use for a couple of months before things got too hot.

Peta sat behind a white Formica desk working her way through a tentative crew list for *Antepenultimate*, confirming daily rates, availability, union status. Tim stood in the small reception area looking at the posters on the walls. There was a one-sheet for *Loggers* showing four sensitive-looking men contemplating the just-cut stump of a Douglas fir. And there was a set of lurid, blown-up video cassette covers – the high points, Tim assumed, of Kid Haldane's porn career: *Bitch Fever*, *Bitch Fever II*, *Who Ordered Sausage?*, *Double Digit Dynamite*.

Credits along the bottom of these posters listed Kid and a small selection of other performers. The director and the production house were the same on all four: Brett Adelaide and Sunnico.

The vids were mid-nineties vintage and Tim wondered what a director did when his porn days were over. Was Brett Adelaide now some guy with a paunch who lived in a flophouse, smoked cheap cigars and got blown occasionally by the drug-fucked wrecks he'd once exploited in such gynecological detail?

The door to Kid's office opened and Chick emerged – leather catsuit, SWAT boots. Through the open doorway Tim saw a man behind a desk – Kid Haldane.

Older than the posters. Weathered, lean and blond. Kid waved and smiled and Chick did a quick "Tim, Kid; Kid, Tim." intro before the door swung shut.

She put her arm through Tim's and they walked down the stairs, out into the warm air, car exhaust, and gritty bustle that was Santa Monica Boulevard in the evening.

Since their trip to see Danny Bartlemann, Chick had let Tim keep the Bonneville. He sat on it while Chick went into a hardware store further down the strip of shops. When she came back she put a can of red spray paint in the pannier of her Thruxton.

"Bel Air, Timbo. You cool?"

Chick had another of her anti-Hollywood raids planned. That she wanted Tim along both thrilled him and freaked him out. Inclusion meant a growing relationship, but setting billboards on fire and wrecking marriages was the kind of behavior that Tim would previously have classed as fucking crazy. Not to mention dangerous. But what choice did he have? He wanted a new life. He wanted Chick. This was the entry fee.

Before they fired up the bikes, Tim asked: "Are you guys close?"

"Me and Kid? Oh, shit, yeah. I mean, *Loggers*, he made that happen for me. He's committed. One way or another he'll get *Ante* off the ground."

"Have you known him long?"

"Couple of years. Met him when I was working in a cafe. Hit it off straight away. Like minds. I said I wanted to direct. He said he'd make it happen."

"Just like that? He didn't even know you and he wants to make movies with you."

"Yeah, I know. It was kind of overwhelming at first. But this, Timbo, is Hollywood."

Chick hit the starter on the Thruxton. Tim hit the Bonnie's. Clutch in, clutch out. Gas. Out onto the boulevard, Chick already ahead, cutting lanes, giving the finger as horns went off.

Denning in his Crown Vic. Just-parked in the strip mall lot. Thirty yards from the entrance to Kid Haldane Productions. There to take Peta to dinner. He could have met her at the restaurant, of course, but then he wouldn't have gotten to see the man she was sleeping with.

He was about to climb out of his car when Tim exited Haldane's office, arm in arm with a leather-clad girl. Denning stayed put and watched till they rode away, simmering in an instant storm of mistrust and suspicion.

Was it all a smokescreen? Was Tim part of it all, part of some elaborate plan to ruin him all over again? Was he a Trojan horse, feeding information to Michael Starck via Kid Haldane? Egging Denning on until Denning had made just enough rope to hang himself?

Denning wished he had some Oxy, something to buffer these thoughts, to calm synapses already snarled with images of Peta being plowed by Haldane. But he'd left his last few pills at home.

And who was the girl? That skanky-looking freak in the Suzi Quatro get-up. Someone yet to come into play? A fresh dose of fuck-up headed his way?

He got out of his car and walked quickly to Peta's office. Inside, up a flight of stairs, she greeted him happily enough, but there was a sad cast to her eyes. She knew this had to happen. It was sick and it felt dirty, but meeting Kid would make it real for Denning, would drive home the fact that what they'd had together was beyond resurrection.

Kid came out of his office, doing his best to be affable, to make a good impression on his lover's father. He shook Denning's hand.

"I was starting to think Peta must be an orphan. Good to meet you, Alan."

"Likewise."

Denning remembered how it felt smashing the windows on the Camaro. He looked around him, lingering on the porn posters.

"Interesting art."

Kid looked rueful.

"I know. I know. That stuff's disgusting and I can tell you flat out it isn't part of my life anymore. They're there to remind me I've got to keep moving forward, got to leave that stuff as far behind as I can. I know this place doesn't look much, but that'll change."

Kid smiled. Denning couldn't resist a thrust.

"Sure it will. Even companies like Mandalay and GHQ had to start somewhere."

There was a small uncertain flicker behind Kid's eyes. Denning saw it and thought, *Yeah, you fuck*....

Denning and Peta sat in a booth in a place on Fourth Street and ate enchiladas. Peta seemed calm to Denning, as though all the worrying she had had to do over ending their relationship was now put to rest and she was reconciled and happy on her new path.

Denning watched her as she ate and wondered what the fuck he'd done with the last ten years. The end of their relationship had sucked the air from that time, taken all the moments they'd shared together and wiped them away like chalk from a blackboard, leaving amorphous smears of memory that Denning could only imperfectly decipher.

Where would he be now if it had never happened? He would have found someone else, perhaps, some other woman out in the world. He would have sent his daughter off to college, to live as other girls lived, to meet boys and to study and to make her way in life. There would have been no ammunition for GHQ to use against him and he would have risen in his profession, prospered perhaps.

He thought of his wife. Why did things change? Why, when happiness seemed so certain, so unassailable, did life take a hammer to it? If Clara had stayed at home that day, if he had been faster and had pulled the guy from his van before he could drive away, questioned him, beaten him senseless and bloody....

There was life ahead of him still. Technically. He could retrain. He could take a loan, study, date fifty-year-old women. But all of that was a dream. His wife had been killed and he had fucked his daughter. There were no new starts after that.

One thing now to sustain him. Not to give him hope, but to keep him going at least, to keep him breathing, putting one foot in front of the other – the book he would write, the book that would destroy GHQ. Maybe, if he was lucky, he'd find a place in it for Kid Haldane, too.

Denning came out of these thoughts to find Peta asking him to pass her a saucer of jalapeño salsa.

He slid the relish across the table and said: "That guy who came out of your office just before I got there, with a woman dressed in leather – who were they?"

Peta shrugged.

"The girl just calls herself Chick. She's directing the film Kid's trying to get off the ground. The guy's her boyfriend, I think."

"Does he know Haldane? Do they work together?"

"She introduced them to each other, so I shouldn't think so. Why?"

Denning shrugged.

"No reason."

Tim hadn't asked who the night's target was. But it was pretty obvious when they parked two hundred yards up the road from a stretch of high white wall on one of the upper streets of Bel Air. Same place he'd followed Skye to. Same place he'd first seen Denning.

Delores Fuentes' movie star mansion.

It was fully dark now. The street lights were on but they were widely spaced and there were dark patches of shadow between them. The road was doing its Bel Air thing – being empty. They sat on their bikes, hidden by shadow, engines off, waiting. Looking both ways for the glow of approaching headlights, making sure they wouldn't be interrupted.

Chick pointed down the street at the wall and spoke in a whisper.

"Thar she blows."

"I know whose house that is."

"Delores Fuentes. I know! What a blast, huh? Queen of the morons. The dickheads at GHQ want to give her a part in *Antepenultimate*. I've gotta take a fucking meeting with her."

Chick got the can of spray paint out of her pannier.

"Rock and roll, Timbo. Let's go."

They left their helmets on and trotted down the sloping road. Tim could hear Chick stifling giggles, the rattle of the ball-bearing in the paint can as she shook it.

There was a camera, but it was pointed at the driveway. Chick started work, moved slowly along the wall until she was about five yards from the gates, her arm making long sweeps and curves. The hiss of the paint sounded loud in the quiet street.

When she was finished the wall was covered in red letters four feet high: *CUNTS LIKE YOU KILL ART.*

Chick walked casually back to her bike. Tim tried to hurry her.

"Let's get out of here. She might come out."

Chick laughed. "Hah! Wouldn't that be a trip?"

They sat on their bikes again, but they didn't start up. Chick wanted to admire her work.

"You know, before the internet and Twitter and all that shit, graffiti on walls was the first indication that social upheaval was brewing. I know that some people might say what I do is just vandalism. For me, it's a declaration of war. You know, if there was some place I could go, all wrapped up in plastic explosive like one of those whacked out ragheads, and blow up the whole of the entrenched Hollywood establishment, I mean like every single one of them – actors, directors, studio heads, producers, even the DoPs who work on that shit – I think I'd do it. It'd be worth the sacrifice to clean out this colony of whores."

Chick scratched her crotch.

"Let's go, Timbo, it's fuck time."

But before she could start her bike a bright spill of light fell through the bars of Delores Fuentes' gates, and then the gates rolled back into the walls and a matte black '78 Trans Am, engine throbbing at low revs, nosed through the opening. It turned left onto the street, away from them, the engine note rose, and then the car was just two red lights, and then it was gone, around a bend, swallowed by the night.

Matte black Trans Am.

Blond head behind the wheel.

In the darkness the driver had not seen them.

But they'd seen him – Sean.

Tim and Chick looked at each other. Chick surprised and smirking. Tim thinking his friend was a fucking liar.

Inside the mansion, Delores Fuentes lay on her super-king bed, the sheet beside her still damp with Sean's sweat, wondering if it was a good idea to be starting up with him again. And then figuring, if nothing else, it was a secret fuck-you to Michael for the way he'd treated her.

Upstairs at Chick's place, the fucking done, eating takeout Chinese in the kitchen alcove, the window overlooking the alley out back black against the night, Chick wearing only a pair of briefs that smelled faintly of urine, her small breasts pale and hard.

"I read your screenplay. It's really good, man. A bit unbalanced in the second and third acts maybe, but you're a shit-hot writer. How come you haven't had more made?"

Tim felt an urge to confess, to blurt that he hadn't been entirely frank about the *Wilderness* script. But it was too late. She was looking at him with such admiration. He couldn't bear to see it turn to pity or disgust.

"Luck of the game I guess. This one I kind of wrote just for me, you know, to examine the effects of artistic decay. It needs more work I know. I'll get round to it one day."

"You should, dude. It'd be a waste not to."

Chick got up, went into the main area of the flat and reached under the bed. When she sat down again, she put an old shoe box on the table, opened it and took out a jar of Hoppe's No. 9 solvent, a small plastic bottle of lubricating oil, a cloth and a cleaning rod and some cotton patches and Q-tips.

Tim watched her, thinking: No, she's not going to.

But she did. Took a dull silver automatic with black grips out of the box, put it next to the cleaning stuff. She looked at Tim and wiggled her eyebrows.

"Bersa, Thunder Ultra Compact. Forty-five."

"Wow.... You have a gun."

"Very observant."

"No, I mean, I'm just a bit surprised, is all."

"You don't approve?"

Tim didn't say anything, watched as she broke the gun down and started to clean it.

Chick said: "Tell you what, Timbo, let me get a couple of big dudes to snatch you off the street, tie you up and blindfold you, then fuck you with something that tears you up, and maybe or maybe not kill you. I'm betting you'd change your mind."

Tim figuring a wrong move here might spoil the beginning of a beautiful friendship, figuring a change of tack was the safest course.

"I'm not judging, I just haven't seen one up close before."

"Well, watch and learn. This is how you clean a handgun. And you don't need to freak out, I'm not gun nut. I just keep it in the house for when I get nervous."

"Did you have to get a permit and everything?"

"Shit no, I bought it on the street. Guy told me it was untraceable, as if that matters."

For a while Chick concentrated on the gun, showing Tim how it worked, letting him push patches through the barrel with the cleaning rod. Putting it back together. Teaching him how to load, rack the slide, use the safety.

When Tim held the reassembled gun for the first time he felt something strange run through him, a charge of frightened excitement, as though he was standing on the edge of a cliff, about to jump off. He wanted to drop it immediately. And at the same time he wanted to hold onto it as long as he could.

Chick had him dry fire the thing, showed him how to grip it, how to stand, how to squeeze the trigger.

Later, after the gun had been put back under the bed and they sat again, chatting idly at the kitchen table, Chick said: "You know what really freaked me, in your screenplay? The reference to Flynn's Flying Fuckers memorabilia."

Tim remembered the scene in *Wilderness*. Chad and Chloe Standish are seen enthusing about a small collection of one of Hollywood's least known and rarest forms of memorabilia. It had nothing to do with the plot and Tim figured Rebecca had only added it for color and a little character enrichment. He'd Googled the term and found a handful of hits describing how, in the 1930s, Errol Flynn had collected about him a coterie of drinking and fucking buddies he dubbed Flynn's Flying Fuckers. As a badge for this informal club he'd had gold "FFF" lapel pins made up for its members. Over the years a small number of other Flying Fuckers pieces had surfaced.

Tim lied through his teeth.

"You liked that? I got the idea when I read something about Dean Stockwell — he did a film with Flynn and got given one of the lapel pins. I did a bit more research and found there was some other stuff out there too."

"I know all about it. We had the most famous piece in the store when Mom was running it. An Oscar statuette with a hardon. Flynn supposedly had it made in retaliation after the Academy withdrew his Best Actor nomination for *The Sun Also Rises*. Incredibly rare, only one ever made."

"A *hardon* Oscar? Do you still have it?"

Chick pushed away the rest of her food.

"No. It was stolen the night I was kidnapped. Taken by the same cocksucker. That's what they raped me with. The little hardon was what split my pussy lip."

"Assholes."

"Totally."

And through Tim's mind a thought skittered, like a bug on a polished floor, quickly moving, scrabbling to find purchase, but there all the same. If Rebecca's screenplay turned out to be a true outline of the Scott Bartlemann murder, and if it also turned out that GHQ were the killers, then what did it mean that something as rare and generally unknown as Flynn's Flying Fuckers memorabilia was mentioned as being owned by two of the *roman à clef* GHQ principals in that same screenplay? Was this thing going to blow out to include not only Bartlemann and Rebecca's murders, but Chick's rape as well?

Rebecca hadn't mentioned the hardon Oscar specifically, just the collection, and there was no indication in the screenplay that the Standish siblings had ever raped anyone. But it was an unusual reference nonetheless.

Chick, not in the mood to dwell on her rape, changed the subject.

"Hey, what was that with Sean tonight? Does he know Delores Fuentes?"

"If he does, he never told me. But, then, he doesn't talk much about women. He's hinted at some kind of relationship in the past, but he won't say with who."

"With Delores Fuentes?"

"Seems unlikely the way he is now. But he was there tonight."

"It's not completely out of the question, if you think about it. I mean, I only know him from *Loggers*, but I checked his acting history before I hired him."

"And?"

"He had a small part in *Turner's Highway*, another bullshit Delores Fuentes movie GHQ did. Maybe they met then."

"But she's a huge star. They don't usually fuck the help."

"You seen photos of him back then? He was pretty hot. Not my type, but he could easily have caught her eye. And that featured extra thing? He wasn't going to stay that way. Back about then he was all set to take off."

"Seriously? The stuff I've seen, he only ever had pretty-boy bit parts."

"I found an old *Variety* piece on him. GHQ had him slated to be supporting male in a big budget buddy movie called *Random Burn*. It would have made him huge, you know, like it was every actor's dream role. And if he had that kind of heat under him, getting with Delores could easily have happened. Ashton/Demi, know what I mean?"

"Wow."

"What's more wow than that is he never did *Random Burn*. For some reason he tuned in, turned on and dropped out, man. Kicked Hollywood in the ass and became a recluse."

"Jesus, why?"

"Who knows? But I admire him for it. Better to do nothing than be associated with shit like that."

"Still, doesn't really explain it, does it? If he didn't want to do *Random Burn*, fine, but why completely turn your back on acting if you're getting that close to becoming a star?"

"I'm not his shrink, Timbo. I just hired him for a few days on *Loggers*."

Tim thought back to his earlier conversation with Sean. Sean had said he'd only ever had one bit part with GHQ, that he didn't know anyone connected with them.

Bullshit, obviously.

He knew Delores, and GHQ had offered him a breakout role, had been ready to make him Brad Pitt. Why keep that a secret? Why not tell a friend of two years that he knew one of the biggest female action stars in the world?

Tim couldn't figure it, but he knew one thing – if Sean was going to lie about his involvement with GHQ and Delores, and if Delores and GHQ were somehow connected to the Bartlemann murder and maybe Rebecca's as well, then Sean had just become another piece of the puzzle that had started with the USB drive in Rebecca's hidden cupboard.

CHAPTER 23

Morning on Delaware Avenue, Santa Monica. Nowhere near the sea. A little south of the Santa Monica Freeway. A long street of wooden bungalows and single-story concrete blocks. The kind of street that had never managed to develop a personality. Lawns too dry and too dusty, not enough trees on the sidewalks, houses with their backs turned. All Denning could afford, Tim guessed. Or maybe he liked the anonymity.

Tim walked up a short concrete path to the front door. Denning opened it before he knocked. Inside, Tim wasn't sure what he'd find. What does a house look like where a man has slept with his daughter? Like Rebecca's when Tim used to pay his visits? Like any other house? Like any other pair of lives?

Denning's house was neat, clean. The carpets were thin and the walls were the usual nondescript rental colors, but there were several well-chosen pieces of furniture and the place felt like a home. His daughter was out at work, but her touch was evident in the small ornaments on windowsills and shelves, in the Ansel Adams photographs that hung here and there.

At this time of day Tim would usually have been fighting a headache from last night's wine, but not today. He was cutting down. He hadn't stopped, but he went to bed sober now more often than not. Spending time with Chick had made him embarrassed at the years of evenings he'd wasted, boiling his brain in a vat of Sauvignon Blanc.

In the living room, heading for the kitchen, Denning turned so abruptly that Tim ran into him and they bumped chests. Denning shoved him away then stepped close again and grabbed the front of Tim's shirt with both hands.

"Kid Haldane."

"What?"

"Kid Haldane. You went to see him yesterday."

"What the fuck are you doing?"

Tim tried to knock Denning's hands away, but Denning was almost as big as Tim and he was angry.

"His office. On Santa Monica. You were there yesterday."

"So what?"

"My daughter's his assistant. I was outside, waiting to pick her up."

"And I was meeting a girl. If you were outside you would have seen her."

"I saw her."

"Okay. Again, so what?"

Denning had wanted this to be a conflagration, a big turning point where fresh information was spilled. Like blood on a floor. The threads of conspiracy revealed. But it wasn't going to happen, Tim was simply too confused. Plus there was what Peta had said about his introduction to Kid.

Denning let go and nodded toward the kitchen.

"Let's have coffee."

He walked through the open doorway. After a moment, Tim followed.

"What was *that* about?"

Denning poured coffee, took two cups to the table and sat down. Tim hesitated, then slid into the booth.

Denning blew on his coffee.

"Okay, I'm sorry. I went off the deep end. But that guy, Kid Haldane, has some sort of connection to GHQ."

"They're financing a film for him. The girl I was meeting is the director. I told you about her before."

"Why would they give *him* finance?"

"People who want to make films borrow, people with money lend. How else do films get made?"

"I know how the industry works, Tim. I meant, what would make a company like GHQ lend money to a guy who's only ever made one pissant arthouse flick? Peta told me the budget's three million bucks, for Christ sake! Does that make sense to you?"

"Hey, it's Hollywood."

"*It's Hollywood, it's Hollywood....*" Denning's voice was scornful. "Hollywood is a business like any other. When money is lent, it's lent because risks are assessed and the investment is figured to be favorable, to have a reasonable chance of turning a profit. Where the fuck is that with Kid Haldane? Besides that arthouse movie, all he's ever done is fuck people in porn vids."

"So he has no track record. It's weird. Yeah. But what's it got to do with us?"

Denning took a breath, held it, then let it out.

"I don't know for sure, but it's not much of a leap to figure he and Michael Starck might have more than the usual business relationship."

"You think they're gay?"

"Jesus, no. Not Michael Starck. Wait there."

Denning fetched a laptop from his room. He'd copied the video of the Super 8 film from his phone onto it. Back in the kitchen he played it for Tim.

"Take a look at this."

Tim watched the video, saw a cabin in the country, forest behind it, smoke, some of the trees burning. Saw Michael Starck come through the doorway, a small backpack over one shoulder, walk to a horse and ride away. Denning hit Stop.

"Okay. This is a copy of a Super 8 film that Kid Haldane somehow got hold of. A couple of weeks ago he went to the GHQ offices and played it for Starck. Someone with a suspicious mind might think it had something to do with him getting that finance."

"As in the Bartlemann murder? You think Kid's involved in that? Bartlemann was killed in a big house up in Isla Vista, not a cabin in a forest. That could just be Michael Starck on vacation. And who's to say when it was shot? It could have been before Bartlemann was killed, could have been years after."

"Why would Kid have it if it's just a home movie of the prick on vacation?"

Tim shook his head. "I don't know. How did you get it? How do you know Haldane played it for Starck?"

"Peta's his assistant."

"I know. You told me. But she isn't going to be handing over his home movies to you."

Denning finished his coffee. He put his mug down and looked at the flat surface of the table for a moment before replying.

"I got the film because I stole it from his car while he was in a bar. He's got it back now."

"He knows you stole it?"

"No. He thinks he misplaced it."

"That's kind of out there."

Denning shrugged. "It is what it is. Call it residual jealousy. And I know Haldane played it for Starck because Peta was there. Not in the room when it happened, but Haldane took the film into Starck's office. Not much point, if he wasn't going to play it."

Tyler, the girl who, back when he was still a journalist, had given Denning the Dictaphone tape of Scott Bartlemann issuing instructions for the shelving of *Maximum Kill*, lived now in a condo in the Wilshire district. It had taken Denning a couple of days in reporter mode to track her down through a string of previous landlords.

He'd phoned and asked for half an hour of her time, said he was doing a follow-up on the Bartlemann kill, something for the ten-year anniversary. Mentioned he'd be bringing along a trainee reporter.

She'd agreed to the half hour, but it had cost three hundred bucks. Tyler had ditched the speed, cleaned up, and become an independent, moderately-priced hooker. These days, she didn't give anyone her time for free.

The condo was on the fourteenth floor. It might have had views, but directly across Wilshire there was another just like it, so the large windows that fronted the place just showed a pattern of glass and concrete. Inside, though, the apartment was spacious and professionally appointed.

They sat around a glass-topped coffee table on soft chairs that were upholstered in Navaho print fabric. Tyler was a tanned and healthy-looking woman in her mid-thirties. She wore a short skirt and her legs were gym-toned and smooth.

Around her eyes, though, there was a lot of wear and her mouth was a hard straight line that spoiled her looks.

Denning flashed an out-of-date press ID at her, introduced Tim as an associate and reminded her about the last time they'd met. Then he played her the tape on a Dictaphone he'd brought along. Tyler said she remembered it and Denning started in on his questions, making notes of her answers on a pad.

"So, the tape is of a document instructing various departments to shelve the film, *Maximum Kill*. What I wanted to know is if there was any likelihood the production company who made the film – GHQ – would have received a copy of that document."

Tyler picked up Denning's Dictaphone from the coffee table, rewound the tape and hit Play. Scott Bartlemann's voice:

"July twenty-sixth, 2002. Strictly confidential; in-house only. Attention: Theo Portman, Joint CEO; Steve Holdsworthy, Marketing; Lionel Weerasinga, Domestic Booking—"

She stopped the tape.

"Big Glass was like junior school. There were rules for everything. You had to log your fucking toilet breaks. Break one of the rules and you were gone that day. *'Strictly confidential; in-house only.'* meant just what it says. No one except the addressees would ever get a copy. And more than that, even the people who got a copy weren't allowed to discuss it with anyone. GHQ isn't mentioned, so they wouldn't have gotten a copy, simple as that. I mean, I can't say what happened to the document after I put it on Bartlemann's desk – I was, like, marched ten minutes later – but in the general run of things, GHQ wouldn't have seen it."

"Are you sure? They were probably in the office a lot around then."

"Wouldn't have mattered. It wasn't like anyone was going to leave a doc marked *'confidential'* lying around on a desk. Not if they wanted to stay working there."

Denning paused like he wasn't sure what to ask next. Tyler checked her watch.

"Is that all you wanted? You've got twenty minutes left, I don't want you to feel short-changed. How come you don't use an iPad?"

Denning ignored her question.

"Tell me about Big Glass, I mean apart from the rules. There were two partners, right? Scott Bartlemann and Theo Portman."

"Yeah. Not a marriage made in heaven."

"Really?"

"Scott was a moralist and an aesthete. He wanted to work with films that had a message, that would refine people. Theo just wanted to make money. So Scott hated the kind of films Theo brought in, and Theo thought Scott was going to run the company into the ground with the arty crap *he* bought. I have to say, from the stuff I saw, Theo was probably right. Scott made some bad decisions."

"You think Theo might have had something to do with Scott's death?"

"Ah, man.... It was a murder/suicide. The maid did it. You think I'm stupid enough to let you quote me saying it was Theo? Apart from the fact that the idea is insane, Theo isn't someone you poke with a stick."

"Litigious?"

Tyler looked at him like he was an imbecile.

"Do you do any research before you conduct these interviews?"

"I like to fly by the seat of my pants."

"Theo Portman came out of the San Fernando valley. Back in the nineties he was a big noise in the porn industry there, definitely a player. You don't get to the top of that heap wearing kid gloves, you know what I mean?"

Back at Denning's place, before Tim got out of the car to collect his bike, they debriefed.

Denning was morose, said: "That was a fucking wash. We still can't tie GHQ to knowing that Bartlemann intended to shelve *Maximum Kill*."

"And without that, there's no motive. But it was ten years ago. There isn't going to be a smoking gun, or whatever, with a big note pinned to it saying, *GHQ knew Scott Bartlemann was going to can Maximum Kill.*" Tim reached into the back of the car for his satchel, took a copy of *Wilderness* out of it, flipped pages. "I think we're going at things ass about face. What we need to do first is get some confidence around whether or not we can actually trust the screenplay as a true record of what happened. Look here."

Tim pointed to the scene where the murder took place.

"Beau Montgomery – Scott Bartlemann, to us – has been shot by Brandon Kane a.k.a. Michael Starck. Maybe. And the maid's come into the study and seen what's happened...."

Tim read aloud:

"Beau lies slumped against a bookcase, bleeding from the chest. Dead. Brandon stands over him, holding a pistol. A MEXICAN MAID, has just entered through a set of open French doors that give onto the second story terrace, a look of horror on her face. Chad, who saw her enter, has already taken a pump-action shotgun from Beau's gun rack. He jacks a round into its chamber, steps toward her.

CHLOE
(Shrieking)
What are you doing?

Chad glances at his sister.

CHAD
Seriously?

He puts the muzzle of the shotgun under the maid's chin and makes her walk around a little, toying with her. They end up standing side-on to the open French doors. Chad smiles at the maid and pulls the trigger. The maid's head explodes. Chad looks at Brandon and Chloe, surprised and kind of turned on.

CHAD
Wow!

He pumps the shotgun once, like he's some sort of gangster.

We see the spent shotgun shell eject from the gun. We FOLLOW it as it spins through the air, out through the open French doors. It lands on the terrace, rolls across the tiles to a corner near the balustrade and falls into an un-grated drainage hole.

Brandon, Chloe and Chad are all transfixed, staring at the now-headless maid on the floor. They haven't followed the shotgun shell's trajectory.

EXT. REAR OF BEAU MONTGOMERY'S WEEKEND HOUSE – NIGHT.

A drainpipe runs from the terrace down the outside wall of the house. It has a right-angle bend in it where it detours around an air-conditioning vent. We HEAR the shotgun shell rattling down the drainpipe, coming to rest inside the horizontal portion of the pipe."

Tim closed the screenplay.

"If it happened like that, the shell could still be there. You said the cops never found it. Those things are made out of plastic and brass. If it hasn't been washed out of the pipe it could still be intact."

"So we go look at the house. Good idea. We should also think about Theo Portman. If our scenario is right, the murder meant GHQ got *Maximum Kill* released, but it also meant Portman got to take over Big Glass by getting rid of a partner he hated. We find some sort of extra-curricular link between Portman and GHQ, then GHQ knowing the film was going to be shelved could be a fait accompli."

Tim rode home thinking things were getting serious. Speaking to an ex-employee of Big Glass was one thing, trespassing on private property and ripping open a drainpipe was something else entirely.

A few weeks ago he would have broken into a cold sweat just thinking about it. Now, ramming through the gears, traffic opening, parting, so that it was nothing, so that it seemed he could go anywhere, could fly above the city if he wanted, he felt a kind of thrill that he was embarked upon something so insane. Something so wild. He was on the way to putting himself in the kind of situations he'd only ever written about before, only ever seen in films. He was tracking down his sister's killer!

As he passed the junction with Melrose Avenue, he thought briefly about buying a pair of leather trousers.

Chapter 24

Chick had made sure not to shower for three days before her meeting with Delores Fuentes, even though she'd fucked Tim every night. The idea of someone like Delores in *Antepenultimate* was ludicrous. Action hero movie star vs. sensitive portrait of familial decay. Dumber than dumb. But there was an upside, too. Delores' name, particularly as she hadn't appeared in a film for four years, would at least triple the opening audience the film might otherwise draw.

Chick was aware there was an element of sell-out in this audience-increase justification. And it was this awareness that had kept her away from soap and water in the days before her sit-down with the action woman. The reek of her catsuit and the tang between her legs were declarations to herself, reminders that she would use Delores only on her own terms, that she would not compromise herself or her film in any way to accommodate either the whims of the GHQ leadership, or whatever movie star insanities Delores might try to foist on the production.

Up to Bel Air, the Thruxton's chrome splintering sunlight, laying long and hard into the bends. There'd been a small quake in Long Beach that day, two buildings had collapsed and a water main had ruptured leaving more than five thousand residents without water. But up here, up in the hills, the world was a calmness of green lawns and sprinklers, white walls and gates and wealth. The leaves of the trees back in the estates turned lazily in a light breeze.

As Chick approached the mansion she saw that the wall out front was a clean white again, the red graffiti had been painted over.

A maid showed her through to the pool. Delores lay on the dark blue cushions of a sun lounger. Her legs were long and tanned, the separation of her quads visible, calf muscles high and hard. She wore a high-cut one-piece swimsuit that showed the borders of a smoothly depilated pubic mound. Chick thought retro-eighties. Thought for Mexican chicks shaving was probably a good idea. A copy of the *Antepenultimate* script lay on the stone tiles beside the lounger.

Chick took a chair, sat like a man, legs apart, an elbow on one knee.

Delores said: "You know I won't end up doing this picture."

"Ally Bannister seemed to think you would."

"It's their way of torturing me. In the last four years they've slated me for six parts. Always, GHQ cancels at the last minute."

"You're a condition of the money. Ally says you're in, you're in. I don't know anything about what you've got happening with GHQ, and I don't want to know. I've got enough to worry about prepping the film. We should just continue on the assumption that you're playing the part of the mother."

Delores drew one knee up and let it fall sideways against the lounger's armrest.

"You know, even if they do let me do the film, it will finish off what's left of my career. Can you imagine how an action star will look playing that part? I'll be a laughingstock. You know what someone painted on my wall? That I kill art."

"That's harsh."

"Do you think it's true?"

"Cinema is a religion for me. I believe what I do is a calling. You're asking the wrong person if you want your ass sucked."

Chick saw the impact of her words, the tightening around Delores' eyes, and relented a little.

"Look, I'm going to make an exceptional picture. Actors, despite what they like to think, are pretty much interchangeable. You've got baggage, sure. But ten minutes in, I guarantee no one's going to be thinking about the shit you've made before. Could be a chance for you to reinvent yourself."

"You think you're that good?"

"You bet."

Delores scratched at the leg of her swimsuit, ran her finger under the elasticized seam, lifting it away from her skin.

Chick knew she was being played, but that didn't stop the rush of blood to her crotch. Delores was a little over-pumped now, but she was still a beautiful woman. And it hadn't been that long ago that she was a household name. Movie star sex. One of the perks of being a director. And what better way to fuck the establishment than to fuck, literally, one of its poster girls? Chick figured she'd play right back.

"Look, I don't like the films you've made, I don't like your whole side of the industry. But if you can be a person and not a star, if you can turn off the whole Delores Fuentes thing, then I can make this film work for you."

Delores laughed bitterly.

"I told you, it won't happen."

Chick shrugged and thought fuck it, if this bitch wanted to wallow in self-pity she could knock herself out. The mother in Danny's story, the part GHQ wanted her to play, was a small role. Whatever anyone did – whether there really was some kind of career-wrecking intent behind her casting, or whether GHQ pulled Delores at the last minute – Chick knew it'd be a simple thing to find a replacement.

Delores sighed and picked up the screenplay.

"We might as well get on with this charade."

For half an hour they batted about questions of motivation and character arc. Delores outlined some backstory she'd dreamed up for the mother. Chick thought it was hokey and paint-by-numbers, but gave her points for bothering at least.

Chick talked about the emotional heart of the character, about truth and verisimilitude. Delores grew a little more enthusiastic. She plucked at the crotch of her swimsuit, complaining that it was a size too small. Chick drew her chair closer. When Delores pulled at the elastic again, Chick slid her hand through the space and touched Delores' laser-bald pussy.

A bedroom. White like so much of the house. Third story, a row of arched windows along an entire wall, long scallops of light. Expensive sheets. Freshly laundered. White....

Chick moved down Delores' body, pressed her face into movie star groin, closed her mouth against labia, rubbing her face in circles. Delores gasping, pulling her knees back, and Chick thinking if only this bitch knew, planning another evening visit with the spray paint.... And then feeling it, a ragged split in the right lip, a tear where she had a tear, a rip where she was ripped.

Chick got to her knees and straddled Delores, moved up her body so Delores would be able to see. But when Delores realized what Chick was doing she threw her off and rolled out of bed, grabbed a robe and walked out onto a terrace through open French doors at the far end of the room.

Chick, who had expected an immediate comrades-in-arms scenario, lay for a moment trying to figure this reaction. Then got up and pulled on her catsuit.

Delores sat at a wrought-iron table, gazing at blue sky and white clouds, smoking a dark-papered cigarette.

Chick crossed the terrace, in no mood to be gentle, ready to launch an inquisition. But Delores spoke first. Turned her head from the sky and calmly stubbed out her cigarette.

"What happened?"

Chick, figuring the calmness to be some sort of coping mechanism, decided to be charitable, pulled out a chair and sat at the table.

"I was raped. When I was fifteen. Abducted from my mother's store, taken somewhere and hammered by two people. They used a hardon Oscar. Know what that is?"

Delores shook her head.

"A fake Oscar statuette. It has an erection instead of a sword. It's the dick that splits your pussy."

"That's ridiculous."

"It was stolen from my mother's store the night I was abducted. The dick's exactly the right size. That's what happened to you, right? Abducted, blindfolded, dildoed with the Oscar?"

"No."

"No?" Chick's voice rose. "You're shitting me!"

"You want me to have suffered as well. I understand. To share it. But I was injured riding a horse. I was thrown. I landed on a fence."

"Oh, really? You fall off a horse and you land on your *cunt*?"

Chick was shouting now. Delores raised a hand to quiet her, but Chick ignored it.

"You weren't taken to a room somewhere where they played movies, or the soundtrack of movies? Action shit like you're so good at? You weren't dumped in Griffith Park with some cash and a bottle of water? Your cunt looks just like mine!"

When Chick mentioned movies, the corner of Delores' mouth twitched, but she didn't say anything. Chick carried on:

"If we compare what happened to us we might find some clue about who did it. Don't you want to know who it was? Don't you want to fucking kill them?"

Delores lit another cigarette, said: "I'm sorry, I can't help you with this." And went back to looking at the sky.

Chick told her she was a gutless bitch and left the terrace. At the French doors she stopped and looked back.

"How do you know Sean Nightingale?"

"Who?"

Chick repeated the name. Delores shook her head.

"I don't know him."

CHAPTER 25

The day after Kid had given Michael the Super 8 film, Business Affairs at GHQ created a production account for *Antepenultimate*/Kid Haldane Productions and transferred three million dollars into it. Kid and the production accountant could draw on this money, but expenses over fifty grand had to be okayed by GHQ Business Affairs. A way for Michael to hold the upper hand a little while longer.

But Business Affairs' control was standard practice, and Kid wasn't bothered by it. And, anyhow, he'd copied the Super 8 film with a video camera. He was confident that funds for *Antepenultimate* would flow unhindered.

Now today. Another step forward. Danny Bartlemann in L.A., in Kid's office. Chick there too, bouncing on the spot and clapping her hands, Danny signing the contract that gave Haldane Productions ownership of the *Antepenultimate* screenplay. Chick stopped jumping around long enough to witness the document, and then Kid slid a check, pre-approved by GHQ Business Affairs, for $200,000 across the table.

$200,000 wasn't a million bucks, wasn't the stuff Hollywood screenwriting legends are made of, but for a picture with a three-mil budget it was a very good figure.

Mainstream U.S. productions generally allotted five percent of production budget for writing expenses – initial screenplay, rewrites, extra writers if needed – so Danny was fifty grand ahead of the curve before they'd even completed development – the period during which a final, rewritten script would be nailed down.

On top of the up-front payment, Danny's contract also gave him three percent of net profits. But everyone in the room, Danny included, knew that on a three million dollar film, three percent of the net was unlikely to ever equal more than zero.

Kid called Peta in from Reception and everyone congratulated each other, and then Kid pulled a couple of bottles of champagne from the office fridge and all of them, except Danny who didn't drink, made toasts to the film and the writer and the director and all the awards they were going to win.

It was a good day. It was a day that made Kid think he really could forget all the lost and ruined women he'd fucked in front of the camera, all the girls he'd fed to Jeffery and Ally. Could make up for what he'd done to Chick.

As the alcohol seeped pleasantly into his cells, he relaxed in his chair and looked about him at the happy little party. He felt, deep in his bones, that something was looking after him, that after all the abandoned years he was now being directed toward a life that would be fulfilling and good.

He watched Peta. She was distant, still, in some ways, close in others. She would not take him to her house, he'd only met her father once, briefly; but she had slept with him and now spent several nights each week at his apartment on Wilshire. He'd told her he loved her and though she hadn't said it back she hadn't freaked out either.

Morning. Nineteen floors above Wilshire. A whole different ballgame. Blinds not drawn and a sharp, bright morning light coming in, flaying the happy certainty of yesterday. Hangover from the booze at the office, or just the merciless light of a new day? Impossible to tell. But during the night some unfathomable realization had occurred, some falling-away of scales. And he knew, just knew, that the optimism he'd felt about his future, with Chick and Danny and Peta, had been an illusion.

Jeffery and Ally had recognized Chick as the first girl they'd raped. They'd want her again. They hadn't called yet, but they would. And then they'd rape her again. Probably worse, considering Jeffery's deterioration.

A world going up in flames.

And Kid, lying beside a sleeping Peta, whipcord muscles drawn tight through the whole lean length of his body, teeth grinding at the utter fucking unfairness of it all. Knowing that it wasn't supposed to be this way, that he should have been a good man, a man good things happened to. And thinking again, for the millionth time, of that cold night at the edge of the desert twenty years ago.

In the mid-nineties the Southern Californian porn business turned over around a billion dollars annually. That kind of money made people protective of their assets.

Back then, Kid was at his peak, riding the crest of the adult industry wave. Good looking, over-hung, in demand. He was a name you could put on the front of a vid and double or triple your sales.

Kid had been discovered in a truck stop toilet outside of Salinas by Ron Le Forge, a guy who, like a number of his competitors, had beaten and killed his way into a significant slice of the porn pie.

Ron liked big dicks and Ron liked money. When he visited the men's room on his way home from a meeting with a small San Francisco-based outfit he was considering acquiring and saw what came lunging through the glory hole in his cubicle, he knew he'd found a way to mix business with pleasure.

Ron was good to Kid and Kid returned the favor, worked hard, did what he was told and earned Ron a lot of money. Between shoots he let Ron express his gratitude physically. Kid liked girls, but he put up with Ron shoving his way into one orifice or another because he figured it was a smart move – keep the boss happy, get the best jobs. Tough guy Ron, on the other hand, was more than a little smitten with his double digit leading man.

That industry, those days, there were no formal agreements, no printed contracts stipulating exclusivity or length of service, but Ron put a lot of stock in loyalty and figured it went without saying that the people who worked for him wouldn't sell their services to any of his competitors. Kid, on the other hand, believed in a free-market economy where loyalty was fine as long as it didn't result in restraint of trade.

A couple of years into his time with Ron, Kid met a director who went by the industry name of Brett Adelaide. Brett worked for another of the San Fernando porn mills, a company whose owner stayed a long way back in the shadows and who didn't fuck the help.

Brett had seen Kid's work and wanted that talent in his own films. A chance meeting in a bar became a regular drinking date. They weren't friends exactly, but they shot the shit and they both liked booze. The first time Brett asked, Kid wasn't dumb enough to say yes. He was not completely blind to notions of obligation.

But time passed and Brett kept asking and Kid started to consider the advantages that working with the guy might hold. Kid was earning good money with Ron, but Brett would pay more. Brett was very definitely heterosexual and so, unlike Ron, had no interest in leveraging Kid's talents into off-screen fun. Most of all, though, Brett's films were far better written and shot than those churned out by the revolving door of directors Ron Le Forge employed.

And so Kid, then still young and brash and convinced of his own importance, made a flick with Brett during a lull in Ron's shooting schedule. It did well. It was a hit with all the sweaty men perched in front of their VCRs. It did too well, in fact, because Ron found out about it.

Ron figured he was a reasonable man. He believed in trying to talk things through. He explained the finer points of their relationship to Kid. He mentioned damage to his business, personal betrayal, the obligation he felt Kid owed to a man who had plucked him from a truck stop toilet. And he sent a guy around to talk to Brett, too. Just talk. Because he was a reasonable man.

But Kid and Brett, not knowing enough about Ron to be properly frightened of him, didn't listen. They made another film, this one a double-hander with one of Brett's regulars, a Mexican dude called Christo, a guy with pocked skin, an equine dick and an aura of lurking violence that cast and crew took care not to ignite, particularly as it was rumored he also worked as a fixit guy for Brett's boss.

And that level of personal and financial betrayal was enough for Ron. For him, there was no point in telling anyone anything twice. If they didn't listen the first time, they weren't going to. So he got two of his guys and went and snatched Kid and then Brett.

The mistake he made was taking Brett as he emerged from company headquarters in the Valley after a meeting with his boss – with Christo parked fifty yards back down the block, waiting to ferry the director to a casting session for a water sports extravaganza he was shooting the following week.

Ron took Brett and Kid on a two-hour drive to an abandoned gas station outside Victorville, around where the mesquite dessert began. There, in the workshop out back, a place Ron had had occasion to visit in the past, the two men were bound with chains and propped against a wall while Ron rooted through rusted lengths of pipe and a few old tools in search of an implement that would suit his purpose.

Ron never found what he wanted, though. Christo had phoned Brett's boss as soon as he'd seen what was going down and the two of them, both men accustomed to taking swift action and keeping cool heads, had followed Ron's van at a leisurely distance along Route 15, and then on through a few smaller streets to the gas station. It was dusk when they parked far enough away not to be heard, and they had no trouble creeping up on the place unseen and stepping through the unlocked workshop door.

Ron's guys had guns, but after Brett and Kid had been trussed, they'd stuck them in their belts. Christo and Brett's boss, therefore, had the advantage when they came through the door, guns in hand.

After Kid and Brett had been freed from their chains, and Ron and his two goons had been lined up against a wall, everyone could have had a chat, could have come to some sort of agreement about Ron loaning Kid's services to Brett.

Could have, but didn't. Brett's boss, whose past was at least as shady as Ron's, knew that Ron wouldn't forgive this intrusion and didn't want to spend any more of the near future looking over his shoulder than he had to.

He had Christo shoot one of Ron's guys. Then he handed a pistol to Brett and made it plain that what they were engaged in there that night was a shared enterprise, that participation was the price Brett and Kid were going to have to pay for being rescued, for the inconvenience they'd caused everyone. For their own stupidity.

Brett, a talented director and a man who was convinced he had a bright future ahead of him, didn't have any trouble reading the subtext: *you or him*. It took a bit of courage, a bit of nerve, but he made Ron, begging and babbling by this time, turn around and kneel on the floor. When Brett pulled the trigger, the bullet went into the back of Ron's head and came out through the middle of his face, blasting away his nose and an upper set of porcelain veneers.

Christo took the gun out of Brett's hand and gave it to Kid. And *this* was the moment, this was when Kid had changed from one type of man into another, from a guy who just did something disgusting for a living, to someone who could take another man's life, someone who could supply girls to a pair of rapists.

When Kid opened up on the remaining goon, he was so fritzed he couldn't stop pulling the trigger. The pistol was a Glock 16. It held a lot of bullets. Kid put all of them into center mass. The hole he made was so big he saw light through it before the guy hit the floor.

Chapter 26

From Jeffery's second-story bedroom, Ally watched Michael climb into his Maserati, head down the driveway and through the gates. She and Jeffery had not seen him in person for three months. What input the business demanded of them they supplied by phone, video conference or email. Just the way Michael liked it.

He'd stayed for an hour, relaying the news that the *Wilderness* screenplay had resurfaced. Only one solution, kill the two women, Skye and her screenwriter lover.

Delores was the source of this idiocy. If she had been killed last time, it wouldn't be happening again. As far as Ally was concerned that made Michael responsible, and if it had been up to her she wouldn't have bothered listening to him, would have told him to fix the mess himself.

But Jeffery had piped up. Jeffery had volunteered. Jeffery had leapt at the opportunity.

A long time ago he'd blown a woman's head off with a shotgun. He hadn't killed since – the Ritual of Freeing had been enough to smooth the edges of his ragged past. But in the last few years the ritual had been losing its hold on him, and as memories of his grandfather clawed their way more and more frequently out of his muddled subconscious, he'd started to talk about killing again, as though, in some way, he believed it would give him back the identity that had been so brutally taken from him.

And now, too, there was the First, a source of terminal excitation Jeffery wouldn't shut up about, that he was chaffing to offer to the gods of his sex-destroyed psyche. But she would take time to arrange, to cajole out from under

Kid's protective gaze. Until then, the women Michael wanted killed would be a convenient stopgap at least.

Even so, Ally might have tried to persuade her brother to leave them to Michael, might have argued that the women were something he should stay out of – why open himself up to all that risk? But Ally had had a phone call that morning before Michael arrived. Ally had spoken to Danny Bartlemann. And she knew it would be far easier to reestablish a relationship with the man she loved if her brother's short-circuiting attention was directed elsewhere.

Ally turned away from the bedroom window. Jeffery was standing in front of a full-length mirror, trying on different 1940s outfits. He seemed energized, there was a little color to his face.

"It's going to be like a black-and-white movie, Ally. There'll be GIs back from the front and hoods and gangsters and dames and dirty cops. And when they write the history of Los Angeles I'll be there, I'll be the guy who rubbed out two mouthy broads."

Jeffery pulled the .38 from his shoulder holster and pointed it at himself in the mirror. He stared at his reflection for a long time. And then he blinked and swallowed like he was going to cry. He put his gun away and threw his arms around Ally and buried his face in the hollow of her neck.

Danny Bartlemann's motel was on Lincoln Boulevard, south of the Santa Monica Freeway – a single-story court around a square of grass and a couple of palms. A semi-okay place, quiet enough for him to work on whatever rewrites Haldane needed for *Antepenultimate*.

Ally arrived mid-afternoon. She'd told Jeffery she was going out to shop for clothes. He'd been busy paging through photos of old-time Los Angeles and seemed not to have heard her.

Danny was grayer, thinner, tired-looking, but still the man she remembered, and the years between them fell away as he put his arms around her.

Their lovemaking was the halfway sex they had become comfortable with when they were last together. A warm world created beneath the bedcovers, a dream of touching and kissing and forgetting about the limitations of their bodies and their minds.

Later. In each other's arms as the afternoon aged and the sun came softly between the blinds. Danny thinking that at last his long loneliness was ended, that those years up at Los Padres could be given meaning after all if they had led to this, if they had somehow been necessary to bring him back, full-circle, to Ally.

There was still Jeffery, of course. That dark and destructive presence who had taken Ally away from him last time. It could happen again. But Ally was different now, he could see it in her face. He thought at first it was because she had become stronger, but later realized he was mistaken. The thing that had changed about her was not her strength but her level of desperation.

When he tried to probe her past, the years they had been apart, Ally talked of inconsequentialities, of business and movies. And when he pressed, would only say that Jeffery was not well – a comment from which Danny took comfort, picturing the Hollywood freak dying in bed.

But what did it matter? Strength or desperation – it was all the same. As long as this time she was willing to resist her brother and stay with him.

Danny made plans. Finish work on *Antepenultimate*, give up cigarettes, maybe cut his hair.... Take Ally up to Los Padres – put as much distance between her and her brother as possible. Maybe move to New York; Paris, maybe....

Next to him, Ally kept her eyes closed and wondered if the happiness she felt at being with Danny again could survive the things she had done. She had helped kill his father, after all. She knew that Danny had not been close to him, but still....

As they started to make love again, she couldn't help wishing that she didn't have so much to hide.

Outside, across the street, sitting in a restored 1942 Packard 180 convertible Victoria with the top up, Jeffery watched the motel, picturing his sister with her legs spread, knowing it must be that fucking screenwriter.

Chapter 27

Chick, blasting into Tim's flat, wanting to talk about her visit with Delores. Tim feeling good. Feeling great. Two days without wine, three pounds lighter because he'd cut out crap since meeting Chick. Feeling strength in his arms and legs, feeling the first hints of a returning youth.

Tim reached for her, wanting to fuck her on the floor, but Chick pushed him away.

"No, man, you gotta listen to this."

She went into the kitchen and sat at the table.

"I had that meeting with Delores Fuentes? What the fuck she's doing in the movie, I don't know. Anyhow, that's not important. What happened, right, is we fucked and—"

"You fucked Delores Fuentes?"

"She's a woman, Timbo. It's not like I'm cheating on you. She doesn't have a secret dick or anything."

Tim saw the logic.

"Okay, cool. What was she wearing?"

"Dude, this is important. She's got the same rip in her cunt as me."

"Maybe it's just how she's made. Some girls are a little frilly down there."

"Frilly? That bitch's right lip is split half an inch. It's not because she's 'frilly'. It's because she was fucked with the hardon Oscar."

"What did she say about it?"

"She didn't say shit. I told her what happened to me. She said she got hers when she fell off a horse. Complete bullshit. And you know what else? I asked her about Sean. I didn't say we saw him at her place or anything, I just asked if she knew him. Know what she said? She said she'd never heard of him. She's a fucking liar, man."

"I can figure she might not want to talk about a rape, being a movie star and all. But why would she lie about Sean?" And, Tim thought, why would Sean lie about Delores? "You think she knows who the rapists are?"

"I don't know. If she does, why not tell me? One woman to another."

She was silent for a while, pondering. And then, shaking her head, said quietly: "Fuck it's a coincidence about that Flynn's Flying Fuckers stuff in your screenplay."

Later, Chick left. She was going to work late at her place storyboarding *Antepenultimate*. After she'd gone, Tim lay on the sofa, staring at the ceiling, feeling bad that he'd told Chick he'd written the screenplay. It wasn't a good thing, so early in a relationship, to be keeping secrets.

Like Chick, he thought the Flynn's Flying Fucker reference in the screenplay was a hell of a coincidence. Unlike her, he knew there was a possibility that the characters in the screenplay actually had counterparts in the real world. She was so obviously fucked up by the rape, so desperate to exact revenge, that it made him feel disloyal, not sharing this knowledge with her.

But now wasn't the time. Chick was too wild. And he had no real proof yet of anything. If he pulled Chick's trigger before he'd properly unraveled the mystery surrounding the screenplay, she'd be firebombing Bel Air before he ever had a chance to find out what had happened to Rebecca.

Night. Up to the bunker on the Bonneville, the thing with Sean bugging him. Sean opening the door not stoned, amazingly. Or rather, on a low, low dose to smooth the withdrawal. If smooth was the right word.

Shivering, nose running, lower back locking.... He'd tried to quit before and failed, but Tim saw something behind those squinting, blinking, red-rimmed eyes now. Something that hadn't been there the other times. A new brand of determination, maybe?

"You don't look so good."

"Feel worse."

"Why now?"

Sean shrugged.

"Why not?"

But Tim could put two and two together. An old love, the one Sean never talked about, a visit to Delores Fuentes.... Kicking because he figured he had a chance again?

Tim had done the supportive friend thing a number of times over the last two years. If he had been the same guy he used to be, the pre-Chick version, he might have done it again. But he had no time for it now; Sean had lied to him.

"I was up in Bel Air the other night."

Sean, on the sofa, hugged his knees and rocked back and forth.

"Oh, yeah?"

"Yeah. Up the street from a big white Spanish mansion with a big white wall. Just kinda hanging out."

Sean leaned over the arm of the couch and vomited into a bucket. He grunted for a while, then wiped his mouth and fell back against the cushions. "Lucky you didn't get picked up."

"I saw you, dude. Coming out of Delores Fuentes' place. You lied to me. You told me you didn't know anyone connected with GHQ. She's got an exclusive fucking contract with them! Everyone in Hollywood knows that."

"Whoa, man. Okay, okay...." Sean held his hands up defensively. "It's no big deal. It's just a personal thing I didn't want to get into."

"We've known each other two years. You don't tell me you're fucking a movie star?"

"Used to fuck. Not fuck*ing.* Well, sort of. We saw each other for maybe eighteen months. It finished two years ago, around the time I met you. We kept it secret when we were going out because Delores thought it wasn't a good look for her to be dating an unknown. When we split up, she wanted to keep it quiet even more. So I never told anyone. You included. We're trying to figure out if we can start it up again, that's all. That's why I was at her place. There's nothing sinister about it."

"Nothing sinister? Are you fucking serious? I told you about Rebecca and the screenplay. I told you she was writing it for Delores – around the time she was fucking *killed* – and you don't say shit to me? You don't think it might be kind of important to me to know what Rebecca was doing when she died?"

"Tim, calm down. My head is fucking killing me. I'm sorry I didn't say anything. I should have. But telling you about Rebecca would have meant telling you about Delores and me. Look at my life, man. I've got nothing. Getting back with her is everything. I mean, fucking *everything*. If she wants to keep things secret, I'm going to keep them secret."

"Yeah? Well, now they're not fucking secret, so you can tell me what you know about Rebecca. When I met you, you said you knew her from a couple of industry parties, that's all. But that's bullshit, isn't it? You met her through Delores. And you knew they were working on a screenplay together. Two actors, sitting down for dinner? There's no way Delores wouldn't have told you about it."

Sean took a damp cloth from beside his bucket and wiped the sweat off his face with it. He took longer than he needed and Tim punched the arm of the sofa.

"Sean!"

Sean dropped the cloth and sat back tiredly.

"There's not really a whole lot to tell.... Okay, I met Rebecca twice, only, when she was at Bel Air with Delores. That's the extent of it. I hardly knew her."

"You only met her twice and you went to her funeral?"

Sean looked a little thrown for a moment, did his best to cover it by looking sick.

"Delores wasn't going to go, so I thought I would. It seemed like the right thing to do."

"That's it? 'It seemed like the right thing to do'? When you didn't even know her?"

"What can I say? She seemed nice. I didn't have anything else to do that day, I took a drive to the cemetery."

"Tell me about her and Delores."

"You're right…. They were working together. Delores had an idea for a film, she needed someone to write it for her."

"*Delores* had the idea?"

"Well—"

"You said Delores had the idea?"

"Yeah. She wanted to do some Faustian Hollywood thing, sell your soul for money, etcetera. I don't know exactly what, she wouldn't let me read anything and she wouldn't tell me the story."

"So it wasn't Rebecca who brought her the idea? She wasn't trying to sell her a spec script?"

"No."

Tim sat for a moment, processing. This was something new. He and Denning had assumed Rebecca had been the source of the *Wilderness* story, passing it on to Delores. Now it looked like things had been the other way around.

Tim could have left it there, could have ridden away from the bunker with this new piece of information, with the truth, if truth it was, of how Sean knew Rebecca. But he was too angry with Sean, too pissed off at being lied to.

"When I asked you if you knew anything about GHQ, if you had any connection there, you told me you'd had a bit part in one of their movies."

"*Turners Highway*. Yeah."

"But that wasn't all you had going with them, was it?"

"Jesus, Tim...."

"You were slated for a breakout role in another GHQ film, *Random Burn*. One that would have made you the next big male star. Chick told me about it. I'd call that a fucking connection. All the back and forth, the contract, the agent, the meetings, the casting sessions.... And you say you don't know anyone there, that there's no information you can give me about the company?"

Sean tipped his head back and looked at the ceiling, his mouth tight and angry.

"All right. Fuck it. When I met you at the cemetery the day of Rebecca's funeral, I felt sorry for you, man, okay? I wasn't looking for a best bud. You just looked like you could have used someone to talk to. Two years later, you're still coming around. You think I owe you something, like you've got a right to my life story, because I put up with you whining about how impossible it is for you to write, or how unfair the film industry is, or whatever other self-justifying bullshit you feel you need to vent? You don't, man. My life's my life. It isn't yours."

Tim was riding a big, cool, English bike now, and banging Chick had made him feel like cock of the walk, but this hurt. This hurt badly. His friendship with

Sean, as limited as it had been, was the only real, human relationship he'd had in the time since Rebecca's murder. And now Sean had burned it.

Tim got up and headed for the door, wanting to get away before he made any more of a fool of himself.

But there was something he couldn't leave without asking. With the door half open he turned back to Sean.

"How come you bailed on that role? You'd be Brad Pitt now."

But Sean had his face in his hands and didn't answer, and Tim left the bunker and climbed onto the Bonneville and sat for a moment in the dark before he fired it up, feeling empty and cold, like the world had fallen away beneath him.

And inside the bunker, Sean got up and got his works together and figured he'd quit tomorrow instead.

Chapter 28

Scott Bartlemann had been killed in a cliff-top ocean-front weekend home he owned a few miles outside Isla Vista, north of Santa Barbara – about a two-and-a-half-hour drive from L.A.

The place had been built in the fifties, on a promontory that stuck out into the ocean like the side of a breast. It was only about two miles in a straight line from the highway, but the trail to it meandered through pine forest, serving two or three other properties hidden back in the trees, and it took Tim and Denning a couple of wrong turns and fifteen minutes to find it. When they did, the first thing Denning said was: "What the fuck?"

The house was a large two-story structure that looked like it was originally intended to be a boutique hotel or a small private hospital. Out back of it there was clear ground for twenty yards, and then the land fell away in a hundred-foot cliff.

Denning had seen a photo at the time of the murder. It had shown a white, wooden building fronted by a wide lawn and a collection of decorative shrubs. There had been trees close to the sides of the house and the place, despite its size, had looked comfortable and homey.

Not now. The white was gone, replaced by institutional gray. The lawn, the shrubs and the trees had been removed, and on three sides of the building there was a wide apron of black macadam. Pods of aerials, radar dishes and microwave links cluttered the roof, and around the entire property, right down to the edge of the cliff, there was a twelve-foot chain-link fence.

In the middle of the fence, directly opposite where the road came out of the trees, a double gate bore the red, white and blue flash and double anchor crest of the 11th District United States Coast Guard. Beside the insignia a sign proclaimed the place to be the Isla Vista Marine Observation Facility.

Scott Bartlemann's house, it seemed, had been co-opted by the government as a watchful eye against untaxed importation, illegal immigrants and waterborne drug runners.

Denning looked at Tim open-mouthed, then both of the men laughed and Denning said:

"A coast guard station? They turned the place into a fucking coast guard station?"

They sat in the car for a while looking at the place. Then, with nothing else to do, they got out of the car and walked aimlessly along the chain link fence.

From what Tim could see, the building conformed to the description Rebecca had used in her screenplay. But that wasn't saying much. The only distinctive external feature mentioned in *Wilderness* was a second-floor terrace. The coast guard station had one that ran across the back of the building and around its two side walls.

Tim pointed to it.

"Terrace."

Denning grunted and pointed himself.

"No French doors."

The section of terrace they were looking at was on the right-hand side of the building and the wall there was just a plain expanse of gray wooden planks – no exit space for a flying shotgun shell.

They were about to move further along the fence to take a look at the rear of the building when the sound of a slow-running diesel engine swelled behind them. They turned and saw a maroon-colored coach come out of the trees and roll to a stop in a gust of air-brakes a little way from Denning's car.

The door opened and a couple of minutes later a procession of senior citizens began climbing uncertainly down the steps, clinging tightly to the handrail and the door frame.

Ten minutes later, twenty of them had congregated in front of the coast guard station's gates. They wore sun visors and check pants and polyester dresses and over-sized glasses. Some of them coughed into handkerchiefs. Mean age, seventy-five easily.

The entrance to Bartlemann's house had been replaced with a set of glass double doors. Two man wearing coast guard uniforms and dark blue baseball caps pushed through them now and walked across the macadam. One of the men had a moustache, he pulled the gates open and smiled.

"Good afternoon ladies and gentlemen...."

The driver of the coach, twenty years younger than his charges, shook hands with the mustachioed guy, and together they looked at something on a clipboard the driver was holding.

Tim nudged Denning. Doing their best to look casual they walked to the group of old folks and got close. Some of the seniors turned to look at them. Tim smiled. Denning smiled. The old people smiled back. One of them, a woman with liver spots up to her elbows, rubbed her hands together and said: "What fun!"

The coast guard with the moustache was saying that the tour was forty min-utes long, that his name was John Trivett and that the man with him was Paul and they were coast guard community liaison officers.

When he was done, he stood aside and waved the group through the gates like he was directing a wagon train. Paul took point and led everyone toward the house. Tim and Denning stayed close to the rear of the group, eyes down, shuffling their feet so they didn't move too fast.

Trivett stood holding one of the gates. As Tim and Denning passed him he called out to them:

"You want the tour, too?"

Tim looked up, making like he figured anyone was allowed to walk in.

"It's a tour?"

Trivett chuckled a little. "Federal land, gotta be accompanied. No problem if you want to tag along, we welcome greater community engagement. Every Tuesday and Thursday. Just stay with the group."

Denning thanked him and the two of them spent a second checking out each other's moustaches.

The ground floor of what had been Scott Bartlemann's house had been turned into a series of administrative offices. The corridors that ran between them showed signs of the place's former elegance – polished dark wood floors, high ceilings, molded cornices – but the decoration now was thoroughly institutional. The walls were white, hung with photographs of helicopters, coast guard cutters and aircraft.

Paul took them on a leisurely circuit, pausing at open doorways to describe the different functions performed by the officers inside or to declaim on the merits of the machines in the photographs. The old folks oohed and ahhed and nodded to each other. Tim figured a little firsthand contact with Homeland Security was probably a comforting thing when the osteo had eaten your bones brittle or you were carrying your shit around in a plastic bag.

Tim and Denning kept their eyes open for anything that would match with the *Wilderness* screenplay, but the action had all taken place in Bartlemann's second-floor study and Rebecca had written next to nothing about the rest of the house. One thing that had given them hope when they'd come in through the glass front doors, though, was a wide straight staircase that led to the upper floor. Rebecca had mentioned one just like it and the two men were anxious to see what it led to. But they had to wait until Paul had taken them through a small bunk room, a kitchen, the office of the base commander, a server room and...more offices.

Finally, after another delay while several of the group lurched to the rest-rooms, they headed upstairs.

The second story was given over to banks of computers and electronic monitoring equipment. Men in dark blue fatigues sat at consoles pushing buttons, turning dials and speaking into headsets. The duty commander, a man at least ten years younger than Tim, gave a short speech on the role of the coast guard, said they helped to gather data on whales and dolphins as well as catching the bad guys. Mentioned that the station was a converted private residence, that the coast guard had acquired it ten years previously from the estate of a man who'd worked in the film industry.

Running across most of the rear of the house was a four-foot window, obviously a coast guard addition. The view through it was quite spectacular – an uninterrupted panorama of ocean and rugged coastal cliffs. Tim tried to see the floor of the terrace that ran beneath it, but a bank of equipment prevented him getting close enough to see anything but the top half of the terrace's balustrade.

The old folks were starting to mutter about lunch by the time the duty commander had finished his spiel. Trivett, who had absented himself from the ground-floor tour, took over from Paul and led the group to the north-west corner of the second floor for one last stop. A medium-sized room. A chapel commemorating members of the coast guard who had died in the line of duty. Photographs, plaques, wreathes of plastic leaves. Wood paneled.

Denning looked at Tim. The screenplay had described Bartlemann's study as wood paneled.

In the corner of the rear wall a set of French doors let in the afternoon sun. Beyond them, the terrace, and then the ocean. Tim took the screenplay from his satchel and read in a whisper:

"He puts the muzzle of the shotgun under the maid's chin and makes her walk around a little, toying with her. They end up standing side-on to the open French doors. Chad smiles at the maid and pulls the trigger."

And then:

"We see the spent shotgun shell eject from the gun. We FOLLOW it as it spins through the air, out through the open French doors. It lands on the terrace, rolls across the tiles to a corner near the balustrade and falls into an un-grated drainage hole."

After a solemn examination of the room, the group began to leave. The coast guard was serving hotdogs and sodas on the lawn out back of the house. Trivett was outside the room, shepherding people along the landing to the stairs.

Denning went to the French doors and tried them. They were unlocked. He opened them and stepped out. Tim followed.

The terrace was about eight feet across. Tim and Denning stood at its inner corner, where it made a ninety-degree turn and ran back down the side of the building. At their feet, something round and dark – the opening to a rainwater runoff, covered with a wire grate.

Tim crossed to the balustrade, leaned forward over it as far as he could to look at the rear wall of the house. Underneath the runoff opening a pipe about four inches diameter dropped toward the ground, made a sharp angle around an air-conditioning unit, then straightened again and carried on until it ended a few inches short of an external drain.

"Pipe's the same."

Denning nodded. "Shame about the grate."

"Ten years ago, might not have been there. Coast guard probably pays attention to things like that."

Trivett came out then, smiling.

"We don't really allow the public out here. Someone might fall off and sue us. Beautiful view, though, huh?"

Denning said it was, then made some more scenic beauty small-talk. Trivett put his hands on his hips and took a deep breath, savoring the sea air. He didn't seem in any hurry to leave.

Denning stuck his hand out.

"Alan Denning."

He and Trivett shook.

Denning continued: "I actually came out to research a book I'm writing."

"Oh, yeah?"

"You know about the guy who was killed here? And his maid?"

"Oh sure. I've been at Isla Vista since we took it over. It was quite a sensation back about, what, ten years? To be expected, I suppose. Hollywood and all."

"In that room there, wasn't it?" Denning nodded at the chapel.

"Apparently."

"Is this place manned all the time?"

"Coast guard never sleeps. This is a twenty-four hour, three-sixty-five facility."

"Since ten years ago?"

"Give or take, yeah."

Below them on the grass a couple of uniformed men were working a barbecue, handing sausages in buns to hungry pensioners. The smell of the meat was good on the air and a thin blue haze rose from the grill.

Trivett turned away from the view and the three of them went back inside.

As they walked down the stairs Trivett said to Denning: "You from Hollywood, too?"

"Not really. Westwood."

"Couple of years ago some movie people came out here. They were doing research, too. Thought maybe you knew them."

"Could be."

"Three of them. Can't remember their names. Did those big action movies, though. *Turner's Highway.* You see that?"

A coffee house in Santa Barbara, across the road from the harbor. Boats in rows, white, quiet at their berths because there was no swell. Cars passing on the road outside the big window, throwing splashes of reflected color against the ceiling. Tim and Denning at a table, with coffee, back in the shadows, away from anyone else. The copy of *Wilderness* on the table between them. Denning reading through the murder scene again, then leaning back, taking a sip, putting his mug down.

"I'd say bingo. No shotgun shell, but it's as close a match as we're going to get. French doors, drainpipe, drain hole just where the screenplay said it'd be. And two years ago, three people who've gotta be GHQ come out and look the place over. They had to be looking for the same thing as us. There's no other reason they'd be there."

"Why not before? Two years ago was eight years after the murder."

"Right after the murder the house would have been too hot. GHQ couldn't have been sure it wasn't being watched."

"But not for eight years."

"You're right. I think the answer is that they didn't know about the shell in the drainpipe until a lot later. You're in the middle of killing someone, you're probably kinda distracted. You know, nighttime, it goes out the door, it's dark, there's blood everywhere, you're shitting yourself...."

"*Someone* obviously knew about it."

"Yeah, but not GHQ. They would only have gotten hold of the screenplay when they killed your sister. Two years ago, right? Could be that was the first they knew about where the shell went, that it might still be there to be found. So they go out to the house to try and remove the evidence. Only thing is, by that time the coast guard owns the place and it's impossible for them to fuck about with

the drainpipe. So they have no choice but to let sleeping dogs lie. It fits perfectly."
Denning's eyes widened. "I might even do my book that way. Start off with Starck
visiting the house, only to find out he has absolutely no chance of getting the shell.
Work back from there. Yeah...that could be cool."

"Still leaves the question of who saw where the shell went. Someone had to,
otherwise it couldn't be in the screenplay."

"Rebecca?"

"No. She would never have had anything to do with a murder. I'm thinking
Delores Fuentes."

Denning snorted. "Delores Fuentes. How the fuck does that work?"

"I found out something yesterday. I know a guy. A friend of mine, kind of.
Used to be an actor. He was seeing Delores Fuentes when Rebecca was killed and
he told me that, at the time, Delores was working with Rebecca on a pet project she
had – a Faustian Hollywood tale, he said she called it. It has to be the same screenplay. A Faustian tale? Right before she was killed? And get this, it wasn't Rebecca
who came up with the story, it was *Delores*. Rebecca was just working for hire."

"Who is this guy?"

"Sean Nightingale. He's no one now, but he was on the way up a few years ago.
He actually had a small part in *Turner's Highway*. Then he got into smack."

"Does he know the screenplay's about the Bartlemann kill?"

"He said he never read it. But I mentioned it might be a *roman à clef* thing, asked
him if he knew anything useful about GHQ."

"And did he?"

"No, apart from what he said about Rebecca and Delores working together.
Forget him, he's not important. But what it means is that Delores Fuentes has to
be involved in Bartlemann's murder somehow, otherwise she couldn't have known
about it to tell Rebecca. Was she in the States when he was killed?"

"I don't know. She didn't make anything until after GHQ had done *Maximum
Kill*, but that doesn't mean she wasn't here. And her relationship with GHQ wasn't
just business. She and Michael Starck had a thing going."

"An affair?"

"Yeah. When *Maximum Kill* came out and hit big, Michael Starck was the hot-
test new director in town. The gossip magazines were all over him and he made a

big deal out of this Mexican girl he was going out with, talking her up, telling everyone she was the love of his life and he was going to make her a big star – Delores Fuentes. They were together for, I don't know, maybe five years?"

"You think the relationship went back before *Maximum Kill*?"

"If it did, then at least the timing's right."

"How do we find out?"

Denning thought for a moment, then smiled and nodded to himself.

"Nancy Epps, a.k.a. Mrs. Nancy Starck."

"Starck was married?"

"Yeah. One of those shitty Hollywood things – they're together ten years while he's doing whatever he did before *Maximum Kill*, then just before he gets successful they split. She was a writer – books mostly, but she also wrote his first film, *Chrysanthemum*. Went home to San Francisco. Pretty successful now in women's romance. I should be able to get an address easily enough."

"You think she'll know anything about Delores?"

"Who knows? But they got divorced, and there's no smoke without fire. Might be that Delores had been hanging around for long enough by then to be the cause."

They were silent for a while, drinking coffee, staring at the boats through the window.

Then Tim said: "You know what I can't figure? Why would Delores, who works only for GHQ, who was plucked from obscurity and made a star by them, commission a screenplay that could have potentially destroyed them?"

"Why bite the hand that feeds?"

"Yeah, exactly."

"I don't know.... Could be a 'hell hath no fury' thing. She hasn't made a movie for a while now. In fact I can't recall one since she and Starck split."

"She wrote it as revenge for not getting parts? That's a pretty extreme reaction."

"This is Hollywood, baby."

Chapter 29

The day Jeffery set out to kill Jocelyn, he spent a long time in front of his mirror getting ready. He wore a twill suit with wide shoulders and pegged pants. He wore a white shirt and a broad tie printed with a pattern of sailboats and autumn leaves. He combed his hair with Bay Rum. The .38 sat heavy under his arm. He had extra shells in his coat pocket.

When he was ready, he stood there, still. His sister had been out again last night, had gone to the motel on Lincoln Boulevard. He'd followed and he'd waited, but she stayed so long he left in the end. This morning, when she came home, saying she'd spent the night at a girlfriend's, he smelled her as she passed him.

The screenwriter. Danny Bartlemann.

Taking her from him.

And Ally going. Lying to him and going.

Last time she had not kept her affair secret. And she had ended it when he told her how unhappy it made him.

But now it was hidden, something private and precious that Ally was keeping for herself, that she was growing in the shadows of a cheap motel room. And if it grew too strong it would take her away from him and he would be anchorless and alone.

Jeffery was glad he had something else to do.

Since Michael had called them together and told them that the screenplay had made its way back into the world, Jeffery had taken several trips to the girl's apartment building, watched it from the Packard. The other woman was staying with her, he'd seen them entering the building together – Delores' personal assistant, the betrayer who'd started this thing. Convenient.

Tonight, the two women would drive to a decommissioned parking station on the corner of Wilshire and South Barrington Avenue. They'd go to the top floor and the assistant would watch while the girl was fucked by whatever group of men had congregated there.

Jeffery thought about wearing a hat. He wanted to. He wanted to, badly. But it was too conspicuous. So he went bareheaded into the night.

He drove the Packard to Nolan's restaurant on South Beverly Glen, had it valeted, went to the bar and ordered a gin and tonic which he didn't drink, then went back out onto the boulevard, walked a hundred yards, hailed a cab. He could have parked his car on any street far enough away from the parking lot not to be seen, of course. But the Packard was worth close to half a million dollars and he didn't want it tagged by some wandering teenage gang.

Jeffery didn't like walking around in Los Angeles, not out in wide busy spaces like Wilshire, it was too hard to continually reimagine them as he wanted them to be, denuded of high-rises, of concrete and steel buildings, cleansed of streamlined cars with satellite navigation devices. Too hard to age the place seventy years.

It was dark, the sky hazy with smog that threw back a pale orange luminescence. In the forties, Jeffery imagined, you would have still been able to see the moon and the stars. In the forties, the area he was walking through probably hadn't been incorporated into the City of Los Angeles. It would have been a strip of dives and flophouses and dark bars where dames and broads got stinko with hoods and cops on the take.

Now, it rose into the sky and its lights hurt his eyes, the air stank of exhaust and there was nothing of the clean fragrance that used to come down from the hills or roll up from the ocean at Santa Monica, salt-dusted and whispering of promise.

Jeffery moved quickly into the nine-story parking lot and worked his way to the top floor. The homeless on the lower levels didn't bother him, not when he had his gun. He kept far enough away from them, though, so that even if they spoke to the cops afterwards they wouldn't be able to provide a useful description.

On the top floor the fucking was in full swing. A mattress on the ground. The girl on her hands and knees, being spit-roasted by two men, three others waiting their turn. The assistant standing behind the open door of a blue Prius, a hand between her legs, the other inside her blouse.

Someone had brought a battery lamp and placed it beside the mattress. It threw long, jerking shadows across the dirty concrete floor, made the place look like some hellish farmyard scene. Jeffery waited back in the dark, unseen, hand around the butt of his pistol.

As the men finished, one by one, they climbed into their cars and drove away. When the last had gone, the girl rose gingerly from the mattress. The assistant came out from behind the Prius's door, lay back on the car's hood, lifted her skirt and began to masturbate harshly. The girl stayed were she was, caught in the light, dripping.

Jeffery scanned the floor. The two women, mattress, lamp, hybrid. No one else. He pulled the .38 from its holster and took the safety off. When the assistant started to come, he stepped out of the shadows and walked swiftly to the girl. The assistant's moans were loud in the hard concrete space and the girl didn't hear him approach.

He held his arm straight out, gun extended. Around him, in the dark air, the skin of Los Angeles peeled away, parted to let the other Los Angeles through – hosts of drape-jacketed, hat-wearing men, sassy women smoking and back-talking, moving like panthers in skin-tight gowns and sequins; cars the size of trucks, the strains of swing jazz, the smell of cigarettes and bourbon, and the soft, warm air of empty roads along the edge of the ocean.

And all of it black-and-white. All of them watching him, opening their arms, making space, making him part of them, taking him back, bestowing meaning, weaving him into the fabric of their own world.

Skye, jerking in orgasm, saw him then and lifted her other hand to point, to warn Jocelyn of what approached. And Jocelyn saw and started to turn, but Jeffery was already there and he pulled the trigger and shot her in the side of the head.

Blood in a mist, then in an arc, like a black rope through the air. The sound of it hitting the dusty concrete, thick and heavy and wet. Jocelyn staggering sideways, like she'd lost her balance, then twisting and collapsing, hitting first with her knees and then falling forward, onto her face, arms outstretched and the blood still pouring from her.

On the hood of the car, Skye lay with the fingers of one hand frozen inside her.

Maybe if she hadn't come, if she hadn't had those split seconds with her head swimming and her legs lax, she might have had time to get away. Maybe if she hadn't met Jeffery while working as Delores' personal assistant she wouldn't have hesitated, trying to understand: the murder of her lover, one of the owners of GHQ....

She was only just beginning to roll off the hood when Jeffery used up the rest of his bullets – two between the shoulders, one in the neck, one in the back of the head.

A lot of noise. Bang, bang, bang, bang. Echoes bouncing off concrete. But outside the building, nothing more than incidental counterpoints to an unremarkable L.A. night.

Jeffery inspected the women and marveled. Though no one but he would know it, they had given him a place in the city. They would be found, there would be newspaper stories – murder and sex, hooks in the public consciousness. The mystery would remain unsolved, would be puzzled over and talked about when people discussed the real L.A., when they sat around tables smoking and drinking, trying to figure out what L.A. really meant.

The girl's apartment. Risky but necessary. Before she was fired, the assistant had lived in a pool house on Delores' property. Michael had seen that it was properly cleared, that no trace of the screenplay remained to be found. Same as he'd removed everything screenplay-related from the first screenwriter's apartment two years ago. Now Jeffery had the same task. Not really too difficult as he'd taken the keys from a handbag he found in the Prius. Be discrete, wear gloves, pick the right moment.

The apartment was sparsely furnished. It made things quicker. An open suitcase of clothes on the bedroom floor, too many toiletries and cosmetics in the bathroom. He found two laptops. He found a pile of loose pages – a work in progress, the *Wilderness* screenplay with different character names. On the first page a handwritten note: *'I've trimmed the dialogue and taken out a couple of unnecessary scenes. See what you think. Tim.*' On many of the other pages notes, excisions, changes marked in blue pencil.

Good to get the pages. Not good to find that someone else had read them.

Jeffery found a laundry bag, took the pages and the laptops, went back to Nolan's and got his Packard. On his way home he stopped beside Stone Canyon Reservoir and threw the laptops into the water. He kept the screenplay pages – Michael would have to figure out what to do about 'Tim'.

Ally walked among the ruins of Raintree. The collapsed center was ribbed with cross-sectioned floors, rooms cut in half and exposed. The furniture was long gone, of course, but she could place exactly where in the house various incidents with her grandfather had occurred – the billiard room, the library, their bedrooms, his bedroom....

It was night and she was alone, having come here hoping that the horrors the place held might send her spinning on some new trajectory of self-preservation, might be converted into a justification for selfishness. She wanted to be gone, to leave her past, to leave the houses and the money, to leave Hollywood. To leave Jeffery and his unseverable ties to the past. To leave the atrocities she had committed in the name of survival. To go with Danny and, like some plane-crash amnesiac, build a life from scratch, with no memories, no brother to worry about and keep safe.

He was out now, killing the people Michael wanted killed. He would come back safely. She felt it. But how long would that last? The killing tonight would unleash a desire for more. And more killing would, at some point, lead to his capture. And his capture would be her destruction as well as his. The rapes, Bartlemann, the screenwriter...all of it would be exposed.

To be safe. To be free. One sure solution. But not yet. Not while there was still one more thing to try.

The Ritual of Freeing. The First. Another death, but one that might fix Jeffery, that might be the psychic peg that held him in place long enough for her to escape to a new life with Danny.

She didn't believe it. But Jeffery was her brother, her twin. They shared things most other humans only ever read about in news reports. They were two halves of one cancerous whole and however sick he was, however much of a threat he was, she could not abandon him while there was still a chance.

Up here, in the Malibu hills, she could pretend Los Angeles didn't exist, could run farm-girl scenarios of what it must be like living in Danny's cabin up at Los Padres. It was late now and the cicadas had stopped. There were clouds in the sky, a smell of trees and dry grass, the dry grass rustling under a hot wind.

She went down to the basement, unlocked the door to the screening room. She moved about, touching the seats, the walls, breathing the faint smells of sweat and fear and sex. How many women? She'd never bothered to keep count.

CHAPTER 30

Michael, putting down the phone from freak-boy Jeffery. The killing done, at least. No pursuing phalanxes of black-and-whites, no screaming choirs of sirens gathering in Beverly Hills. Two silly women who didn't know what they were playing with, removed.

Should have been an end to it. Status quo restored. Except that someone called Tim had read the screenplay pages, had read them with enough attention to make notes.

Delores had said Sean had supplied the information, that he'd seen the girl read pages at some writers' group. That he'd learned of it by chance. Michael didn't believe it. Sean had shouted the warning and probably wasn't out to make trouble. But he hadn't told the whole of the truth.

Someone else was involved, someone named Tim. Delores didn't know about him. She would have said if she did – not to do so would have made the deaths of the women pointless.

But Sean knew. Michael was sure of it.

At least two more people to deal with now, both of them men – Sean, to find out who Tim was, and maybe in the process eliminate as well; and Tim himself, whoever *he* turned out to be. Not something he could delegate to Jeffery. Too much planning, too much investigation. Not something Michael wanted to do alone, either. Not when there were two men involved. Not when Tim was an unknown quantity.

In the study, in his Beverly Hills house, Michael unlocked the cupboard where he kept his weapons. A rich filmmaker, famous for putting firepower on film, connections with armorers, productions in Southeast Asian countries – it hadn't been hard to build a small collection. Assorted handguns, half a dozen assault rifles, a McMillan Tac-50 sniper's rifle, a tactical longbow.... It gave him comfort to look at them, but he knew things were escalating, expanding beyond a point where he felt competent to protect himself and his company. Expanding to a point where he needed help.

He closed the cupboard and thought about Delores, cause of this current shitstorm. He dared himself to imagine what his world would be like without her in it. Funny thing, it wasn't that hard.

Pacific Palisades. Theo Portman's white stone mansion, styled like some European country house – Tudor arches, stained glass, slate roof, castellated parapets. But back from the road. Way back. Big money, but quiet. Like Theo had always been, even in the porn days, strings in his hands, but a gray curtain between himself and the world.

They were bonded. Theo owned Big Glass, Big Glass distributed all GHQ product. An exclusive agreement, locked in from *Maximum Kill* onwards. But the ties went deeper, went back to Scott Bartlemann. Back further, to the desert.

Theo Portman was a big guy in his mid-sixties. When he'd run Sunnico, his long defunct porn company, he'd been sixty pounds lighter and considerably less polished. Now, his hair was white and the pale linen suits he wore in summer, though beautifully tailored, could not hide his body's creeping expansion.

He had become an anglophile, cementing over rough, east coast origins with what Hollywood thought of as class. He collected manuscripts and first editions, he hung his walls with seventeenth-century hand-drawn maps of the British Isles. He had a suit of armor in his entrance hall.

But neither the fat, nor the Anglo-affectations did anything to alter the fact that he was still a very dangerous man. At least not for Michael, who knew him better than most.

They shared a Hollywood genesis. *Maximum Kill* had made them both; Michael as a director/producer, Theo as an independent distributor. Their relationship was based not on friendship, but on the utility they had afforded each other in the past, on the checks and balances required to keep level the scales of a shared but beneficial guilt. They saw each other rarely, and only then on matters of business.

A library on the first floor, like the inside of a church. Stone walls, arched windows, books and wood and sun-warmed silence. Theo sat in a leather wing-back chair, a book of Medieval illuminations on his knee, a Malamute curled beside him. Michael stayed standing, moving around the room as he spoke, inspecting curios, books, a case of pinned butterflies.... Apprising Theo of the *Wilderness* resurgence, of the steps he had already taken.

Theo fondled his dog's ears and followed Michael with his eyes, wondering exactly how whipped you had to be before you did something about it. This Australian asshole swallowed people whole in his business life, but couldn't do something as simple as breaking an attachment to a Mexican bitch who cared nothing for him. And here it was again, more of the same, more cleaning-up because some emotional disease had prevented Michael from blowing her head off on the two previous occasions when it had been so clearly mandated.

Michael's twanging accent cut through the sun-soaked air; matter of fact, no trace of obsequiousness or begging. The one thing Theo liked about him – his sense of entitlement, the expectation that things would conform to his will.

"....we track Sean down, make him tell how he really found out about the screenplay, who this Tim person is. We remove Tim, it should fix things."

"Except for Sean. Except for Delores."

"I don't think Sean's a problem in himself. Without him we might not have known about the situation until it was too late. Pointless incurring more risk if we don't need to."

"It would be much cleaner, though, Michael. It really wouldn't do for him to become another Delores in a few years' time."

"It's not Delores' fault if her assistant turns out to be a thief."

"Ask yourself why she kept a copy of the screenplay."

"You're insulated, Theo. There's nothing linking you to any of this. Bartlemann, the screenwriter, the women Jeffery just did, nothing. Let me deal with things my way."

"But to do things your way, you need my help."

"You made ten million dollars off *Maximum Kill*. My pictures since have earned you more than a hundred million. This is just the cost of doing business. I've already taken care of the women, but this is getting beyond what I can keep a handle on. We've got to track down Sean — a guy who went off the grid two years ago — and we've got to make him tell us about this Tim guy, and then we've got to find him and kill him. And I've still got a business to run. I need Christo."

"Christo has his own business concerns. It may take several days for him to get away."

"But you'll bring him up?"

"I'll bring him up. But I want this thing dead, Michael. I want this to be the last time. That means Sean goes. At the very least."

Michael shrugged.

"If that's what it takes."

"At the very least."

In his Maserati, on the way back to the office, Michael thought about his relationship with Theo. About how Theo and Christo had saved his life that night with Kid on the edge of the desert. How Theo had cashed in this sandy debt by pointing Michael at Scott Bartlemann, skillfully leveraging Michael's own self-interest to get rid of a business partner he despised. How, despite his own misgivings, he'd shown Michael that Delores could be saved, that there was a woman Christo could snatch....

And he thought, too, of the thing that Theo did not know, the spool of film that Kid had shot out in the forest. He'd burned it, but if Theo ever found out, or if there was a copy that was yet to surface, Theo's own instinct for self-preservation would set Christo on a far less helpful course.

Today, his directive had been clear — clean up the loose ends. Kill Sean, kill Tim. Make the fat man happy and kill Delores too.

Michael had caved to Sean, what did he care? Hadn't caved to Delores. Not yet.... A clear stretch opened up on Wilshire, Michael put his foot down and let the engine howl.

Chapter 31

Hollywood time again. Go mix with the movers and shakers. One of the perks, the mark by which you are known. Lunch with Jeffery and Ally at one of their houses. An address in the Malibu hills that they'd been insistent about her not mentioning to anyone – privacy, and all that.

Blast the Thrux over unpaved trails, a little off-road experience, happy to get dusted, for it to cling to the sweating creases of her catsuit, another unspoken fuck-you to these entrenched assholes.

The place was wild. Some huge mansion with its guts burned out. Miles from anywhere. Chick rode around back, as Ally had instructed, found an open graveled area and a row of trees. A table with food standing in the shade.

In the wall of the house there was an open garage door. Inside the garage: a vintage Packard and a classic Mercedes coupe from the 1960s.

As she climbed off her bike she got a call on her cell – Kid, wanting her okay on the number of Panavision lenses the cameraman had ordered. Kid read through the list, Chick vetoed half of them.

"I already told him I want to keep it real, man. Like you're there, in the film, not half a mile back at the end of a fucking telephoto. Maybe we should look at someone else."

They chatted for a moment about possible replacements. As they were about to hang up Kid asked, without really caring, what she was doing. Chick, disinclined to obey Ally's request for discretion, told him about her lunch date.

Kid would have screamed down the phone for her to get out, to get on her bike and come back to the office, would have used any excuse. But Ally and Jeffery chose that moment to come through a door at the back of the garage and walk out into the sun, all smiles and welcome, and before Kid could speak, Chick killed the call. When her phone rang again she didn't answer. What Jeffery and Ally stood for disgusted her, but there was no point in being rude. Not to their faces. Not until *Antepenultimate* was in the can.

The three of them sat at the table, Chick digging the Addams Family vibe of the burnt house behind them, digging the isolation. Like going out to the forest to see Danny, a change from the daily Los Angeles headfuck.

No servants, a hamper from Hatfield's. Ally served. French-Californian – date and mint crusted lamb, guinea hen, Tasmanian ocean trout. Food Chick hadn't tasted before. Sauvignon Blanc, a wine she had. Jeffery and Ally didn't drink, Chick's glass was always full.

They talked about *Antepenultimate*, about progress toward a principal photography go-date. The film in pre-prod now, cast and crew finalized, locations halfway locked down, wardrobe firing up, transport and equipment being bargained for, a line producer working up a preliminary shooting schedule, hampered by the incomplete location list....

Exciting for Chick. The stuff dreams are made of. Boring for Jeffery and Ally, done a score of times before, bigger, better, and with a far larger budget for pyrotechnics.

The talk drifted to gossip, to industry reshufflings and financial realignments, areas in which Chick was adrift. Ally kept up the patter, a smokescreen of words. Jeffery sat tense and expectant, seeing in his head a rainstorm of blood, a whirlwind of sexual savagery. He made pointless comments, spoke in non sequiturs, torn between visions of Oscar-raping this girl to death and a mounting desire to stand up and scream into Ally's face that he knew about Danny Bartlemann.

Chick had pegged him as a psycho the first time they met and, after trying to fathom a couple of his comments, largely tuned him out. She noticed Ally's eyes lingering on her crotch, drifting over the partially unzipped bodice of her catsuit. She gave it back, figuring another A-list roll in the hay. But Ally crossed her legs and turned side-on and began another anecdote about some bullshit mind-rotting piece of crap she'd made.

A few minutes later Jeffery stood up while Chick was still eating, face bright, lips drawn back in something that was meant to be a smile, all sudden enthusiasm and excitement.

"Hey, you know what? We should show Chick the screening room."

Chick, interrupted mid-mouthful, made a note to find this fucker's car some-day and set it on fire.

Ally reached for the wine bottle now and filled her water glass with Sav, knocked it back in four quick swallows and stood abruptly.

"Jeffery's right. This estate was built in nineteen-sixteen. The house burned down more than twenty years ago, but part of the basement survived. The screen-ing room is really worth seeing."

Chick was just beginning to stand when Kid's yellow Camaro rocketed around the far end of the house and slid to a stop near her bike.

Jeffery snatched a glass from the table and hurled it at the wall of the house. It smashed with such force that small pieces of glass flew back and fell into the food. He stalked into the garage and stood in the shadows. Chick thinking, there goes a dude who needs some sedation.

And Kid climbing out of his car, a tight anxiety draining from his face as he took in Chick still alive and breathing.

Ally looked at the glass-sprinkled food for a moment, then said to Chick: "I liked the lamb, didn't you?"

She took Chick by the hand and led her into the garage. Kid followed. Jeffery was standing by the door in the rear wall, back under control, resigned to joining in the game that everyone but Chick knew was being played.

There were stairs on the other side of the door, leading to the basement. On the way down, Kid made noises like he and Chick had to leave, like there were things at the office they just had to go through.

But if Jeffery and Ally couldn't enact the ultimate instance of the Ritual of Freeing that day, they were at least going to toy with their prey a little. Ally took Kid's arm and said she wouldn't hear of them leaving so soon, not when Chick hadn't seen the screening room.

Kid wanted to wrench his arm away, bundle Chick into his car and get gone. But he was vulnerable. Puncture this charade and Jeffery and Ally might feel the need to explain to Chick the details of how she was abducted from her mother's store. And then go ahead and kill her anyway. He knew Jeffery often carried a gun.

At the bottom of the stairs. A long corridor. Jeffery led them along it, past a couple of doors to another one at the end – soundproofed. As Jeffery swung it open Kid tensed, figuring if they'd set up the rape bench already Chick was going to freak.

But when the door was open and they were in the room, Kid saw that the space in front of the screen was empty. And immediately thought, maybe not such a great thing after all. Probably meant that their fucking ritual had escalated, that what Jeffery and Ally had planned to do there that day involved something beginning with M.

The lugs for the feet of the bench, embedded in concrete beneath the carpet, were still visible, however. Kid saw Chick eyeing them, saw her turn her head, back and forth, as though trying to catch some scent in the air. But after a moment she spun in a circle and said:

"The projector still work? You still watch films here?"

Ally nodded. "Oh, yes. We've got quite a library."

"Oh, man, fucking celluloid. Thirty-five millimeter. The way movies were meant to be seen. No dried out digital files, no digital fucking projection."

Chick flopped onto one of the two-seater leather couches.

"They shoot movies specifically for 3D and IMAX now. It's all about the fucking delivery system. Five years from now they'll be shooting twenty-minute movies because that's what Apple will have decided the optimum viewing time on an iPad is."

Ally laughed a little, but not like she really cared.

"It's a business, Chick. We make what the people want."

"They don't *want* your shit. They don't want a 3D *Titanic*, they don't want *Clash of the Titans*, they don't want two hours of explosions and killing and vacuous special effects every single fucking time they watch a movie. They just think they do, because movies like that are like crack for the senses. They over-stimulate the surface, but they don't nourish anything underneath. And you've fed them to people for so long that they've become hooked on sensory stimulation. They've forgotten that they're actually human beings, they've forgotten that they used to give a shit about what other human beings did and felt and thought."

Kid looked at the twins to see how they'd taken this insult to their genre. Ally was cleaning something from beneath the nail of her index finger. Jeffery, in his forties suit, had a dreamy look on his face. Kid figured he was running *The Big Sleep* in his head, maybe thinking Chick wasn't all that wrong.

Chick, having vented, started to fidget, wanting to get back on her bike and get back to work and build a film that would show these fuckers what the future of cinema ought to be.

"I'm shooting *Ante* on thirty-five. We should screen it here when it's done."

Jeffery smiled, broke out of his reverie.

"You know, maybe we should!" Then, "I've got something else to show you."

They went back along the corridor to one of the doors they'd passed before and Jeffery ushered Chick into a room where the twins stored mementos of the movies they'd produced.

The walls were hung with promotional posters, signed pictures of actors, a series of photos taken on various sets. Along one wall there were shelves that held small props – handgun replicas, light fittings, costume jewelry, a few items of wardrobe, a selection of children's toys, a clock, a pair of shoes....

Chick cast a professional eye over it. Tools of the trade – so what?

Then Jeffery, mischievous psycho-child that he was, drew her attention to a display case fixed to the wall at the end of the room. He took her hand and pulled her close, pressing his finger to the glass as he pointed.

"Something a little special. Do you know much about Errol Flynn?"

And Chick, spying a gold lapel badge that bore the initials FFF and that had a buttonhole pin styled in the shape of a penis, breathed: "Flynn's Flying Fuckers...."

"Yes, indeed. Perhaps the most rarefied of all Hollywood memorabilia. We bought that one off an ex-child star who worked with Flynn on *Gunga Din*. There must have been quite a number more – Flynn's erotomania, like misery, required company. We haven't been able to find them, though."

"And this?" Chick pointed to a ship's flag which displayed the same FFF legend and covered the back of the case.

"From Flynn's yacht, Zaca. He'd fly it, apparently, when sailing into port. The girls would line up on the dock."

Jeffery pointed out other items, all with the FFF logo – a handkerchief, two cigarette lighters, a penknife and a pair of boxer shorts.

"I want to think the shorts were Flynn's, but there's no way of knowing. They're about the right size."

Jeffery lingered on the last word. Chick rolled her eyes.

"Please don't tell me about how he used to play '*You Are My Sunshine*' on the piano with his knob."

"Hard to separate the man from the legend. There aren't many people who, when they hear the name Errol Flynn, don't immediately think: 'twelve inches'."

"Jesus...."

"He was a man obsessed with penises. Did you know that he once commissioned a statuette—" And here, Kid saw him flick a look at Ally, a barely suppressed smile. "—of Oscar. The Academy Award trophy. He was nominated in 1957, toward the end of his life, for *The Sun Also Rises*, but the nomination was withdrawn for some reason. His revenge was to have a statuette made for himself, only in true Flynn style this one had—"

"A dick."

"A hardon, to be precise."

"The hardon Oscar."

"You know about it? It isn't mentioned in any of his biographies. We only learned of it from our grandfather. He knew David Niven, Flynn's friend."

"My mother owned a movie memorabilia shop. She had the Oscar. She bought it off a Parisian dealer who got into Sean Flynn's flat after he went missing in Cambodia. Errol had left it to his son."

Jeffery put his hand to his mouth and looked wide-eyed at Ally.

"Oh my God. Tell me you still have it. Please!"

"No, it was stolen. A long time ago."

Jeffery tired of the game abruptly. He turned and looked hard at Kid, and Kid saw in his eyes the weighing of opportunity, the calculation of outcomes – pull gun, shoot Kid, overpower Chick. Kid saw the thoughts ticking off. But Jeffery was not a strong man and Kid was ready for him, waiting for him to make a move.

In the end Jeffery deflated, declared that he had to go back to Bel Air to sleep. He pushed past Kid and left the room. A moment later Ally, and then Kid, headed out into the corridor and back up to the garage. But Chick lingered in front of the display case.

Flynn's Flying Fuckers memorabilia. How many people even knew about it, let alone had a collection of it? It was possible, of course, that the man who abducted her stole the hardon Oscar simply because he thought it looked cool, that he had no idea at all of its connection to Errol Flynn. But it was also possible that he, or someone else involved in her rape, did. And that it was taken to add to a collection.

She'd been raped by two people. The movie soundtrack had masked what little they'd said, but she'd been able to tell one of the voices was female. Jeffery and Ally? An insane notion. Two super successful filmmakers abducting a girl and raping her?

But Jeffery was patently a freak, and Ally was so battened down anything could be lurking under that anemic facade. And, this *was* Hollywood.

Still, ridiculous. And anyway, in the second or two before she'd lost consciousness out back of her mother's memorabilia store the night she was taken, she'd seen the blurred outline of her abductor, and she remembered him as a man larger and more robust than skinny-ass Jeffery.

Unless.... Unless they'd paid someone to do the abducting.

Chick would have stopped herself there. She had too much going on with *Antepenultimate* to divert her energies into speculation about something that had happened to her twelve years ago. She would have stopped, but there was something else.

In Tim's screenplay, some murder thing about Hollywood, there were two characters who were brother and sister. Brother and sister were part owners of a film production company. And Flynn's Flying Fuckers memorabilia was mentioned. Just a couple of lines. Just a daub of scene description. Nothing, really.

But Jeffery and Ally were brother and sister.

And they had a case of Flynn's Flying Fuckers memorabilia.

How could Tim have known?

Chick stepped out into the hallway and walked back to the screening room. She stood in the area of open floor between the screen and the rows of couches.

She closed her eyes. Had it been here? It was a room that could certainly have produced the soundtrack to her ordeal.

It was only as she was leaving that she remembered Delores Fuentes' torn pussy. If, by some insane chance Jeffery and Ally had raped her too, then Chick was not the only one who had spent time in that screening room, listening to action movie segments as the Oscar's metal cock left its mark on her.

CHAPTER 32

Telegraph Hill, San Francisco. Nancy Epps, formerly Nancy Starck, owned a modern two-story wooden house at the top of Kearny Street, right at the edge of Pioneer Park. Tim and Denning had made the drive in a little over six hours. They'd both taken 40mg of OxyContin to smooth out the car aches and the drive hadn't been too much of a chore.

Denning had spun his usual story, backed it up with his out-of-date press card. Tim posing as photographer, carrying a camera Denning had lent him.

The room Nancy received them in was all about her and the books she wrote. There were marketing posters on the walls, shelves of her romance novels, various formats, various translations. There were several award statuettes and a number of photos showing Nancy receiving them.

Nancy was an attractive woman in her late forties, she had coiffed blond hair and she wore expensive jewelry. She was no Barbara Taylor Bradford in terms of sales, but she was doing okay for herself.

Denning's spiel was that he wanted to explore the life experiences that had shaped the author, a cover that necessitated an hour of playacting – Denning scribbling notes on his pad, Tim looking attentive – during which Nancy held forth on the farm in Nebraska where she'd spent her childhood, the formative role her parents had played in her literary career, her relocation to California in her twenties and the burning desire to write that she never lost, even during the years in Los Angeles. Eventually, she got round to Michael Starck.

She'd divorced him more than ten years ago, during the making of *Maximum Kill*. When she spoke about him, her tone was dismissive.

Denning played it cool, like it was just one more event in her life story.

"So, the divorce, was it a difficult decision?"

"Some relationships don't have legs, ours was one of them. We'd been together fifteen years, we were too young when we married. Michael was a very focused individual. In the early days it was fun; his drive, his need to succeed. But after he started GHQ it wasn't fun anymore. He used to talk about art, about creativity. Once the company got going, though, that went out the window and nothing mattered except becoming powerful and famous."

"Not what you wanted?"

"I felt stifled. The first thing they did was a film called *Chrysanthemum*. I wrote the screenplay, but really, as far as the production went, I was nothing more than an unpaid personal assistant to Michael, expected to lay down everything and dedicate myself to the great god GHQ."

"So...alienation, drifting apart, the pressure of Michael's work, the loss of your own identity...." Denning made more notes.

"All of the above. The fact that he started fucking Scott Bartlemann's maid during *Maximum Kill* didn't help either."

Denning's pen stopped moving. He leaned forward in his chair.

Nancy took it as a sign that she was being especially interesting and explained: "Scott Bartlemann was the owner of the distribution company that was going to distribute *Maximum Kill* when it was finished."

"The guy who was murdered. I remember."

"Yes, shot in his weekender or something like that."

"The maid did it, then killed herself."

"Maria. I could say it was a terrible shame. But when another woman is one of the reasons your marriage fails, your sympathies become a little...diluted."

"Do you mind speaking about the affair?"

Nancy made a face like it didn't matter to her.

"It was like any other affair, I suppose. He met her at Scott's house when he was there on film business. She was Mexican, an illegal, not long in the country.

That she happened to be sweeping floors for his distributor was pure coincidence. Michael fell in love. Deeply, passionately, the kind of love where you go a little bit insane. A love, I realized, that he never felt for me. I didn't know it at the time, but Michael has a *type*. I wasn't it, she was. To a tee."

"A type?"

"Feisty, Mexican, hot body. Look who he hooked up with after Maria, once he'd become famous – Delores Fuentes. She and Maria could have come from the same mold."

"Did you ever meet Maria?"

"Once. I walked in on them in bed together."

Denning nodded seriously.

"Must have been tough."

"It was. But without that kick in the pants I wouldn't have this." Nancy gestured at the posters and the awards.

"Michael must have been broken up, when Maria killed herself."

"I was long gone by then, but I spoke to him on the phone after it happened and he really didn't seem that affected by it. Seemed strange to me, but then Michael is Michael – he doesn't waste energy on things which can't benefit him, like grief or guilt. Maybe he'd already met Delores Fuentes by then. Who knows?"

"I did a piece on the killing when it happened. Not much is known about the maid. She was an undocumented illegal. It's not part of this article, but I wonder, is there anything else you could tell me about her?"

Nancy seemed a little miffed that the spotlight was drifting from her, but she did her best to hide it.

"Mexican, early thirties, attractive, great body. What else can I say? I didn't ask her her life story."

"I don't remember ever seeing Michael linked with the maid, in the press or anything."

"He wasn't. Michael kept the affair very quiet. I was the only one who knew. Even Scott Bartlemann didn't have any idea. And when she killed herself, Michael certainly didn't say anything to anyone. It was a very important time for him. *Maximum Kill* was heading to market. He didn't want that kind of publicity around himself. He asked me not to say anything, and I didn't. I don't suppose it matters now, ten years later."

Remembering Michael had obviously brought old resentments to the surface and Nancy said this with a certain relish, as though, even if it did matter, she didn't care.

Denning focused on her again for appearances' sake, asking about the experience of establishing herself as a successful novelist, life in San Francisco....

Ten minutes later, after Tim had photographed Nancy and her awards, they called it a day and headed for the door. Nancy opened it for them, courteously showing them out, pleased with the attention, with the free publicity.

Denning paused to thank her for the interview.

"It must be sweet revenge to have become so successful through your writing. What does Michael think about it?"

Nancy looked like she was going to burst out laughing.

"Michael? I don't expect he's thought about it at all. It would be next to meaningless to him."

"I guess you can get pretty dissociated when you're that successful."

"And he's nothing if not successful. No mean achievement for a poor boy from Australia who learnt his craft in the San Fernando Valley."

Denning frowned. "Michael directed porn?"

"Oh, yes. He doesn't like people to know it, but before *Chrysanthemum* and *Maximum Kill*, that's what did. Even had a porn pseudonym – always thinking of the future was Michael – Brett Adelaide, after his home town. He was considered quite the flesh maestro.

A truck stop an hour out of San Francisco on I-5. Burgers, Coke, fries. Fueling up for the long haul back to Los Angeles. Denning and Tim sat at a table sunk into a concrete slab out front. Diesel fumes, air-brakes, huge engines left idling, rattling the late afternoon air while men with beer guts and heavy metal T-shirts drank coffee, smoked and ate grease.

Tim, still trying to reduce the amount of trash he put into himself, had considered a healthier option. But a salad and some tuna wasn't the kind of food a sane man chose when he still had five hours of road ahead of him. Plus, they'd both taken another 40mg for the homeward drive, so what did it matter?

Denning looked morose, disappointed, anxious to get back to Los Angeles and have the fucking day over with.

Tim started the debrief: "So the maid and Michael – no one saw that coming. You could figure it kind of fucks the whole GHQ-killing-Scott-Bartlemann thing, at least how the screenplay portrays it. If Michael was in love with the maid, it's hardly likely they would have killed her."

Denning, not wanting to let go of the theory, said: "On the other hand, a connection like that with the maid does put Michael and GHQ closer to Bartlemann. Easier for them to know when he'd be alone, to get access to the house."

"Still...."

"I know. It's not great. But it's only Nancy saying he was in love with the maid. And she also said he didn't seem that affected by her death. Maybe she was wrong on the first count. It didn't take him long to start up with Delores, after all."

"Be good if we could find out more about this maid."

"I tried when I covered the killing. No one knew who she was. She'd only worked for Bartlemann for six months and she wasn't close to any of the other help. She didn't have any friends or relatives who could be traced because there was no paper on her. Bartlemann's personal assistant, who did the hiring and firing of domestic staff, had her down as Maria Morales. But it turned out the social security number she'd given was false. There weren't even any photos of her. And they couldn't take one post-mortem to show around because she didn't have a head."

"I can get to Danny Bartlemann through Chick. He told me he ID'd the maid's body. Won't hurt if I talk to him again."

"ID'd how?"

"I don't know, but that's what he said."

"I don't think the maid's got much to do with anything. Michael was fucking her, she happened to be out there when they offed Bartlemann, they had to get rid of her. End of story. What we need is some sort of previous connection between Michael Starck/GHQ and Theo Portman, because that's about the only way I can see GHQ knowing *Maximum Kill* was going to be shelved."

Tim smiled, leaned back, laced his fingers and stretched his arms.

"Well, you're going to love this. Nancy told us Michael used to direct porn vids, right?"

"Yeah. And Tyler told us that Theo Portman ran a porn company. It's close, but it's not a connection. Starck could have worked for any of a hundred outfits."

"Except that Tyler told us Portman's company was called Sunnico. And Nancy just told us Michael used to call himself Brett Adelaide."

"So?"

"So, in Kid Haldane's office there are a bunch of posters for the skin flicks he did—"

"Yeah, I've seen them."

"Read the credits at the bottom?"

"No."

"I did. Guess what they say. *'Produced by Sunnico, directed by Brett Adelaide'*. Michael Starck used to work for Theo Portman."

Denning's mouth opened. For a moment he just stared at Tim, then he punched the air and shouted:

"Fuck, yeah!"

Across the tarmac of the parking lot, a trucker climbing into his cab turned to look in their direction.

Flat land. Dry scrub, dusty soil, rainfall down by thirty percent in this part of the golden state. Long, desiccated swathes of agriculturally modified landscape, uniform rows of low, parched trees, trees bled dry for oranges, for soft fruit, for olives, trees that looked like they were in pain.

Bare land, rutted and gouged, crumbling without moisture to hold it together, sandy grains separating, moving away from each other. And off to the right, low hills, like the backs of whales, dark in the dusk, outlined by the dying light in the west. On and on. Mile after mile. To the left, vast plains, swallowed in shadow, their margins sandy white; a ghost land lit by the peripheral glow of passing headlights.

Business done, talked to death. Denning at the wheel, Tim beside him. Two men in a small steel box, mildly bombed on OxyContin, lulled by the soft hypnosis of the road. Miles rolling beneath the wheels, headlights oncoming, exploding as they passed, and the red lights of the cars ahead, small beacons, fellow travelers, more men in steel boxes with their own mysteries and dreams and sorrows.

And in the silence of the car, in the warm air between the men – now that there was nothing more to say about Michael and GHQ – the other thing they shared. The thing that had made some deep and essential part of them forever lonely, that had set them at a distance from other men. A distance that could never be traveled back over, or reeled in, or made to be small.

Peta and Rebecca. Daughter and sister. Names and relationships that had changed meaning. No longer markers for lists of childhood events, for bedtime stories and games of hide and seek. No longer anchor points for memories of sibling adventures, shared playtimes, birthdays and Christmases.

Peta. Rebecca. Names to hold in your arms, to throw your weight on, to pin to the sheets and empty yourself into. Names to long for through sweating, hardon plagued nights.

Fully dark now, three hours in. Denning shifted in his seat, spoke almost to himself.

"Do you ever wish you hadn't done it?"

"Rebecca?" Tim watched half a mile of road unreel before he answered. "No. I was in love with her. To me, it felt preordained."

Denning nodded and didn't say anything. Tim looked at him.

"You?"

"It's an impossible situation. You've got something, but you haven't. She's an adult, she's willing, it's consensual, but the world won't allow it and you have to spend your whole life hiding it." Denning clicked his indicator and overtook a Winnebago. "Peta and I are done. She's with Kid Haldane now. And that's...good. But I look at those years and I think they could have been so much more, for both of us. Especially her.

"You say it felt preordained with your sister. I get that. With Peta, the best way I can describe it is that it was transcendent. In the sense that you enter this universe that's always been there but which, normally, you'd never have access to. It's a huge thing, being given that. Here's this person, this woman, who you know so completely because she's half your DNA to start with, and you've spent all of her life guiding her and loving her and you're so much a part of her, literally, in the way she acts, the way she behaves, her sense of right and wrong, who she is. But you only know her that one way. When you look at her, you only see that one side of her. And then to have her naked, underneath you, to have her kissing you and holding you and *wanting* you to be there – then she becomes this whole other person. But it's not like this new person replaces the old one, it's like she's two people now, like this whole side of her that only her lovers would normally ever have seen is yours now as well."

Denning rubbed his hand over his face. He was silent for a long time, and then he spoke again.

"One minute everything's normal, the next we're thinking about each other's bodies and what we're going to do in bed. At the time it's so overwhelming it carries you along like a whirlwind. But afterwards, you realize you've lost something. You're not Daddy anymore. And she's not your daughter, not like she used to be. And you can never get that back. Even when the sex is finished, you can never make it not have happened."

Tim looked out the side window – black glass, black country beyond. Light from the dash making a dim reflection of his face. Unlike Denning, the only incest-related pain he felt was the pain of not being able to sleep with his sister anymore.

Chapter 33

Thunder in the alley. 865cc of chrome steel and red and white paint. Then boots on the stairs and someone pounding on the kitchen door. Tim waking groggily from a post-San Francisco sleep, wondering what the time was, what the fucking noise was all about.

In the kitchen, track pants and a t-shirt, thinking he needed another three hours and a gallon of coffee. Chick slammed in, dropped her gloves and helmet on the table and stood there, eyes narrowed.

"Flynn's Flying Fuckers."

"Okay...."

"Don't fucking 'okay' me, Timbo. You put that shit in your script. A brother and sister, film producers, who have a case of the stuff. And then I go to Jeffery and Ally Bannister's place for some bullshit lunch and they show me *their* collection. And they're fucking twins!"

Tim felt blurred and vaguely nauseous from the OxyContin he'd done the day before. He was glad of it, though. Glad of his tiredness and his just-woken disorientation. Admitting to Chick that he'd lied was something more easily done with a little cognitive distance.

"I didn't write the screenplay."

"Oh?" Chick slid into a seat at the table and pointed for him to sit opposite. "This is going to be interesting."

"My sister wrote it."

"You have a sister?"

"Had."

Tim spent the next twenty minutes talking about Rebecca, about her screen-writing success, about how he found the *Wilderness* screenplay and passed it off as his own in an attempt to impress Chick. When he told her that Rebecca had been murdered outside a village called Mule Ridge, near Devore in the San Gabriels, Chick interrupted.

"I know Mule Ridge."

"Oh, yeah?"

"Yeah, it was one of the locations we considered for *Loggers*."

Tim carried on, told her that Rebecca had been writing the screenplay for Delores Fuentes and that he suspected it was based on a real-life killing. And that the people responsible for that killing may also have been responsible for his sis-ter's murder.

"What real-life killing?"

"Scott Bartlemann. Danny's father."

"Danny's father? You're shitting me!"

Tim shook his head and outlined the kill for her, told her how the cops thought it went down, pointed out how the screenplay had a different take on it.

She thought for a couple of seconds, then started ticking off points.

"The brother and sister in the screenplay have a collection of Flynn's Flying Fuckers stuff. Jeffery and Ally have a similar collection. Jeffery and Ally are the brother and sister. Which makes the third guy in the script, the boss-man, Michael Starck. You're saying GHQ killed Scott Bartlemann. And then, later, your sister, because she wrote the screenplay and the screenplay could expose them."

"That's how it looks."

"Are you going to tell Danny?"

"Later, maybe. Not now. I want to be a hundred percent sure – he doesn't look like a guy who'd keep quiet about that kind of news."

"How did you find all of this out?"

So, then Tim had to tell her about Denning, how they'd met, that GHQ had destroyed his career, about the various investigations he and Denning had so far undertaken.

Chick asked: "How'd they destroy his career? I mean, I know companies like GHQ have a lot of clout, but even they can't stop a guy from working in Los Angeles just because they don't like him poking around."

"Denning had made himself vulnerable."

"Sounds juicy. Go on."

Tim didn't really want to betray the implicit confidence Denning had placed in him when he'd told him about Peta, but if it turned out that Jeffery and Ally Bannister were Chick's rapists, Tim knew there may well come a time when she, he and Denning might need to work together. And if that ever happened, she'd need to know enough about Denning's past to trust his motivation.

"They got some film of him boffing his daughter. Don't worry, it was consensual, she was eighteen."

"Some gals do love their daddies."

"You ever meet him, don't say anything."

"Duh! A little daddy/daughter action is the least of what's going on here, Timbo. Murder, rape.... I could care less what he does in the bedroom."

Chick looked levelly at him for a long moment without speaking, then nodded slowly to herself.

"Tell me, Timbo, how come you haven't gone to the pigs?"

During the whole of the time he'd spent looking into the Bartlemann kill with Denning, following the dim pathways between it and Rebecca's murder, Tim had never once seriously considered involving the police.

His relationship with Rebecca had been too intimate, too deeply embedded in the physical and sexual parts of himself to allow anything but an intimately physical response. He was not a violent man. He was not a killer by nature. But he knew that his retribution could not be exacted by proxy, could not be handed off to a uniformed bureaucracy. Whatever had to be done, had to be done with his own hands. And yet, he was still reluctant to say it out loud.

So he said: "We could be wrong about the screenplay. It could just be an alternative take on a story anyone with an internet connection can read about."

"But you don't think that. I was watching you, dude. I know what was going through your head. You haven't gone to the pigs because you don't want to. This is a do-it-yourself thing for you."

She put her chin on her fist and smirked at him.

"I gotta tell you, I'm kinda impressed, Timbo. I mean, I think you're cool, but it wasn't like you had a whole lot going on on your side of the fence, know what I mean? Turns out you did, though. Secret-agent man."

She smiled dreamily at him for a while. Then she shook herself and straightened and said:

"In the screenplay you've got two people collecting Flynn's Flying Fuckers stuff, and there's those two real-life whack jobs doing the same thing. If you're right, and like the screenplay says, they really did kill Bartlemann and his maid, then it doesn't take Einstein to infer that they could be the assholes who raped me."

"Look, I wanted to tell you before, I really did, but I didn't have anything concrete on the Bartlemann kill, let alone the rape. And you have your film happening – I didn't want to raise suspicions and maybe jeopardize the picture unnecessarily."

"Don't sweat it, Timbo. I've been waiting twelve years. Without you, I might have been waiting a whole lot longer. It's good enough that I know now."

"Hey, wait a minute. Just because there's the screenplay and Jeffery and Ally happen to have this Flynn stuff, you can't—"

"Go ghetto?"

"Well, fuck, that's what you're thinking, right?"

"Totally."

"Don't. Not yet. Please. One, you don't have enough proof to be sure. It might just be that Rebecca met Jeffery and Ally sometime and used them as models for the characters in the script. And, two, if you move too soon it could alert Michael Starck to what Denning and I are doing. If we're right about the murders, then these are dangerous people. I don't want them to find out about us before we're ready for them."

"They deserve to die for their films alone."

"Chick, please. This isn't some billboard you can go set on fire. These are powerful people who'll fight back with everything they've got. Just wait a little longer."

Chick pressed her lips together, considered for a moment, then let her breath out and nodded.

"Okay. But in return you don't tell this Denning guy about me and the rapes, okay?"

"Sure, but why?"

"Because these assholes took away part of who I was. Without them I'd be a different person. It might not show, dude, but there's a huge fucking hole in the middle of who I am. And I don't want someone else being a part of that. Nothing you've told me about the murders of Bartlemann and the maid and your sister connects to my rape. Denning doesn't need to know anything about it."

Tim held his hands up.

"Okay, I promise. I won't tell Denning."

"Good."

"There's something else, though. Have you thought that Jeffery and Ally might know who you are?"

Chick looked shocked. "I was fifteen. I looked totally different. Different hair, fucked up skin, *baaad* clothes."

Tim pointed to her missing finger joint.

"How about that?"

Chick turned it in the light.

"I did it a year before the rape."

"How many girls do you think are missing part of their little finger?"

"Oh, fuck. And that Jeffery freak was totally pissed off when Kid turned up at the lunch. Were they, like, grooming me?"

"That's what I'm saying, these aren't people you fuck around with."

Tim got up from the table, went to the stove and put a pot of coffee on. While it was heating he came back and sat down again.

"I want to ask you about Kid."

"What about him?"

"He has some sort of relationship with Michael Starck."

"Yeah, they go back, so what?"

"They go back a *long* way. Michael Starck used to direct Kid's pornos. He was called Brett Adelaide back then."

"I didn't know that."

"The thing is, knowing someone, even for a long time, isn't usually enough for them to give you three million dollars."

"It is if you've got a killer project."

"Not GHQ. They exist to make money. A lot of money, from great big movies. *Antepenultimate*, and I know you'll make it brilliantly, but that kind of story? It's going to have a limited market."

"Which is why it has to be made, so that all the dumbasses who think—"

"I know, I know.... But let's just focus on murder and killing and rape, okay? Kid has never done anything except porn and your first film."

"*Loggers*."

"Yeah."

"He did a diploma in film production – three months at USC."

"Kind of my point – he's got no track record, nothing to say to GHQ they can be confident they're going to get their money back. It's fucking weird, don't you think? Him getting three million bucks to make a film with – and no criticism intended here – an inexperienced director; from a script that you have to admit is a little heavy on the navel-gazing side of things."

"You think he's blackmailing Michael somehow? Is that what you're after? You think he can give you some ammunition to use against GHQ?"

Chick's tone was incredulous, but Tim could see doubt flickering in her eyes, an uncertainty about the man who was doing his best to turn her into the next hot maverick director. And as he watched this brief play of emotion, the meaning in her words set a small, wavering flame to the dry tinder of memory.... Denning's phone playing a video. A forest. A cabin. Michael Starck exiting. The video a copy of a Super 8 film Denning had taken from Kid's car. A celluloid ticket to three million dollars?

"How much do you know about Kid?"

"I've known him three years. We worked closely on *Loggers*, of course. I hang out with him sometimes, not so much since I met you."

"Were you...intimate."

"Oh, Tim, intimate? Nice!" Chick laughed. "No, we never fucked. Though, to be truthful, I did try. He didn't want to. Like really no way. I think he sees himself as a father figure to me. And fathers don't fuck daughters, I guess – unless you're Denning. Lucky escape, probably. I would have been walking bowlegged for a week – have you seen any of his vids?"

"Uh, no. But on that – he can't have been doing porn up to when you made *Loggers*, he's too old."

"He stopped all of that years before he met me. I think he's embarrassed by it now."

"What did he do in between?"

Chick shrugged. "I don't know. Had some money put by, I guess."

"And you met by accident?"

"Timbo, it might be strange about the three mil, but where's this going? Kid didn't kill Bartlemann, and he's not part of GHQ."

"But?"

"Yeah, by accident. He walked into the cafe where I was working, ordered a coffee, kept looking at me the whole time and when I asked him what the fuck, we started chatting. We went out to some bars. I told him I wanted to be a director, showed him my student stuff. Couple of weeks later he promised he'd make it happen for me. I thought it was just the usual Hollywood bullshit, or some sort of sympathy thing because I'd told him about being raped and he felt sorry for me. But then he set up *Loggers*."

"You must have impressed him."

"Classic discovery story. Look, his thing for me, this daughter thing, or whatever it is, is a little crazy, for sure. On the other hand, he *wants* to be a producer, he wants to legitimize himself – so, we help each other. Hollywood is a sewer, but it's where these sort of things happen. It's a place where, on nothing more than a gut feeling, someone gambles on someone else, and twenty years later you read about them and they've changed the face of entertainment. And either way, I'm not complaining. Out of my class at UCLA I'm the only one who's done a feature. Everyone else is still doing corporate videos or toothpaste ads."

Later. Down to Venice Beach on the bikes. On the grass at the edge of the sand, eating souvlaki and drinking lemon soda. High blue sky, gulls, here and there white clouds like cotton candy, sharply outlined in the clear air. The beach weekday peaceful, an onshore breeze moving Chick's blond hair, both of them smiling, eyes alight, and laughing at nothing, and their bodies touching at arm and hip and thigh, and Chick's manic energy, all those wild and churning thoughts, stilled, quieted by the ocean and the sun and the soft crump of the waves. And Tim's heart expanding, marveling at this gift, this change, this rebirth....

And on the beach – life. Children with their happy shouting, adults loose and open against the dazzle of the water; as though with their clothes, piled now by beach towels and coolers, these Los Angelinos had thrown off, for the day, their cares and their trials, had given them back to the city, and at the edge of this ocean, on this warm yellow sand, had said: you will not come here, this day is mine. It is not yours.

And for this snatched time, these minutes, an hour maybe, Tim and Chick, each in their own way the most alienated of people, felt a gentle tugging on the long disused strings that bound them to the world of others. And though they could not put a name to this feeling, both felt it, and wishing to say something, to share this buoyancy of spirit, turned to each other with the words upon their lips, but then did not speak, silenced by the realization that they were in love.

Chapter 34

Tim in leather now, jacket and pants. Had figured why the fuck not? He was riding a Bonneville, after all. L.A. hipster. Marlon Brando resurrected. Stretched black cow skin an armor against the terror of the day that was fast approaching, the day when speculation would give way to action, when Tim, by his own hand, would be forever changed.

But not now. Now there was still time to ride through sunshine, to take pleasure in the warm air and the wind, to blinker the mind with the rushing invigoration of speed. To just...be.

On Lincoln Boulevard. With Chick on the Thruxton next to him. Lost in the clatter of their engines, sunlight on chrome, tarmac, concrete, white lines. All the shit and the beauty of Los Angeles smashed into one average street of cars and ragged palms and buildings that needed fixing and too many people. And none of it meaning anything when you were so far above it.

Looking at Chick as she pulled ahead, at her ass in tight leather, and wanting to fuck her, wanting to stay on this bike forever and ride down all the long, straight streets of the world with her.

Danny Bartlemann's motel. Piggybacking on a meeting about the *Antepenultimate* script. Tim ran his palm over his stomach as they dismounted. He'd lost more weight, the paunch was gone, his stomach was flat under his T-shirt.

Blinds drawn, room dim, food wrappers on the floor, the bed heavily used. Danny turning locks and pulling bolts when they knocked, checking the street as they entered, locking up behind them. Muttering, when Chick asked, that he thought someone was watching his room. And Chick winking at Tim behind Danny's back, twirling her finger at her temple – fucking nutcase.

Danny had emailed a rewrite the day before and Chick wanted to go through it with him. Tim knew from experience that dialogue between a director and a screenwriter could last forever, so he got in first, before the nitpicking began. Told Danny he was interested in the story of his father's murder, that he was thinking of writing a screenplay based on it.

One screenwriter to another. Danny saying okay, but he really didn't know that much about it. And distracted, running his hands through his long graying hair, filling the room with smoke from his hand-rolled cigarettes, looking like he wanted to be somewhere else. Or with someone else.

Chick happy to wait, knowing Tim's agenda but playing dumb. Sprawling on the bed behind Danny, giving Tim looks and spreading her legs.

Tim said: "So, you said, when we were up at Los Padres, that you were estranged from your father?"

"Estranged? Nonexistent. He left when I was eleven. It wasn't until *Maximum Kill* was shooting that I had any even halfway meaningful contact with him. I went out to his house a couple of times around then."

"Was he into *Maximum Kill*? Did he like it?"

"All I know is that Big Glass bought the film. I don't know how much input he had personally in the decision. It sure didn't change his attitude toward me."

"Did you meet the maid? Maria? The one who killed him?"

"Yeah."

"Impressions?"

"Hard, is the word that comes to mind. Like she saw all this good American stuff around her and she *wanted* it."

"Doesn't really fit with her blowing her own head off."

"No, it doesn't. I mean, she wasn't super beautiful, but she was close. She had a killer body. A little bit of work, she could have gotten somewhere for sure. Here."

Danny brought up a photo on a battered flip-top phone, handed it to Tim. A woman, from the waist up, naked. Probably early thirties, beautiful breasts, long curling dark hair, low hairline accentuating her Mexican-ness, nose a little heavy. Nice-looking, but like Danny had said, not quite there.

It wasn't the kind of picture you'd expect a son to take of his father's maid. Tim looked closer, saw that she was sitting on the edge of a bed, her body presented for the camera, as though this illegal immigrant had had some innate sense of how to work the lens.

Out of nowhere, Tim thought: A star is born.

A meaningless piece of brain chatter, the usual head noise.... But then he realized why he'd thought it.

He asked Danny to message the photo to his cell. Danny didn't know how to do it, so Tim pressed the buttons for him.

"How come she's naked?"

Danny took his phone back, looked solemnly at the photo. "I took it at my father's place. I'd, um, just gone down on her."

"You're kidding?"

Danny shook his head. "She knew I was the son. Daddy was in the film business. She thought I was an opportunity, that's all. Next time I visited, she didn't want anything to do with me. Must have figured out how the land lay, that I was not favored in the house of Bartlemann. I was too embarrassed to give it to the cops."

Tim nodded understandingly, wanting to keep the info flowing.

"Was there anything idiosyncratic about her? Something I could use to flesh out her character, maybe?"

Danny shrugged, then said facetiously: "One of her labia was split."

Over on the bed Chick sat up straight and opened her mouth. Tim looked quickly at her. She closed her mouth and stayed silent.

"Really?"

"Yeah, like that." Danny held his thumb and forefinger half an inch apart. "She got it fixed, though."

"What do you mean?"

"I had to ID the body. They don't wear clothes in the morgue."

"You looked at her pussy in the morgue?"

Danny's face colored.

"She was uncovered, I couldn't help it. Christ!"

Tim backpedaled quickly. "Of course. I'm sorry. Go on."

"There's nothing to go on about. Her labia were intact. Ergo, she'd had it fixed. Vaginoplasty is not uncommon in L.A., one suspects."

From the bed Chick squealed: "Ouch!"

"How come you had to make the ID?"

"Maria was illegal, so they couldn't trace her relatives. And the only other people she worked with were two women – a Mexican cook and my father's personal assistant. Maria didn't have a head. It's not really something a woman should have to see. I was at the morgue to do my father, so I guess the cops just thought, two birds with one stone."

"How did you ID her if she didn't have a head?"

"There was some of the back of the skull left and the hair was the same. And the body looked like her body – Mexican, built. But, tell you the truth, you're in this room with the cops and your father is on the next table and there's this...*thing* lying there.... You don't spend too long looking at it. But who else could it have been? There was only her and my father out at the house that night."

Chapter 35

A hot night. Kid had the large sliding windows along the front of his apartment open. Gritty currents of air rolled like small breakers over his bare chest. He sat in a replica Eames armchair and gazed at the lights of the apartment buildings across the street.

Antepenultimate rolling along, heading toward Go. Chick finalizing rewrites. Budget locked down. Key cast and crew in place, a post-completion plan of festivals already mapped out. Kid hoping for a crossover hit.

A busy time of long days and hard work. A time that demanded confidence, optimism.

Not exactly what he was feeling.

Jeffery and Ally wanted Chick as part of their insane self-administered psychotherapy. And sooner or later, unless something was done, they'd find a way to get her. Kid couldn't keep tabs on her twenty-four hours a day.

And tonight, another helping of shit. A phone call from Christo – Theo Portman had asked him to come to Los Angeles. Christo wouldn't say what for, but he wanted to be sure he could count on Kid if he needed an extra pair of hands.

What could Kid say? For the last twelve years he'd worked with this pock-marked Mexican to subject innocent girls to kidnapping and rape. Not a situation where you could say: "Sorry, dude, not really in the mood."

And the night getting worse.

Peta in the bedroom, door closed, asleep. The intercom buzzing. Chick striding into the apartment all leather and gasoline, swinging her helmet, eyes on fire.

They sat by the windows. Sounds of traffic nineteen floors below, like a pulse in the hot air. Chick didn't bother with preamble.

"Jeffery and Ally's place. Why'd you turn up there?"

"I thought it might save time. Give us a chance to update them on *Ante* together."

"But you didn't talk about the film at all."

"Just the way things turned out."

"It seemed to me like all you wanted to do was get me out of there."

"What's this about, Chick?"

"You thought they were going to hurt me."

Kid looked out the open window and thought: Oh, fuck. Said: "Jeffery and Ally are seriously damaged people. They can be dangerous in the wrong situation."

Chick laughed. "You know, even though you've talked about Michael on and off ever since we did *Loggers*, you never said shit about Jeffery and Ally. Never mentioned them. So how do you suddenly know them well enough to tell me how dangerous they can be?"

"It's just the impression I get."

Chick went on like she hadn't heard. "Because if they *are* damaged and dangerous, and they *were* thinking of hurting me, and you came out there to make sure they didn't, then I'd have to figure you had some way of knowing how and why they were dangerous. And not just dangerous, but dangerous to me, specifically."

"This is crazy. I don't know what you're upset about. You're special to me. It's called caring."

Chick could see he was lying, this man who had listened to her hopes and dreams for the last three years, who had made *Loggers* and *Antepenultimate* a reality. Chick had not cried since she was fifteen. She'd figured if she wasn't crying, then she couldn't be too badly hurt. She'd trained herself in the year after her rape by pushing needles into the skin between her thumb and forefinger. So she was damned if she was going to cry now. Even though her chest felt like it was going to split.

"Kid, did I ever show you my pussy?"

Kid lifted his hands.

"Hey, hey, hey.... We talked about this a long time ago. I want to help you. I don't want to fuck you."

"And why is that? I mean, shit, you made a career out of fucking anything that moved. I'm skinny. I've got blond hair down there, man. What's wrong with you?"

Kid stood up. "Jesus fucking Christ, Chick! Stop it."

"I know you're doing your receptionist now. But before her, you still didn't want it. Don't get me wrong, I'm not dying to get drilled by that thing in your pants. But I wonder why you didn't even want a random fuck. Do you feel bad about something, Kid? Something about me?"

And right then he could have told her, he could have blurted it all out – the abduction, the rapes. He could have begged for mercy, he could have held up *Loggers* and *Antepenultimate* as proof of how much he'd tried to make amends. But he didn't. He knew Chick too well. He knew about the firebombing, the destroyed marriages, the vandalism. And he knew about the dark core of hatred she'd lived with since Jeffery and Ally had gone to work on her in their screening room. She would not forgive him.

So, he lied and told the truth at the same time, said that the only thing he wanted in the world was for her to be happy, to achieve her dreams.

And Chick read the evasion in his face and heard it in his words and felt, on that evening of hot winds, more abandoned and lonely than she had in all of her abandoned and lonely life. She stood up, blinking hard, and pulled down the zip of her catsuit, pushed the leather to her knees, lay back on the couch and pulled apart the tear in her labia.

Kid turned his back so he wouldn't have to see.

"Oh really? You're not even going to look? Well, maybe it's not pretty enough for *you*, but I like it. Know why? 'Cause it means I'll never forget what happened. I'll never fucking forget."

When Chick left Kid's apartment a few minutes later she didn't know anything more than she had going in, not in words, not in a way she could point to and say, yeah, now I know what he did. But she knew something. She knew that Kid had lied to her.

In bed with Peta, curled against her sleeping back, with the night hot and the blinds open and too much light coming from Wilshire into the room, Kid felt the cold approach of change. Somewhere, something had woken and was now tracking him, still in the shadows, still beyond clear sight, but closing, his scent in its nostrils – the beast of his past come hungry to the present.

He held onto Peta, pressed his stomach against her, but her heat would not penetrate his rape-fucked skin. Safety – it seemed to him at that moment the most valuable of commodities, a thing to be desired above all else. But how to achieve it? How to take the threat of his part in the rapes and make it not exist? The answer obvious – kill Jeffery and Ally. Revisit that scene in the desert. Hold a gun, pull a trigger.

Chick might have her suspicions, but without the twins there could be no confirmation. Not a perfect solution, but good enough. Good enough when *Antepenultimate* came out and all Chick could think about was her place in cinema history.

Chapter 36

late, late night. A world of streetlights and the lit windows of empty offices. Concrete guard walls, green freeway signs: *North, 5, 110, No Trucks*.... Tall buildings craning their necks at lonely travelers, squat apartment blocks disinterested as lizards. Idiots, criminals and shift-workers the only traffic during these dark hours.

And then long, empty stretches of road with dusty banks, here and there planted with ivy, with creeper, with dry tufts of grass. But mostly raw, untended, the stony, sandy, ragged edges bleeding into a landscape of warehouses and commercial buildings. Pre-fab concrete, pressed-tin walls, a hundred thousand acres of flat metal roofs. And overpasses and exit ramps and banal, talentless graffiti, and lone, defiant palms that would not die, and small stands of gum trees grimed from a lifetime spent sucking gas.

Cross the Hollywood Freeway, cross the L.A. River, pass Golden State and hang left, low, leaning out, one cog up going in, and another down coming out, and another.... Down onto North San Fernando Road, common denominator Los Angeles, everything low-rise and utilitarian, railroad tracks behind overgrown plants, auto wreckers, blank box buildings, places that stripped paint and, in a setting just so right for the poverty-struck misery it dealt with, the L.A. County Public Defender's office.

And on up the long straight road, trailing smashed sound waves, leather clothes shining for brief pulsed seconds as they passed from streetlight to streetlight, set grim and hard upon their bikes, the prime directive: keep rolling. Because you don't stop on North San Fernando, not that late at night. Further up, a purple snow of jacaranda blossoms. Tree after tree.

And Chick sad and fucked and angry, looking to burn the pain away with gasoline. And Tim there, not part of her thing with Kid, not knowing about it, but cool with the gig, and this time not feeling the trepidation of the times before, not feeling out of place, but making it something for him too. A chance to add a little more steel, a little more fortitude. A training ground for a man who knew that someday soon he would have to commit murder.

Down to a post-production facility – Full Circle Media – at the end of a dead-end cross street. A place that rented non-linear editing suites and supplied computer graphics services to Hollywood production companies. A place that had worked on five of the largest opening weekend grossers of the last twelve months – sci-fi and action flicks, of course.

There was a large circular parking lot, barrier up and unattended at this time of night, laid out around a rear corner of the building. Tim and Chick left their bikes a few yards up the street, away from any cameras that might catch a license plate, and jogged across the lot and around to the back of the two-story building. They carried cans of gasoline and a road flare.

It was dark here, and out of sight of the street, and the building's back wall was blank except for a pair of locked steel fire doors. The millions-of-dollars' worth of equipment inside meant penetrating the building would take something explosive. But Chick wasn't interested in getting inside. There were other ways to fuck up these contributors to the degeneration of cinema.

A few yards away from the building, set against a chain link fence, there was a metal container about ten feet long and four feet high. It had a number of pipes that exited one end and disappeared into the ground, on both long sides there were vents, and on top there was a small air conditioning unit. This was the electrical routing box for Full Circle Media. It distributed the large amounts of electricity needed to run the AVID editing machines and the banks of image processors that created the special effects Chick despised so much.

On previous jaunts Tim had noticed an excitement in Chick, an almost carnal delight in the destruction she was about to wreak. But it was absent tonight. She doused the routing box with gasoline silently, no banter, no gleeful anticipation. After Tim had emptied his can too, they backed off and Chick lit the road flare. The world around them turned rose and smoky.

Then she muttered, "Fucking cunts," and lobbed the flare and they turned and sprinted back to the bikes and behind them the box went up in a sheet of flame.

Tim looked over his shoulder once as they pulled away, but the box was hidden by the angle of the building and all he could see was a bright orange glow that spread across the asphalt of the parking lot and out past the chain link fence to weeds and stones and the dim glimmer of railway tracks.

CHAPTER 37

Delaware Avenue. The house lonely now. Peta at Kid's most nights of the week. Her bedroom, the lounge, the kitchen, the bathroom – all of them somehow dead and flat, all of them somehow wrong, like a pattern he had committed to memory a long time ago but had now lost the ability to recognize.

Denning had a pile of notes for the book he was planning. He had the first half of an outline – a reconstruction of what he and Tim had found out about the Bartlemann kill and GHQ. His hopes for the future, his roadmap for revenge. Still not complete.

In the long nighttime hours, he sat at the kitchen table making changes and notes, ticking off questions yet to be answered. And later, on those nights, when he could do no more, he would take an old shoebox of photographs into the sitting room and torture himself, not with images of Peta, but with those of his wife.

Clara.... Back to first causes, back to his only real love. Mapping out the life he could have had if she had not been taken from him.

And then he would pace the rooms, fighting the realization that even if he ruined GHQ and brought them to justice, there would be no resurrection, not for the happiness he had buried ten years ago.

But the next day, waking and finding nothing else to believe in, nothing to replace his need for revenge. And so carrying on, like some dog, faithful to a single master.

Mid-morning. Tim rolled up on his bike, tired and a little fritzed from last night's fire attack. They sat in the kitchen. Denning made coffee.

Tim showed him the photo of Maria that Danny had given him. They transferred it to Denning's laptop, brought up a picture of movie star Delores, put them side by side. Hairline different, nose different, Maria a little fuller in the face, cheap hairstyle contrasting with Delores' Hollywood locks. But nothing that couldn't be fixed. A good stylist, a nose job, some laser depilation, a diet.... Illegal immigrant to Tinsel Town star.

Denning looked at the screen for a long time, from one picture to the other.

"It could be her. I mean...it could be her. God, I wish we had something more to go on." He was silent for a moment, pondering, then he asked, "How come she's naked?"

"Danny Bartlemann wrote the *Maximum Kill* script, right? So, one day while the film's in production, he goes around to see his father, and while he's at the house the maid gets cozy with him, thinks he's Mister Hollywood or something - ergo the nude pic. But what's important, and bear with me here, is he ends up going down on her, and he sees that she has a ripped pussy."

Denning looked irritated. "What?"

"One of her labia was split in the middle."

"One of her labia was split...." Denning screwed up his face trying to figure out what the hell Tim was talking about.

Tim carried on: "After the murder, the cops ask Danny to ID her. There's no one else who can do it. But she's got no head and he's all shook up from ID-ing his dad and he's sure it has to be Maria anyhow, because who else would it be? So he says yes it's her without really knowing. One thing he notices, though, is her pussy."

"The ripped pussy."

"No. *This* pussy is intact. Danny just assumed she got it fixed sometime before she got killed."

Denning looked like he was about to throw his hands up and ask what the fuck. But then he caught himself and his face went flat. He said quietly: "But that's not what you think."

"No. I think the woman in the morgue was someone else. Look at what we've got. We couldn't figure out how Delores knew what happened at Bartlemann's house, how she knew all the information she passed on to Rebecca, right? But this explains it. Maria didn't get her head blown off at all, she changed into Delores. Delores was *there* that night, as Maria. She saw the whole thing go down and then walked away and became a movie star."

"Because Michael was in love with her."

"Yes! Nancy Epps said that when Maria supposedly killed herself, Michael didn't seem upset, even though this was a woman he'd been so in love with he'd chucked his marriage for her. But you wouldn't be upset, would you, if your lover was still alive? And look who Michael's with just a few months after *Maximum Kill* comes out – long enough for a nose job and some electrolysis – Delores Fuentes. He was seeing the *same* woman."

Denning set his mouth in a hard, straight line. Tim had expected him to be at least a bit excited by this deduction and he didn't understand why he looked so grim.

Denning said: "Michael substituted someone else's body. If the maid vanished right after Scott Bartlemann was killed there would have been a huge hunt for her. She would never have gotten away. They had to have a body in order for Delores to resurface safely."

"And the whole thing in the screenplay about one of GHQ blowing the maid's head off is just Delores hiding her tracks, keeping herself out of it."

"We find out that one of Delores' labia is split, that would pretty much clinch it."

"Well, funny thing...."

"Bullshit. How could you possibly know that?"

"Chick fucked her."

"Your girlfriend?"

"Yeah. Jeffery and Ally Bannister, apparently, want Delores to have a part in Chick's film. Chick met with her, they ended up in bed. Chick got a good look."

Denning pressed the heels of his hands against his eyes.

When half a minute had passed and he still hadn't taken his hands away, Tim asked: "Are you okay, Alan?"

Denning dropped his hands, took a breath and nodded.

"Headache."

Tim figured it must have been pretty severe because Denning's eyes looked raw and wet.

Denning said: "How did Delores get that way?"

Tim dissembled, keeping his promise to Chick, staying clear of the rape scenario.

"She wouldn't say. But she's Mexican. Who knows what happened to her growing up."

Denning got up, took the mugs to the sink. He spent a moment washing them, absorbed in his own thoughts, then turned back to Tim.

"Well, that's it, then. As far as GHQ and Delores go, we're done. Bartlemann was going to shelve *Maximum Kill*. Theo Portman had a relationship with Michael Starck from their porn days and most likely tipped him off about the shelving. GHQ kills Scott Bartlemann to ensure the release of *Maximum Kill*, Danny inherits Scott's share and sells it to Theo, Theo gets control of Big Glass, GHQ gets rich. Michael was in love with the maid, the maid morphs into Delores, who Michael turns into a star and has a relationship with. Five years later they split and her career takes a nosedive. Couple of years after that, Delores employs your sister to write the screenplay. What Delores hoped to accomplish, given that she was exclusively signed to GHQ, is anyone's guess, but it isn't too insane to figure she was probably trying to force them to put her back in the game."

"We still don't have anything concrete on Rebecca, though. Someone from GHQ killed her. And—"

"And you need that before you can do what you have to do."

Tim nodded. Denning stuck his hand out. Tim took it.

Denning said: "We're in this together. I'm not going to bail just because I've got what I need. We'll find out who killed your sister. Worse comes to worst, we'll beat it out of Delores Fuentes."

After Tim had gone, Denning sat alone on the sofa in the living room. He knew who GHQ had substituted for Maria. He knew whose head had been blown away by that shotgun blast. And any notion he might have had about taking his revenge from a distance by writing a book, by disgracing GHQ and possibly exposing them to the law, was now forgotten. Was now buried under a red, burning need to feel blood on his hands.

Chapter 38

Bel Air. Jeffery had forgone his usual mid-morning Zopiclone and was instead very much awake. Too awake, in fact, to stand the world around him.

Ally was out. But he knew where she was. Knew that the writer was on top of her, and that she was thinking only of him, of a life together with him.

He went into her suite, stared for a moment at her unused bed, at the small collection of cosmetics on her dressing table, the freshly placed flowers in front of a window. All too neat and unlived in. A setting that screamed 'She's gone'.

He opened her laundry hamper and rummaged through clothes, pulled out a pair of briefs. He examined the crotch. No semen, but the smell of sex. Unmistakable.

Jeffery moaned, tried to tear the material with his teeth. But it was too strong and he threw the garment on the bed so that she would see he'd been there and know that he knew.

In his own suite, he dressed in his darkest, most favorite 1940s suit – midnight blue with a narrow chalk stripe. White shirt, black brogues, waistcoat, a tie with clocks on it. Dark and deadly, clothes fit for the occasion. No .38 for this outing. Instead, double leather shoulder holsters and two Colt .45 automatics circa WWII – Elisha Cook Jr.'s rig from *The Maltese Falcon*.

He looked in the mirror. Thought the hell with it and put a hat on his head this time. Looked in the mirror again and felt just right.

He went down to the garage and got the Packard out and drove through the city, killing time until dark, until Ally would be back in Bel Air and the writer would be alone.

Landmarks in a noir cityscape. The Bradbury building – *Double Indemnity*, *D.O.A.*, *Shockproof*. MacArthur Park – *The Bigamist, Too Late for Tears, The Unfaithful*. Union Station – *Criss Cross, Cry Danger*. The Hollywood Bowl – *Man in the Vault*, Fred MacMurray chatting with Jean Heather in *Double Indemnity*. Old City Hall, the L.A. River, the Hollywood sign.... Retinal burns in black-and-white, the scars of a thousand late nights living in another world, stacking celluloid memories against the door, trying to pile them high enough to keep Granddaddy out.

Two a.m. A moon over Los Angeles. Silver light turning the streets monochrome. The Packard in an alley out back of the motel.

Through a service entrance, pulling on gloves, racking the slide on one gun and then the other. Safeties on, reholstering. Into the paved area around which the motel units formed a court. The centerpiece of plants dense and black in the metallic light.

Empty space. No movement. Too late for anyone to be heading for the pool, to be putting quarters in the ice machine.

Jeffery knocked quietly until Danny called out to ask who it was, kept on knocking until he opened the door. Then pushed in, kicked the door shut behind him.

A sidelight by the bed. Danny's bladder went as soon as he saw who it was.

Jeffery wanted to make a hard-boiled speech, to toss some tough-guy slang out the side of his mouth. But there was nothing to say. As long as Danny was alive, Jeffery wouldn't have Ally. Words weren't going to change anything about that.

So.... Double hand draw, the sides of his coat flying open. In his head, everything in slow motion, lit by James Wong Howe. Safeties off, the Colts exploding in his hands, spurts of fire, heavy recoil making them hard to keep centered.

Danny reaching out with his arms and opening his mouth and saying, "No, no, no...." And the first of the big slugs taking away fingers and part of his hand and blood in all its forms – mist and spurts and heavy globs – beginning to fly around. And the hard, sharp cracks of the guns filling all the corners of the room.

Jeffery pulling triggers like he was playing an instrument. Bang, bang, bang, bang. Danny's chest pulverized by lead, recoil dragging the grouping up, ripping out the side of his throat, the carotid on one side erupting. Danny pinned to the wall, flapping about like washing on a windy day and the bullets still climbing, seven shots in each mag, biting pieces from his chin and his jaw and his cheekbones and then his head splitting raggedly, a lump of it falling away and Danny deader than dead before he even slid down the wall.

Jeffery stepped out into the court. No one. Not even lights behind blinds. Only idiots draw attention to themselves when guns start going off. It was only when he got back to the Packard that he realized he was still holding the Colts. He paused before he climbed in, took a breath, reholstered, the barrels still hot. He looked around, memorizing the alley, making sure it stayed real in his head. Books on the city would have photos of this place.

Morning. Bel Air. Out by the pool. Jeffery had slept well. Ally read the trades, waiting until she could decently leave, until she could resume making plans with her lover. Jeffery told the maid to bring bacon and French toast with powdered sugar. He watched his sister, impatient for her to go and come back.

They were wheeling him out as she arrived. The body bag was zipped but Ally knew it was him. She could see through the open door of his room, the mess in there, like someone had thrown a paint can of blood at the walls. She stood on the sidewalk, against the tape, and listened to bystanders talk about shots in the night, the ones early on the scene recounting descriptions of massive cranial damage.

In her car, later, at the edge of the ocean, she ran the air conditioning with the windows closed, as high as it would go, wrapped in the noise and the cold.

She didn't feel fury, or hatred. She had been pushed beyond those permutations of anger. Finally.

Finally, had come an end to it all. To the nights when her grandfather's cock moved inside her like a calcified arm. To the memories. To the endless worry about Jeffery; the constant remolding of his melting personality, the reining-in of his lusts. To the rapes, to the killing. And to all the things she had hoped life, in its compassion, might have brought to her eventually – absolution, freedom...love.

All things now settled.

All the infinite raft of decisions that life demands, no longer hers to make.

She looked through the windshield at the sea, trying to remember what she was like before her parents died. And found a small kernel of joy in remembering herself, sunlit, laughing, loved, as innocent as any other child. There had been a chance for her then.

And there had been hope along the way, too – the dream that the Ritual of Freeing really did hold the key to liberation. And when that dream died, for her though not for Jeffery, the hope that it would at least keep them sane.

But it had been a delusion. They were broken beyond fixing, and all the acting out and all the supposed transference of pain had not altered their rocketing trajectory to this point by a fraction of an inch.

So now, home to her beloved brother, home to begin the end, to spend the last hours and days together.

Jeffery was swimming laps naked in the pool when she arrived back in Bel Air. She watched him as he climbed from the water – this man, her DNA copy, the only other in all the world who shared what she had been through. How lonely it would have been to be without him, to have had no one to look after.

She handed him a robe, then took his hand and together they walked along pathways between ornamental shrubs, between hibiscus and bougainvillea, kicking their feet through purple drifts of jacaranda blossoms, and she spoke to him of how important it was that they perform the final Ritual of Freeing, that they use the girl, the director, the First. Soon.

CHAPTER 39

A hotel room in Santa Monica. Christo up from Mexico at Theo's behest, fixing shit for one of Theo's pals – a guy Christo knew too, by another name, from his porn star days. And from a certain night out in the desert. A hassle to take time away from ferrying peasants over the border, but Theo paid better than good. Same as he had ten years ago when he wanted that woman snatched – Christo's only other active Stateside gig in all that time. The thing with Kid just cross-border transportation.

In the hotel room now, a view of blue sea and beach out the window. Christo poured himself a drink and wondered idly what Theo had wanted the woman for all those years ago, what he'd done with her. He remembered it well. You snatch a woman from the streets of Los Angeles, it isn't something that's going to get fuzzy.

She'd been one hot chika. A Mexican beauty living in a white neighborhood; kid, married to some slob. Who could figure what went on in this shithole city? Doing something with dogs. What a waste.

It hadn't been difficult. Drive up, get out while she's messing with dog stuff at the side of her truck. Hit her in the head and put her in the van. Wore a ski mask but didn't need it – he knew she wasn't coming back from wherever Theo planned to take her. Tape her up, leave her in the back – a modus operandi that had served him well in the years afterwards, when Kid found whoever it was who wanted four girls a year. Park the van where Theo had told him to, and get the fuck back to Mexico. Easiest fifty grand he'd ever earned.

Today, earlier, a meeting. Hardly a meeting. Just telling this crony of Theo's what the dude already knew. Michael Starck his real name. Big man in the movie industry, now. How things turn out....

Someone named Tim had to be found. Someone named Sean knew where he was. Sean lived off the grid. Movie Star Delores Fuentes was fucking him. The solution so simple Christo let the dude finish his sentence – get Delores to set Sean up. Don't let her say no.

Christo considered calling Kid for backup. But figured not yet, save him for later, an available resource. Michael had looked strong enough to help out. And it kept things safer all round, that sort of personal culpability.

Michael drove his Maserati to Delores' place in Bel Air. Santa Monica Boulevard, South Beverly Glen, Stone Canyon Road. Leafy, past a leg of the golf course, narrow roads, flowering shrubs – a back-pocket paradise.

He knew he'd have to come down hard. She'd refused to give Sean up before. Cajoling wouldn't work.

Her favorite room to receive visitors. The white one overlooking the pool. Michael knew it was because she thought all the white set off the color of her skin. Made her look more exotic. She wasn't wrong.

He had loved her for eleven years. But looking at her now, arranged on the brocade couch, a little too muscular, a little too cut, smiling up at him as though she knew he wanted to fuck her, he realized at last that he was finished with her.

He'd always known she was greedy and vain, ruthless to the point of psychopathy when it would serve her. It hadn't bothered him, it had fit too well with his own assessment of himself. But she had added betrayal and stupidity; and the collection of problems she now represented, unleavened by any love for him, had, during the past week, tipped some set of emotional scales. All he saw on the couch now was an issue that needed to be dealt with. Theo had been right, as Theo usually was – she had to be removed.

But not yet. Not before Sean had been found.

He took three quick steps across the floor, watched her expression change to an irritated frown as he approached, and slapped her as hard as he could across the face.

Delores bounced against the back of the couch then fell onto the floor. The blow had been hard enough to stun her and it took a good two minutes before she was able to pick herself up and regain her seat. She opened her mouth. Michael knew she was going to start yelling, so he slapped her again, not quite as hard, but hard enough to make her shut up. He started speaking before she could recover.

"The girl who had the screenplay, and your assistant? They're done. Two people dead because you were too fucking stupid to delete the screenplay. Or too fucking devious."

Michael saw her change in front of him. Something about the eyes. For the first time he saw fear there. It wasn't the beating or his raised voice, though. She'd seen that his love was gone.

Michael said: "How did you know about the script?"

"I told you. Sean."

"How did he know?"

"Some stupid writers' group he goes to. I told you that, too."

"No."

"That's what he said."

"When Jeffery took care of the women, he found a copy of the screenplay. Somebody called Tim had signed his name and made notes on it. Somebody called Tim had read it. Who's Tim?"

"I don't know."

"Delores—"

"I don't know! Fuck you, Michael. All I know is what Sean told me, and I came to you with it. You can't treat me like this."

"It isn't just me now."

Delores was silent for a moment, then she whispered: "Theo?"

"What did you expect?"

Delores put her hands together like she was praying. "Michael, I did the right thing. I came to you. I told you. It's not my fault. You've got to tell Theo I did the right thing. Please, Michael."

"Theo thinks you need dealing with. Has done since Bartlemann. I had to beg him when I told him you'd kept a copy of the screenplay. And now, someone else knows about it. He doesn't think you're worth the trouble anymore."

Delores got up and poured herself a glass of Scotch at a bar that was built into one of the walls. Michael saw that the side of her face was beginning to swell.

She came back and sat down, held her glass with both hands. After a moment she looked up at him and asked: "What do I do?"

"Sean lied about the screenplay. He knows more than he told you. I need to speak to him."

"I don't know where he lives. I already told you that."

"But you have a number for him. You can arrange to meet him somewhere."

Delores looked woodenly at him. She knew what was being asked.

Michael spoke again: "You don't have a choice. Theo's already brought his guy up from Mexico."

CHAPTER 40

Night. Delores a little bombed on the painkillers and Scotch she'd taken for her face. A thousand people she could call for company, but none she wanted to see. A world where she was still remembered, where she could still step out and be adored. But movie star love wouldn't stop death from visiting if Theo wished it.

The house was empty. She'd sent the servants home. Delores walked the long halls and passed through the oversized rooms, wondering how long she had left to enjoy the place.

She thought, a little light-headedly, that there would be a fitting symmetry if she was killed. After all, her rise to stardom had begun with a death. With Bartlemann. And even before that, though not quite a death, there had been something that felt very much like it at the time.

She'd been thirty years old. A young woman who'd learned English at church-sponsored classes and then taught it to students herself. A woman for whom La Hiedra, at the top of Baja California, had ceased to be home and had become instead a place she had spent ten years trying to escape. A woman with a body men would kill for.

Some girls in the village sold themselves in a shack behind the cantina. But Maria – strange to think of herself by that name now – Maria valued that body too highly, knew it was too good to be entered by sweating farmhands who could do nothing for her. So she'd worked in a laundry, washing and ironing in temperatures that regularly hit a hundred and ten.

Until one day she had saved enough.

It hadn't been hard to find the coyote. A woman with money who wanted the North American dream – it was almost enough just to think it.

He'd been waiting in her room when she returned from work one night. A man, handsome in a blunt way, with pockmarked skin. Someone she had never seen before, someone who was not from her village, or the next. They made the arrangements. She had been ready to go for too long by then to complain that she only had two days to pack up her home.

The next time she saw him was again at night. A mini-bus with the name of a church on its side. Fifteen other men and women, all of them wide-eyed with fear, their skins grainy under the roof light. She was handed a bible and a cheap rosary as she took her seat. The man with the pockmarked skin drove. Rolling out, La Hiedra dark in the hour before morning, cats prowling the edges of the main street, sliding like mercury under wooden porches at the first touch of the headlights. Her parents long dead, no family, no relations, no one who would miss her. No send-off, no party. The town as useless to her now as an amputated leg. One small bag, all she was allowed, all she needed – there was so little she wanted to take with her.

An eight-hour drive to the parking lot of a church on a desert stretch of Carretera Federal 2D, parallel to the border, between Tijuana and Tecate. And sleeping through the day there, in the bus, pissing on the dust behind the church, sweating and talking hardly at all. Everyone superstitiously frightened that some small detail about themselves might bring about their downfall, might mystically alert Border Patrol. And in the early evening the pastor bringing warm tamales and putting them down without speaking, looking for a moment and shaking his head sadly, then going back to his church.

When it was dark they left the bus, followed a different man for two hours on foot to a hole in the fence. Some of the travelers muttering it was too dangerous, only a little placated when they were told Border Patrol had been bribed for a half hour window.

Scrambling through. And then running, running, running, through the dust and the dark, pushed on by their herder with shoves and punches. Colliding with prickly pear and cholla cactus, tearing thorns from skin and stumbling on again, the world a cartwheeling nightmare of black sky and stars and sand and chest-burning breath. And fear, that someone out there in the night would start shooting.

And then a road, like heaven, like salvation, and the bus and the pockmarked man waiting. And then driving, Maria not believing it, staring through the window like a kid. Road signs passing: Chula Vista, National City. Then the orange-lit sprawl of San Diego and she knew she was really there – the United States! Streets clean, buildings big, cars shiny and all of them brand new, everything brand new. Like every TV show she'd ever seen. She could smell her future in the scents of ocean, freeway, city and car exhaust.

More signs: La Jolla, Del Mar. And then the bus pulled into an abandoned parking lot on the dark edge of a small town. Solana Beach. Nowhere near Los Angeles, their paid-for destination – she knew L.A. was three hours from the border. The pockmarked man letting the other man take the driver's seat, coming to her at the back of the bus and leading her out, onto the broken concrete. The bus driving away, its door closing. But the man telling her not to worry, that this was a much safer way. He could see she was special and he wanted to make sure she got to L.A. without trouble.

There was a white van parked against a half-demolished building. They sat on the doorsill of the cargo bay and he shared some food with her, gave her a fruit drink and insisted she finish it – he wasn't thirsty. Forty minutes later she was unconscious.

She woke once. Could not open her eyes or mouth, could not move her limbs. She heard the sound of an engine, felt the movement of the van, the warm metal of the floor beneath her cheek. Blacked out again.

The next time she woke she wasn't in the van. A room, large by its acoustics. Bound, naked and face-down, over some sort of bench, arms and legs secured, eyes, mouth, most of her head covered with tape. Whispered voices somewhere – a man and a woman, she thought. And then a great tearing jolt of noise, a mix of music and explosions and a giant's voice. So unexpected she had to fight to understand it. Eventually – a movie, as though played in a cinema. But not a movie, a segment of one, a few minutes long, and then another and another, different sounds, but the same – gunshots, cars, strident men, explosions again.

And then they were behind her, two people, working a cold, hard object into her. She was dry as dust and it stretched her painfully, and when she thought she could take no more of the burning, ripping pain, when she was full of this metal thing inside her, some spur or spine on it began to gouge at the tender flesh between her legs.

She tried to pull away, to ease the dreadful pressure. But the bench would not allow it, and the thing rammed in again and again, tearing, hot blood running down the inside of her thigh, and Maria begged and cursed, and jerked at her bonds, craning her head up and back as far as it would go, as though by some sort of spastic contortion she could draw away those parts of her that were being so mercilessly tortured.

And through everything the sound of movies.

Death a certainty, she'd assumed. But when it was over she was put back in the van and someone sponged the blood from between her legs and dressed her. And then driving. And then the sound of the van's door sliding open, the tape at her wrists and ankles being cut. A man's hands helping her out, her head still swathed in tape, and placing in hers a phone and a bottle of water and a small craft knife.

The sound of the van going away on an unpaved road. And then silence and Maria not daring to move. For a long time not daring to move. Until, through the muffling tape, small sounds came to her that were not of men or of pain or of horror, but of the breeze, and grasses moving, and a bird a long way off.

So she dropped the phone and the water and cut away the tape with the knife, peeled it from her face and her head, the sting of it and the torn lumps of hair nothing to the red throbbing inside her, and saw around her the nighttime countryside of Griffith Park. And spread out below, the city of her dreams, the million-mile lightshow: Los Angeles.

Delores thought about Sean. They'd seen each other several times. The loneliness of not working, and the fear she'd had to live with since his first visit, had made the idea of falling back in love with him a cozily attractive proposition.

But unlikely.

She had forgiven him for what he'd done with *Wilderness*, but she would never entirely trust him again. Add Michael and these two new deaths, add Theo and the shallowness of her own emotional engagement, add Sean's drug addiction – a weakness she abhorred – and there wasn't much of a chance for a happy ending.

So make the phone call. How could you lose something if you didn't have it in the first place?

One call. A simple thing. But a shitty thing too, because Sean wouldn't come out of it unscathed, if he came out of it at all. She hated Michael for putting her in this position, for forcing her to hurt a man who was in love with her.

But even if she did it, would she be safe? Michael was sick of her, she'd seen it in his eyes. Jeffery, Ally, Theo – they'd been sick of her for a long, long time.

Only one way to find out.

But not tonight. She couldn't face lying to Sean tonight.

So, take a different tack.

Chick. The leather-suited hotshot with the unwashed pussy. The girl who had been raped the same way she had. She looked wild enough. She looked like if she found the people who raped her she'd respond physically. Looked like she'd go off like a bomb.

When Delores had been tied down and the movies had played, she'd been too terrified to think much about them. And, anyway, most of the American films she'd seen up to that time had been dubbed in Spanish. So she had not come away from her ordeal with a list of titles stored in her head.

But in the years afterwards she had seen a lot of movies. And there had been a handful where one scene or another had triggered a cascade of anxiety, where the music and the voices had brought back that time when she was strapped down and violated.

She'd written them down, she knew them by heart: *Caribbean Crisis, Braughtigan, Halfway to Hell, Full Clip, The Seventh Sea.* A string of action movies from 1968 to 1982. All of them made by Randolph Bannister, a successful producer of the period who just happened to be Jeffery and Ally's grandfather.

Delores had thought it an interesting coincidence, more interesting still when she'd learned that they'd lived with him after their parents had died.

But back then the possibility of a connection to her rape was not something she had wanted to pursue. Not when the idea was patently ridiculous. Not when she and Jeffery and Ally shared something like Bartlemann. Not when being a movie star depended on the twins' cooperation with Michael.

Now, things were different. GHQ had taken away her movie star baton. And suddenly things didn't seem so ridiculous at all, now that there was someone else who had a story about a split in her pussy. Now that if Chick could be primed and set to detonate within Jeffery and Ally's sequestered world, maybe Michael would be too busy dealing with the fallout to bother with one waning movie star.

Thruxton to Bel Air. A late night booty call. Sort of. Chick hoping for a payoff in information.

Fuck first, then talk. Delores stressed by some movie star concern or other, needing to blow off steam. Needing to blow. Writhing and grinding on the super-king. At the end of it, the air in the suite heavy with the smell of fish. Chick wiping herself with a handful of sheet, figuring ways to start the conversation, surprised when Delores beat her to it. Surprised even more when the Mexican Spitfire admitted she was raped.

"The coyote who brought me across the border drugged me. I woke up, my eyes and mouth taped over, tied to a bench. There were two people. They used something that tore me up. Yes, just like you."

Chick fought to stay calm, repaid Delores' information with some of her own.

"I was abducted in L.A. Guy in a ski mask Tasered me, knocked me out. Dumped me in Griffith Park after."

"With water and a phone?"

Chick shook her head. "Just a pad to soak up the blood. What year?"

"2001. You?"

"2000. Maybe they refined their technique."

"Did you recognize any of the movies they played?"

"Man, I was fifteen. All I remember is they were dumbass action flicks. Your kind of thing."

Delores rolled across the bed and took a piece of paper from a nightstand drawer, lay back against Chick and showed it to her.

"This is what I remember."

Chick read through the titles.

"They don't mean anything to me. I hate that kind of shit."

"Give the soapbox a rest, sweetie. All these movies were produced by Randolph Bannister. Randolph Bannister was Jeffery and Ally's grandfather."

Bingo. A puzzle piece that plugged straight into the scenario Chick had been building since she'd seen the case of Flynn's Flying Fuckers memorabilia in the Malibu hills.

Chick said: "You think it was them?"

"They're crazy enough."

"They're a lot more than crazy. I told you that the thing we were raped with was a hardon Oscar, right? That it was stolen from my mother's store. So, this hardon Oscar is the prize piece in a certain kind of memorabilia created by Errol Flynn. He had a group of guys he called Flynn's Flying Fuckers and he made up lapel pins and things like that for the members."

Delores sat up, Mexican eyes flashing, and said: "They have a collection. Ally showed it to me once."

"Out at Raintree, that place above Malibu."

"Yes. They're crazy about it."

"And who else but someone obsessed with that shit would bother to steal the hardon Oscar during the abduction of a fifteen-year-old girl?"

"But there is no Oscar in that collection."

"Doesn't mean they don't have it. They're not going to put it on display if they rape people with it, are they?"

"*People?* You think there were others?"

"Well, there was you and me. And that was ten years ago. I don't think we'd be the only ones, it's too fetishistic. Plus, Danny Bartlemann— You know who he is?"

"Of course, his father used to own the company that distributes all GHQ product. He wrote *Maximum Kill.*"

"Okay. Well, he told me he met someone who had the same thing with her pussy."

"Who?"

"His father's maid. Mexican. Might have come over with a coyote like you, who knows? She's dead now, though, so we can't ask her."

"Pity."

CHAPTER 41

Mule Ridge. Off Angeles Crest Highway, Angeles National Forest. The village a cluster of buildings around an intersection in a one-lane road – a general store, a tourist info place, a restaurant/bar, a gas station, a couple of antiques shops and a stand where some local women sold pottery.

Up in the hills, pine, fir. Cabins for rent along rutted, unpaved trails, for those who craved isolation or wanted to play at being frontiersmen. Snow in the winter, but now the ground dusty beneath the trees. A sign on the side of the road saying fire danger was high.

Tim there to connect with Rebecca, a pilgrimage he'd been putting off since her death. Denning, driving his Crown Victoria, showing solidarity, quid pro quo for Tim's involvement with Bartlemann and GHQ.

Two years ago Rebecca had emailed Tim directions in case he'd wanted to come up for a day. He hadn't taken her up on the offer, but he had a printout of that email now and he gave Denning instructions as they passed through the village.

Another two miles, four different trails. An occasional double-rut driveway leading off, but nothing visible from the road, no cabins, no houses. Once, they passed a string of horses, ridden by city folk in shirtsleeves and big hats, children covered in sunscreen.

The place Rebecca had rented stood with its back to a section of forest, a small cabin with its porch facing out over a meadow that dropped gently down and away in green, knee-high grass, and then rose to climb a slope and become pine forest again.

None of the crime scene photos the cop had let him see after Rebecca's murder had shown the cabin's exterior. But Tim still recognized it immediately. Denning, too.

Denning stopped the car at the edge of the meadow, fifty yards away from the cabin. He pulled out his phone, muttering "Holy shit!" and brought up the video of the Super 8 film he'd stolen from Kid. He played it with Tim looking on.

The cabin, Michael exiting, a backpack over his shoulders. And behind the cabin the trees full of smoke, some of them burning.

Denning put his phone away.

"It's the same fucking place!"

Tim gazed across to the wall of forest on the opposite side of the meadow, figuring whoever had shot it must have been filming from just inside the tree line. Unseen.

They drove along a trail that cut across the meadow, rolled up to the front of the cabin. The place was untenanted. Up on the stoop, peering through windows. The rooms inside looked pleasant – cozy furnishings in bright colors, wooden walls. Tim tried the door, but it was locked. Above it a hand carved sign read: *Lansdowne Cabin.*

Tim was secretly grateful he couldn't get in. There was a reason he hadn't been out here before: proximity-sparked images he didn't want to see – guns firing, holes in flesh, blood at his sister's mouth.

Tim and Denning walked around to the back of the cabin and across the twenty-yard margin of dusty ground that separated it from the edge of the forest. Inside the tree line, scattered amongst healthy green vegetation, the black trunks of burned trees stood ranked back into the shadows like some sort of charred army.

Out front again. Replaying Michael's exit. Following the way he'd gone – right, out of the cabin, along a narrow trail that led toward the forest on the opposite side of the meadow, away from the fire. Mounting his horse, then riding along the trail and into the trees. Rebecca's laptop in his pack.

Tim and Denning spent an hour following the trail on foot. The sky was clear with small patches of high white cloud, sun fell warmly between the trees, lifting the scents of pine and soil. They saw the marks of horse hooves, occasional piles of dried horse shit.

The trail led to a network of similar trails. Michael could have ridden out of the area in any number of directions, easily hiding the fact that he'd been anywhere near the cabin.

Back at the car, Denning leaned against its fender and drank water from a plastic bottle, gazing up at the tree line.

He said: "You reckon Kid knew what Michael was going to do up here? That he was waiting for him?"

"If it was Kid who shot the film."

"That's a point."

"We've got a porn link between him and Michael. And there's the movie finance thing, of course. But he's never turned up in anything about Bartlemann or Rebecca."

"Until now."

"Chick told me that two years ago they scouted Mule Ridge for locations to use in the first film she did. Maybe they shot some footage while they were here and just happened to catch Michael on it. Maybe that's all it was, I'll ask her."

"And then Kid somehow figured out what it meant and realized he could put the bite on his old buddy."

"If the film was shot on the day Rebecca was killed."

"You know it was. There'd be no point to it otherwise."

On the way back through the village, Tim stopped to make sure.

The tourist information office doubled as a letting agency for many of the cabins in the area. Tim spoke to the woman behind the counter – gray hair, t-shirt with an eco-slogan, a long-term resident of the area.

"Lansdowne Cabin."

"Free till next Wednesday, then there's a week in September. Lucky Lansdowne is a popular rental."

"'Lucky'?"

"Sure. Two years ago we had fires up here, only time in the last forty years. Nothing big, mind you, the village was fine. But a couple of properties down that way got burned out. Not Lucky Lansdowne. Fire came within twenty yards of it, then turned back on itself. Cabin wasn't touched."

"Do you remember the date?"

"Of course I do. I remember it because—" and here she leaned across the counter and dropped her voice to a rough whisper "—it was the same day that poor girl was shot to death there. August twenty-third."

She straightened and smiled at him.

"Do you want that week in September?"

Chapter 42

Delores had made the call, hadn't had much choice, told Sean she wanted to see him. Suggested a day by the ocean, a small place she owned on the coast south of Santa Barbara. Told him to meet her there tomorrow, to let himself in if he got there before her.

She put down the phone and wiped her eyes, cursing Michael for making her do this. She felt beaten by him, prostituted, disgusted with herself.

Delores had a small pistol, a .25 automatic. She spent the afternoon firing it in her garden, blowing apart expensive vases and pieces of Wedgwood china.

Sean, happy as a lark. An invitation from the woman he loved.

He hadn't quit heroin yet. He felt too bad about the way he'd pissed on his friendship with Tim. He'd had to do something, with Tim asking all those questions about his past. But it still tasted like shit in his mouth.

He'd cut back, though. He'd gone way down, knowing it was a prerequisite for anything good to happen with Delores. He figured a few more weeks and he would cross the line. Get clean for the first time in two years. Figured he could do it if Delores was waiting on the other side for him.

But for now, a kiddie dose, just enough to kill the aches and the nausea. Not enough to get high. He wanted to show Delores how important she was to him.

Pacific Coast Highway on a summer's day. Trans Am a black smudge on the road. Roof panels off for the very first time, warm wind, sea sparkle, space, whispers of a new way to live.... Behind the wheel, behind the power of the four-hundred-cubic-inch engine, it wasn't too hard to imagine that the wound he'd inflicted on himself with Rebecca was starting to heal.

He drove fast. He made it in an hour and a half.

He'd been there before, when he and Delores had been lovers. A secluded bungalow on a bluff overlooking the sea. A low-key, non-movie star place for assignations that needed to stay unreported.

He stepped out of the car and stretched, smelling the sage and lavender that grew against the front wall and down the borders of the driveway. No other cars. He'd beaten Delores there. He used the key she kept under a rock.

It happened immediately. He put his bag down, walked along a short hall to the living room that faced out over the sea. Saw Michael Starck step out in front of him. Felt something hammer behind his ear.

Ten minutes later he came to, duct taped to a heavy wooden chair, the glass wall showing wide sea and a pathway to the sun.

Michael off to one side. Another guy he'd never seen before standing in front of him. Impassive stare, Mexican, pocked skin. They hadn't taped his mouth. It didn't matter if he screamed, there was no one close enough to hear.

Michael asked: "Who is Tim?"

Sean didn't have time to process the question before the Mexican guy hit him, a hard short right to the side of the head. Hard enough to make Sean throw up over his thighs.

They waited until he'd finished. Then Michael spoke again.

"You told Delores you saw the *Wilderness* screenplay at a screenwriters' group. Some girl called Jocelyn."

"Yeah. What the fuck is this? I told Delores to tell you. I was trying to help."

"Who's Tim?"

The Mexican guy hit him again. Blood ran from one side of Sean's nose and for a while he couldn't see properly out of his left eye. It wasn't like in the movies, where some guy can get punched in the head about a thousand times and still be walking around in the next scene. Sean knew a couple more hits and that would be it – brain damage, fractured skull at the very least.

And the fear, too, was overwhelming. He wasn't sure why he hadn't pissed himself yet. Taped to a chair, some Mexican gangster and a Hollywood psychopath reprising *Reservoir Dogs* – he could have been forgiven.

"Who's Tim?"

Another punch. A sound like a monstrous handclap, followed immediately by a high-pitched tone that sizzled through all of the cells in his head, climbing in volume until he thought his ears would burst.

And the fear and the pain not even all of it. Even worse, the thoughts of Delores. Two possibilities. They got her before he arrived. Tortured and killed her trying to get info she didn't have. Dumped her in a bedroom. But Sean didn't think so. These guys didn't look like they'd just finished killing someone else.

Possibility two: Delores had set him up.

Had to be. If Michael had found out about Tim.

But she could have warned him. They could have disappeared together, fought back together, run away to Brazil.... There were alternatives.

He spoke before Michael could ask his question again.

"Tim is the brother of the woman Delores paid to write *Wilderness*." Sean turned his head to look directly at Michael. "The brother of the woman you killed. Delores didn't know about him, but I went to her funeral. I met him there."

"He gave the script to that Jocelyn girl? Skye was bullshit?"

"No, it happened like Delores said. Skye stole the file, gave pieces of it to Jocelyn. But Tim was seeing Jocelyn, too. He recognized the screenplay."

"He has a copy?"

Sean didn't answer. Michael hit him himself this time, split Sean's lip, wiped blood off his knuckles and screamed: "He has a copy?"

Sean didn't want to speak, didn't want to make another sound. Wanted his beaten mouth to stay closed for ever and ever, so that he wouldn't be someone who'd handed over a friend to this motherfucker. But as Michael wound up for another pop, the fear in Sean reached a point where notions of loyalty or friendship or love or anything else at all became secondary to the need to keep on living. And to his horror he heard himself scream back:

"Yes, you fucker! He has a copy. All right? He has a copy."

Early morning. Delores sitting by her pool, smoking. There before the sun came up, unable to sleep. Light now. Golden Bel Air light, filtered and polished and sprinkled with birdsong. But Delores saw only her hatred of Michael and the dreadful thing she'd done.

She flicked the butt of her cigarette into the pool, watched smoke curl on the water's surface and then vanish. Beside her, on a table, her pistol shone as the morning sun caught it.

It was still early when the garage door rolled up and Delores, wearing a SWAT harness and a pair of tactical boots, ran her eyes over the long slope of her Bentley Continental, figuring it was a better fit for today than the Mercedes.

Death seemed likely. The subject matter they were discussing – wasn't really something everyone was going to shake hands about afterwards. Especially as Michael had told him Jocelyn and Skye had been killed.

So, even though his conscious mind rebelled against it, even though he hated himself more with every word that passed his lips, Sean kept talking. Because as long as he was doing that, he wasn't dying.

"He lives in his sister's old apartment. He found a copy of the file."

Michael said: "I cleaned that place out. There were no screenplays left to find."

"It was hidden. On a USB drive."

"Does he know what it means?"

"He knows it's about Bartlemann. He's been asking questions about GHQ."

Michael cursed and balled his fist. Sean figured what the fuck.

"He's a smart guy. If he's figured you killed Bartlemann, he'll know it was you who killed his sister."

Michael drew back his arm, he knew everything he needed to know. He wouldn't gain anything more by hitting this piece of wreckage again. But he was too angry to stop himself.

His fist was already traveling toward Sean's neck when Delores stepped into the room, pearl-handled, nickel-plated .25 gripped firmly in two hands, knees bent, arms extended. Five years of action movies, her shooter's stance was perfect.

The .25 went off with a bang like a small firecracker and put a slug through Michael's left shoulder, knocking him sideways and sending a fine mist of blood over an armchair she'd had imported from Italy.

Delores was mildly surprised she'd pulled the trigger, but surveying the scene it looked like the best thing she could have done. The Mexican guy with Michael had a gun in his waistband and had started to reach for it when she'd entered the room. Her shot stopped him mid-reach. She kept him covered, told him to take his gun out using his thumb and forefinger and throw it toward her. She'd spoken the same line to Alan Rickman once.

Michael sat on the chair he'd sprayed with blood, holding his shoulder.

"You fucking mad bitch."

Delores couldn't make herself speak to him. She was too frightened she'd lose her nerve, that she'd drop her gun and just give up in the face of his anger. She waved her pistol at the Mexican, forcing him back across the room, giving herself space to get to Sean. As the man moved backwards, she ran her eyes over the scars on his face – chicken pox as a kid. Something familiar about that ravaged skin.

Close to Sean, she pulled a Ka-bar utility knife from the shoulder sheath on her harness and used it to slice the tape that held his left wrist. When his hand was loose she gave him the knife and covered the Mexican while Sean cut the rest of himself free. The Mexican didn't make any sudden moves, just watched her, patiently, as though he knew he'd get another chance to resolve this situation.

Sean levered himself upright, picked up the Mexican's pistol and stepped behind Delores. Together they walked out of the room, Delores backwards, Sean holding her harness, guiding her while she kept her gun on Michael and the Mexican. He'd seen his share of action movies too.

Michael shouted after them.

"Don't do anything stupid, Delores. Let us deal with Tim and we can all go back to our lives. I'll even forget you shot me. Promise."

But Delores and Sean were already outside, running for the Bentley.

Life changing. One afternoon and nothing was the same. Michael's words meant nothing, both of them knew it. Sean would have died in that chair, Delores would have been dealt with as soon as Tim was no longer a problem. Michael would do everything he could to make today's escape nothing more than a deferral.

Sean drove. Delores watched to see that they were not followed, and then looked for a long time at Sean. It felt good to have saved him, to have not used someone who loved her to save her own skin. She liked what it said about herself.

Despite his throbbing head and the pain in his mouth, Sean smiled as he drove. Delores had set him up, but she'd rescued him, too. True love overcoming self-interest, a pure statement of forgiveness, of how much she wanted him.

But there was a cost to this reconnection. Tim. Sean had spilled everything Michael needed to know. If he'd known he was going to be rescued he would have held out longer, endured more for his friend. But it hadn't happened that way. The only thing he could do now was do his best to keep Tim safe, do his best to come clean. He used the car phone, dialed Tim's number – a recorded message said the phone was turned off or out of the coverage area.

Delores looked at him questioningly, he told her everything he knew about Tim.

Later, on the other side of Oxnard, Delores saw a white van parked on the side of the road. It was only then that she remembered where she'd seen the Mexican before.

Solana Beach. Handing her a fruit drink. More than ten years ago.

Chapter 43

Tim, back from Mule Ridge, dropped off by Denning. Sean waiting on the steps outside the kitchen, face bruised and cut, looking like shit. A Bentley parked in the alley.

Tim let him in and sat down at the table. He didn't speak, remembering their last interaction. Sean sat across from him, reached out and put his hand on Tim's arm.

"I'm your friend, man. What I said last time was bullshit. I only said it because there was something I couldn't face telling you."

"What happened to your face?"

"Michael Starck knows you've got the *Wilderness* screenplay. And he knows that you know it's about Bartlemann."

"How the hell would he know that?"

"He had Jocelyn and Skye killed. He found a note from you on the script."

"Jocelyn's dead? Jesus.... Lucky he doesn't know who I am."

"Uh, well, about that...."

Sean pointed to his face and told Tim everything that had happened at his meeting with Michael and the Mexican.

"I'm sorry, man. If Delores hadn't turned up they would have killed me. She's staying with me at the bunker, you should too. It's the safest place. Also...."

He took the Mexican's gun out of the back of his pants and slid it across the table. Tim picked it up, remembered Chick showing him how everything worked. This one was bigger. It had a plastic-looking olive-drab frame. At the base of the grip there was a "Walther" logo and the black slide was stamped with "P99". He pictured himself pulling the trigger, blowing away pieces of Michael.

Tim said: "What was it you couldn't face telling me?"

"You might want to put the gun down."

Said as a joke, but there was a current of sadness in his voice that made Tim look at him. Tim popped the magazine, racked the slide and ejected the barrel load. He put everything on the table.

"Gun's down."

"My breakout role. *Random Burn.* You were right. It would have made me a star. It was one of those parts every actor dreams of, that lifts you out of obscurity and puts you in front of the world. I'd been waiting for it all my career."

"You got it because of Delores."

"No, that's the crazy thing. I got it because the people at GHQ liked my work. Delores was out of favor by then, wasn't working. No one was going to listen to her about casting."

"But you were seeing her."

"Yeah."

"And Michael fired you when he found out."

Sean shook his head sadly.

"No. The part was mine. No one took it away."

"What happened?"

"About four years ago Delores dumped Michael. Michael stopped putting her in movies. Delores rode it out as long as she could, but after a couple of years she'd had enough and she started hassling Michael for parts. He wasn't interested. You don't dump a man like Michael Starck. A little while later, GHQ put *Canvas Carousel* into development. A perfect comeback vehicle for Delores – female wrestler on the skids at the end of her career wins back her title and her institutionalized Down's syndrome son. Action *and* credibility. Would have done for her what *From Here to Eternity* did for Frank Sinatra. Delores had to have the part. She was obsessed. She begged, threatened – everything she could think of. Michael wouldn't budge."

Sean got up and ran himself a glass of water at the sink, sat down again.

"Then Delores got the idea for *Wilderness.* She'd met Rebecca at some industry function or other and she hired her to write the screenplay. I bumped into her a couple of times when she was over at Delores' place for script meetings, but I didn't have a clue what they were working on, not then. Delores wouldn't say anything about it. Eventually, though, they got a first draft finished and Delores couldn't help herself. She had to show it off to someone, so she let me take a look at it."

Sean broke off and swallowed. When he spoke again, there were tears in his eyes.

"Man, you gotta believe me, I never thought they'd go after Rebecca. I thought Delores would get slapped on the wrist and that would be the end of it."

Tim looked at his friend and felt a sense of creeping dread. Since he and Denning had tied Michael to Rebecca's cabin with the Super 8 film, he'd just assumed Delores must have been the one who told Michael about his sister writing the screenplay. Things looked worse than that.

Tim said: "You figured out what the screenplay was about."

"I guessed what it *might* be about. Everyone in the industry had heard about Scott Bartlemann. And here was a screenplay that had an alternative take on a murder that could have been his. I didn't know anything for sure. I mean, Delores could have been making the fucking thing up. But she was still after *Canvas Carousel* and there wasn't really a big part for her in *Wilderness*, so I thought maybe there was some other reason for her and Rebecca writing it. But I didn't *know*, man. I didn't know about GHQ and *Maximum Kill* and any of that shit."

"But you couldn't risk it being true. Because if it was and it fucked GHQ, there wouldn't be any more dream role for you. There wouldn't be any movie."

Sean put his face in his hands. Tim listened to him sob and wondered if there were any limits to how insanely awful life could get.

Sean raised his face.

"All I did was give Michael a copy. That's all I did. Why would he even go after Rebecca? Delores was the one driving the thing."

"So you wouldn't have cared if he killed Delores?" Tim couldn't keep the sarcasm out of his voice.

"No! God, of course I didn't want that. All Michael had to do was give her *Canvas Carousel*. Why would he risk killing a movie star when he could so easily do that? I didn't think anything bad would happen. All I wanted was for things not to get fucked up. I thought if he had some warning it'd be safer, that he'd be able to control the situation in case Delores did something stupid."

"You fucking whore."

Tim looked at the pistol, the magazine, the bullet, and thought about putting them back together. But the rage suddenly left him, replaced instead by an overwhelming fatigue. Michael was the killer. It was Michael who deserved to die. Sean was just another filmland casualty; too venal, too vain, too Hollywood-infected to be truly blameworthy.

Tim said: "If you knew all of this, if you knew you were going to have to hide it from me, why did you come up to me at the funeral? Why make contact at all?"

"Guilt. I lived with what I'd done every fucking day. You were the only way I could do anything about it. Not fix it, or anything. Of course not that. But I thought by being your friend I'd at least be helping you through what I'd caused. Does that make sense?"

"Why Rebecca and not Delores? Why didn't Michael kill her?"

"He was still in love with her. He used Rebecca to send a message instead. And it worked. Scared Delores so badly she never asked him about another film again. She dumped me because she thought I'd betrayed her by taking the screenplay to Michael, then just lived in her mansion like Norma Desmond. I figured Michael might get nervous about me, so I disappeared. Bought the bunker and pulled my head in."

Tim glanced through the window at the Bentley.

"But now it's all happy families again."

"Time's passed. Plus Delores was always going to show Michael the screenplay at some point anyhow, otherwise there would have been no reason to write it. She's probably accepted that he would have reacted the same way regardless of who gave it to him."

"Did she ever tell you how she found out about the story for the screenplay? How she knew who killed Bartlemann?"

"No."

"You didn't ask?"

"I didn't want to know."

"So you don't know if she was there the night he was killed?"

Sean shook his head.

"Why no breakout role in the end? Michael take back the offer?"

"No. I was sick of myself. I didn't kill Rebecca, but I put her in Michael's sights. Once I heard she'd been murdered, even though the cops said it was a robbery, I knew what had happened. And I just couldn't do it anymore. I didn't *deserve* to do it. So I gave up acting and took up junk." Sean paused, weighing his words, frightened that they'd sound trite. "You know, man, I got next to you because of Rebecca, but after that it wasn't just for her."

They were silent then for a long time. Tim stared out the window, trying to determine how he felt. Points for finally telling him. Points for feeling bad enough about what he'd done to give up a movie career. Points for becoming a junkie. But lying for two years, knowing about the screenplay and how it figured in his sister's murder? That was a scar that was going to take a long time to fade.

It was only when Tim saw the Bentley pull out from the curb in the alley below that he realized Sean had left.

CHAPTER 44

Ally in the wild grass out front of Raintree, staring at the wide clear sky as she spoke on her phone. And then sitting with Jeffery in his car, parked on the gravel out back of the ruined house. Looking through photograph albums, her arm around his shoulders as he turned the pages. Pictures of their childhood, their parents. Lives on track, a smiling, sun-drenched Californian family with everything to live for.

They spoke quietly together and laughed. Ally held him close to her. Between pages of the photo album he turned his head and kissed her childishly on the cheek. A little later they went down to the basement.

Kid in New York on a two-night stint schmoozing potential exhibitors. Peta along as a perk of the job. Chick at the office, Ally Bannister on the phone wanting a progress meeting out at Raintree later that day. Chick making excuses, turning it down flat, thinking: smarter not to be alone with those two.

And what was the point of a meeting anyhow? *Antepenultimate* pre-prod was under control. Nothing Jeffery and Ally had to say would make any difference. Maybe they'd wanted to talk about Danny Bartlemann being found shot to pieces in his motel. Chick had been shocked and saddened when she was told about it. Danny had been a nice guy and an overlooked talent. But Haldane Productions owned the rights to the screenplay and the death of the writer meant next to nothing as far as getting the film made went. If they needed rewrites she'd get Tim to do them.

A half hour later, Chick's phone vibrating, the message changing her mind. A picture, a few inches square. Digital code. In a way, not even real. But more than real enough to begin the final act in a drama that had begun in her mother's memorabilia store twelve years ago: Jeffery in a large dark room with a few rows of leather couches behind him. Holding a golden statuette turned sideways to show a phallus in profile. The hardon Oscar. In Jeffery's hand. In the screening room at Raintree.

Chick didn't think about consequences, about the risk of getting caught. She'd lived with the horror too long. Blood to the head and groin, pressure at the front of her skull, the burning rush of impending retribution.

She called Delores' cell, then burned tarmac from the office to her flat in North Hollywood, took the Bersa Thunder Ultra Compact .45 from under her bed, put a leather jacket on over her catsuit and got back on her bike.

Five minutes' ride. Laurel Canyon Boulevard. Elrita Drive.

The Bentley out front of Sean's bunker. Chick in the passenger seat, smells of leather and money and gun oil. Delores behind the wheel in her action woman get-up: black singlet, black assault pants, tactical boots, SWAT harness with upside-down Ka-bar. Hair tied back, mirror aviators. She wanted high-five when Chick climbed in. Black leather gloves.

Chick figured the bitch was whacked, but what the hell? It'd work for today.

They could have had male muscle. Could have enlisted Tim and Sean, apprised them of the situation. But this was a girls-only gig. Entrance fee: one ripped pussy apiece. A treat that couldn't be shared.

Malibu-bound. The Bentley moving without sound. Delores saying things like 'boo yah' and 'let's get this fucker done'. Trotting out lines from her movies. Checking out her biceps as she turned the steering wheel. Chick knew she was shitting herself, but she had to admire her front.

On the floor, under Chick's feet: Delores' weapon – a TEC-9 full-auto machine pistol with a twenty-round clip. An 80s gun she'd been given as a present after a production affair with the weapons guy on one of her movies – a period piece about cocaine running in Miami. She'd fired it during filming, but not since. She figured it would say fuck you a lot louder than her .25.

After a while, Delores dialed down her gung-ho and told Chick she wanted information about the coyote who brought her into the States. Now that Jeffery and Ally were confirmed as the rapists, Delores pegged him as their source. Chick wasn't convinced, but figured it wouldn't hurt to ask.

Raintree. The basement screening room. Above them the ruins of the house. And beyond that the sky and the sun and the limitless world. But in the room, shadows and dim walls, the screen alight with their grandfather's films, a loop of clips they'd put together twelve years ago when they first hit on the idea that they might be able to cure themselves.

The rape bench bolted to the floor. The hardon Oscar specially displayed in a niche in the wall opposite the door, softly spot-lit, unmissable.

Jeffery stood beside the bench, running his hand along it, staring at the images on the screen. He'd spent a lot of time thinking about how to do it. A gun had seemed too crude, too noisy, and a knife just wasn't his thing. He'd found the answer in his wardrobe – a brown leather belt, softened with age. It had needed more holes to make it neck-size, though.

He and Ally wore white robes, nothing underneath. Jeffery knew that Kid was in New York, but Ally had reassured him that he wasn't needed this time, that she'd organized everything. Jeffery hadn't asked questions – there was no need, using the First could not be anything but perfect.

He adjusted his hat. His favorite. Fred McMurray, *Double Indemnity*. Ally held his hand and looked at her watch.

Out of the Bentley and running. SWAT boots perfect for the gravel behind the house. Chick leading, the Bersa in her hand, nickel slide glinting in the sun. Delores close, TEC-9 on a strap, ready to go. No plan. Just get to the screening room ready to kill.

Quiet through the garage entrance. Delores coiling through doorways, the TEC-9's barrel pointed at the ceiling like she'd been taught by technical advisors. Chick going in with hers leveled, not giving a fuck about gun safety.

Stairs.

Corridor.

The long hall in the basement dark, the screening room door illuminated at the end. On the left, the memorabilia room. Empty. Another room with a sofa in it. Nowhere else to look. No more seconds between them and what they were there to do. Chick's cunt chafing against the seam of her catsuit, a reminder of what had happened in the room ahead. The Bersa held seven rounds, the spare clip in her jacket pocket made fourteen. She planned to use them all.

Tag team. Chick threw the screening room door open and stepped inside, Delores covered with the TEC. The scene in front of them everything they'd dreamed, everything they'd feared. Nightmare imaginings made real at last. The rape bench, the movies on the screen, high volume sound bytes, exploding macho bullshit. And across the room, proof-positive that this was the end of the road – the hardon Oscar.

Jeffery turning as they entered, mouth wide. Looking at Ally, wondering what the fuck? And then, seeing her face, seeing the acceptance there, understanding what she'd done. His eyes filling with tears, reaching for her with his hands, not caring now that he would never have the First, that he had been betrayed. Possessed only by a dreadful sorrow, by the knowledge that he was now to be parted from her.

And Ally cupping his face with her palms, holding his eyes with hers, wanting this to be her last sight, the only image she cared to take from the world.

And both of them in that moment, in that instant, knowing there was no other way, no other exit or conclusion for them, and feeling a letting-go, a divine relaxation, understanding that this was their cure, their long-dreamed liberation, their freedom at last.

Chick, the Bersa held one-handed, arm straight, ready for conversation. Wanting the details of her abduction, the name of the man with the van. Wanting to give this final tallying the weight it deserved.

But Delores too amped, too frightened if the truth be told, standing a little behind Chick and to her right, opening up with the TEC, burning full-auto through the clip, the shitty gun shaking like a jackhammer as the overweight one-pound bolt pistoned back and forth. And holding on grimly in the smoke and the noise, fighting recoil as a river of brass cartridges arced from the breech.

Halfway through the clip Chick turned and opened her mouth to scream at Delores to stop shooting. But saw Delores' frown, her look of incomprehension as her bullets ran out and Jeffery and Ally stayed standing, and turned back to see the white robes unstained, to see the twins slowly opening screwed-shut eyes as they tried to figure out if heaven was really supposed to look like the inside of a screening room.

Blanks. Delores' armorer lover, she understood now, had given her only what he could lay his hands on – movie-set ammo, of course.

Jeffery, not entirely unused to situations involving firearms and death, recovered quickly, started to move across the floor toward the two women, laughing.

Until Chick squeezed the trigger on the Thunder Ultra Compact and ionized the air in the room with a single hideous bang. Sent a heavy .45 slug into Jeffery's knee, blowing away his patella and most of the joint behind it.

Jeffery fell face-first, but not feeling the pain yet, tried immediately to stand. And fell again, this time twisting, dropping sideways, so that he came to rest with his back against the base of one of the couches, his legs straight out in front of him.

His robe had fallen open. He looked down at the hole in the middle of his leg, at the blood and the splintered ends of blue-white bone, and said: "Huh?"

Ally looked from her brother to Chick, assuming the kill shot was coming, waiting for it to be over, waiting for it to be her turn. And when it didn't come, shifted her gaze to Delores, not understanding why she was there.

"Delores?"

Chick stepped in close and hit her backhand across the cheekbone with the side of her pistol. Ally dropped to the floor and lay still, Chick walked past her to the far side of the room and took the hardon Oscar from its niche in the wall.

Twelve years since she'd seen it last, twelve years since she'd been dragged across the threshold that separated a safe and ordered world from one where violence and lack of accountability were the norm. She hefted it in her hand, felt its weight, rubbed her thumb over the smooth golden metal, over the vicious spur jutting from its middle.

Everything was in it. All her anger, all the dignity they had taken away from her, all the injustice, all the screaming impotence – all of it crystallized within this thirteen-and-a-half-inch piece of metal brought into being by some brain-rotted piece of shit sixty years ago.

Ally had regained consciousness, had pushed herself into a seated position on the floor, leaning her back against the stage. Jeffery groaned and squeezed his thigh, trying to stem the flow of blood from his knee. Delores unsheathed her Ka-bar.

Chick came back across the room.

Jeffery looked up from his wound and smiled at her.

"The First...."

Chick shot him in the shoulder. Jeffery slammed back against the couch and screamed, slipped sideways leaving a bright smear on the leather behind him. On the screen a gas tanker ran into a house and a guy with muscles lit a cigar. The sound of the explosion sent tremors through the floor. Chick located the speakers on either side of the screen, emptied rounds into them until her gun was empty and the movies played silently.

She slapped in a new clip and racked the slide, turned to Ally and asked a question.

"Why me?"

And then shot Jeffery in his other shoulder. Jeffery now jerking on the floor, screaming and begging, upper body and the sleeves of his robe slick with blood, but not near death yet.

Chick asked her question again, and Ally, with no allegiance to anyone but her brother, had no reason not to answer. But Jeffery was in agony and she could not bear to see it. She called to him and told him she loved him, that they would be together forever. And then looked at Chick and told her she'd tell her everything she wanted to know if.... And signaled toward Jeffery with her eyes.

Chick stood over Jeffery and kicked him until he looked at her. She gazed at him for a full minute before she shot him twice in the center of the chest.

When he was dead she turned back to Ally and Ally said: "Why you? Because you were there. We asked for a girl and you were what we got."

"And me?"

Delores' voice was high. Ally looked at her and shook her head slowly.

"I don't know what you mean."

"I was raped here, too. I was strapped to that bench, torn with that fucking statue."

"When?"

"Ten years ago. Eleven. Before I worked for Bartlemann. You never recognized me?"

"The girls have their faces covered with tape. It's part of the ritual that they remain anonymous to us, otherwise they couldn't be vessels for our pain. You? You were one of them?"

Delores lunged forward and cut a deep slice into Ally's left breast with her Ka-bar. Ally drew in her breath and made a small coughing noise, but she didn't scream. Chick pushed Delores back.

"Wait!"

"I want to know who the coyote is!"

Ally looked at her breast, then at Delores.

"I don't know what you mean."

"The pig I paid to bring me to America. The pig who delivered me to you."

"All the girls were delivered by Kid Haldane. We never asked where he got them. But they were all Mexican, so perhaps...."

Chick felt her head swim, as though the world had shifted sideways around her.

Kid.

She'd known.

She'd known that night at his apartment on Wilshire. But to hear it, to have it made real.... A man who had been the closest thing she'd had to a friend for three years, who had done his best to make her cinematic dreams come true. It seemed impossible that something as destructive as her rape could be made even more so, could send its fissures through even more of her life. But there it was.

Chick said: "I'm not Mexican."

"No. You were the first one. Kid took you himself. But white girls, in Los Angeles...too dangerous to do more than once."

"And he took the hardon Oscar when he took me?"

Ally nodded.

"It became part of our ritual."

"How many girls have there been?"

Ally shrugged.

"Three or four a year, for twelve years...."

Chick shot her five times, from crotch to stomach. Delores stuck the Ka-bar into the side of her neck and left it there.

CHAPTER 45

A white van in the alley. Christo in the driver's seat. Deep night in Santa Monica. The aches that had started a few hours ago in his legs and back trimmed to nothing now by a line of brown smack. But not the irritation, not the anger at having to sit in a van for four hours when he could have been drinking Jose Cuervo Silver and partying with an American whore. Instead of waiting for the fucker who was supposed to live in the apartment he could see above the fence of the alley.

He'd climbed the steps to the back entrance just before dusk, seen an empty kitchen through the window, an empty flat. He'd tried the door but it was locked and the place was too overlooked by surrounding properties to risk kicking it in. Plus he didn't want to leave any marks that would alert its occupant.

So now he was waiting, but the lights in the flat hadn't come on, Tim hadn't come home. Michael had said kill the guy, but Christo was up here because Theo Portman had asked him to come. And Theo had said something else – kill the guy, then kill Delores.

Delores was a movie star, a high profile target. Christo had sucked air through his teeth until Theo pointed out that if she started blabbing, a certain job Christo did for him ten years ago might come back and bite both of them in the ass.

Tim either had himself a girl somewhere, or that streak of piss they'd had in the chair had tipped him off. Maybe both.

But Christo didn't have anything else to go on, so he stayed there, watching the flat, waiting for a man who had a bullet coming his way.

Denning sweating. On his bed. Thick legs tangled in sheets. Dark body hair holding the heat, face unshaven, fingers clawing the coarse growth on his chest, leaving red marks. A glass of whiskey, half empty, ice melted, on the nightstand. A small light. And Denning staring at the ceiling, the whites of his eyes made yellow by the light.

Tim had called, told him about this guy Sean's part in channeling the *Wilderness* screenplay to Michael Starck. Told him he, Tim, was now on Starck's most wanted list and couldn't go home. And, more bizarrely, that Delores was now on that list too, that she'd rescued Sean, saved him from Michael and one of his thugs.

Michael was striking back.

Denning smoked, watched the gray coils rise and break apart, and listened to the silence of the house around him. Its emptiness. Peta with Kid Haldane. He made a conscious effort not to picture it. Failed. Got out of bed and pulled on some clothes.

Pacific Palisades. 2457 Mesa Road. Denning had had the address for a while now, a credit card and an internet connection all he'd needed. But there had been no reason to visit it. There was no real reason now, except that Denning couldn't sleep, couldn't stop his mind from working. Couldn't stop thinking about Peta.

Windows down on the Crown Victoria, late night air, the smell of eucalyptus and the sea not far away. Air-brushed California. The wealthy, the empowered. Mansions with ocean views, the winding street thick with flowering sub-tropicals, orange-golden light spilling from windows and lights above doors.

Portman's white castle, set back from the road. Wide green lawns gently spot-lit. Movie money making dreams real. Denning cruised past. He'd seen photos. A fat man with white hair. Regularly listed in the one-hundred most powerful Hollywood players.

There was a small T-junction a hundred yards on from the house. Denning parked there for a while and watched. But it was late and there was nothing but the light and the grass and the white walls, nothing that told him anything more about Theo Portman than he already knew.

Denning stayed for an hour, then headed for town.

Santa Monica Boulevard. West Hollywood. Denning aware he was acting obsessively, but unable to stop himself. An hour in a retro porn store, sifting through old VHS fuck tapes transferred to disc. Full-bush flicks revived for the connoisseur. Pizza delivery men, TV cable guys, moustaches and ponytails.

Denning bought three, all of them part of Kid Haldane's back catalogue. Wanting to see what Peta was getting. Sick but true.

Some kid in the alley behind the store sold him a blister of Oxy. At home he swallowed 80mg and fired up the player.

On the sofa in the sitting-room, lights out, TV on. Denning watching. Kid, twenty years younger, the star. Plowing his way through women with bad perms and too much tan. Monster cock the focus of attention. Denning aghast, substituting his daughter for the posturing skanks on the screen. Wondering if he'd ever be able to look her in the eye again.

Dumbass scenarios from back when porn producers thought their audience was interested in story. Denning kept watching, floating on Oxy, determined to see it all. Hoping it would help him let Peta become a daughter again.

Kid was the lead in every video, supported by a changing roster of equally equipped but less handsome men who mostly looked like they'd been hired off a construction site. Three films into the first disc, Denning started paying attention to one of them in particular – a heavy-set Mexican guy with pockmarked skin.

At first he was just one more body slamming itself into whatever orifice Kid wasn't plugging at the time, a brutal man who fucked hard and grunted a lot. But then there was a scene where he went down on a woman, a close shot of his face from the side. And Denning saw a pattern of pockmarks, like a ragged question mark running across the man's cheekbone and down his cheek. A pattern he'd seen once before and never forgotten.

The man in the white van across the street from his house the day Clara had gone missing had worn black wraparound sunglasses. A partial disguise. But Denning had got a good look at the left side of his face. Same mark. The guy in the video younger, but the same man. Denning knew it for sure.

Denning fast-forwarded through the remaining disks. The Mexican tag-teamed with Kid in another eight films. Looked like they'd been a popular duo.

Denning got a pen and wrote down the credits at the end of each one. The same every time.

Kid Haldane.

The Mexican billed as Polla Villa. A stage name without doubt. *Polla* Spanish for cock, *Villa* from Pancho, probably.

Directed by Brett Adelaide.

Produced by Sunnico.

Denning staring at his piece of paper. Sunnico equals Theo Portman. Brett Adelaide equals Michael Starck. Polla Villa, the man who took his wife.

But why Clara? How had they even known about her? She had been abducted two years before Denning had had any contact with GHQ or Delores Fuentes. Where was the connection?

When Clara disappeared from her dog grooming gig the police canvassed all of the clients in her appointment book. Denning had gone through the book as well, afterwards, staring at names and addresses, begging them to reveal the secret of her fate. But none of them had given him anything.

He killed the TV, went into his bedroom and sat at his desk. The cops had returned the appointment book when they figured there was no chance of Clara turning up. He took it out of a drawer and opened it.

It went back six months from the date she'd disappeared. Most of the clients repeated on monthly or two-weekly cycles. Clara did around five jobs a day.

The book was a handwritten ledger: name, address, time, breed and number of dogs, services required. Denning started at the beginning, running his finger down pages. Had he read the name Michael Starck all those years ago and forgotten it? Was that why he had not seen the connection before?

Almost a hundred and thirty days of entries. No Michael Starck. He did it again. No Theo Portman, no company names: no GHQ or Big Glass. Not even an entry for Sunnico. But finally something that clicked. A number. A street.

2457 Mesa Road. Malamute. Wash and groom. Nail clip. Flea and tick treatment. Monthly entries. Booked by Carmelita. Booked by Mariana.

Denning had missed it on earlier passes because he'd been concentrating on names. But, he realized now, the kind of people who could afford a Malamute and to have someone else wash it probably wouldn't be making the booking themselves.

Would be getting the maid or the housekeeper or the assistant to do it. So no Theo Portman printed neatly in Clara's hand.

But 2457 Mesa Road was there – Theo Portman's address.

And that meant Portman could have known Clara, could have seen her, could have taken note of that body. And when the time came, when the need was there, arranged to have her given to Michael. Used a Mexican thug who worked for him back in the day.

Could have. Who was there to ask for proof? Not Theo. Not Michael. But there was Delores. On the run. Hiding out. Maybe ready to talk if it would help save her skin. If they promised to remove the threat Michael had become to her.

CHAPTER 46

Mid-morning. North Hollywood. Chick's place. Tim in his leathers, packing the Walther P99. Chick, white as a sheet, cleaning the Thunder Ultra Compact at a coffee table in the flat's main room. Talking as she rubbed and oiled, telling Tim how she and Delores had killed Jeffery and Ally. The hardon Oscar standing golden at the end of the table.

"It ain't like setting fire to a billboard, I can tell you that, Timbo."

"You regret it?"

Chick looked up.

"Jesus, no. Someone rapes the shit out of you, there aren't too many other effective solutions. It's just...visceral, is all."

Chick looked down at the table for a while, not speaking, then said quietly: "It's a hell of a thing." And then, pulling herself together: "And it's fucking more of a thing finding out about Kid."

"Does he go too?"

"I don't know. Maybe. I want to, you know? Just wipe that fucking slate clean. But I don't know.... Delores wants to kill the Mexican guy, the one who supplied Kid."

"With your help?"

"No, that shit's her deal."

"And she says the Mexican guy is the same one who interrogated Sean? The one who's coming after me?"

"The very."

"You think she can take care of him by herself?"

Chick laughed. "Maybe if she gets some real bullets. Probably not. One has to assume coyotes are bona fide bad-asses."

Tim watched her put the Thunder Ultra Compact back together. The killing had started. Two-thirds of GHQ were pushing up daisies. His own target was waiting, unambiguously guilty. Worse than waiting, had started to hunt him back. *It's a hell of a thing....* He figured he'd get to feel what it was like for himself soon enough.

Denning called Tim's cell. A half hour later he stepped into Chick's flat. Tim had previously told him about Sean's interrogation and escape, about Tim's own fugitive status. Now, Denning learned a whole lot more – that Chick and Delores had killed Jeffery and Ally. That Kid and a Mexican guy had been involved in supplying rape girls for twelve years. That Delores and Chick had been two of the victims.

Denning marveling that Jeffery and Ally were dead. Marveling more that Delores was involved. Looking at Chick like she might explode.

And then thinking about Peta, vacationing with Kid in the Big Apple. A second or two of total fear. Then telling himself she was okay, that if Kid was going to hurt her he would have done it long before now, that he wouldn't try anything so far away from his home turf. And then wondering if he was just deluding himself.

He put a porno disc in Chick's player, fast-forwarded to a face shot of the Mexican, wondering if Chick's Mexican guy and Clara's were the same. But Chick had only heard of him via Delores. She'd never actually seen him.

Tim and Chick waiting for more, an explanation of this cheesy twenty-year-old fuck vid. Denning nodded at the guns on the table.

"You got one of those for me?"

Tim looked at him incredulously.

"I thought you were writing a book."

Denning said: "Not anymore."

And then told them about the man with the wraparound shades and a question mark of chicken pox scars, the man who'd followed Clara, who'd been parked across the street on the morning of the day his wife disappeared.

He pointed to the TV, to the frozen face of Kid Haldane's big-dicked wingman.

"Him. Clara was taken July twenty-eighth, the day before Bartlemann was killed."

Denning fast-forwarded the disc, froze it again when the credits came up, pointed out Polla Villa, pointed out Brett Adelaide, pointed out Sunnico.

"So, we already figure Michael Starck and Theo Portman are linked. They made porn flicks together in the old days. Big Glass distributes all GHQ product. And both of them profited massively from Scott Bartlemann's death. Now, the Mexican guy who took Clara turns out to be part of Sunnico's old stable. He must have known Michael, and he probably knew Theo. And Theo was one of Clara's dog customers. He would have known her, known what she looked like."

Denning took a deep breath, shuddered as he let it out.

"The body at Bartlemann's was Clara. They substituted her so that Maria the maid could disappear and come back as Delores the movie star."

Denning got up from his seat and took the disc out of the player, sat down again, looked hard at Tim and said: "So I don't give a shit about a book anymore. These motherfuckers killed my wife."

The three of them were silent for a while, Tim and Chick digesting this info, Denning staring at Chick's gun. Then Chick said: "Hang on, wouldn't the cops have taken fingerprints off the body? If they were Clara's they would have matched the print on her driver's license."

Denning shook his head.

"Clara got her license when we lived in Nevada. Nevada licenses don't require fingerprinting. She never changed over to a Californian license."

Later, Chick made coffee and they talked for a while about guns and the reality of killing, Chick the only one of them with any first-hand knowledge. Denning so far gone, so fucked by the world, he didn't care how he'd feel after he pulled the trigger.

Tim listened to the conversation, but didn't say much, frightened that if he got into it too deeply, if he imagined it too clearly, he'd choke when it came time to actually do it.

He turned the dialogue toward a Rebecca-related loose end. Asked Denning to play the video of Michael coming out of the cabin at Mule Ridge.

Chick recognized it immediately.

"Yeah, Super 8. Totally real. Look at that color. That was one crazy day, man. The fucking trees were on fire!"

"Who shot it?"

"Me, of course. I told you I scouted Mule Ridge as a location for *Loggers*."

"With Kid?"

"No. Just me. But I gave him everything I shot. Once we'd processed the stock we watched it, decided if the location was suitable or not, then Kid stored it at his office. We didn't use that cabin. How did you get hold of it?"

Tim nodded at Denning. "Kid's car got broken into. Long story. The film found its way back to Kid, anonymously, a little while later." Tim tapped the phone's screen. "You know who that is, right?"

"Sure, Michael Starck. I figured he was on vacation or something. I was back in the trees, he couldn't see me."

"This film is how Kid got finance for *Antepenultimate*."

"Huh?"

"The fire. That was the only time they'd had one up there in forty years. Dates the film to August twenty-third two years ago. And August twenty-third two years ago was the day my sister was killed. In that cabin up at Mule Ridge, while she was finishing rewrites on *Wilderness*."

"Jesus Christ...."

"All it would have taken was for Kid to have seen a news report about Rebecca's murder. Once that happened, Michael was fucked. Cough up three mil or else."

Chick shook her head slowly, like un-fucking-believable.

When the video was done, Denning went out of the room and called Peta in New York. No answer, her phone was turned off. When he came back in, Tim said it was time they had a talk with Delores.

CHAPTER 47

Denning in his car, Tim and Chick burning asphalt on the Triumphs. Visors up, digging the breeze. Both of them strapped, personal armament part of their lives for now. Until things were finished.

Dusk. Orange in the sky, smog-powdered brown at the horizon. But high up, a dome of pure, fading blue. A false clarity, but still beautiful.

Tim feeling sharp and light and fast. Body-fat now down to an ab-revealing percentage. Trying to feel fated, like the thing with Michael was out of his hands, like he had no choice but to do what he'd set himself to do. But a background fear in him still, a white noise hiss behind everything he did.

And Chick changing gears, twisting the throttle, but feeling in her hand the kicking of the Thunder Ultra Compact. Feeling blank. Feeling expended. The killing of Jeffery and Ally something she didn't want to examine. Not now. Enough to hope that it had done some good.

Wondering how much everything meant to her now. Her hatreds, her attacks, Hollywood.... Even her own film, slated to start principal photography in four weeks.

Not sure how it happened, but knowing her life had been turned on its head. That there was love in it now, something she'd never expected.

And Denning, bombed on Oxy and too little sleep, driving, windows up, air-con off, the overheated cell of his car feeling like it was the only thing holding his head together, knowing that when this thing with Michael Starck and the Mexican and Theo Portman was done there would be nothing left of him.

Sean's bunker. The five of them there, sitting on the sofas or standing around. A cool distance between Tim and Sean. Introductions. Explanations. Everyone knew what everyone knew. With a Mexican movie star exception. Delores knew a whole lot more.

Denning looking at her like he'd found the holy grail, like everything he needed to know was contained in that over-trained body. Eight years wandering through the wreckage of his life, finally come full-circle.

The first person he'd ever been able to ask why.

Delores remembered him. Remembered their interview, his pestering, his enquiries into her background. Remembered telling Michael, and how Michael said he'd take care of it. Remembered thinking Denning got off lightly, considering what Michael did to Bartlemann.

The guy in the leathers was the Tim Michael and his Mexican thug were looking to kill, BF of the girl she'd killed Jeffery and Ally with.

They knew about the screenplay. They wanted their suspicions confirmed, they wanted to hear the truth spoken by someone who knew.

Delores had little choice. They knew enough to make her their enemy if they wanted. She knew enough to point them at Michael and pull the trigger.

With all three of the GHQ principals dead the link between her and Scott Bartlemann's murder would be severed forever, the company would dissolve, and she would be free to resurrect her career. Why not? She wasn't much older than Jennifer Aniston.

Denning put his porno disc in the player, fast forwarded to a face shot of the pockmarked Mexican guy, watched for Delores' reaction.

Delores shouted: "Motherfucker!" and looked at Chick. "That's the coyote!"

From off to the side Sean added: "And the goon who worked me over. You need to be careful, Tim."

Denning ticking boxes. The pockmarked Mexican: his wife's abductor, an old porn buddy of Kid Haldane's, Kid's partner in the rape girl business.

Thinking about Peta, praying she was safe.

Delores figuring one more reason to side with these people – wipe that raping animal off the planet. Making the decision. Give them what they want. She started with Maria.

"I crossed from Mexico illegally. I was raped. I had a second cousin in Boyle Heights. I stayed there while I healed and then I got a job as a live-in maid for Scott Bartlemann. He had a lot of film people come round to his house. I met Michael and he fell in love with me. But he was married so no one could know. Not even Scott. Michael had made a picture, *Maximum Kill*. Scott's company, Big Glass, owned the distribution rights. Scott changed his mind about the picture and decided to delay its release indefinitely."

Denning cut in: "How did Michael find out it was going to be shelved?"

"Scott's partner, Theo Portman, told him."

"And Portman liked the movie?"

"Theo liked Big Glass, he wanted it for himself. But, yes, he liked the movie, too. He had a lot more money than Scott, but he didn't own enough of the company to override him. When Theo bought in, Scott had made sure to keep a majority share. So it didn't matter what Theo thought."

"At least while Bartlemann was alive."

"Yes."

"So Theo and Michael came up with a plan."

"You've read the screenplay."

"You set Bartlemann up?"

"I told Michael he was going to be at Isla Vista, that he was going to be alone. I unlocked the doors. I turned off the alarm."

"And Michael said he'd make you a star."

"And he did."

"In the screenplay, the Michael character kills Bartlemann, then the Jeffery character kills the maid. But that's not exactly the way it happened, is it?"

"No, it's not."

"There was another woman."

"You know about that?"

"Oh, yeah, I know. But I want to hear it from you."

"It was a terrible thing. I didn't know anything about it until after Michael shot Scott and they brought her in. They'd had her in a van outside all the time. I begged them not to do it. Michael said I'd never get out of the States, that the search would be too intense if the police didn't have the maid. Or her body. I told them I didn't care, that I'd take my chances. This poor woman.... But Michael loved me too much."

Delores dropped her head and looked at her hands. Her fingers twisted against themselves and her knuckles went white. Denning didn't care whether this display of emotion was real or not. All he saw was the woman his wife had been killed for.

Denning said: "Who killed her?"

"Jeffery. The same as in the screenplay. He put the gun under her chin, told her if she put her hands on the gun and prayed he wouldn't pull the trigger. But he did. It was horrible."

"Do you know who she was?" Denning's voice broke.

Delores shrugged. "Someone whose body was similar to mine. I never spoke to Michael about it. I never spoke to any of them about it. I wanted to forget it ever happened."

Denning moved close to her, bent down to where she sat on one of the sofas, put his face close to hers.

"Lucky you, that you had that luxury. She was my wife, you fucking spic bitch!"

Delores looked at him and nodded, allowed a tear to leak from each eye and whispered: "I'm sorry."

Denning balled his fists and screamed "Fuck!" into her face, then turned abruptly and walked across the room and leaned his head against the wall by the bathroom door.

Tim took over, figured he'd cross a few Ts. He showed Delores the photo Danny Bartlemann had given him of his father's maid.

"You, as Maria?"

Delores took the phone, looked at the photo for a long moment.

"Yes. Before...everything. Taken by the son...."

She handed the phone back and said: "After it was over Michael gave me money and Ally took me to the airport. I went to Mexico City. I stayed there four months. I had my hairline raised, some work on my nose. I spent every day in the gym, lost seven kilos, changed my hairstyle. All part of Michael's plan, all arranged before he killed Bartlemann."

"If you came over illegally, how did you get back into Mexico?"

Delores looked at him as though he was stupid.

"I had my passport."

"In what name?"

"My real one – Delores Fuentes. I brought it with me, but when I stayed with my cousin I bought fake ID. Maria Morales – supposedly a legal identity. If you get picked up, the first thing ICE does is check immigration records. There would have been no permanent residency listed under Delores Fuentes, I would have been arrested, deported. Using a resident ID, even if it's fake, at least you have a chance."

"And then you came back to the States."

"Under my real name, as a tourist. *Maximum Kill* had been released by that time and Michael was becoming an important man. I had residency in six months."

Denning returned to the sofas.

Calmer now, he asked: "And that was all it took, a little work on your nose, a tourist visa, a change of name? And no one ever knew you'd been Maria or worked for Scott Bartlemann?"

"Why should they? I only worked for him for six months. He was divorced from his wife, his son only came to see him two or three times. Mexican maids are anonymous, part of the furniture. No one pays attention to them. And what was there to connect me to him anyway? The real Maria Morales probably died before I even entered the country. The rest of Scott's staff knew nothing about me, about my family, what village I came from. I'd never been fingerprinted here or in Mexico. And when I became famous, if anyone noticed a slight resemblance to some 'spic' maid they'd once seen, they wouldn't give it a second thought. The idea would be just too preposterous."

Tim said: "Tell me about Rebecca and the *Wilderness* screenplay."

"I met your sister socially. I forget where, some party or other. I liked her. We were close for a short time."

"Close?"

"Sexually. Just a few nights. But we stayed in touch. Four years ago I left Michael. I asked him to release me from my contract. He refused. From then on, GHQ wouldn't put me in anything, they wouldn't allow me to work for anyone else, either. I had to do something. When they put a picture called *Canvas Carousel* into development I knew I couldn't wait any longer. It was perfect for me. It could have changed the whole direction of my career. Michael, of course, wouldn't even talk to me about it. So I decided to persuade him."

"With Rebecca's help."

"I had the story, but I'm not a writer. I wanted a gun I could put to Michael's head. Something he'd understand, that he'd know was dangerous. I paid Rebecca to write it. The story wasn't one hundred percent the truth. I left myself out of it, of course. But it was close enough to be very dangerous to Michael and GHQ if it ever circulated in Hollywood. Too many people in the industry knew about Scott's murder."

"The shotgun shell."

"Yes, that was part of it. But a breakout film, three principals, a film distributor victim.... These were parallels that would draw attention."

"Why did they leave the shell there?"

"They didn't know where it was. I was the only one who saw where it went. I turned away when Jeffery pulled the trigger. After they killed the woman they were too frightened to stay and look for it. And they weren't worried anyhow, there were no prints on it – they all wore gloves. I was too shocked at the time to say anything. And later I didn't dare. I was frightened they'd think I'd stayed quiet deliberately."

"But you were under contract to GHQ. If you fucked them with the screenplay, you'd be fucked, too, because they wouldn't be making movies anymore. Plus, if they ever got busted, they'd implicate you for sure."

"I wasn't making movies by then anyhow. But the screenplay was only ever supposed to be a bluff. I just wanted Michael to see what *could* happen if he pushed me too far. I was never going to show it to anyone else. I'm not stupid. But Sean made a mistake and showed it to Michael before I was ready, before I'd had a chance to set the stage."

Sean was in an armchair off to one side of the group, watching, listening, but playing no part in the discussion. When Delores mentioned his name he shifted uncomfortably. Delores didn't look at him.

Delores continued: "So, Michael assumed I was actually going to use the screenplay. When he told Jeffery and Ally, they demanded he deal with the supposed problem. They wanted him to kill me. He chose Rebecca instead." Delores put a pleading look on her face. "Believe me, if I'd known what he was going to do, I would have warned her. I liked her very much."

Tim counted through those responsible for his sister's death. Delores, who must have known the danger she was putting Rebecca in. Stupid, self-serving Sean – a man who had so terribly miscalculated his own need for fame. Jeffery and Ally, dead now. And Michael, the man who had pulled the trigger.

Of those still alive, only Michael was worth killing, only Michael had deliberately set out to murder his sister. Sean and Delores were just Hollywood cripples.

Denning, too, was doing his share of thinking, watching Delores while she talked with Tim. How strange to be this close to her now, after stalking her so relentlessly eight years ago and learning almost nothing.

He ran his eyes over her body – hardened and sinewy now from her obsessive training routine. It was still there, though, the pattern that had matched Clara so closely. And of course, that was why she had been taken – same nationality, same color, same body shape.

Denning pointed at the TV screen, at the Mexican's face.

"This is the man who abducted my wife."

Delores spat: "And the pig who sold me to Jeffery and Ally!"

Chick said: "Actually, who provided you to Kid, who sold you to Jeffery and Ally."

Tim said to Denning: "How do you know Kid wasn't involved in snatching your wife too? He made a bunch of pornos with this guy, then later the dude's supplying him with Mexican rape girls."

"I don't. Clara saw a Mexican guy following her, then next day the same guy's parked on our street. I go to talk to him, he drives off. I didn't see anyone else. But, you're right, it's a possibility Haldane was involved."

Chick cut in: "Wait a fucking minute. I've got my own business with Kid. Don't go putting him on your list."

She was sitting on the back of one of the sofas, feet on its seat cushions, parted legs revealing the salt rings on the catsuit's crotch. Denning looked at her and wondered what it was with L.A. that brought so much crazy to the surface.

"I haven't put him on a list, whatever the fuck list that is. But if he helped take Clara then he's a target."

"And he's also a target because of my rape. He's on *my* list. And I know what my list is, because it's got a whole shitload of people on it. Jeffery and Ally got scratched already. If I decide that Kid's gotta go, then I take care of it, not you."

"Are you fucking serious? You're arguing with me about who's going to kill Haldane? She was my fucking wife!"

"And it was me who got kidnapped when I was fifteen. You don't even know if Kid was involved in taking your wife. Just because he knows this Mexican guy...."

Denning took a breath, held it, then let it out.

"Okay. But the Mexican guy, we're clear on, right? He knows Michael, he knows Theo Portman. And he took Clara. That makes him my target."

Delores stood up abruptly, and planted herself in front of him.

"Who made you the boss?"

"No one. But we need to figure out what to do next."

"So you decide to put the coyote on your list?"

"*What fucking list?*"

"You don't think I have a right to him, too? You think because I'm Mexican my rape doesn't count?"

"Oh, what the *fuck*?"

"You have no idea how much damage I suffered. I deserve a chance to heal myself."

Denning was about to say something about the damage you suffer when you find out your wife had her head blown off so some venal skank could become a movie star, but Tim, figuring this little confab had run its course, told Delores to sit down and shut up and if there was a problem killing the Mexican then she and Denning could do it together.

Fifteen minutes of pointless bickering later, the meeting broke up.

Sean tried to catch Tim's eye as Tim headed for the door with Chick and Denning, but Tim avoided his look.

As they filed out into the night, Denning stopped in the doorway and turned back to Delores with one final question.

"Why did GHQ destroy me? Eight years ago, back when I interviewed you. You know what happened to me?"

"I know."

"So, why?"

"They didn't know what you were looking for. It was only two years after Bartlemann. You were too persistent."

"I was researching a portrait piece on the company, I wasn't trying to solve the murder."

"You were asking questions at Big Glass. You were looking into my background. Scott Bartlemann and me together? Too many red flags. You should have been more discreet."

"But I didn't have anything new on Bartlemann's death. I just wanted some color for the piece."

Delores shrugged.

"Why take the chance?"

Outside, Denning called Peta again. She was due home tomorrow. Still no answer.

CHAPTER 48

Michael in his mansion in Beverly Hills. His left shoulder fixed by a doctor Theo had on tap. The pain down to a radiating ache, dulled by morphine sulfate. A small wound that had nicked the bone. Not life-threatening, not by a mile, but something that would be there for the rest of his life, telling him when rain was coming, aching in the snow at Aspen.

In his study, back to the windows. Outside, the mass-produced beauty of another Southern California day. *Chrysanthemum* playing on a flat-screen. GHQ's first feature. His one statement of artistic intent, the only honorable film he'd ever made. The beginning of his rise to success, the start of his fall.

He'd come a long way from the flat heat and dry red earth of South Australia. From a childhood spent kicking footballs around, fighting with other kids in dusty paddocks, guzzling American TV and wanting the life he saw on that black-and-white screen. Wanting to escape to the wide roads and bright lights, to a place that was bigger and better than anywhere else on the planet. Wanting money and glamour and fame

And he'd done it. He'd got out of that drab, directionless world of small houses and back yards and corrugated-iron fences. He'd got out, and with his brains and his talent he'd built himself the life he'd dreamed of. Beverly Hills. Millionaire. Movie producer and director. A winner amongst winners.

Once he'd committed to films like *Maximum Kill*, he'd never allowed himself to think about the statements he could have made, the art he could have created. But now, when Delores had so little time left to live, he couldn't help thinking that there might have been a better way to do things. Without so much money, without the houses and the cars and the A-list.

He watched the screen for several minutes. *Chrysanthemum* was so damn good. Why couldn't it have been enough for him to just create art? He had the talent. And even a director of arty independent films was still something to be. Bartlemann would never have had to have been killed. And Delores would never have risen high enough to leave him, would never have done something as stupid as that fucking screenplay.

Chrysanthemum had been written by his ex-wife, Nancy. He'd directed. A team that had fallen apart not long afterwards, during the early days shooting *Maximum Kill*. Nancy had hated *Max Kill*. She'd hated more the fact that he was seeing Bartlemann's maid.

On an impulse, Michael picked up the desk phone and called her. They'd spoken only infrequently in the ten years since the divorce. She'd hated him at first, but the success she'd had with her books had eventually tamed her anger and later phone calls had at least been civil.

She answered. They spoke. Michael talked about the old days, how they met, the good times they had had, struggling together in the Valley, their move to the small flat in Venice, the excitement of *Chrysanthemum....*

Nancy figured the call was a symptom of an approaching mid-life crisis, took a certain delight in the tones of unhappiness his voice carried. But they'd been married for a long time and those early shared memories were pleasant to reminisce about now that enough time had passed to stop them hurting.

Toward the end of the conversation, overtaken by a flush of the affection she'd once felt for him, she mentioned her recent interview with a journalist from the Hollywood Reporter and how Michael's name had come up and that she was sure he didn't mind, after all this time, that she'd mentioned he used to make porno movies and that they broke up because he was seeing Scott Bartlemann's maid.

Michael thought 'Hollywood Reporter', thought 'questions about his past'. Remembered another journalist who had worked for the same magazine eight years ago. He kept his voice even.

"Did he give you a name?"

"Of course. He's not going to interview me without telling me his name, is he? Hold on, I've got his email."

Michael heard her mouse clicking, and then: "Alan Denning. Looked a bit, you know, rumpled. The photographer was nice, though."

"Did the photographer have a name?"

"What do you care?"

"I like to keep track of who's interested in me."

"They weren't asking questions about you, they were interviewing me. I see the megalomania hasn't improved any. I think it was...Tom?"

"Tim?"

"Yeah, Tim. How did you know?"

A couple of minutes later Michael put down the phone, all his maundering thoughts of earlier replaced by the realization that there was more going on than just the reappearance of the screenplay. Someone was actively investigating him. The hack he'd exposed for incest, after all this time out for revenge? Hooked up with the Tim who'd left his name on the screenplay Jeffery had found.

Michael spent a few minutes on his computer. The private detective who had planted the camera in Denning's bedroom had emailed Michael, six months after the D.A. dropped the incest case, that Denning had moved house.

Michael picked up the phone and called Theo.

And then Theo called Christo's cell and passed on an address.

Chapter 49

Late night. Kid and Peta back from New York. Full of the sights – Empire State, Guggenheim, Brooklyn, Central Park. Matching *I Love New York* T-shirts.

At Kid's apartment. A shower and a vodka tonic. Glad to find her charger under his bed. She thought she'd packed it, had spent most of the time away with a dead phone.

Messages from Denning, wanting her to call him urgently. She connected. He asked if she was safe. She had no idea what he was talking about. He asked if Kid was there, if he could hear them talking. Peta said she was too tired to talk, that she'd meet him at the house lunchtime tomorrow. Not earlier. She wanted to sleep off the flight.

In the alley behind the porno store where he'd bought the DVDs, Denning found the kid again and scored two more blisters of 40mg OxyContin. After the money changed hands, Denning asked about a gun.

They took a ride to a street corner on the eastern edge of Hancock Park. A group of youths hanging around under a streetlight. Denning starting to shit himself, realizing they could just roll him for the wad of cash he had in his pocket. Realizing he could end up in a dumpster.

One of the youths asked what he wanted. A white boy who spoke well, who had hair like a Marine. Denning said he didn't care as long as it worked and there was enough ammo to practice with. Army boy went off and came back with something wrapped in a towel and a couple of boxes of rounds.

As he passed the gun through the window he said: ".38 Special, Smith and Wesson Airweight 642. Internal hammer, light, small; perfect pocket gun."

Denning forked over twelve hundred bucks and drove the first kid back to his spot in the alley.

At home he loaded the thing and held it. The black rubberized grip felt solid in his hand, not something he was likely to drop. Short barrel, under two inches, five-round cylinder, aluminum frame.

Denning had never fired a gun before but he knew the effective range on these things wasn't great. Still, he figured when he started putting bullets into the Mexican he'd want to be standing nice and close. Denning snicked the safety up and down, couldn't figure what was on and what was off. Did the dot mean danger, the thing's ready to go; or beware, if you need this to fire, it ain't going to happen?

Morning. Time to kill before Peta came around. Denning put his .38 Special and a box of ammo in the trunk of his car and drove to LAX firing range in Inglewood. Next to an adult video store on West Manchester – a strip of single-story small businesses, car lots and gas stations. Denning thought if he got through this whole GHQ thing, if he was still alive at the end of it, he was going to get the fuck out of town, find a shack a long way up the coast somewhere, maybe up past San Fran, maybe Oregon. Someplace where there was just the sea and a whole lot of trees. Someplace where it wasn't commonplace to find guns and porn side by side.

He paid for a lane, chose zombie targets and had the pro spend ten minutes with him showing him how to use the gun. After that he spent twenty minutes burning rounds. He'd heard it was great for stress relief, empowering, that you became your own personal action hero. But all it was for him was noisy and nasty and the pistol kept jumping around and he couldn't stop thinking about how easy it would be for one, or all, of the gun freaks on the other lanes to turn his way and see what their bullets did for real.

By the end of the session, though, he was hitting his targets most of the time. And, more importantly, he'd gotten over the fear of what happened when you pulled the trigger on a gun – a very loud bang and an upwards recoil. Plus he knew how to work the safety.

He washed up afterwards, but his hands still stank of cordite. Eleven a.m. A late breakfast in a diner down the road. Killing time, trying not to think about Peta too much. Trying not to worry about her being with Kid, a man who knew the man who'd stolen his wife. Who maybe was involved in that, too.

Christo. A night of tequila, coke and some barmaid who'd wanted to see what it was like to be drilled by a porn-sized cock. A late start on the alternative directive he'd received from Theo.

Alan Denning. Ex-journalist, pal of the other guy, Tim, who seemed, at the moment, to be in the wind. If you can't get one, get the other. Theo conveying that this shit needed sorting. Upping the pressure, upping the paycheck. Conveying that Michael wanted, when Denning was safely trussed somewhere, to have a chat with him, to find out what he knew.

Parked in his van on Delaware Avenue, watching the bungalow. Waiting for Denning to drag his ass back from wherever it was. Calling Kid. Women weren't a problem but a man, it was better if you had another pair of hands. Or fists.

And Christo needing a place, too. Hard to do the kind of dirty work Theo expected in the back of a van.

Calling Kid and getting no answer. Getting the impression Kid was screening his calls.

Light coming into Kid's apartment too early, his phone ringing at intervals. Peta giving up on the idea of sleeping in. Turning in bed, putting her arms around him from behind, feeling the lean body, the dry, tough skin. Their weekend away had been fun.

She liked being with him, liked the excitement of the movie business, liked that he thought so much of her. But she wasn't in love with him. He was a jumping-off point, a gateway back into a world where who you spent your nights with wasn't a secret that had to be kept at all costs. She knew that she would move on. He was hardly two kids, a dog and a white picket fence. But for now he was sexy and exciting enough to stay with, even if she did find the size of his cock revolting.

Five minutes later she got up, figuring she'd go see Denning earlier than planned. Grab coffee and donuts on the way, surprise him.

Delaware Avenue. Mid-morning. All the workaday Joes had left for the plant, for the office, for the store, for the warehouse, the construction site. All the girls were behind their desks in town, thinking about a liver-cleansing juice or the next hit of caffeine and sugar.

She parked on the street. Black asphalt. The surf sound of traffic on the Santa Monica Freeway. A woman with a young child and another in a stroller, walking on the sidewalk. Telegraph poles, black wires against a bleached sky. Cars at the curb – Japanese, Korean, ten years old, nothing flash, a white van a few yards along from her driveway.... A quiet day on a quiet street where people kept to themselves.

The side of the house had a tin-roofed car port and a door that opened directly into the kitchen. Denning's car wasn't there.

Peta went across the small lawn and in through the main door at the front of the house. The place smelled of cigarettes. Denning had obviously taken to smoking inside since she'd been gone. He wasn't home. She walked through the lounge, down the hall, to his room.

The bed, unmade. The place on the pillow where his head had been. The scatter of pads and pens on his desk, a pair of pants over the back of the chair. These things were still dear to her. She had woken in that bed, she had straightened its sheets, had held him in it when he cried for her mother. Had slept deeply and safely with his strong hairy body beside her.

She realized, looking at the room, that he was not some husk to be sloughed off, he was not a memory she could overlay with a new life. What they had done had changed them both, had made them more a part of each other than they should have been. And however far she went from him, whatever new relationships she forged for herself, those nights together would always form the base definition of who they considered themselves to be.

She did not regret what she had done, did not regret that she had stepped close and kissed him that night in the kitchen. But this was what it looked like when a man lived alone, and this was how it would be for him from now on. And for that, she knew, she bore a measure of blame.

She lay on his bed and pressed her face into his pillow, breathing, wishing that his life could be happier, that her own need for happiness had not left him so terribly bereft. She closed her eyes and imagined him next to her, curled against her.

Christo had watched the girl enter the house, had seen her open the screen door and knock, had heard her call out, "Hey, Dad, it's me," before taking a key from her bag and unlocking the door and entering.

Theo had mentioned a daughter. The relationship with the daughter being the cause of some kind of engineered destruction years ago, that destruction being the motive for Denning having become a thorn in Michael Starck's side.

If Denning didn't feel like talking, if his hatred for GHQ ran deep enough to give him some backbone, Christo figured the daughter might be a useful tool when it came to initiating conversation.

He got out of the van, walked casually across the road, up the drive and into the shadow under the carport roof. It took him less than ten seconds to force the door that gave onto the kitchen.

He walked through the house. He moved quietly, but he wasn't overly concerned about being heard. He'd been waiting outside long enough to know that she was alone. And he was used to dealing with women in situations like these. It made things easier if you could surprise them, grab them from behind or something before they knew you were there. But it didn't really matter too much. Not if you didn't care about hurting them.

Hallway. Living room back down it to the right. To the left, a bedroom, obviously a woman's, the bed made and a general air of the place not having been used for a while. Further along on the other side, a bathroom that he didn't bother checking. A final room on the right, it's door open, an infinitesimal increase in temperature as he approached it, a scent, a sound that wasn't a sound – breathing unheard but there all the same, disturbing the air – the subliminal announcement of another human being.

Christo stepped through the doorway, saw the woman on the bed coming out of a light doze, pushing herself up on one elbow, blinking, squinting, trying to make sense of the fact that there a was a man in her room, opening her mouth to yell. But Christo fast and confident. Two long steps and a hard right to the side of her jaw. Out like a light. It hadn't failed him yet. Not with a woman.

Christo got the van, parked it under the carport, lined up its sliding side door with that of the kitchen. He went back to the bedroom with a roll of duct tape, did ankles, wrists and mouth, then dragged the woman through the house and put her in the back of the van. Slid the door shut and locked it. Like all the vans he used, the cargo bay was windowless.

He drove away from Delaware Avenue, cursing Kid under his breath. He needed a safe place to dump the van and the girl, and he needed a ride back from wherever that was so he could continue his wait for Denning.

Pico, 20th, Wilshire. He pulled into 7th, down the side of some park. Called Kid for the tenth time. And got an answer.

Kid's screen showed a list of unanswered calls. An unknown number, but he knew who it was. Peta off out somewhere, shopping maybe, maybe at the gym. Impossible to put off talking to Christo any longer.

Kid knew he owed him for that night in the desert, if he and Theo hadn't turned up Kid would have been one dead porn star. But Christo was also part of the rape girl thing and Kid really didn't want to see him or talk to him or have anything more than absolutely necessary to do with him. Trouble was, you get on that kind of rollercoaster, you're stuck on it. At least till the wheels fall off.

The phone rang again.

Kid knew he should check in with Chick, make sure she'd stayed away from Jeffery and Ally. Make sure she was still safe. But the last time he'd seen her things hadn't gone so well.

So he'd put it off. Hadn't called her from New York. Hadn't called her since he'd been back in L.A. And now Christo was calling. Another excuse not to do it.

Kid answered his phone.

His Mexican accomplice wanting a place to store a girl. Not a rape girl, though, nothing to do with that. Something entirely different. No big deal. Not wanting him to help kill someone, or rob a bank. A small matter of needing a hand snatching a guy. The dude not a tough guy, just a shlub Christo needed to extract some info from. Kid didn't have to watch, didn't have to apply any pressure. Just help with the snatch. And provide storage away from inquisitive eyes. One day max.

Kid knew the perfect place. Raintree. Jeffery and Ally only ever used it for their nut-job rituals, the occasional meeting. He hadn't had any contact with them since a few days before he and Peta left for New York, so he figured it'd be safe enough. And if it wasn't, who gave a shit? If Jeffery and Ally met Christo, maybe it'd be a good thing. Maybe it'd facilitate an exit from the whole fucking rape mess he'd gotten himself into.

He rang the office, spoke to the production manager for twenty minutes about a series of read-throughs Chick wanted to do with the cast principals, filled him in on the exhibitors in New York, and said he wouldn't be in that day. Then he got in the Camaro and drove to 7th Street.

The white van at the side of a park. Always a white van. The sight of them now a great glaring sign pointing to all the wrong turns Kid had made. A woman inside. Bound, no doubt. Hidden behind the thin metal walls. Kid was glad he couldn't see her, glad he didn't have to know anything about her.

He didn't bother to get out of his car, just pulled alongside and signaled Christo to follow. Down to PCH, along to Malibu, up into the hills, to Raintree.

Kid drove around back of the gutted mansion to the garage. Christo rolled the van past him and parked it in the shade of a stand of oak trees. The men got out of their vehicles and shook hands. There wasn't a lot to say. They'd known each other a long time, they were bound by terrible things. But they weren't friends.

So they said their hellos and made tough guy small talk. Christo outlined his reason for being in Los Angeles – talk to a couple of guys who were making trouble for Michael Starck, find out how much they knew, how much danger they were. The woman in the van the daughter of one of them – leverage, bait. Christo not bothering with names. Christo's improvised plan: go back to where he got the daughter, snatch the father, bring him back here and do what was necessary.

Kid held up is hands and shook his head.

"I'm not doing any killing."

"Did I ask you, bro? All I need is a ride back to town, then you and me hang out at the house. When Daddy gets home we ask him to come for a ride out here – look at the beautiful sea, check out the trees, get some sun. Be good for his health. I point out his daughter's not having a great time, he sings like a bird."

"And then what?"

"You go home and never think about it again."

"And you waste them."

"And you never think about it again."

Christo looked at the ruined house.

"Some place."

"What sort of trouble is Michael in?" Kid wondering if there was a threat to the *Antepenultimate* finance here.

Christo tapped the side of his nose.

"Nothing that can't be taken care of." He gestured at the house. "How'd you find this place?"

"Did some business with the people who own it. I want to check it out, make sure they're not planning to use it any time soon."

Christo looked dubiously at the charred rubble.

"Use it?"

Kid unlocked the door to the garage — no cars, no sign of caterers, cleaners or the impending arrival of Jeffery and Ally. Christo got into his van and drove it inside, then Kid unlocked the connecting door and the two of them went down to the basement.

There were lights on in the long corridor. Not a good sign, Kid figured. Lights meant people, and in this place that meant Jeffery and Ally. No sounds, though. No feeling that anyone else was there. But something else as he and Christo walked along. Something that made the air heavier, something like a thick sweetness, something that got worse as they got closer to the screening room.

Christo smelling it too, frowning, pulling a nickel-plated .38 auto from the back of his waistband. Looking at Kid like what the fuck's going on here, bro?

Kid put his hand on the heavy soundproof door thinking about Chick, holding a scream in his chest, figuring if she was dead, if these psychos had already used her for their fucking ritual, then he would be deservedly beyond redemption forever.

He pushed the door open. The sweetness in the air was stronger, a smell of meat and blood, not yet a stench of decay. There were flies, but not many — the basement was cool and the door closed tightly.

Two bodies. Jeffery and Ally.

Kid sagged with relief, steadied himself against a wall. Christo scanned the room, gun raised.

Jeffery, seated on the floor, legs splayed. Dark dried blood from his shoulders, his knee, his chest. Bullet holes, ragged chunks of flesh torn away, face the color of a bruise. And facing him, seated much the same way, Ally with a knife in the side of her neck, her breast slashed and a line of holes up the center of her body. The robe she was wearing open and stiff, a pool of congealed blood between her legs. Blood everywhere.

Christo looked questioningly at Kid.

"Know them?"

"They own the place. Michael's partners in GHQ – Jeffery and Ally Bannister." And then, because there now seemed no reason not to: "They were the people who bought the girls."

Christo laughed.

"Seriously? Hollywood dudes?" He shook his head. "And people say Mexico's a shithole…. No more paydays, now, bro."

Kid nodded, looking at the scene, processing. "This is where they raped them."

"You thinking payback? Some girl figured out who they were and bought herself a gun?"

"Too many wounds to be someone who wasn't angry."

Christo shrugged. "It was gonna happen sometime."

But Kid wasn't really interested in Christo's opinion. He was thinking about the night Chick had come to his apartment and shown him her ripped pussy. This kind of anger – the knife wounds, the number of shots – this was how Chick would do it.

And if Chick had figured out Jeffery and Ally were the people who raped her when she was fifteen, then it was possible she had also learned of his part in it. Something made a little more than likely by the way she'd been with him when he'd seen her last. Did she have this kind of bloodbath in mind for him?

Christo jerked his head at the door.

"Let's go. I want to get back before the dude comes home."

"You still want to use this place?"

"Why not? The owners ain't gonna bust in and disturb us, that's for sure. And I bring him back here and show him this, he's gonna shit himself. I probably don't even need his daughter now."

"So let her go."

"Don't be stupid."

Upstairs, outside, Kid walked around in the sunlight while Christo checked to make sure whoever it was he had in his van was still breathing.

When Christo was finished, Kid went over and locked the garage door and then they drove to Santa Monica in the Camaro and parked outside a rundown bungalow on a low-income street, waiting for the man Christo wanted to speak to.

Chapter 50

Sean sat outside the bunker on the step in front of the door, moderately stoned. He felt the sun on his legs and shoulders and around him the canyon slopes were peaceful in the warmth. Delores was still in bed.

He had slept badly and in the long dark hours, staring at the bunker's ceiling, he had come to the realization, certain, profound, unarguable, that there was nothing left for him. Not as an actor – that had ended a long time ago; not in his friendship with Tim; not, even, with Delores.

He was a junkie who would never get clean. He had betrayed Tim, had lied to him about Rebecca, had, if not killed her, then at least hastened her death. And though Delores had risked her life to save him from Michael, he knew he'd never be enough for her. She was already distant with him, complaining about his addiction, chaffing to escape the confines of the bunker. To be somewhere else.

When this thing with Tim and Michael was done, if Tim came out on top, Delores would be out in the market again, maybe not as big as she had been, but big enough. Big enough to need a high profile man. Certainly big enough not to need a junkie ex-bit-part actor on her arm.

He felt an overwhelming sadness at the way things had turned out. But not self-pity. He was thirty-three years old. He had had the world at his feet. The decisions he'd made, he'd made on his own.

He'd lived for two years with the guilt of what he'd done to Rebecca eating him from the inside out. What little of him remained had been taken away when Michael and the Mexican had had him in that chair. Dignity? Balls? Guts? Honor?

Some last thing that, despite all he'd done up to that point, had allowed him to still consider himself a man.

And not just Michael and the Mexican, but Delores, too. Before she'd changed her mind and made her action-hero play, she'd been the one who'd set him up.

Another piece of him gone.

Good to be saved, yes. Better not to have been betrayed in the first place, because some things once taken can never be given back.

But who was he to talk about betrayal?

He'd betrayed Delores two years ago, taken her screenplay and given it to Michael. He'd betrayed Tim by lying to him every day of those two years. And, if he could stomach the psychobabble, he'd betrayed himself with heroin.

So, how to complete that character arc? How to compensate his own shredded sense of justice for the damage that had been done to it?

The answer simple, the fate of all doomed lovers and heroes. Give something back, then go out in flames.

Chapter 51

Midday. Windows wound down on the Camaro. The smell of asphalt heating up, exhaust fumes from the freeway, a faint scent of eucalyptus, the sound of cicadas.

Christo relaxed, eyes on the bungalow. Eating marshmallows, pink and white, from a bag on his lap. Powdered sugar on his fingers. Kid faintly sickened by the smell, thinking of the screening room. And nervous. Driving a girl in the back of a van was one thing, snatching a man from his house was another. He'd given that sort of thing up after Chick. Too frightening.

Kid stared out the side window at all the small, happy houses. Flowers, pot plants, a fake flamingo. Even a gnome out the front of one place. And wondered why the fuck he was doing this. He didn't need Christo for rape girls anymore – the demand for that supply was gone. There was the desert, but that was a long time ago and Christo had only been there because Theo told him to be. And with the money he'd put Christo's way over the last ten years Kid figured that debt was long paid off.

So why risk this shit?

Kid figured, no reason. Unless, maybe, Christo pulled his gun and forced the issue. Kid thought about a compromise, lend the guy his car. Get out, walk away, hope to get it back when Christo was done. Worth a try.

Kid was reaching for the door handle when a white Crown Victoria pulled into the bungalow's driveway and drove up under the carport and Christo said:

"Bingo."

Kid kept reaching until he saw the man in the car get out, carrying a small box in one hand, and stand looking at the door in the side of the house for a moment before pushing it open and going inside.

And for the second time that day Kid wanted to scream. Felt for one hot moment that his bladder would let go, that he'd piss himself with fear and the sudden desperate need to get back out to Raintree.

Because the man who had just entered the house was Peta's father, Denning. And that, of course, made it pretty fucking obvious who the girl in the back of Christo's van was.

But Kid held it in and got out of the Camaro with Christo and walked across the road to the bungalow with him.

Denning walked quickly through the house. Empty. He went back to the kitchen and stood looking at the take-out cups of coffee and the box of donuts on the kitchen table. Peta had been there. But she wasn't now. And the lock on the kitchen door had been forced.

Denning put the box of ammo he was still holding on the table beside the donuts. He took the short-barreled .38 Special out of his coat pocket and loaded it. Thinking who the fuck was he, Serpico? But what else do you do when you have a gun and it looks like something bad might have happened to your daughter.

He was just pushing the final slug into the cylinder when a Mexican guy stepped into the kitchen from the carport, pointed a silver automatic at his head and told him to put the .38 Special down on the table.

The first word out of Denning's mouth sounded corny, even to him.

"You?"

And Christo, too, paused fractionally. He'd had a name, Alan Denning. Denning...it had sounded vaguely familiar, but he hadn't placed it. And he'd never been to this house before.

But he knew this man. Older, heavier, a lot more life-fucked, but still the man from ten years ago, the man who had seen him parked outside another address, who had walked across the road toward him. The man whose wife he had stolen for Theo Portman.

Kid came into the room behind the Mexican, and Denning's face began another sunburst of recognition. But Kid held his eyes hard and made a small move with his head and Denning, not knowing what was going on here but understanding it was more than it seemed, froze his face and looked blank and asked: "Where's my daughter?"

Christo said: "We're going there now. It wouldn't be smart not to be smart. Walk out to the car like we're all friends."

As Denning moved toward the door, Kid stepped past Christo, picked up Denning's pistol and put it in his jacket pocket. Looked at Christo and shrugged. "Can't hurt."

Raintree. Straight into the garage, the door closed behind them. Denning surprised the place had electricity. The first thing he saw: a fucking white van. The next thing, while the Mexican covered him, Peta being dragged out of it. Alive, thank God. Kid cutting the tape at her ankles, supporting her until she could walk around. Leaving the tape on her mouth, whispering to tell her not to recognize him.

All of them down to the screening room. Denning figuring out pretty quick whose place this was, trying to understand the connection here. Two bodies – Jeffery and Ally Bannister. Killed by Chick and Delores. And now Kid and his porno buddy were here too? Fucking mad. Fucking crazy.

Peta crying behind her face tape, figuring she and Denning were next. Denning wanting to tell her it was okay, that everything was going to be all right, but really not having a clue how things were going to turn out. Hoping that Kid had a plan, that this wasn't simply the end of some serial killer game.

Christo sat Peta down, right next to dead Ally, made sure they were touching. Peta retching behind her tape. Denning pushed into place on Ally's other side, shoved roughly down by Kid. And then the Mexican standing in front of them, casually waving his gun at the blood and the bodies, a message that couldn't be clearer. Don't fuck around.

Christo pulled out his cell, nodded for Kid to watch Denning and Peta. Kid with the stubby .38 Special making like grim, making like whatever the fuck went down here was okay by him.

Christo punched out a number, spoke into the phone, said: "I've got him."

Raising an eyebrow at Kid and Kid telling him the name of the road, telling him a property called Raintree.

"Get on over. Don't waste time. There's something else here that's gonna give you a real big kick."

Denning figuring Michael, getting a pretty good idea now how things were going to turn out. But wanting to know anyway, speaking when the Mexican put his phone away.

"You took my wife."

Christo looking at him, thinking this guy wasn't walking out of here, thinking no reason to be more of a cunt than necessary.

"Yes."

"And you gave her to Michael."

"Michael Starck? I left her in the back of a van in a parking lot near Venice Beach. Got out and walked away. I don't know what happened to her after that."

"Why?"

"Why her? Why did I take her? A man told me to, same man paid me a lot of money. No other reason."

"Theo Portman?"

The Mexican smiled and shook his head.

"No wonder they're after you, *hermano*."

And Kid thinking, no more time left. Someone on their way. Michael, most likely. Theo not the type to get his hands dirty, not these days. Whatever. Christo plus someone else would be too much to handle. And Peta would wind up dead.

Kid said: "Theo know I'm helping you out? I'm getting something out of this right?"

Christo said: "Theo doesn't want to know any more than he needs to know. You're a subcontractor, dude. I'll take care of you out of my end, don't worry."

Kid thinking, something, at least. Might get out of there without putting himself in anyone's crosshairs.

Christo looked at Peta for a moment, watched her crying and sniffing and struggling to breathe, and then tucked his gun in the back of his pants and bent to peel the tape from her mouth. As he began to straighten again, Kid slammed the .38 Special against the side of his head. The Airweight 642 was a small gun, but it was metal and it was hard and Christo hit the floor unconscious. He had a two-inch gash above his right ear, blood ran from it, down the side of his face and the back of his neck.

Denning powered to his feet, looked at Kid for a second to make sure there wasn't any violence coming his way, then hauled Peta upright and held her as she sobbed against his neck.

Kid took Christo's gun out of his pants and stuck it into his own waistband. Then he got Christo's phone and checked the last number dialed, no name against it, but he recognized it as Michael Starck's cell.

"We have to get going. I can't be here when Michael arrives."

Peta's hands were still taped behind her back. Denning stepped away from her, hesitated, then bent and pulled the Ka-bar from Ally's neck and used it to cut his daughter free.

He nodded at the bodies, said to Kid: "You know who they are?"

"Yeah."

"You know who killed them?"

"I have an idea."

Kid held out the .38 Special for Denning to take. Messages in the gesture. Pleas. I saved your life. I saved your daughter's life. I won't hurt her. Don't destroy my relationship with her. Don't say any more about Jeffery and Ally, about why they were killed. If you know something about me, don't say it.

Denning weighing the small gun in his hand, the knife in the other, and knowing what else had to take place before they drove away from Raintree, thinking Peta's safety with this guy was pretty much guaranteed. Figuring quid pro quo was fair enough.

Peta went to Kid and kissed him and pressed herself against him, and still holding him turned back to Denning and started to ask questions. What happened here? Who are these people? Why did the Mexican guy on the floor kidnap me? What did he want? All of it in a stream, flooding out as though her words, if they were fast enough and there were enough of them, could wash away all of the blood around her, could carry with them all of her fear. All of her horror.

And the biggest question of all – was this really the man? Was this the man who had taken her mother, who had taken the normal world away from them?

Kid said the Mexican's name was Christo, that he was someone he'd made porn vids with back in the day. Told Peta that it was probably him who'd killed the two people here, but he didn't know for sure.

Denning said Christo was the man who'd taken Clara. That there was no doubt.

Kid said they were leaving it too late, that they had to go now, and started to lead Peta out of the room.

When his daughter realized that Denning was not following, she looked back at him and stumbled. Looked back at him holding the knife and the gun, and her eyes filled again with tears, knowing what was going to happen when she was gone, knowing that it had to happen, that for her father and, even for her, there was no other way. But hating it anyway, hating that he would end up even more hurt by it than he already was.

Alone in the screening room. Christo coming around, holding his head and groaning. Denning letting him stand, watching as he took a couple of steps across the open space in front of the stage, then stop for a moment and sway, then carry on and collapse on one of the leather couches.

Christo looked up at Denning, started to wonder if the guy had the stones to go through with it, then stopped before he was halfway done with the thought, seeing that this man had been broken too badly to care about consequences. Knowing that his own life had always been going to end in some kind of scene like this. And here it was.

He could make a lunge, a last attempt to survive. But he knew he wouldn't make it across to where Denning stood. So he sat back in the couch, made himself as comfortable as he could with the throbbing in his head, and waited.

Denning looked at the weapons in his hands, at the pistol, at the Ka-bar crusted with blood.

He tightened his grip on the Ka-bar, raised it a little, said to the Mexican: "Who else was with you when you took my wife?"

"No one. Women I can handle alone."

"Not Kid?"

"Not Kid. There was no need for him. This was something Theo wanted done without anyone else knowing. I did it. I didn't ask questions. Do you know how to use a knife?"

"Push it in and pull it out. Don't fuck with me."

"It isn't that easy, not if you want to kill. Most people who haven't done it before freak out. They stab, figuring once will do it, but it doesn't. So they do it again and again and again because they know how bad it must hurt and they just want it to be over. But it takes some time. Sometimes it takes a long time."

"Lucky I've got a gun, then."

And Denning raised the .38 Special, saw it sharp and clear as though under a too-bright light. Saw the black edge of the grip, the shining silver body, the numbers and letters stamped into the metal, the slim, fluted cylinder, the sloping sight on the stubby barrel.... Saw the man beyond it, pressing back into the couch, back as hard as he could, but his mouth tightly closed, not going to beg or plead or make excuses. And Denning thought, you motherfucker – all of this was work for you. All the dismantling of lives, all the terror and pain Clara must have felt, all the sorrow, all the loss...this was just work.

And he pulled the trigger and sent a round into Christo's head. And for that instant, as blood and brain flew backwards, it felt good and right and a thousand times justified. So good that he kept pulling the trigger until the other four bullets were gone.

CHAPTER 52

Night. Rain on a hot city. Black-mirror roads full of colors. Cars shiny, sidewalks empty, streetlights haloed. The swish of tires through water.

Chick in her apartment. Tim, lying on the sofa, reading through a screenplay he'd written a few years back, thinking that parts of it weren't too bad. Denning had phoned, told him Michael's Mexican was dead. Tim now trailing the field.

Chick at a table across the room, making notes on the latest shooting schedule for *Antepenultimate*. The script pages, the locations, the required cast – all of it everything she had dreamed of for so long. Now just words on paper. The film seeming dull and pretentious. Since the screening room, since killing Jeffery and Ally.

She knew what would happen when it was made. A few festivals, some good reviews on arty websites, a release across maybe fifty theatres in a few of the larger cities. And then gone. Without a ripple. The fuck-you she so much wanted to howl at Hollywood nothing more than a whimper.

Why hadn't she seen it before?

Probably, she figured, because before she hadn't turned a gun on two people and blown the shit out of them.

The rumble of a large engine down on the street. She got up and looked out the window, saw a yellow Camaro. Told Tim to go into the bedroom, to listen if he wanted, but to stay out of sight – this conversation was Chick/Kid only.

As he left the room, Tim said: "Don't shoot him here."

He left the door open an inch.

A minute later, Chick let Kid into the building.

She sat at the table where she'd been working, the Thunder Ultra Compact within reach, half-hidden beneath a few sheets of paper. Kid stayed standing, beads of rain in his hair catching the light. On the table, beside Chick's laptop, the hardon Oscar shone in the light, too. The first thing Kid saw when he walked upstairs.

He picked it up, turned it in his hand, put it back down.

"Jeffery and Ally are dead."

"And you know why."

Kid looked at her for a long moment.

"Yes, I know why."

"I was fifteen!"

"I didn't participate, if that means anything."

"No, you just kidnapped me, Tasered me, taped me up and drove me to Raintree."

Kid nodded.

Chick said: "I want to tell you how frightened I was, how certain I was that I was going to die. I want you to know how much was taken away from me that night. But I can't do it, because no matter what I say to you, I can't make you feel what I felt. You'll say I know how terrible it was, blah, blah, blah, but you won't feel part of yourself dying."

Kid could see the barrel of Chick's gun poking from beneath the papers.

"Are you going to shoot me, as well?"

"I don't know."

"I never did it again. Abduct someone myself, I mean."

"You became a deliveryman."

"Yes. For a long time. None of the girls was ever killed, though. It wasn't anything like that."

"*Loggers. Antepenultimate.* Your way of making things right?"

"You wanted to be a director. It was the only way I could give you something back."

"You got finance because you were tight with Jeffery and Ally?"

"And because I had something on Michael."

"The location footage I shot at Mule Ridge?"

"How the fuck do you know that?"

Chick ignored the question.

"It puts him there when a woman was murdered. Do you know why she was killed?"

"No. And I don't want to know. I don't want to be any closer to it than I have to be. I saw the film after you shot it. Then I saw a news report."

"What about *Loggers*? I'm sure Michael didn't just hand over the money for that."

"I leveraged something else."

"Your friendship?"

"We shared an experience a long time ago."

"I'm all ears."

Kid told her about the time in the desert when Theo Portman and Christo had saved him and Michael from being killed by a rival porn outfit. Told her how Theo had made both of them kill their attackers.

Kid said: "You aren't the only one bad things happened to."

"That's your excuse? You were so fucked by that, you just had to start supplying girls to those freaks?"

"I did it for the money. But being made to kill someone isn't the best recipe for becoming a better person."

"Did Michael know about the rapes?"

"God, no. If he had, he wouldn't have stood for it – too dangerous for the company."

"And Jeffery and Ally didn't know about him being at Mule Ridge?"

"I don't know what they knew. I just know that he was there. I never told them about the film."

Kid glanced at the gun again.

"That day out at Raintree, when I turned up uninvited? When they showed you the memorabilia room?"

"Yeah."

"They were planning something for you. The rapes were part of a ritual for them. You were important because you were the first one they ever did. They figured it was the circle closing."

"So you interrupted."

"Might have saved your life."

"Might have. Wouldn't have had to if you didn't abduct me in the first place."

Kid had no answer for that. He stood silently for a while and then he nodded and turned and went downstairs to his car.

Outside, the rain had stopped and the air was heavy against Kid's skin. He got into the Camaro and sat staring through the windshield for a long time, hands on the wheel but the engine dead.

Then he put the key in the ignition and turned it and pulled away from the curb, figuring things with Chick had gone about as well as he had any right to expect. Figuring, keep his head down, get the picture done, spend time with Peta and try to become the man he wanted to be. One plus: Jeffery and Ally were dead. Another one: Christo was dead too. The whole rape thing severed at its roots. Never again. Chick now its only ghost. And maybe she would forgive, or at least not do anything about it.

Later that night, Tim rode over to his apartment in Santa Monica. He sat in front of the TV, watching the DVD of his sister, the P99 on the couch next to him. Rebecca was still beautiful to him, still stirred him. But it was different now. Different than it had been. Different enough not to need to be watched.

After five minutes he ejected the disc and took it into the kitchen, put it in the microwave and watched through the glass door as it sparked and flared.

If he had destroyed the disc a few weeks earlier he would have felt he was cutting some vital link to Rebecca, to the essence of who she had been to him. But now...now the disc was not her, was not what was important to him about her. It was just a collection of lovers she'd had, part of a private life captured on film.

As he took the crinkled plastic out of the microwave he was overtaken by a fresh grief. A grief not for the loss of a lover, but for that of a sibling, a girl he had known from birth, who had shared the landscape of childhood with him, whose face had smiled beside his in albums of family photographs.

It had taken until now, until he had fallen in love with Chick, for him to be set free of his doomed hunger for her. Until now, for Rebecca to become again truly his sister.

He went back into the lounge and picked up the P99, closed his hand around the olive polymer grip. Twelve rounds of .40 ammo. Muzzle velocity 1,128.6 feet per second. Short recoil-operated, locked breech. He'd looked it up on the net. Space the rounds closely enough, it'd cut a man in half.

Chapter 53

The water in Michael's indoor Jacuzzi was hot enough to make his belly turn red. He had a balloon of thirty-year-old brandy within reach, his second in the last half hour. The jets of water and bubbles were maxed – Michael trying to distract thought with physical sensation.

It didn't work.

He'd been out to Raintree. He'd gotten Christo's call. He'd opened his weapons cupboard before he left. Equipped himself with a handgun and an HK-416 assault rifle: 5.56mm NATO cartridge, 850 rounds per minute. Driven out there in a Merc G63 AMG.

None of the hardware mattered. Because when he went down to the screening room Christo was dead and Denning was gone. And he found out why he hadn't been able to reach Jeffery and Ally the last couple of days.

Michael thinking some major shift in motivation going on here. Denning took his ass-fucking eight years ago without so much as an abusive phone call. Now he gets hold of the screenplay and turns into a killing machine. Figuring, what? It gives him impunity? Him and Tim, the screenwriter's brother.

Things were way too wide now. When it was just the two women, Skye and her rug-muncher pal, the resurfacing of the screenplay hadn't posed too much of a problem, particularly with Jeffery so willing. And when it turned out someone else, this Tim, knew about it, and Christo had come up to help, there had still been a chance of containment.

But with Denning in on it now, Tim obviously eyeing revenge for his sister and Christo out of the game, Michael knew that things had gone a little too far. After he'd found the bodies at Raintree he'd relocated to his ranch, cancelled all GHQ-related commitments, phoned Theo.

But Theo had said he'd done all he could, that he was mainstream now, had been for more than a decade. Christo had been his last link to the old days, the last piece of muscle he could call on. Hear that? The sound of hands being washed. Dealing was Michael's responsibility now – he'd done Bartlemann, the dog woman, the screenwriter. A disgraced ex-journalist and someone called Tim were not beyond his abilities. Pointing out, when Michael got shitty, that Theo was not tied by a single thing to any of the murders. Saying he wouldn't be able to take his calls for a while.

So Michael had hired two security guys from a firm in Beverly Hills – large guys with sunglasses and handguns under their coats – whose job it was to watch the approach to the ranch and stop anyone getting near.

Because Jeffery and Ally, all swelling and shot to bits, strongly suggested that Denning and Tim's prime objective was not so much the exposing of the Bartlemann kill via the *Wilderness* screenplay, but rather that of exacting some form of terminal retribution.

Michael was looking across the floor of his bathroom at the assault rifle he'd brought with him when his cell phone rang.

Delores sitting bored, or pacing irritably around the bunker. Wanting to get to the gym, wanting to maintain muscle tone, fitness, flexibility.... Muttering that maybe they should work with Michael, feed him Tim and Denning. Why should she suffer because two idiots wanted to go digging up the past? Not really serious. But serious enough. Needing only a yes from Sean to tip those scales. To let her own self-interest convince her that she could buy Michael off with that information, that he'd let her return to her ex-movie-star life unmolested. Nothing that Sean would ever agree to, of course.

Convincing herself eventually that she was Delores Fuentes, that however desperate Michael was, he was not likely to attack her on the streets of Beverly

Hills. Changing into sweats and climbing into the Continental to make a high-end Pilates reformer session at a studio off Rodeo.

And Sean watching her go, thinking that actors had to be the sickest people in the world, himself included. And then going back inside and calling Michael's cell.

Tim, waking next to Chick, looking at the sun coming through the net curtains, at the pale green paint on the walls, at Chick's catsuit thrown on the floor. Knowing that today was the day. That he could not bear the fear of what he had to do any longer. Figuring he'd take Sean up on his offer, not seeing any other easier way. Realizing Chick was awake too and looking at him, reading his face.

Tim and Chick on the Triumphs. Summer turning cool. A crisp blue sky and the smell of salt. Pistols: Thunder Ultra Compact, Walther P99. Tim's stuck in the back of his pants, Chick's in the pocket of her leather jacket. Frightening firepower if you weren't used to guns, but not enough for Tim. Wanting a chain-gun mounted on the Bonneville, wanting an air-strike to call in. Blanket devastation that, once set in motion, couldn't be stopped, wouldn't let him back out.

Michael's ranch was in Boney Mountain State Wilderness, so PCH through Malibu, then Sycamore Canyon Road about ten miles further on. Another three miles inland. Cowboy country, chaparral, wide dry fields of grass and sage on the sides of hills, valleys of olive-green: oaks, sycamores, native walnut. Mountains in the east.

Sean following the bikes in a rented Suzuki Vitara. Two stories in his head – the one he'd told Michael, the one he'd told Tim. Driving with the sunroof open. Such a nice day. Figuring, might as well make the most of it. A good-sized hit before he'd left the bunker, a loaded syringe in the glove compartment in case he needed a top-up. Or extra pain relief. And in his jacket pocket, Delores' .25, taken after she'd left for Beverly Hills. He'd wanted the TEC-9 too, but he wasn't sure he knew how to use it, and it was out of ammo anyhow.

Michael alone at the ranch now. The security guys sent back to the agency, a little nonplussed at their quick cancellation. Michael figuring if he knew what was

coming, if he was in control of how things went down, he'd have no trouble han-
dling it. Figuring he didn't want witnesses. For sure.

Taking a ride on a large chestnut gelding, riding the trails and the fields laid
out in the forty acres behind the ranch house. Centering himself, a little mental
preparation. The HK-416 slung across his back. Plenty of time to get back for the
meet.

Running his conversation with Sean again. For a million dollars and a promise
to leave him and Delores alone, Sean would arrange things. No problem — if it all
stopped here a mil wasn't a bad price. Leave them alone? Say yes now, see how
things played out later. Not out of the question that the three of them could coex-
ist. Maybe throw Delores a part or two, bring her back into the fold.

Sean will tell Tim that Michael wants to make a deal, that Michael is broken
by the deaths of Jeffery and Ally and his Mexican goon. That it's enough already.
That Michael is willing to pay big to have Tim go away, to forget about his sister
and her screenplay.

Sean brings Tim out to the ranch to seal the deal and get his cash, then looks
the other way while Michael hoses the fucker with rounds instead. Sean sets up
exactly the same scenario with Denning the very next day. Easier to handle one at
a time.

Michael tethered his horse to a tree, walked twenty yards out into a field and
burned a clip. Blew the shit out of a lone sycamore. Smooth action. No jams. Ready
to roll. Glad it was his left shoulder that had been shot, the recoil would have made
him faint.

A trail cut into the side of a long hill. Rocky and rutted. Running parallel to a wide
valley floor. Tim and Chick stopped the bikes. Below them, Michael's ranch house
sat in the sun. A big place, made out of logs. It had a corral built out back and a
couple of out-buildings off to one side. Thin blue smoke came from one of the
chimneys and a saddled horse was tied to a rail outside the corral.

They were high enough not to be visible from any of the cabin's windows, but
still Tim made sure to stay back in the shadow behind the scrub that grew along
the edge of the trail.

Sean pulled up behind them and got out of the Vitara. His presence there the payment he'd demanded from Tim for setting up this phony meet, for working things so that Michael didn't have any muscle with him. His one chance at retribution.

Sean had told Michael that Tim wouldn't play ball unless Michael was alone. The rules for the meet were that Sean would leave Tim on the trail, come down and check the cabin out. If there was no one else there he'd go back to Tim, give him the all-clear, make him feel safe. Then bring him down so that Michael could work the old double cross.

Tim's version: when Sean came back with the all-clear all three of them would go down and attack the ranch house. No SWAT tactical plan, no professional risk minimization. Just the pistols and the three five gallon jerry cans of gasoline in the back of the Vitara.

Sean looked at the cabin for a moment, then stuck his hand out.

"Well, I guess this is it."

Tim took his hand and they stood for a while, both of them searching for something to say. Neither of them found it and Sean let go and walked back to the Vitara without saying anything else.

Tim called after him: "Don't get shot."

Sean looked over his shoulder and smiled thinly.

"He wants Denning too much."

Then Sean got in the car and rolled past them and turned onto a smaller trail that ran diagonally down the hill to the valley floor and on to the packed-earth apron out front of the ranch house.

Chick stayed on her bike. Tim got off his and stood close to her.

Chick said: "The objective here, Timbo, is to come out alive."

"You bet."

"And then we're done. With all of this shit – Denning and GHQ and the screenplay and Bartlemann. It's over."

"And Kid?"

"He's getting a pass. I've had enough. I just want to make films."

Down in the valley Sean had reached the cabin. They watched him get out of the car, walk across fifteen yards of dirt and up the steps that led to an unroofed porch. Sean knocked on the front door with one hand, he kept the other in his jacket pocket.

In the car. A last minute alone. The engine ticking. Feeling the sun through the glass of the windshield. The smell of the upholstery, some sort of deodorant the rental company used. A paper pine tree hanging from the rear-view mirror. A bubble of peace. And Sean wanting to stay there forever, wanting this moment to stretch and stretch and stretch...into the future, with the silence and the warmth and the wide blue day all around him.

Thinking, he could turn the car around, drive back to Los Angeles, not do what he had come here to do. But knowing that he wouldn't. Because outside the car all the things he'd done would still be waiting for him.

He opened the glove compartment, took out the syringe and shot up. Sat with his eyes half closed, riding the warm tsunami that was everywhere in his blood and cells and brain and stomach. Tasted the brown Afghani at the back of his nose.

Thought about Delores. About the things that might have been, if they'd both been different people. Took a last look at the day. Sighed. And got out and walked to the cabin and knocked on the door.

The door opening. The ranch house dim beyond it. Michael standing there with some kind of hi-tech rifle leveled at him. Motioning him in with his head.

Sean said: "It's cool, man. He's up on the trail like we said. Let me come in, two minutes, make like I'm looking around."

Michael walked backwards into a large room that took up half of the ground floor. There was no one else there. Michael kept his rifle pointed, kept a good distance between Sean and himself. Sean kept his hand around the pistol in his pocket, thinking he'd figured Michael would trust him more, wouldn't be making this so difficult.

Michael said: "When you bring him down, let him out of the car about where it is now. Tell him to come into the house. Drive away as soon as he starts walking."

"No problem. I get my money tomorrow, right?"

"It's sorted, don't worry."

The smack in Sean's system was suddenly gone. He'd wanted to be out of it enough to put a buffer between him and what he had to do. But he was clear now. The man before him, all the things in the room, were sharp and present and colored and real, and for a moment, one brutal, beautiful God-gifted instant, he remembered what it was like, before the smack, before Delores and Rebecca, when he was young and the days were made for him and he had a place in the world.

And then Michael lowered his rifle a little and Sean thought, fuck it, time to get it done. But then Michael noticed how long Sean's hand had been in his jacket pocket and he frowned and began to raise the rifle again, and Sean reacted too quickly, jerking up the hand inside his pocket, squeezing the trigger, the first small slug blasting through the material, going wide.

And despite himself, feeling his feet starting to step backwards, the fear of that rifle pushing him toward the door. But still pulling the trigger, sending bullets at Michael, only the pistol, trapped in his pocket, wouldn't point the way he wanted and the bullets went close but didn't hit, except for the last two in the clip – one into the top of the left side of Michael's chest, one into Michael's injured left shoulder, the wound Delores had made using the very same gun.

Too little, too late. Because, even though his left arm was dangling uselessly by his side, Michael had the HK-416 up and was holding down the trigger, the gun hammering out rounds in one long burning chainsaw explosion, ripping up from Sean's right hip in a blood-fountaining diagonal, across his stomach and his left lower ribs. Exiting in a meat spray. Punching Sean out of the ranch house and across the porch.

Up on the trail, Tim and Chick listened to the shooting, watched Sean back-pedaling like a cartoon character, falling down the steps, leaving blood everywhere. Lying sprawled and still on the dirt at the bottom, his right hand still in his coat pocket, the ripped material smoldering.

Michael sat slumped on a leather Chesterfield, the HK across his thighs. Gun smoke haze in the air, the smell of cordite. Blood down his left sleeve, down the whole left side of his shirt. Breathing in wheezes, the hole in his chest bubbling each time. He'd made enough action movies to know that Sean's bullet had gone through the top of his lung. Leave it long enough he'd drown in his own blood.

Thought, irony. Thought about the bullets he'd put in Scott Bartlemann's chest all those years ago.

He looked at the HK, eight rounds left in the clip. He wanted to reload, but his left arm would barely move and doing it one handed, fighting to breathe, was out of the question.

Sean had set him up. Obviously. Might mean Tim had never been part of the deal. Might mean he was up on the trail getting ready to come down, a B-team to take up the slack. Either way, screenplay containment was something that looked like it just wasn't going to happen.

A vague plan. Stay alive long enough to get to Theo's pet doctor, hope that his wounds could be treated without involving a hospital. Then get out of the US, go someplace without an extradition treaty. Say goodbye to everything he'd built. He had a lot of money. It could be done. Maybe he'd even make movies again someday, win a Best Foreign Film Oscar, accept it by video-link.

Outside, up on the hillside, the sound of engines starting. Motorcycles. Starting up and heading down. Michael thinking that Foreign Film Oscar might be a bit of a stretch.

Sean dead. Tim and Chick up on the hill, looking down on the tangled blot of his body, the smear of blood around it. Tim knowing what Sean had done, recognizing this attempt to make good. Thinking, one more reason Michael had to die.

Waiting, expecting Michael to come out waving a gun, to check what was arrayed against him. Waiting longer, wondering how many others there were in the ranch house. But nothing. No heads poking from windows, no shouted taunts, no blasts of gunfire.

Weighing possibilities. There had been two guns going when they heard the shooting. Maybe Michael was dead. Maybe incapacitated. Maybe waiting to ambush them....

The Thrux and the Bonnie exploding into life. Tim and Chick leaving their helmets behind on the trail. A simple plan – get down level with the house, see if they could see inside. Keep getting closer as long as no one shot at them. If things got difficult, there was always the gasoline in the Vitara.

The bikes slid and fishtailed on the stony surface of the cut-back that led down to the valley floor. It was better when it leveled out, became hard earth and grass. They paused there, about three hundred yards out. Far enough to feel they were probably still safe. Unless Michael had spent a lot of time on his marksmanship.

No gunfire. No shot across the bows telling them to stay the fuck away.

Black leather, bikes idling, a low thunder.... Chick ran her hands through her short blond hair. Tim took the P99 out of the back of his pants, racked the slide, flipped the safety and just held the gun for a moment, feeling its weight, its deadly potential. This would be the first time. Chick had shown him how, that night in her flat, but this would be the first time he'd fired a weapon.

He gripped the gun with both hands. It felt natural. It felt exactly right for this moment. He squeezed the trigger, fired two rounds at the ranch house. The recoil nowhere near as bad as he'd expected, the noise louder. The house was way beyond the accurate range of the Walther, but he wanted to see if his shots provoked a response.

No movement. They could see the windows of the cabin from where they were, but not through them. The afternoon sun had turned them to mirrors.

Chick said: "Gonna have to get closer, Timbo."

Tim said: "Yeah."

And put the gun away and kicked the Bonnie into gear, held the clutch in and revved the engine, thinking, just ride across, a hundred miles an hour, fuck what came out the door, go straight up the steps and blow the cabin apart. A personal 9/11.

He was about to let the clutch out when Chick grabbed his sleeve and pointed. Michael, on a horse, rifle slung across his back, a long way across the fields that lay between the back of the ranch house and the start of some woods about a mile further on.

Tim said: "Here we go."

And set his jaw grimly and let out the clutch as Chick kicked the Thruxton into gear and their rear wheels spat dirt and stones and they blasted around the ranch house, around the far side of it, in a wide sweep and came around the back, past the corral and the out-buildings, the juddering shocks of the uneven ground punching up through their forearms and the dust rising around them so that they blinked and spat and squinted their eyes until they hit the sage field and the dust was gone and their tires felt like they were floating on the long slippery grass.

And out ahead, out with a long lead, Michael galloping full speed, left arm flopping wildly, rising and falling like one side of him was trying to fly, heading for those woods, where the land started to rise into the hills, where the bikes wouldn't be able to follow because of the grade and the close-growing trees.

Tim and Chick riding side by side, speed limited because of the grass, feeling it slap against their shins, whispering against leather, making their wheels want to drift away from under them. But holding on, pushing it, as fast as they dared, looking across at each other sometimes, thinking what fucking movie are we in?

Michael still with a good lead, riding his horse hard, low in the saddle. Tim pulled out the P99, left-handed because of the throttle, started blasting away, firing too high, worried about hitting the horse, struggling to hold the bike steady with one hand. And too far away anyhow. The bullets doing nothing but spiraling off into the hillside.

Sticking the gun in his jacket pocket because the barrel was too hot to stick down the back of his pants and concentrating on getting closer to the man up ahead. Chick keeping pace. Hard for her to shoot from the Thrux because of its racer design, but that wasn't the reason she didn't join in. She knew this was Tim's deal, that if she took it from him he'd be missing something for the rest of his life. Even if that thing was dirty and dark and full of horror.

Michael now a couple of hundred yards from the trees, getting close. But Tim and Chick closing. Close enough to see the blood lifting into the air from Michael's useless arm, to see the splashes it made on the rump of the horse. To see Michael looking over his shoulder at them, gauging how much time he had left, his face pale and drawn.

The ground was rougher now, under the grass, and Tim's bike lurched as it hit a corrugation. The Bonneville slewed sideways, but Tim fought it and held it and brought it back straight. And Tim and Chick came up on the right side of the horse, Tim closest, Chick riding flank. And they could feel the fall of the horse's hooves through the ground and see the foam at its mouth, smell the horse smell, hear its panting breath. Michael looking down at them, then back at the trees, then down at them again. Trying to unsling the rifle on his back, but too injured to ride without hands at full gallop and almost falling and giving it up to hold onto the pommel and hope for those trees. Refusing to look anymore at the two bikes roaring alongside him.

The time now come. Tim ready. Thinking how Michael had also ridden a horse to the cabin where he killed Rebecca. Playing that scene in his head. More than ready. Reaching left-handed into the pocket of his jacket, but finding the P99 gone. The big pistol had fallen out when he'd almost lost control of his bike.

The trees a hundred yards away now. Tim looked at Chick. She'd figured what had happened. She motioned him to fall back a little, pulled in closer, took the Thunder Ultra Compact out and though she hated to do it, pointed it at the horse's head. Michael would escape if he made the trees.

The trees rushing up. Chick riding with her left arm extended, out to the side. Wishing to fuck she didn't have to do this. Seeing the horse's teeth around the bit, its wide nostrils, its dark round eyes and its mane flying back. A big, beautiful animal that had no place in the cesspools men created for themselves.

And thumbing the safety and thinking 'fuck' and pulling the trigger and at the last minute turning in a long sweep to the right, running parallel to the trees. The enormous bang the Bersa made filling the valley and the heavy .45 round smashing into the side of the horse's head, filling the air around it with a red mist that blew back over Michael.

Tim slowed his bike and stayed close, watched as the big chestnut's momentum carried it on for a few more strides, so that it looked, for a second, for half a second, like the horse was okay. But then its legs gave way, up from the hooves to the knees to the thighs, folding up on themselves so that the horse went chest-first, then neck, into the ground, its hindquarters coming up and up and over and the neck twisting and bending back on itself, the big body rising until it was almost vertical and then seeming to pause and then falling sideways.

And Tim, stopped now and off his bike, hearing above the terrible thunder of its impact, the screams it made, of agony and fear, trumpeting through that long head, because the horse was not dead yet, something in it still lived, something that felt pain, felt life leaving. And it screamed and screamed and screamed and screamed and lay on the ground and one of its back legs jerked like it was still trying to run.

Michael had been thrown when the horse fell. He lay on his back in the grass, the rifle trapped beneath him, blinking up at the sky, too damaged by the fall and his gunshot wounds to raise himself.

Tim walked over, looked down at him. First sight in the flesh. A big man with a belly. Levis and a striped button-up shirt, mostly soaked with blood. A Hollywood player reduced to a bloody stain on a field of grass.

"You killed my sister."

Michael took a breath and blinked. The hole in his chest fizzed wetly. The horse was still screaming, so that Tim wanted to plug his ears, to stop that dreadful sound coming into his head, to stop himself going mad with the horror of standing there by a dying horse, over a man he was going to kill.

He straddled Michael and sat on his stomach, pinned his arms with his knees. Michael moaned with pain, too weak to throw him off.

Tim put his hands around Michael's neck.

Michael said: "I can give you a lot of money."

And Tim started to squeeze, to force his thumbs into the windpipe, feeling the Adam's apple crunch, pressing harder, his whole bodyweight behind it, squeezing so hard his nails cut the flesh on the back of Michael's neck. And Michael gurgled and choked, and blood and spit ran out of his mouth and his body started to heave as though he were some giant fish plucked from the water. And Tim looked into his eyes, saw the blood vessels bursting there, the eyes bulging, the whole head swelling, turning dark, and the tongue suddenly protruding as though it had been vomited out, and heard the horse screaming, and screamed along with it himself. And felt that the world had torn itself open around him and that he had fallen into hell.

And then, mercifully, there were two monstrous reports behind him and the horse was quiet at last.

It took a long time for Tim to force his hands to stop squeezing. When they finally loosened about Michael's neck, he sat back on his heels and looked into the dead face of his sister's killer. And then he stood and turned and saw Chick by the horse, the gun down by her side, smoke rising from its barrel, looking at him. And both of them stood like that and felt that they might never move again.

And then Chick said quietly: "It's a hell of a thing." And started to cry for the first time since she was fifteen.

CHAPTER 54

When staff at GHQ realized there was no one at the helm the cops were called in. A search of the various properties owned by the company directors eventually led them to Raintree and the discovery of Jeffery and Ally Bannister and some Mexican guy. Michael was found in a field behind his ranch when a group of horse trekkers went to investigate what a bunch of crows was feeding on.

Given the movie industry connections and the indications of torture on the bodies of Jeffery and Ally, the press did their best to draw parallels with the Sharon Tate/Charles Manson murders, but Jeffery and Ally were unknown to the public and the level of brutality was not sufficient to make the sensationalism stick.

As Jeffery, Ally and Michael had all been in business together, the murders were assumed to be related – an assumption supported by the fact that two shell casings found out front of Michael's ranch house, along with a tangle of motorcycle tire tracks, bore partial fingerprint matches to the dead Mexican in the Raintree screening room. Chronologically, this didn't make a whole lot of sense as the Mexican was determined to have been killed two days before Michael.

Matching the prints with old California driver's license records did, however, enable the police to identify the Mexican as an ex-porn actor who had worked with Michael almost twenty years ago. Interestingly, the other body found at Michael's ranch was that of Sean Nightingale, a failed actor who was also connected to Michael through a small role in one of the films GHQ had produced.

Porn, plus shell casings, plus previous association prompted the theory that, for reasons unknown, the Mexican and Sean and one or more other accomplices – the existence of which was easily enough arrived at by the variety of bullet calibers and shell casings in the Raintree screening room – had grudge-killed Michael's associates. For some reason they had then revisited the Raintree screening room two to three days later and had apparently had a quarrel that resulted in the Mexican's death. Before leaving this time, the remaining members of the gang took the Mexican's .40 caliber pistol with them.

Sean, driving a rented Vitara, and the accomplices, possibly on motorcycles, later tracked Michael down at his ranch. There was a gun battle, Sean was killed, the remaining accomplices chased Michael into the field, shot his horse and strangled him. The bullets in the horse matched those in Jeffery and Ally Bannister. Proof positive that whoever had offed the Bannisters had been involved in the whole trifecta.

Though the posited scenario was less than elegant, and only one of several possible explanations the police came up with, it was the best they could do. The official statement, released six weeks after the murders, was that Michael Starck and Jeffery and Ally Bannister had been murdered by a team of individuals, possibly made up of disgruntled ex-associates, two of whom had been killed during the commission of their crimes, and one or more others who were still unidentified and unlocated. As to the exact motivation for the killings, the cops had no idea.

A significant portion of the Hollywood filmmaking community – basically anyone who had a personal connection to the victims, or who had had business dealings with GHQ – was interviewed. No one presented as a viable candidate for the missing accomplices, including Chick and Kid who were interviewed because of their deal with GHQ for *Antepenultimate*. Their questioning was perfunctory, a matter of ticking boxes – after all, why would a pair of filmmakers whose film depended on the flow of funds from GHQ jeopardize their project by killing the very people providing those funds?

In the end, the file ended up as another Hollywood unsolved, and anyone who had business with GHQ was left to deal with the fallout.

The temporary management team brought into oversee the running of GHQ until probate was settled for its murdered owners put an immediate freeze on all projects that had not yet started principal photography. *Antepenultimate*, two weeks away from kick-off was one of the victims of this freeze. Chick and Kid could have put a brave face on things and settled down to weather the delay, hoping that they'd still end up with a movie eventually.

But Kid knew better. When the wheels started turning again at GHQ, the bottom line would be the first thing to be scrutinized, and a three million dollar angst-laden film about father/son problems set on a hippy commune in the seventies was not going to stand out as that fiscal year's money maker. And when it was found that there had been no due diligence – no script appraisal, no market testing, no company enforced rewrites, no traceable progression from project submission through to story department sign-off – they'd figure something was off somewhere and cancel the project, simply because it would be the safest thing to do. Kid knew *Antepenultimate* was not just frozen, it was dead.

So he sat down with the temporary management team and it didn't take much to convince them that putting *Antepenultimate* into turnaround, allowing Kid to take the project to other studios or production entities, was probably going to be a win for them. If Kid got it off the ground somewhere else, they'd get a finder's fee. So what if they lost the million bucks Kid had already spent on development and production prep? It was less than the bath they'd take if they actually went ahead and made the dog.

What they didn't know was that Kid and Chick had Delores Fuentes.

When Delores had learned of Sean's death she'd spent a few days doing her best to grieve, to milk that sadness and put it away to draw on in her next downbeat scene. But her relationship with him had been both too uncertain and too complex for her to feel any genuine sense of loss. The most immediate emotion she experienced after the shock of his murder wore off was that of relief, relief that she didn't have to try to figure out what she felt for him anymore.

While her relationship with Sean was unknown to the world at large, her previous affair with Michael Starck was not. She was asked for her reaction to his murder ad nauseam by the tabloids, and held a number of press conferences where she wore dark glasses and practiced her craft by expounding on his merits both as a film producer and as a man.

Behind the scenes, though, the first thing she did, after Jeffery, Ally and Michael's deaths were made public, was have her attorney challenge the exclusive contract she'd signed with GHQ.

The mandate of the temporary management team was to act, primarily, as a caretaker body. As such they were reluctant to expose the company to a potentially costly legal battle. So, when Delores' attorney made his challenge on the grounds that Delores had signed the agreement only because of her personal relationship with the three principals of the company and that, regrettably, those principals no longer existed, GHQ let her go with their best wishes, and a ten percent lien on all earnings over the next ten years. Including residuals.

Now, it was a question of mutual advantage. After four years of zero cinematic exposure, Delores, with the playing field suddenly wide open before her, had the chance to use her comeback to segue from gun-toting eye-candy to serious actress. And Kid, by formally attaching her to his project as female lead, rather than as a supporting player, had the chance to catapult Chick into the ranks of hot new directors who actually meant something outside the arthouse scene.

They had a meeting, Kid and Chick and Tim and Delores, and *Antepenultimate* as they knew it bit the dust. Tim would rewrite Rebecca's *Wilderness* screenplay focusing on a strong female protagonist. Chick, of course, would direct. And Delores would play the lead, a role she couldn't have said no to, even if she'd wanted to, given what everyone else in the room but Kid knew about her.

Relations between Chick and Kid were frosty. But mutual advantage operated there, too. *Antepenultimate*, as heartfelt as it was, would have had minimal impact on the entrenched Hollywood filmmaking community. It was true that it rejected the conventional demands for action over character, for a rocketing plot over philosophic introspection. But these were merely challenges of style, and all any of the big-time execs, directors and producers would do, if they heard about the film at all, would be to shake their heads in amusement and carry right on making the juvenile dross they'd built their careers on.

By working with Kid to re-engineer the project, Chick saw that she had an opportunity to stick a far more effective finger up Hollywood's collective ass. With Delores attached as star, the bargaining power they had when it came to getting finance was enhanced to the point where budget dollars hit eight figures. And that meant a movie guaranteed to be seen, because the only way a financing entity could make back that sort of money was to market it strongly and open the picture across a shitload of theatres.

And Kid, even though he knew Chick could barely stand to be in the same room as him, told himself that the bigger the film, the more he was making up for what he'd done to her.

Finally, for Tim, reworking the *Wilderness* screenplay was an opportunity both to pay homage to his sister and to breathe life into a writing career he'd given up for dead.

Kid hawked the project around town, got a deal with Sony, and eight months after their meeting, *Wilderness* was in the can. Written by Tim, directed by Chick, produced by Kid and starring Delores, the film was the kind of Trojan horse Chick could previously only have dreamed of.

A blistering castigation of Hollywood greed and excess, and a sensitive examination of the effects of prostituting artistic integrity, the film tested strongly in advance screenings. And why not? Murder, Hollywood, a star making her comeback, the gloss and polish of a mainstream budget – all of it shot with every ounce of anger and manic energy Chick could muster.

Sony, scenting possible future awards for *Wilderness* and seeking to establish it as a contender in the minds of the filmmaking community, held a number of industry screenings at theatres around Los Angeles. Though Sony had its own distribution arm, when the suggestion came through from Haldane Productions that word of mouth might be helped along by inviting the heads of independent distribution companies to one of these screenings, the company was only too happy to oblige.

Night. A theatre in Venice. Names in lights. The end of the show. Hip film people flooding the sidewalk. Fat Theo Portman climbing into the back of his towncar, thinking it was a fucking good thing that Michael and Jeffery and Ally were dead. When this film was released it wouldn't take long for some smartass journalist to draw a parallel with the Bartlemann case and start asking questions. With the heads of GHQ now safely buried in expensive graves, there was nothing left in the world of the living that could serve to link him to the death of his old Big Glass partner.

He told the driver to take PCH, drive along the side of the ocean. It was late, traffic was light. Here and there the dark water was streaked with gold from the light of the city.

Ten minutes later the driver turned inland on Entrada Drive and headed for Pacific Palisades. Entrada was a small street, deserted at that time of night, and when an old matte black Trans Am rolled out of a cross street on the left and blocked his way, the driver was thinking about bed and his wife and only just managed to stop without hitting the muscle car.

Theo swore and asked what the fuck was going on. The driver figured the Trans Am would make a proper turn and carry on down the road. But the Trans Am just sat there, its over-sized engine rumbling. Black paint, black glass. The towncar driver figured the smart move was to just wait it out, better than start something with the kind of guy who'd drive an asshole-mobile like that.

While they were waiting, a Vespa without plates turned into the street behind them and pulled up alongside the rear of the towncar. Denning, wearing gloves and a full face helmet with a mirrored visor, pretended to survey the blocked road ahead and then tapped good naturedly on Theo's window. Theo rolled it down, hoping for more help than his rent-a-driver was prepared to give.

Denning lifted his visor, looked at Portman long enough without speaking for Portman to frown and start reaching for the window button again.

Denning said: "Remember my wife?"

Portman stopped reaching, frowned even more and said: "Your wife? What the fuck?"

"Ten years ago. She used to wash your dogs. Mexican."

Portman's eyes went round and his mouth started to move, but he didn't get to say anything else. Because Denning took the .38 Special out of his jacket and put all five rounds into Portman's face.

For half a minute Denning sat with the Vespa burbling beneath him, looking at the ragged, leaking mess of the man whose idea it had been to take his wife from him.

Portman was the last link in the chain of horror that stretched back to the day his wife disappeared, the last thing of any meaning in Denning's ruined and empty life. With his death, there was no mystery left, nothing more to find out, no one else to track down, no one else to kill. Add Peta now living fulltime with Kid Haldane, and it had seemed a safe bet to Denning that when the gun smoke cleared, he would simply flicker and go dark.

But though there was nothing for him any longer in Los Angeles, though the book he had planned would never be written, though Clara could never be made to be alive again, there was now in Denning the faint and surprising notion that perhaps this did not have to be the end, that perhaps that final giving-up could be put off a little longer.

He was sitting on a scooter, the L.A. night was warm around him. He could go. He could ride until he ran out of gas, then fill up again and keep going. He had money from the sinecure Tim had arranged for him as technical advisor on *Wilderness*. Peta was safe and happy, and though their relationship would always be colored by the nights they had spent together there was between them now, at least, the knowledge that they had not destroyed each other completely.

He twisted the scooter into gear and rolled slowly forward. As he passed the Trans Am he paused and nodded once to the dark windshield, and then U-turned and accelerated and drove back along the street and out onto Pacific Coast Highway.

The road north was wide and open. As he started along it, Denning tried to figure out how long it would take him to get to Oregon.

Tim turned the wheel of the Trans Am, drove slowly, wound his way to the coast and the large parking lot by the beach where he'd first met Denning and where he'd sat with Sean a year ago when Sean was still alive and they were still friends.

He left the car there, clean of prints, and went and sat at the edge of the lot.

All chips cashed – Chick for her rapes, Denning for his wife, Tim for the murder of his sister. He looked out at the bright sand, felt the warm air against him, felt the pressure of his leather trousers against the skin of his thighs, felt the weight of his jacket across his shoulders, the leanness of his stomach....

High above him the floodlights hummed in the glowing night sky. Beyond their spill the sand darkened to a charcoal-mauve, and beyond this the sea was thick and rolling and dark, gashed by white lines of surf.

Tim knew he was changed. With Michael's death something of Rebecca had been lifted from his heart. His grief was not gone, his love for her was not gone, but the loss that had strangled him since her death was no longer there. Rebecca had become, at last, a memory, placed within her own time, her own life, freed now of the dreadful pull between two worlds – that of the dead, and that of Tim's need to keep her always with him.

Life.

Again.

He rarely drank now, and he was writing. When the back-end from *Wilderness* kicked in he'd be a moderately wealthy man. And there would be more films, more screenplays, a career if he wanted it. But it was Chick, of course, who had changed him in the only way that really mattered. Her love for him. His for her. A twenty-eight-year-old girl in a black leather catsuit. A girl with more than enough horror of her own.

Behind him, the clatter of the Thruxton entering the parking lot. Engine decelerating against second gear. And then she was beside him, stretched over the racer chassis, holding the clutch in and popping the throttle, smiling softly at him through her helmet.

And saying: "It's finished now, Timbo. Let the sea have it. You and me, we've got all the rest of the world."

Tim stood, and for a moment put his hand on her, then walked to where he'd parked the Bonneville earlier that night, and both of them thundered out of the lot and onto the road.

Three minutes up Santa Monica Boulevard they pulled a tight U-turn and stopped. Chick took a bottle out of her pannier and lit the rag stuffed into its neck. They started again, heading back down the slope, Chick's hand trailing flame. Twenty yards later, her left arm went up and the firebomb arced through the air in a long burning streak and shattered against a billboard advertising that summer's latest action movie. And as they moved on down the road, Tim, riding a little behind, watched the burning gasoline throw colors across the back of Chick's catsuit, orange and yellow....

And then, a little further on, Chick slowed, reached behind her into the pannier again and took out something else. She held it for a moment, tight in her hand, then tossed it away, not looking to see where it landed.

It hit the sidewalk and bounced and then rolled, and came to rest on the concrete apron of an empty bus stop. And as the two hot new filmmakers headed for a midnight test screening of *Wilderness* in Santa Barbara, the light from the boulevard came through the slats of the bus stop bench and fell against the golden skin of the hardon Oscar.

The End.

ABOUT THE AUTHOR

Matthew Stokoe is the author of three previous novels: *Cows*, *High Life*, and *Empty Mile*. His work has been translated into French, German, Russian and Spanish. In 2014 he was nominated for the Grand Prix de Littérature Policière. He lives with his wife in Sydney, Australia.